DEAD DROP

BERKLEY TITLES BY M. P. WOODWARD

THE HANDLER
DEAD DROP

DEAD DROP

M. P. Woodward

BERKLEY
New York

BERKLEY
An imprint of Penguin Random House LLC
penguinrandomhouse.com

Copyright © 2023 by Michael Patrick Woodward
Penguin Random House supports copyright. Copyright fuels creativity, encourages
diverse voices, promotes free speech, and creates a vibrant culture. Thank you for buying
an authorized edition of this book and for complying with copyright laws by not
reproducing, scanning, or distributing any part of it in any form without permission.
You are supporting writers and allowing Penguin Random House to continue to publish
books for every reader.

BERKLEY and the BERKLEY & B colophon are registered trademarks of Penguin
Random House LLC.

Library of Congress Cataloging-in-Publication Data

Names: Woodward, M. P., author.
Title: Dead drop / M.P. Woodward.
Description: New York: Berkley, [2023]
Identifiers: LCCN 2022056155 (print) | LCCN 2022056156 (ebook) |
ISBN 9780593441664 (hardcover) | ISBN 9780593441671 (ebook)
Classification: LCC PS3623.O6857 D43 2023 (print) | LCC PS3623.O6857 (ebook) |
DDC 813/.6—dc23/eng/20211223
LC record available at https://lccn.loc.gov/2022056155
LC ebook record available at https://lccn.loc.gov/2022056156

Printed in the United States of America
1st Printing

Book design by Ashley Tucker

This is a work of fiction. Names, characters, places, and incidents either are the
product of the author's imagination or are used fictitiously, and any resemblance to
actual persons, living or dead, business establishments, events, or locales is entirely
coincidental.

For Wendy

CAST OF CHARACTERS

THE AMERICANS

Meredith Morris-Dale—Senior operations officer in CIA's Counterproliferation (CPC) Center; ex-wife of John Dale. Meredith uses the aliases Maggie O'Dea and Margot Henri.

John Dale—Retiring CIA case officer living in rural Washington State. John uses the aliases Reza Shariati and Etienne Crochet.

Grace Dale—Daughter of John and Meredith; midshipman at the US Naval Academy.

Ed Rance—Department head of CIA's CPC Center based in Langley, Virginia; assigned on temporary duty (TDY) to the diplomatic mission in Vienna, Austria.

Jeff Dorsey—Director of CIA's National Clandestine Service.

THE ISRAELIS

Maya Shaheen—Mossad Operations (Caesarea) director based in Tel Aviv.

Werner Davidai—Chief of Mossad's Caesarea operations based in Tel Aviv.

Daniel Mitz—Chief of Mossad's Junction (covert intelligence collection) division based in Tel Aviv.

Noam Galin—Brigadier general in the Israeli Defense Forces (IDF) military intelligence wing (the Hebrew acronym is AMAN). Commander of AMAN's Unit 8200 (signals intelligence arm).

Eli—Mossad Caesarea *katsa* (intelligence collection operative) on the American station.

Ari—Mossad Caesarea *kidon* (special activities operative) on the American station.

Rina—Mossad Caesarea *katsa* on the American station.

Mia—Mossad Caesarea *katsa* on the American station.

Nahshon—Mossad sniper in Bayonet special forces unit.

THE IRANIANS

Kasem Kahlidi ("Atlas")—Quds lieutenant colonel based in Lebanon; a former adjutant to the late General Soleimani, former head of Quds Force. Atlas is his CIA code name.

Siamak Azad—Iranian Ministry of Intelligence and Security (MOIS) major based in Beirut.

Naser Maloof—Iranian MOIS colonel based in Tehran in charge of Iranian counterintelligence.

Kasra Khani—Girlfriend of Kasem Kahlidi.

Ramin ("Roger") Gulrajani—ex-fiancé of Kasra Khani working as a doctor in London.

Zana Rahimi ("Cerberus")—Former CIA asset, now defected to the US. Before his defection he had been sabotaging Iranian centrifuge arrays; his CIA code name is Cerberus.

Walid Zafir—Iranian MOIS officer posing as a Foreign Ministry diplomat in Vienna.

Nabil—Lebanese Hezbollah cell leader.

CIA CASE OFFICER OATH

I do solemnly swear that I will support and defend the Constitution of the United States against all enemies, foreign and domestic; that I will bear true faith and allegiance to the same; that I take this obligation freely, without any mental reservation or purpose of evasion; and that I will well and faithfully discharge the duties of the office on which I am about to enter. So help me God.

MOSSAD OPERATIONS OFFICER OATH

I swear and commit to maintain allegiance to the State of Israel, its laws, and its authorities, to accept upon myself unconditionally the discipline of the Institute, to obey all the orders and instructions given by authorized commanders, and to devote all my energies, and even sacrifice my life, for the protection of the homeland and the liberty of Israel.

DEAD
DROP

PROLOGUE

THE CAPTAIN HAD TO RELY ON THE OLDEST, MOST RELIABLE NAVAL sensor of them all—his eyes. He pressed his brow to the viewfinder and squinted. Sidestepping, he rotated the large metal cylinder all the way around the bridge. He was under strict orders to avoid using the surface search radar, but after completing the periscope's sweep, he'd concluded that on a night like this, his eyes would do just fine.

For once, conditions up top were just as the intelligence briefers had said they'd be. There were no visible marine navigation lights and only a few winking streetlights on the distant shore. Even better, a thin, silvery sheen from the half-moon reflected on waves that were barely above a ripple. Only a heaving swell undulated the surface of the otherwise flat sea fifty feet above them.

The captain scanned again. This time he paused in the middle of the three-sixty, aiming the reticle at the northern end of the lights on the land. There, he zoomed in to identify the old sandstone ruins, still lit for the tourists at ten o'clock on this summer Saturday eve. The crumbling sixteenth-century Ottoman fort known as the Sidon Sea Castle was easily visible from this distance. With the reticle centered on it, the skipper pressed a button to take a laser navigation fix.

"Point X-ray. Two point four kilometers, bearing zero-eight-three," said a young seaman, reading off the numbers, scribbling in the log.

That sounded about right to the captain. He cross-referenced three more points in the same way and found that *Tekumah*, the Israeli navy diesel-electric Dolphin class submarine he commanded, was right where she was supposed to be.

"Down scope," *Tekumah*'s captain said, folding the handles. As the periscope retracted, he turned to a hard-faced man standing next to him who stoically awaited the report. This man wore a wetsuit pulled down to the waist, exposing a tight black T-shirt.

The captain caught his eye. "Good news, Reu. You and your boys won't have to panic in the tubes tonight."

Reu shrugged, his mouth flat. "Don't surface on our account. We don't mind going out the torpedo tubes."

The captain smiled. "Stow your SDVs and tanks. It's a nice night for boating."

As the frogman went below to break down the Swimmer Delivery Vehicles, *Tekumah*'s captain angled his head toward a petty officer manning the diving planes, then looked at the young lieutenant in charge of the shift. "Officer of the deck, make surface profile zero. Ten degrees up angle. Two knots, dead slow."

Fifteen minutes later, Reu barely bounced as his rubber boat skimmed along the smooth, oily sea. *Nice night for boating,* he repeated inwardly to himself, grateful to have dodged the submerged egress and its claustrophobic hell in the torpedo tubes. Up here there was no wind, a flat sea, good visibility. The rubber boat was making a quiet twenty knots. Ideal conditions, really. The frogman cursed himself. No mission ever had ideal conditions.

He and his three men, commandos of the Israeli Navy SEAL team equivalent known as Flotilla 13, were squatting on the rubber dinghy's sponsons as cool salt air rushed past them. Behind them, *Tekumah* had already submerged in a frenzy of bubbles. Clad in shining black wetsuits and neoprene balaclavas, Reu felt that they were alone on the sea now, invisible in the dark.

Two racing kilometers on, he sensed a warmer shift in the air temperature and signaled his coxswain to stop. Almost immediately, the dinghy's way fell off and began to drift with the Mediterranean current.

The man at the tiller killed the humming engine. All was quiet now, save for the sound of water lapping against the semirigid hull.

"NVGs," the Flotilla 13 commander whispered to the chief petty officer next to him, his number two. A moment later, Reu adjusted the night-vision goggles over his forehead, waiting for them to warm up before scanning the beach. It looked empty—but looks could be deceiving. With an outstretched fist, he signaled his men to remain still, waiting, drifting.

After another minute, the Flotilla 13 commander saw what he'd been looking for. Just beyond the surf line, a van slowed by the side of the road. The tall Mercedes Sprinter then did a three-pointer and turned itself toward the sea. About ten seconds after that, it blinked its headlights—once, then a second time a beat later. Reu's pulse quickened. One blink would have meant mission-scrub. Two meant the op was a go.

Retrieving an angled waterproof flashlight from his combat harness, Reu blinked twice in reply to the van. He then tapped the chief on a knee and stowed his NVGs. The engine coughed back to life and the dinghy surged forward.

Much of the coast in this part of Lebanon was jagged rock, smashed by pounding surf. But they'd planned for landfall on the ladies' beach at the extreme edge of the Damour Beach Resort, just north of Sidon. With a strict night curfew on the female-only enclave, the Damour made for a good exfil point—provided they got back to it before sunup.

Gunning the boat's engine into the back of a breaking swell, the coxswain finally cut power and pulled the engine up. With oars in hand, the men paddled the dinghy to catch the momentum of a roaring wave, then swiveled their legs over the sponsons. They raced in on white water until the keel skidded on sand.

With well-oiled practice, the frogmen pulled the heavy boat ashore, lifting it by its handles, pausing now and then to rest. Once to the dunes, they kneeled beside it to extract their IWI assault rifles, spare magazines, and body armor from their rubber bladders. Finally, with weapons at their sides, they ran low and fast toward the Sprinter van.

The driver, a woman in heels and skirt, helped stow the weapons in the Mercedes's overhead cargo area. The interior stayed dark since the dome lights had been disabled. Catching a glimpse of the woman in the spare moonlight, Reu thought the pretty brunette looked to be all of twenty years old. But then, he admitted to himself, the older he got the younger they looked. He unzipped his wetsuit.

Showing some modesty, the female intelligence officer slid behind the Sprinter's wheel as the men changed into the dry clothes that had been waiting for them. Once dressed in jeans and a polo, Reu got into the front passenger's seat next to her.

"How long?" he asked.

The woman, a Mossad intelligence collection operative called a *katsa*, was busy typing a message on her phone. "Twenty minutes," she said without looking up. "And we're late."

Forty kilometers to the north, the phone lying just to the right of Maya Shaheen's sweating club soda began to buzz. The senior special operative, known in Mossad parlance as a *kidon*, glanced at the glowing screen: *Rendez-vous au Blanc 20.*

Without missing a beat, Maya swiped the message clear and continued the slight nod of her head in time with the throbbing bass, thinking about the op. The team had made landfall. They were a little late—but then so was the man she was to meet here at the club. Maya sipped her soda, mentally choreographing the next set of moves, deciding that the op was still a go.

Despite Lebanon's deepening economic crisis, the nightclub, Beirut White, was packed on this Saturday night. A striking brunette who stood nearly six feet tall, Maya was pressed on all sides by young people ordering drinks, yelling to be heard over the throbbing music. Ignoring the clubgoers, she carefully composed a text to the man she was waiting for.

Mo, où es tu? Je me sens seul.

That should do it, she thought, putting the phone down again. Men tended to hurry whenever Maya said she was lonely. She took another sip of her soda and tapped her foot in time with the beat.

Maya had met Mo at a hotel in Paris about a month back. A Persian who resided in Damascus, Mohammed Baramzedeh preferred the Prophet's first syllable as his sobriquet. Mid-forties, slim, bespectacled, bookish, the Iranian liked to drink when away from his dry homeland. Maya had stalked him to the hotel lobby bar, where Mo had been having his quiet dinner, reading his phone while sipping a Chardonnay—behavior spot-on with her pre-op brief.

She'd taken the corner barstool, just off Mo's elbow. Dressed in a snug suit, she'd crossed her long legs slowly to give a full-body view before asking him how the food was. Even at thirty-nine, the one-time youth model could still pull it off.

Acknowledging that they were both single business travelers in a foreign city, Maya had talked Mo into sharing a bottle of her favorite Bordeaux, conveniently unavailable by the glass. Mo was soon shocked to learn just how much he had in common with this rare beauty. She lived in Beirut. But since she spoke no Arabic, she admitted to feeling sometimes lost in the polyglot city. Mo confessed that as a native Farsi speaker, his Arabic was also poor. In French, he proceeded to tell Maya how much he loved Beirut, how he visited often, how he favored a particular boutique hotel by the sea called Mer Azul. Twirling a finger through one of the J-shaped curls of her shining dark hair, Maya had smiled widely.

Halfway through the second bottle, she'd suggested that with summer ripening, perhaps Mo would be in Beirut again soon. Mo eagerly assured her that he would. She'd made approving noises and glanced at her watch. It had been just long enough. She'd made excuses to leave. But not before scrawling her number on a cocktail napkin.

Now in Beirut, sitting at the bar in Beirut White, Maya saw the predictable response from Mo. *En retard mais j'accélère! Je te verai en dix!*

She acknowledged the message with a winking emoji and a heart.

She then composed another text, meant for a different man.

Ten minutes, she wrote.

Maya's text landed in a bunker two hundred kilometers to the south in Tel Aviv. There, Werner Davidai, head of the Mossad operations directorate called Caesarea, retrieved his buzzing phone from his pocket. The bald sixty-seven-year-old nudged the deputy next to him. "Maya says ten minutes," he said.

The deputy nodded before quietly passing the word to the uniformed men at the scopes.

Werner was sitting along a wall in the darkened Joint War Room, JWR. It was a hardened warren under the Matcal Tower, the general staff headquarters of the Israeli Defense Forces (IDF). Before Maya's text had come in, the Caesarea chief had been listening to the uniformed soldiers of IDF's Unit 8200 swap jargon over their boom mics. Much like the American National Security Agency, Unit 8200 was the Israeli group that processed Signals Intelligence, SIGINT, which included intercepting voice and electronic communications.

Werner put his phone back in the breast pocket of his thick, army-style shirt. Over the soldiers' heads, he watched a grainy infrared video feed from the four Heron drones circling Beirut. The unmanned aerial combat vehicles, UACVs, still had more than two hours' time on station. "Tighten up on Beirut White," he said to one of the operators.

As the view changed, the Caesarea boss watched the telemetry data flashing at the bottom of the screen, indicating flight attitude and weapons status. The flickering numbers reminded him of the heads-up display of the F-15 he'd flown for the Israeli Air Force (IAF) way back when. And then, as often happened to Werner, an involuntary memory fired. He was suddenly glimpsing the sun reflecting off a canopy, a smudge of brown desert beyond the sea. He was watching the red-and-black roundel on the Syrian MiG's wing angling down, away.

A young 8200 soldier brought him back to the present. "Sir—fix on the HVT's phone." It was a reference to Mohammed Baramzedeh, Mo, the Iranian High Value Target they were pursuing, the one on his way to see Maya at Beirut White.

"Can we get him on video?" asked Werner.

"Triangulation on two . . . now three cell towers. Wait one," came the reply. The drone video swung back and forth, retargeting. With the assistance of electronic gimbals, the image improved. Zooming in tight, the men in the JWR identified the car as a silver Honda Accord. And zooming tighter still, they saw the HVT himself—Mo, on his way to meet Maya at the club. Hurrying.

Gotcha, Werner thought.

Reu got out of the van first. Standing still, the Flotilla 13 frogman paused, ensuring that all was as it should be in the parking lot at Beirut White. The nightclub's bass-heavy music shook the Sprinter's windows. But things were otherwise still. Poking his head around the van, Reu surveyed the egress routes and decided they were good, just as they'd been depicted in the satellite photos. Satisfied, he rapped the vehicle's sliding door. Fully dry and clothed as civilians now, his men got out, snugging down the pistols each carried in an ankle holster. They headed toward the club.

At the corner of the building, near clusters of straggling partiers who'd either just left the club or were about to go in, three attractive women approached. These additional Mossad *katsas* put on an ostentatious show of greeting, kissing Reu and his Flotilla 13 men like boyfriends. Now, strutting proudly, holding hands, the girls led their dates past the line of young men waiting at the door. The bouncer winked at the lead brunette and unclipped a velvet rope, letting them all pass. The pretty young *katsa* blew him a kiss on her way through.

"Oh, to be a frogman," said one of the IDF drone operators back in the Tel Aviv JWR bunker, watching on monitor one. The sergeant zoomed in on the front door to Beirut White, confirming that the team had entered as planned. He relayed it to the officer over his shoulder.

With the team inside, Werner turned back to the video of Mo's Honda, mentally urging the Iranian to hurry the hell up to Beirut White. But just as the Caesarea boss willed the silver Accord to make a pivotal turn toward the club, the sedan slowed to a stop on the shoulder.

"What's he doing? Where'd he go?" Werner asked no one in particular.

Caught unawares, the drone's tracking video momentarily lost the vehicle. It then swerved and circled before reacquiring the target. But the Honda was no longer alone. A white Mitsubishi Montero SUV had arrived. It was slowing to a stop behind Mo's now-parked Honda. Alarmed, Werner watched as the Mitsubishi's front seat passenger and driver got out and walked toward Mo's window.

"Who the fuck is *this*?" the Caesarea chief said to the lead 8200 Network Intelligence Officer, NIO, charged with the SIGINT plan. "Has our HVT gotten any calls? How do we not know about this?"

The NIO struggled to respond. "HVT's phone has been active on WhatsApp," a subordinate rescued him. "He's using a VPN. Can't read the contents."

Werner clenched his mouth and stared. The Caesarea boss watched two men approaching Baramzedeh's Honda in the drone video. Both were fit and bearded. One of them cautiously opened the front passenger door of the Accord and slid in next to the HVT. The other stood looking at the street, watching, his right arm at his side. It was poised as though ready to reach for the sidearm that was surely inside his jacket.

The fucking bastards, Werner thought.

Inside Beirut White, Maya watched the Flotilla 13 team and their *katsa* dates as they came through the front door. She'd been one of those young *katsas* before entering the elite *kidon* special activities program more than a decade ago. Approvingly, the now senior Mossad operative watched the four pretty women thread the crowd toward the teeming dance floor. But while the younger Flotilla 13 men were able to blend in, the oldest one looked uncomfortable.

Paying little attention to his assigned date, the Flotilla 13 leader's eyes were resting on the door, watching. *Military men*, Maya thought.

The best of them, the ones you really wanted when the shit hit the fan, simply couldn't pull off an alias like this. Then again, she thought, if the snatch went sideways, that flinty bastard with the thousand-yard stare would be just the man for the job.

Her phone buzzed. Mo texting again. *Excuse moi-je peux pas venir après tout-c'est mon boulot.*

Maya kept her face neutral. It wasn't easy because Mo's message was a disaster, a showstopper. He was abandoning her for work, standing her up. She responded with several coquettish replies. None worked. Mo was adamant.

On pourrai faire rendez vous à la plage à Azul, demain? the Iranian finally offered.

Maya bit the inside of her cheek. *Demain.* Tomorrow.

That was it, then. The op was off, scrubbed. They'd all be heading out now, using their pre-planned egress routes to get back to Israel. There was no sense in pressing further. Werner would lose his mind as soon as he found out, she knew.

But projecting a breezy calm, the beautiful *kidon* composed a final message for Mo. *À demain, chéri!*

Then she texted Werner.

"*Chara!*" Werner cursed in the JWR bunker, reading his buzzing phone. "Maya says the HVT's not going to the club."

Up on monitor three, Werner watched in disgust as the Montero and Honda made a U-turn together. The two vehicles were headed back to the southwest, toward the southern Beirut Shia neighborhoods collectively called the *dahiyeh*, Arabic for "suburb."

"Has to be an IRGC security detail," Werner's deputy said, watching the cars on monitor three. IRGC was the Islamic Revolutionary Guard Corps, the elite backbone of Iranian military ops. They were all over Lebanon, especially the *dahiyeh*.

Not just IRGC, Werner was thinking in response, jaw muscles moving. "They're Quds."

The specialty of IRGC's elite Quds Force was to gin up Shia proxy armies around the Middle East. *Armies of freedom* as the Iranians called them. In Lebanon, that Shia army was called Hezbollah, *Hizb' Allah*, the Party of God.

Someone burned us, Werner thought, crossing his arms.

The vehicles were conducting a surveillance-detection route, an SDR, turning randomly. Regular IRGC officers wouldn't conduct fieldcraft like that. But Quds officers would.

"They seem to be headed southwest. Probably going back to Mer Azul, the HVT's beach hotel," Werner's deputy said, crossing his arms in imitation of the chief.

More like the dahiyeh, thought Werner. Once there, they'd disappear for good into some Hezbollah-run safe house. So much for the planned snatch at Beirut White with the easy transit back to the sub *Tekumah*.

As a grandson of German Holocaust survivors, the old Yiddish saying fired from somewhere in Werner's mind: *Mann tracht, un Gott lacht*.

Well, Werner thought. *God's most certainly laughing now.*

But he still had a play, he thought. He texted Maya.

Inside Beirut White, Maya tried to make sense of the new orders. According to Werner's message, they were now to intercept Mo and suspected Quds escorts somewhere in the middle of the Christian section of East Beirut, an armed ambush of two vehicles.

Not only was it lacking in any detailed planning—dangerous enough—but it would be messy. It would mean a firefight, followed by a running, gunning escape across two-thirds of the city before they got to the exfil point down at the Damour Beach Resort.

Maya knew Werner as well as any man on earth. She wasn't surprised the old man would gamble an active fight with Quds in the middle of Beirut's best neighborhoods. She knew how desperately they needed Mo. But a public gunfight? A hot war with Quds? Still. Orders were orders.

The leggy *kidon* left a three-inch stack of highly devalued Lebanese pounds on the bar and made her way to the dance floor. She nodded a subtle hello to the *katsas* that worked for her and danced her way to the hard-faced Flotilla 13 leader.

Maya took him by the elbow and rotated her hips seductively against his. Feigning a kiss, she pulled his ear close to her mouth. "New orders," she said with a playful lick to his neck that tasted like salt. "Get the team back to the van. Now."

Soon she was bumping over potholes in the speeding Mercedes Sprinter, studying Werner's latest text—his third since they'd entered the vehicle. The Caesarea boss was insistent. Failure wasn't an option, he'd said.

Maya was trying to make sense of the intercept point now, comparing it to the map on her phone. It seemed an unlikely, if not impossible, spot to get to in time. She thought of calling Werner directly to talk him out of this. But she didn't want to break protocol. "Left here," she shouted over the straining diesel, looking again at the app. "This road should cut across Rue Bastille. Let's hope they stay on it. Left. Here, *here!*"

The tires squealed. They were out of East Beirut now, across the old green line from the civil war of the eighties, into the western Sunni zone. It was a place that had seen its share of kidnappings.

"Widen the shot," Werner said to the lieutenant piloting the UACV in the Tel Aviv JWR. The Caesarea boss watched the progress of the team's Mercedes Sprinter in one monitor, the path of the Quds Montero and Accord in another. Since the Quds men were doing an SDR, it was almost impossible to fix a reliable intercept. But for the moment, it looked like there was at least a chance—there were only so many roads the Iranians could use to get down to the *dahiyeh*.

"If they can cut them off there," said Werner, watching the converging vehicles, "then we've got them. Maybe find a shortcut to this point, here." He was interrupted by his buzzing phone. Maya again.

HVT kill ok?

Dragging his eyes from the phone, Werner looked at the monitor and thought through his response. If the Israelis simply eliminated Mo Baramzedeh, as they'd done with a half dozen other Iranian scientists in the past year, they'd lose their best lead into a Quds initiative to arm up Hezbollah with indefensible cruise missiles.

But letting Baramzedeh escape was even worse.

Werner knuckled his head and thought. Up in his office on the top floor of the building, he had the "Red Page" authorization that authorized the assassination. The Red Page had been endorsed all the way up to the prime minister. And Maya could certainly make a clean job of the kill. But if she did, they'd lose their best intelligence lead.

The phone in Werner's hand buzzed again. Maya was still asking what he wanted to do.

Werner's involuntary memory flashed. For a moment, he glimpsed the Syrian MiG through the HUD, a black triangle against a white sky. The old man blinked, shrugged it off, then glanced up at the UACV telemetry data. The Spike missiles were armed and ready. They still had plenty of time on station.

After another moment's consideration, Werner thumbed out his reply to Maya.

KILL ok, Maya read from her perch in the van. She dropped her phone to her lap and relayed the news to the team.

Against the sway of the careening Mercedes, the *kidon* twisted under her shoulder straps, accepting the Sig Sauer P320 with its extended suppressor barrel. She looked down the length of it, ejected the mag, and put a thumb on the top round. Hollow points. She'd put two in Mo's heart, then aim for his forehead.

But only if she couldn't subdue him with drugs first. The Flotilla 13 commander, who Maya now knew as Reu, had agreed that Maya would be the one to approach Mo. She'd take one more chance at getting him alive after the Flotilla 13 people had gunned down the Quds people. But if things went to shit, Maya would use her hollow points.

She rammed the mag back into the grip and pulled the slide to chamber a round. She could hear the men behind her gearing up similarly. Each would carry both the Sig Sauer and the compact version of the Israeli-produced IWI X95 assault rifle.

Maya faced Reu again, holding out her phone. "This intersection," she said, zooming in on the map of the city. "Will that work?" Her hand bobbed as the van jumped a curb.

Reu nodded. The weapons slid and clicked.

"*Shit!*" the young *katsa* behind the wheel suddenly shrieked. "We've got a cop!"

Werner watched as the Beirut City PD BMW flashed its lights and swerved into a U-turn. Though the drone video was silent, the old Caesarea boss could imagine the screaming siren. He could envision the radio calls going out over the Beirut police network, the summons for backup, the dashcam video of the Mossad van stuffed with killers, the headlines that would show up on Al Jazeera, and immediately following, the political outcry in Tel Aviv.

But far worse than any of that, if he kept the team on the op, he could foresee his band of spies being caught, dying under torture from the ruthless Quds operatives who'd inevitably get them from the corrupt Lebanese security forces. The first rule at Mossad was that no officer gets left behind. Ever. To Werner, it was an inviolate sacrament. Rule number one.

Maya texted, interrupting Werner's thought spiral.

Take out cops?

Werner looked up at the monitor with the Honda Accord and Mitsubishi Montero. The two cars were one minute from the intersection at most. An abduction of the HVT was still possible if they disabled the cop car. Maybe the snatch was worth it. To hell with the political outcry.

"More cop cars on the way," relayed one of the SIGINT operators, having intercepted Beiruti police comms.

Take out cops??? Maya messaged again, just seven seconds later.

Werner knew his team was fast. And good. But what if they got bogged down in a gun battle? What if there were more Quds people nearby, blocking the team's escape? On top of compromising his operatives, Werner might even miss Baramzedeh.

Gott lacht.

The Caesarea boss knuckled his head again. He looked at the path of the Mercedes converging on the Honda Accord and Montero. It would be close. He swore under his breath. The F-15 memory flickered. Condensed into a blink, Werner saw the MiG-21 Fishbed in the heads-up display, his own corkscrewing, heat-seeking Sidewinder missile. And the Syrian diving away, escaping.

He still had to answer Maya. He held his thumbs poised over his phone keyboard, pausing one last time. *ABORT*, he finally typed. *RTB*. Return to Base. He released a long, gravelly breath and threw his phone in his pocket.

To his deputy, he said, "Snatch op is *scrubbed*. This is now an egress. Have the team disable the cop car as cleanly as possible and clear the area. I want them back on *Tekumah* ASAP. All of them. And turn on the jamming drones, kill all police comms."

The men around him got to work.

But Werner wasn't finished.

The Caesarea boss turned to the IAF colonel in charge of the UACVs. "As soon as our team is clear, I want a targeting assessment on the Honda and the Montero. Both. Understand?"

Without waiting for the colonel's answer, Werner turned back to watch the other drone's video.

Bright muzzle flashes from the Sprinter van strobed the screen as the Flotilla 13 team lit up the engine block of the Beirut City police car. Smoke poured from the front of the police vehicle, drifting as a ghostly plume in the IR video. The cop car slowed, stuttered a few times, then stopped along a curb. The Sprinter wheeled into a turn.

With his team egressing to the south, Werner shifted his eyes to the drone crosshairs on each of the Quds vehicles. The lead car turned again, following through on the confused urban SDR pattern. From the drone's angle, the tall buildings momentarily scrambled the optical targeting solution, causing a series of dashes where the telemetry numbers had been.

"Well? Do we still have the shot?" Werner asked the IAF man.

"It's a crowded civilian area," responded the colonel.

"Not what I asked you," said Werner.

The colonel cleared his throat. "If those cars go much farther into that neighborhood with the high-rises, we may lose our chance."

"Then fire," said Werner. "Now."

From an altitude of 30,000 feet, the Israeli Heron UACV's two Spike missiles each locked on a separate target, using independently slaved Forward Looking Infrared (FLIR) targeting sensors. The TV screen in the JWR suddenly split, moving from the drone's main FLIR sensor to those of each missile. On the left was the Mitsubishi Montero. On the right, the Honda Accord. One missile per car.

Around a core of TNT, the Spikes' warheads were packed with dense tungsten cubes. They were relatively small, as warheads went, but they'd be good enough.

Werner, the ex–fighter pilot, did the missile math out of habit. Now launched from the drone's wings, the two Spikes were traveling at 1,000 miles per hour, 1,400 feet per second. To cover the 30,000 feet of altitude and the twenty-degree angled offset at the drone's position to the south would take twenty-five seconds. A lifetime.

When his countdown eroded to five seconds, the targeted cars turned again, taking another detour in their confused SDR. Trying to keep up, the missile video swerved, scanning, too close to see much more than a bumper, a taillight, the ground rushing up.

And then the video whited out. All the TV monitors in the JWR blinked for two seconds, as though there'd been a power outage. Then they came back on with a view from the still-circling drones, which watched and waited over the destruction like vultures.

Werner saw billowing black smoke, white-hot flames, long black marks scarring the street. Two buildings were on fire, dark chunks falling from high floors. One of the buildings was already leaning, about to collapse.

And now for the blowback, the Caesarea boss thought as he watched the building tumble, disappearing in a white deluge of fire.

But this time, Werner hadn't missed.

PART ONE

READY

CHAPTER 1

SQUASHED UPON THE OTHERWISE FLAT LINE OF THE DARK PACIFIC
Ocean, stretched wide by blazing yellow clouds, the sun, Meredith
Morris-Dale thought, looked for all the world like a broken egg yolk.
Far from the soul-stirring grandeur that had been promised, Meredith
found the famed Maui sunset a bit disappointing; if anything, a mere
runny mess.

Though preening couples to either side of her erupted with the predictable oohs and aahs, the vacationing CIA operations officer privately
found it all rather ordinary. *The sun going down off Hawaii. Big deal.* She
thought it more or less like the millions of sunsets that had preceded it,
and, barring one of the man-made disasters she'd spent her entire career
preventing, just like the multitudes that would follow.

Sitting by a plastic table on the sand, Meredith wore a backless
white halter dress that hugged her lean torso, showed off her athletic
shoulders, and revealed just enough of her long, brown legs. The heeled
espadrilles she'd removed to make it across the beach were piled with
her handbag on the seat next to her. Her ex-husband, John, was supposed to have been in that chair, sharing this sunset.

But he wasn't.

She glanced at her smartwatch and confirmed that John still hadn't
messaged her. She tasted the salt of her frozen margarita and squinted
at the oblong sun. For all she knew, John had gone straight to the airport and caught a flight back to Seattle. He was more than capable of
that kind of stupidity, she thought.

She sighed. She deserved this—or at least most of it. She'd engineered it, set herself up, raised her own expectations. But who could have blamed her? It had only been two months since she and John had been on that last op in western Iran, working well together.

Maybe—just *maybe*—Meredith had thought back then, the sparks had been strong enough for a rekindling. *Maybe*, she'd hoped, she could even talk John into coming back to CIA as a case officer, ending his self-imposed exile out there in the Pacific Northwest.

For Christ's sake, she thought now, fingering the ice-cold glass in her hand. They'd been married for fifteen years, shared a daughter, traveled the world together in the cloak of a clandestine service that really made a difference. How could she not have at least *tried* to put things back together?

She'd planned this mini-vacation months ago to coincide with the short novice triathlon she'd completed that morning, a fundraiser for a veterans' support group. But in the sparky excitement after that last op—regrettably—she'd decided to invite John.

More judiciously, to sound neutral to her ex—to not scare him away—she'd spun the trip as an opportunity for him to decompress, a reward of sorts, since he'd done that Iranian op as a favor to her. And to her stunned surprise, he'd agreed to come along to root for her in the triathlon. It had been a homing beacon of a signal if ever there was one, she'd thought. How could she not have at least *tried* to make a go of things?

That's when she'd gotten stupid, she realized now, her head pounding after a large gulp of frozen slush. Like some pie-eyed schoolgirl, she'd bought John his own room and paid his airfare. While he said he'd only come for a few days to support her race, she'd stretched her own room reservation to a week, splurging for the ocean view, nurturing a dim hope that he'd stay on with her.

A hope that had taken root, branched out, strengthened, grown with every sunlit day on the beach together. And to her pleasant surprise, she'd even nudged him into talking sense again. Though he hadn't yet fully committed, she'd thought he'd started to consider a return to the Agency. It had all been going so well—until Meredith had gone and raised the old argument about his seven-year-old affair.

She swallowed what was left of the margarita.

Why, Meredith, why?

Now, conspicuously alone at her table, watching the sunset, she could feel the occasional eye upon her. More acutely, she noticed a man at the thatched-hut bar in a red flowered shirt who pretended to ponder the looming cliffs over her shoulder. An expert at counter-surveillance, Meredith recognized this for what it was.

But just then, she didn't care about the man in the red flowered shirt. For once in her life, she wasn't in disguise. She wasn't pretending to be someone else, using an alias on nonofficial cover in some distant hellhole or on her best behavior in some dull reception at an embassy.

No. Far from it. She told herself she had every *bleeping* right to be here by herself. She had every *effing* right to enjoy this drink, this sunset—even if rather ordinary—in solitude. Ogle away, Red Shirt. Enjoy the view. *I'm on vacation. That's right—alone.* She licked the salt on her empty margarita glass.

Sitting up a little straighter, Meredith faced into the ocean breeze. The rising wind tousled her hair and flung it behind her shoulders. Gazing at the backlit Pacific, she dropped her fake smile and allowed her real expression to take hold. Her mouth was firm, chin jutting. Her eyes glittered as they watered in the wind.

A final ray of orange sunlight burst through a cloud. It reflected brightly off the waves, lighting her as if on a stage. With her shining blue eyes and ruffling white dress, she'd instantly blossomed to the full extent of her considerable beauty. Even men with wives sitting directly across from them stole secret glances at this lovely woman sitting all by herself. Another umbrella-topped drink arrived. It was from Red Shirt.

I'll tell you why I did it, Meredith was thinking, unconsciously tossing her head in the breeze, ignoring both the drink and its aloha-shirted procurer. *I did it because no matter what John says, he sure as hell DID cheat with that woman on the Red Sea. He sure as hell DID lie about it right to my face. Bastard's STILL lying about it!*

She glanced at the mai tai now in front of her. She pushed the umbrella and pineapple garnish out of the way to take a lusty swig. And with the rum warming her throat, she told herself to forget all about that stupid triathlon, where she'd finished somewhere in the middle of the over-forty women's division.

Remember who you are, she said to herself, staring at the glowing line on the horizon where the sun had been. She was Meredith Morris-Dale. A force, a warrior, defender of this fucked-up realm. She was strong, resourceful, and self-sufficient. She gave no quarter, expected none. And she would master this setback just as she'd mastered all the rest of them.

Hell, she thought, quaffing more of the booze. *What am I even doing here?* She needed to get back to Langley. After that last successful op, she had every right to believe she might even be up for a chief of station slot, her only real aspiration for the past ten years.

That's the only thing that matters, she told herself. A COS slot was *certainly* more important than stupid, *stupid* John Richard Dale.

And to think she'd switched the Hawaiian invitation from Steve Chadwick—her Istanbul-based sometime-lover—to John. What had she been thinking? Chadwick—an almost station chief himself—would have been at that triathlon this morning, cheering her on. *Hell*, she thought, sipping the mai tai. *Chadwick had even said he'd run the race with me.*

But now, with the horizon line cooled to crimson, she reminded herself that she didn't need Chadwick's validation either. What she needed, she thought, was to get back to Langley where the real action was. There were rumors beginning to circulate that Nick Drault, Paris chief of station, might be moving on.

Paris Station! Meredith bit the juicy pineapple garnish. Yes. It was high time to get back to DC. Now. It was high time to seize the day. *The world waits for no one*, she told herself. *Carpe di*—

"I just wanted to introduce myself," said Red Shirt.

"Oh," she said, squinting up at him, blinking against the wind, swallowing the pineapple. "Hello."

"Enjoying the sunset?"

"I suppose," she said. "It's quite nice."

"How about the mai tai? Enjoying that too?"

Red Shirt took a seat.

Meredith flexed her old training muscles. She could endure this interloper just as she could wait out any contact in the field. The drinks were twenty bucks apiece. She'd pay her damned dues.

She dodged his innocuous questions. Yes, she'd competed in the triathlon. No, she didn't recall seeing him there, but yes, she was glad it was over and that they could all relax now. He asked what her name was. She changed the subject. He volunteered his own as Alex, though she hadn't asked. He was good at keeping up his end of a one-sided conversation.

Later, when the sun was long gone, when the ice in the drinks had melted and the tiki flames blew sideways in the thickening breeze, Alex suggested dinner. He positioned it as a reward for the race they'd both completed that day. Somewhat to her own surprise, Meredith said yes.

Stuck here at this resort, she couldn't think of anything better to do, and if she were honest, she found him rather good-looking—if a little quick to laugh at his own jokes. A second mai tai had helped.

Wafting frangipani and roaring surf accompanied them on their walk up the hill to the restaurant. Soft landscape lighting lent vivid shadows to the crowded banana leaves. Innocently, Alex again asked where she was from, what she did for a living. Meredith continued to redirect. She commented on the stars, the brilliance of the moon, the silvery sea.

But she was running out of runway. She had to give him something.

Instinctively, she used the well-worn details of her Maggie O'Dea cover, the green-eyed international business consultant with red hair, a disguise created by colored contacts and a wig that used to drive John mad. Though she didn't have the wig or contacts on, the more Meredith assumed the role of Maggie, the more comfortable she became.

There was a stopping point along the way, a lookout. Beyond it, large floodlights from the hotel roof lit the waves that thundered against the lava rock a hundred feet below. Alex slowed his pace. She felt the touch of his hand against hers. She felt the touch, yes, but also something else, a buzz.

"I feel something," Alex said earnestly, turning to her, his eyes gleaming in the reflection of the floodlights. "It's as though we—"

Meredith held up her wrist. Resisting the movement, his hand stayed locked on hers, fingers interlaced. "It's my smartwatch," she said, cutting off whatever noble thing he was about to say. "Call coming in."

"Oh," he mumbled, still holding her hand at an awkward angle. "Well, can't you just—"

Meredith had already twisted her wrist to see the number, expecting it to be John calling with an apology. But it wasn't John. It was a number that was . . . *the operations line*. She jerked free of Alex's grasp, shaking him loose. "No," she said. "I can't."

Her wrist still buzzing, Meredith fumbled through her handbag and dug out the phone that lay pressed up against her smallest pistol, a snubbed, seven-round Glock 43. "Hello, Ashley," she said into it, using the prearranged greeting that would tell the dispatcher she needed to free herself before she could speak.

A female watch officer in Langley responded, "Hello. How are things there? We're in Arizona and it's blazing hot."

Holy shit, thought Meredith. *Arizona and it's blazing hot*—the code for an Alpha, an issue that required her to authenticate through the secure app right away. In her entire twenty-one-year career, Meredith had maybe had an Alpha come over the line two or three times. "One minute, Ashley," Meredith said, hitting the mute, her pulse pounding.

Alex had taken a step back, watching, dismayed at the sudden intensity that slanted this fit woman's eyebrows into an intimidating V. When she looked up at him now, she seemed a different person.

Because she was a different person.

Maggie O'Dea was history. It was Meredith Morris-Dale who now held the glowing phone near her heart. "Listen, *ah* . . ." In the sudden turn of events, she'd completely forgotten his name. She bit her lip.

"Alex," he said over the crashing surf.

"Right. Listen, Alex. I've got to go. It was nice meeting you."

He cocked his head. "Wait. What? Do you really have to take that?"

"Yes. It's work."

"Work? Well, can I get your number? Can we pick this up tomorrow?"

Fifteen seconds had ticked since Meredith had put the phone on mute. She'd noted every one of them. *Sixteen . . . seventeen . . .*

"No," she said. "We can't. And I really must go."

He swept his arms to indicate the strip of moon on the sea. "And leave all this . . . alone? For . . . *work*?"

"Absolutely," she said, turning away.

"Really. Work calling you from the middle of the night on the mainland . . . where it's like three in the morning." He thrust his hands into the pockets of his shorts. "Are you . . . married or something?"

Meredith thought it over for a second. "Yes, I'm married . . . or *something*."

"You could have said so," shot Alex.

The phone in her hand felt like a grenade with a pulled pin. "I'm sorry to have . . . led you on. Not what I intended. Now—good night."

"Does it help that I'm married too?"

She laughed and turned her back to him.

"Bitch," he said.

"*Hah!*" she laughed louder, quickening her pace.

She walked as rapidly as her espadrilles could carry her back down the path toward the beach. Glancing back, she saw that Alex stood there in the floodlights, watching. She ducked onto a darkened footpath, completely sober, grateful for the call back to reality.

She opened the secure app, authenticated, and spoke quietly into the phone. Her breath was rushed, heart racing. "Morris-Dale. Up secure. Go."

"Wait one for Officer Rance," said the disembodied voice of the watch officer in Langley. Ed Rance was her boss, head of the Agency's Counterproliferation Center, CPC, charged with stanching the flow of nuclear, biological, and chemical weapons around the world. She was surprised to hear from him. She'd thought he was on a temporary assignment in Europe.

"Meredith," he said, coming on the line after a series of beeps that indicated they had two-way encryption. "Sorry to interrupt your vacation."

She doubted that. She pressed the phone hard against her head to hear him over the surf. "No problem."

"Hope you've been enjoying yourself," he said.

"Not really."

She heard him grunt. "Well. Anyway—we have another Atlas problem. I need you back to HQS. ASAP."

"*Now*, Ed? Why? What's going on with Atlas?"

"I'll fill you in when you get here. Suffice to say we have an urgent meeting with Dorsey and the director. I'm putting you through to Ops for travel. See you later tonight."

"You mean tomorrow night."

"Whatever."

Prick.

CHAPTER 2

MEREDITH SAT RAMROD STRAIGHT ON THE BARELY PADDED CHAIR OUT-
side the director's office. She'd been in this ninety-degree position since
takeoff from Kahului in the dark some fourteen hours earlier. She
wanted to slouch. But she'd be damned before she'd let them think she
was anything but sharp.

As if, she thought now, smoothing the work trousers she always kept
in her bag for just such an emergency. She hoped the makeup she'd
hastily applied in a stinking Dulles restroom was still holding. She'd
barely slept on the long trek over the Pacific and the connecting flight
from LA, trying to ignore the ear-splitting babies in the rows ahead of
and behind her. For at least three hours it seemed the infants had
worked in concert.

But it wasn't just the babies. Meredith had worn a groove through
her brain with Rance's ominous summons. *Another Atlas problem.* She'd
formed at least five theories as to what this latest problem might be,
each a fresh headwind to her career.

She'd gotten to the seventh floor an hour late, having weaved pointlessly through DC's crawling Beltway traffic. Now, at eight p.m. in the
anteroom outside the director's office, sore from the triathlon, she was
dying to get horizontal. But no case officer outside this door ever expected a good night's sleep.

A glowing red light indicated the director's office was secure, not to
be entered. Since Meredith had arrived late, she had no way to get in—
a fact confirmed by either of the two ancient assistants that sat thirty

feet away, posed like a pair of sphinxes outside a temple. Now and then, the one who faced Meredith looked up from her monitor and offered a tepid, wrinkled smile.

Partially to avoid the assistant, Meredith stared vacantly at a TV tuned to CNN on the opposite wall. Though muted, she watched a reporter standing in front of flashing emergency lights in the dark. "Beirut car-bomb kills thirty, sets off sectarian violence," read the chyron below the video. She'd caught snippets of the bombing during her travels. It had been a big one. The Sunnis were blaming the Shias. The Shias were blaming the Christians. The Christians were blaming Hezbollah. Hezbollah swore it was Israel.

Another Atlas problem, she thought. Could this be it?

Doubtful.

Atlas wasn't in Beirut. He was in CIA custody, enduring debriefs in downstate Virginia.

But Atlas had once been the lead Iranian Quds weapons dealer for Hezbollah before Meredith had gone and snatched him on that last op in western Iran.

Probably, she thought now.

On that Iran op two months prior, strapped into that escaping Black Hawk, Meredith had had only thirty seconds to decide whether to kill or keep the surrendered Quds man, whom they'd since codenamed Atlas. With a SEAL's rifle at his throat, the Quds lieutenant colonel had hurriedly convinced Meredith he could be a valuable CIA spy, an agent sent back to Iran, working for her. She'd bought it. Running a highly placed asset on the inside of Quds would be a career masterstroke, she'd calculated at the time.

Perhaps not, she thought now, staring at the light over the director's door and the mess unfolding on CNN.

The light blinked off. The door opened. A short man in a gray suit came through the threshold. He was bald, mid-sixties, compact, stout, in a hurry. As he walked past Meredith, their eyes met briefly. The man passed the old sphinxes and hustled out the door.

Two taller, dark-haired lackies followed. Both carried hard-sided briefcases. Meredith could feel a mild rush of air as they passed. Whatever the agenda of their meeting with the director, it hadn't gone well. The red light over the director's door came on again.

Another eight minutes. When the door finally reopened, Meredith stood and squared her shoulders, ready to apologize for being late. But just as she was about to cross the threshold, Jeff Dorsey, her boss's boss, came straight at her.

Rance, her direct superior, trailed Dorsey by a half step. Both men were suited up, ties knotted, faces grim. Tucked snugly under Rance's elbow were three classified folders with candy-cane stripes. Neither of them broke stride.

Meredith got out of their way.

"You missed it," Rance said over his shoulder as he passed her. "Come on."

Per the customs of their service, they switched to small talk in the elevator. They asked after Meredith's trip, her performance in the Maui triathlon. Dorsey, wispy-haired, a foot shorter than Rance, looked pained. He apologized for calling her back. Rance asked how John was doing. Meredith answered with a shrug. The three of them rode in silence.

Another Atlas problem.

A few floors down, an attendant opened Dorsey's personal SCIF in the operations section. Pronounced *skiff*, it was a vault for only the most sensitive conversations. Before going in, the attendant confiscated their phones and watches, which weren't allowed in the hardened room. The rows of cubicles on the rest of the floor were lightly staffed by junior CIA analysts from the various country desks. The full complement had gone home for the evening. Rance pulled the heavy door shut.

Dorsey removed his suit coat and yanked at his collar, lowering his tie to half-mast. He collapsed into a chair. His head fell into his hands as though his neck had just broken.

"Well, that was fun," said Dorsey, the head of CIA's National Clandestine Service. His red-rimmed eyes remained fixed on the tabletop.

Rance placed the stack of classified folders on the table. He pushed them toward the middle with his fingertips, as though they might infect him. But, ever courtly, he offered Meredith a chair before taking one of his own.

With the studied concentration of a surgeon, Dorsey focused on unbuttoning his cuffs, rolling up his sleeves. "So—Meredith. You recognize the man who came out before us? The old bald guy?"

"No—should I have?" She thought of the brief eye contact she'd exchanged with the man.

"That was Werner Davidai," answered Dorsey, pronouncing the W like a V. He shifted his concentration to the left sleeve.

"*That* was Davidai? What's the head of Mossad Caesarea doing here?"

"Delivering these files," said Rance, tilting his head toward the striped stack at the table center. "That's what."

"Does this have something to do with that car bomb in Beirut?"

"Yup," said Dorsey, exhaling. "Beirut. Again. Fucking Mossad . . ."

Dorsey's voice died away. The spy chief swiveled his chair and rummaged through a credenza drawer. He turned back with a Bic and legal pad in his hands, then drummed the pen on the paper. "I suppose you may as well brief her up now, Ed. Director wants me back up there as soon as we're done. He's waiting."

Rance crossed his legs and pinched the skin near his Adam's apple. "Okay. I'll give her the abbreviated version."

Dorsey nodded.

Rance cleared his throat. "You know, Meredith, that I've been TDY in Vienna, right?" TDY meant temporary duty, a short-term overseas assignment.

"Yes," she answered. "Working for State on the new Iranian nuclear deal."

"A strategic *advisor* to State, yes."

Friendly way of putting it, she thought. Months earlier, Rance had unwittingly fallen for a Russian SVR honeytrap. Meredith had been the one to expose the affair. Though a counterintelligence investigation had cleared Rance of *criminal* wrongdoing, the CI team had recommended giving him a temporary assignment with State as a precaution.

The Bic in Dorsey's mouth had already been viciously chewed, an old cigarette-substitution habit of his. He removed the pen to speak. "The administration really wants this new nuclear deal, Meredith. Ed's over there in Vienna to make sure State doesn't agree to anything stupid—and who knows? Maybe he can even recruit some of the Iranian foreign ministry people to spy for us."

Another charitable description. Meredith looked at Rance. "Makes sense. And how are things in Vienna, Ed?"

Rance played with his loafer tassel. "Oh, you know, Meredith. I've met a few of their diplomats—but they're all on a tight MOIS leash." MOIS was the Iranian Ministry of Intelligence, CIA's opposite number in the Islamic Republic.

"But I will say," Rance added, "the actual deal negotiations are going well. The sanctions are biting. And we finally got the French and Germans to come around. State thinks we're getting close—at least that's what they thought before this goddamned Beirut thing happened."

Dorsey sighed. "Yeah. The, *uh*, quote-unquote car bomb story that was leaked to the media is about to fall apart. Al-Manar, Hezbollah's mouthpiece, is already making noise about Israel. You'd expect that . . . but Al Jazeera's raising questions now too. Pretty soon the whole world will know it was a Mossad drone strike on . . . on . . . Shit." The spy boss snapped his fingers. "What was the guy's name, Ed?"

Rance flipped open a file. "The Iranian scientist was named Mohammed Baramzedeh."

"Right," said Dorsey. "According to Werner, this Baramzedeh guy was an aerodynamics guru working on missile guidance. Werner was making the case for the hit in the meeting with the director—the one you just missed."

"Why would he need to come all the way here to make the case?" asked Meredith. "Mossad's been whacking Iranian technical experts for years."

"Yeah, but they usually check with us first," said Rance. "And this time it's caused us big problems. The Iranians have left the negotiating table. Right when we had all the other cosigners on board—the Brits, the French, the Germans . . ."

"Even the Russians," added Dorsey.

"Right," said Rance. "Even them. Anyway, right when we had everyone about ready to agree to a multilateral deal framework—Caesarea goes and whacks an Iranian scientist in the middle of Beirut, killing a bunch of civilians along the way. The director's furious. He called Mossad. They sent Werner."

"Ah," said Meredith. "No wonder Werner didn't look too happy when he came out of the director's office."

"To put it *mildly*," said Dorsey, gnawing on the pen, sighing. "I can't relive that car-crash of a meeting. Tell her the rest, Ed."

Rance pulled one of the striped folders free of the stack and flipped it open. Meredith saw an annotated missile schematic, a blueprint, edged with squared-off Hebrew markings. "This missile," Rance said as he tapped the schematic, "is why Baramzedeh got the Red Page."

Meredith nodded. She looked at the schematic and noted an Arabic word printed on the lower right: *Taniyn*. "I don't know if Arabic and Farsi use the same word—but this missile seems to be called *Taniyn*. Means 'dragon,' " she said.

"We know," answered Rance. "Werner told us."

"And Werner thinks this Baramzedeh was critical to this new Iranian missile, *Taniyn*?"

"Yeah. But it's technically not an *Iranian* missile. *Taniyn* is a Hezbollah weapon," said Dorsey. "Mossad's research directorate says the schematic is a modified SAM, an old Soviet SA-5, imported from Damascus years ago for Hezbollah in Beirut."

"Right," said Rance. "Werner thinks Baramzedeh was working on a plan to modify the old Hezbollah SA-5s to deliver a different kind of payload." He paused to clear his throat elaborately before going on. "Possibly . . . for nukes."

"*Nukes?*" shot Meredith. "Fitted to old surface-to-air missiles? What's to blow up at 50,000 feet?"

"Well, if you're to believe Werner," said Rance, "the payload isn't the only change."

"What else, then?"

"Enhancements to the wings, the control surfaces. That's what has Werner giving out Red Pages. The revised guidance package of this thing is based on the Chinese CJ-10, which itself was reverse engineered from our Tomahawk. We're talking about tech like enhanced GPS and DSMAC—Digital Scene Matching Area Correlator for optical geographic target recognition."

Meredith noted that Rance pronounced the acronym as *dee-smack*, as though he'd been familiar with it for years. "Range?" she asked.

"The SA-5 has a liquid-fueled rocket with solid fuel boosters . . . max range is something like two hundred miles. Enough to reach most of Israel from Hezbollah-held territories in the Beqaa and southern Lebanon."

"Long range for a SAM."

"Yeah," said Dorsey. "The Soviets got real creative on anti-air in the Cold War. This thing was designed to knock down B-52s over Siberia."

"Exactly," said Rance. "The Sovs exported a ton of these missiles, including to Assad, who handed them over to Hezbollah to fuck with the Israeli Air Force."

"Right," said Dorsey, shoving at his sleeves. "But it's more than just the guidance that has Werner all spun up. The missile casing's been altered too."

"See here?" Rance's finger settled on the nose cone. "Mossad's research team says the *Taniyn* design specs are a composite of ceramics and carbon fiber—same material used in new hypersonic missiles. At Mach 2, it would corkscrew into just about any target."

"That casing matches our intel for the new Russian hypersonic," added Dorsey.

"Love this new cold war," said Meredith, studying the schematic. "How many of these old SA-5s does Syria have?"

"Nobody knows for sure," said Rance. "Twenty, thirty . . . something like that. We don't know how many have made their way down to Hezbollah either. And, obviously, we don't know how significant this is. It's all Mossad intel. And you know how they like to . . . well . . . *influence* us."

"What's our Russia desk got to say about it?" asked Meredith. "Russia and Iran are pretty cozy in Syria. Any sign SVR's involved?"

"There's no sign of direct involvement from Russian intelligence," said Rance, enunciating carefully.

"We sure?" asked Meredith. After his Russian honeypot fuckup, Rance probably never wanted to hear the letters S-V-R again.

"I concur with Ed," said Dorsey. "After the meeting upstairs, the Russia desk told the director they hadn't seen any direct SVR presence in Iranian weapons sites." He fiddled with his sagging tie. "This is all about importation of components through Quds front companies, then coordinating Iranian aerodynamic experts to modify the missiles—guys like Baramzedeh."

"Did Werner tell you how Mossad got *this* missile schematic?" asked Meredith.

"Yeah. They stole it directly from Baramzedeh," said Dorsey. "A Caesarea *kidon* honeytrap lured the scientist to a bar in Paris last month. Mossad broke into his room and hacked his laptop while he was at the bar with her. Werner at least gave us that much."

"I can't read Hebrew," said Meredith. "But the engineering marks look similar to ours. Does this schematic actually indicate anything about nukes?"

"*Uh*, no," said Rance. "*Nothing.* The warhead cavity's a blank canvas—at least in the schematic."

"Then why is Werner making that leap? This could be a conventional cruise missile."

"Exactly," said Rance.

Dorsey sighed. "Well. Werner has his reasons." He nodded to Rance.

"A few weeks ago," said Rance, "Hezbollah fired a SAM in the general direction of an IAF F-16 off the Lebanese coast. But the usual electronic signature was different. No active radar. After skimming the surface, the mystery missile went into the sea. No explosion."

"Right," said Dorsey. "And, thinking that strange, the Israelis sent a sub out to recover the wreckage. The recovered fragments match *this* schematic. *Taniyn*." He tapped the blueprint.

"Okay," said Meredith. "But why fire it into the sea?"

"Mossad thinks it was a dry run against a terrestrial target package. But they acknowledge they don't know what that target might be. And, as it turns out, the recovered warhead was a dummy—twenty kilos of concrete."

"So—worst case," said Meredith, "Werner thinks that dummy warhead may have been simulating a nuclear payload—courtesy of our good friends in Iran?"

Dorsey nodded. "Uh-huh. A fast, low-flying hypersonic that could obliterate Tel Aviv."

"How'd Hezbollah get this thing built?" asked Meredith. "I haven't seen anything about a missile like this coming through our cables."

"No shit," said Dorsey, frowning. "Surprised all of us."

"It seems," started Rance, "that Soleimani's Quds Force built up the front companies that face Russian and Chinese suppliers. The whole weapons-import network's a mishmash. Even Mossad couldn't put it all together. They've detailed what they could in that second folder there. It's translated for us. Pretty sharp intel, if it isn't just Israeli disinformation for our benefit."

Meredith pulled the thin folder free of the stack and looked through it. "I still don't see how Mossad's making the nuke leap," she said after ten seconds of reading. "The warhead in this schematic's a solid dark color, no details. The recovered warhead was concrete. So, what's the *actual* payload?"

"That's the trillion-dollar question," said Dorsey.

Rance drew Meredith's eyes back to the drawing. "The warhead cavity is a big blank in the schematic, you're right. But according to Werner, the dummy cement core appears to have been a sphere surrounded by a plastic shell with . . . blast caps."

"Blast caps," repeated Meredith, looking up. "As in . . ." She didn't need to verbalize the rest. The design Rance had just described had the basic elements for a simple nuclear weapon. Touched off by blast caps, a spherical implosion would compress a ball of Highly Enriched Uranium, HEU, to start the chain reaction of atomic fission. A nuke.

"Exactly," said Dorsey, playing with his tie.

"Or the caps were just there to disintegrate the missile so the Israelis couldn't analyze it," said Rance. "There's no *real* proof of a nuclear design. And we have no intel to suggest Iran's exported any of their HEU. As part of the deal negotiation, we've had IAEA monitors keeping track of Iran's small existing HEU stockpile."

Meredith stared at him. "We're going to rely on IAEA inspectors?"

"Iran has every incentive to keep their HEU in country," said Rance. "They want the sanctions removed. Low Enriched Uranium for their nuclear reactors will be stored in a bank governed by the UN. Whatever HEU they have now, they keep—but UN monitoring will ensure they don't make more. That's the deal we've all agreed to. And it's as good a deal as we're going to get."

"Where's the LEU bank?" asked Meredith.

"Russia," said Dorsey.

"The missile's Russian," said Meredith.

"Soviet," corrected Rance, grimacing. "And all Werner really has are fragments of a dummy that could just be an anti-ship missile, a cheap copy of a Chinese Silkworm. It was fired into the sea, wasn't it?"

"After being designed by an Iranian missile expert with a payload that seems deliberately disguised," said Meredith. She looked at Dorsey. "What if Werner's right? What if they could smuggle a radiological warhead into Lebanon? They got the missile guidance revisions into the country somehow, right? Why not use the same distribution channels?"

"Exactly," said Dorsey. "And if it's as Mossad says, if Hezbollah has really taken possession of an Iranian nuclear delivery capability, then Israel's fucked. They have no defense for this thing."

"Iron Dome knocks down Hamas rockets from the Gaza Strip every other week," said Meredith.

"Those rockets fly in an unguided high-altitude arc," countered Dorsey. He tapped the schematic. "This thing's control surfaces indicate it as a low-altitude cruise missile. And its solid fuel engines would get it traveling at Mach 2 or better. Iron Dome couldn't touch it. Our Patriots couldn't either, for that matter."

"Sounds like a job for Israeli F-15s," said Meredith. "Bunker busters. Take out the SA-5 stockpiles up in Beirut."

"If they knew where they were," said Dorsey. "And of course, even if they did, Hezbollah keeps weapons labs under hospitals and day-care centers. No Israeli politician would ever go for another war in Lebanon. And—God forbid—if there really is any kind of nuclear component, the radiation leak in the middle of a dense city could kill millions."

"That," Rance added, "and you can't bomb knowledge. Iran and Hezbollah would just find a way to rebuild this thing somewhere else. It's why the Vienna deal matters. If we have the right verifications in place, we can tolerate a nuclear Iran."

"How about a nuclear Hezbollah?" asked Meredith.

"You sound like Werner," said Rance.

"Because he's making sense."

"There's not enough intel to support that angle," said Rance. "All Werner has is a modified SAM with a concrete warhead and the guidance system of a Chinese anti-ship missile that was fired into the sea. Meanwhile, the Vienna deal covers the Iranian HEU warhead risk."

"I'm guessing Werner wants us to back off the deal now," said Meredith.

"Yup," said Dorsey.

"He's off the rails," said Rance. "If anything, Werner should be *rooting* for us to finish the negotiation. Instead, he's using hits like this to sabotage it."

"Which brings us back to you, Meredith," said Dorsey, sighing. "I'm not buying Werner's suspicions off the rack—but it at least casts some doubt on our current intelligence analysis. I'll need that resolved in the National Intelligence Estimate before we can certify the Vienna deal."

"I didn't realize the NIE was still in play," said Meredith.

"I haven't endorsed it yet," said Dorsey. "And the director's plenty pissed at me for taking so long. But I was trying to be extra thorough. Last thing I want is to be hauled before the next Select Committee to explain our latest intelligence failure. Now I think we need to run this *Taniyn* thing down to ground truth—figure out what it's for. I told the director the same thing upstairs after Werner left."

"Every other country that's a signatory is already on board," said Rance. "We're the only ones who have this extra NIE step."

"Right," said Dorsey. "But, lucky for us, we do. Now, I've had the Iran desk running with the NIE so far. But given this new technical aspect coming in from Mossad . . . well, Meredith, I want *you* to run it, finish it off, vet this mystery missile for us. The director agrees with me on giving you the job."

Meredith sat bolt upright. Running an NIE was a *massive* career opportunity. "Yes, sir," she said before Dorsey had a chance to reconsider. "Happy to. Of course. Right away. On it."

"And the reason we want you," said Dorsey, "is because of the other thing that happened in the meeting. An Atlas thing."

Meredith's eyebrows pressed inward. "Oh?"

"Yeah," said Dorsey, watching her. "As Soleimani's main weapons procurer, Atlas should have been all over this. He'd know what the warhead is, what it's designed for, what the target is. I need you to put the screws to him. Yesterday. If we don't get the story quick, Werner's going to continue whacking Iranian scientists."

"More deal sabotage," muttered Rance.

Meredith ignored Rance and said she'd be honored to take it on.

Dorsey raised an eye at her. "I know the director had his doubts about your call to snatch Atlas and recruit him . . . but it looks like you got it right, Meredith."

Meredith clenched her toes. "You know, Atlas's psych profile shows he's not ready yet. He's still—"

"*Make* him ready," said Dorsey, cutting her off. "We're out of time. The Iranians might be getting wind of Atlas's status soon."

"More deal sabotage," said Rance. "But from our own shop."

"Wait," said Meredith, ignoring Rance. "Why do we think the Iranians might hear about our Atlas recruit? I've put out a huge deception package to suggest he was taken by Kurds to Iraq."

"May not be working," said Dorsey.

"What makes you say that?"

"Because Werner suspects we have Atlas."

"*What?*" cried Meredith. "Only about ten people in this whole building know about Atlas."

"It's Mossad," said Rance.

Meredith swore under her breath, ignoring Rance. *No one* could know about Atlas if her plan was to work. Least of all Mossad. She looked at Dorsey. "What exactly did Werner say?"

"Among other things, that Lieutenant Colonel Kasem Kahlidi, Soleimani's chief weapons importer, disappeared the night of April ten," said Dorsey. "He was very deliberate about the timing. Probably why he came over himself. He clearly knows about the Iran exfil op you ran and thinks we took Kahlidi along for the ride. I think half the reason he came to Langley was to ask for a share in the take."

"Fuck," said Meredith. "And?"

Dorsey sucked on a cheek. "I didn't spill anything. Yet. We can't risk a share at this early stage with Mossad, given the Israeli attitude on the Iran deal. Mossad could deliberately leak it back to Iran, which would *really* fuck the deal. And us."

"Well," said Meredith, eyes down. "At least we didn't give anything to Mossad. That will keep my plan to reinsert him alive."

Dorsey nodded. "No need to worry about us collaborating with Mossad on Atlas. Not after the meeting blew up."

"*Blew up*," said Meredith. "What do you mean? How's that?"

Dorsey cupped an elbow with one hand and held the Bic to his mouth with the other. He nodded once at Rance.

Rance exhaled noisily. "I helped coordinate a demarche from State, cosigned by the national security advisor. It directs the Israelis to stand-down offensive ops on Iran while we're negotiating the nuclear deal. The director delivered it formally to Werner upstairs. And Werner . . . ripped the doc to shreds. Cover letter and all."

Meredith rubbed her narrow chin. "Oh."

"Yeah. Right in front of us," said Dorsey, chewing the Bic. "Director hit the roof. Threw Werner out of his office. That's how you saw him coming out."

"Literally told him to get the fuck out of the country," added Rance, head still shaking.

Meredith thought about the man who had made brief eye contact with her in the director's lobby.

"You see now why I need this NIE tuned up fast?" Dorsey asked Meredith. "If Mossad keeps up the Red Pages, then this Iran negotiation is *toast*."

"Fucking disaster," said Rance.

"And worse," continued Dorsey. "Suppose Werner's right? If this *Taniyn* missile becomes an operational hypersonic, then Iran could turn Hezbollah loose with it as retaliation for the Red Pages."

"Precisely," said Rance.

"And what if it really is radiological?" Dorsey continued. "Then Israel hits back *hard*. Really fucking hard—with their own goddamned nukes. That loops in the Iranians, the Syrians, the Chinese, the Russians—"

"A world in flames," finished Meredith.

"Maybe what Hezbollah is really after," said Dorsey. "The Twelfth Imam coming back to preside over Armageddon. Destruction of the decadent West. Et cetera."

"The irony," said Rance, crossing his arms, "is that Werner's Red Pages might well be ruining the deal that could prevent the entire thing."

"That's the director's point," said Dorsey. "Which is why, Meredith, one way or another we need Atlas to tell us what this goddamned *Taniyn* thing is all about and get it into the NIE."

She nodded.

Dorsey checked the time on the wall clock. "Now, I reviewed a few of the Atlas debriefs this morning. The psych team seems to think our man might be more cooperative if we brought John back in, given his history with Kahlidi."

Suppressing a grin, Rance sucked in his cheeks.

"John has nothing to do with any of this," Meredith said immediately, tapping the schematic.

"Sure he does," said Rance.

"No. John and Kahlidi happened to intersect in another life, years ago, just by chance. And it was before any of this. They're *not* friends. There's no particular rapport between him and Kahlidi. I won't need John."

Dorsey drummed the Bic on his legal pad, taking a moment to think. "This needs to move fast. And it's your NIE now."

"Of course, sir," said Meredith. "But I won't need John."

The spy boss stared at her for five full seconds. "Whatever you think. Atlas is *your* prospective agent. And John's your—"

"Ex-husband," she finished for him. "And I won't need him."

CHAPTER 3

THE JEEP SEEMED TO HAVE A MIND OF ITS OWN AS JOHN DALE AT-tempted to steer it down the slippery red trail. The red mud was famously obstinate here on Maui's rainy easternmost tip, and even Dale's borrowed '76 CJ-7 was falling victim.

First he felt the rear wheels fishtail on a downshift, which turned him thirty degrees to starboard. Then he felt the front wheels spin, which rammed the grill's brush bar into a weedy bank. Soon, gunning the engine, red mud was flinging up from all four tires, painting the hood in slimy mud as the Jeep tilted further into earth.

Oh, for fuck's sake, thought Dale. *Again?*

In the Jeep's tiny cargo bed was a just-completed twelve-by-eighteen oil-on-canvas painting. Dale had brushed it out in the breaking dawn. He'd done it with a borrowed set of decayed equipment—three frayed brushes, five crumpled oil tubes, and a wobbling easel. But enough. Plein air was all about austerity.

Dale knew a lot about austerity.

He considered the sunrise painting to be good enough to get, say, two hundred bucks for it at the little tourist gallery down in Hana. That would be just enough to earn back some of the cash he'd laid out for his two nights in the guesthouse he'd found. That's all he'd really wanted the painting to do. Since CIA still hadn't fully straightened out his bureaucratically knotted pension, painting was his only source of income. And though they'd given him an advance on his pension for coming out of retirement to complete that last mission, Dale had become dismayed at how quickly it was already dwindling.

Accordingly, to fund his vacation, the prior evening he'd climbed a hill to paint a sunset, capturing an outrigger crew as they plied their craft across Hana's shining bay. The gallery owner had liked it enough to buy it on the spot. He'd even wanted another. To get it, he'd loaned Dale the Jeep for a crack at the sunrise.

A Jeep now hopelessly mired. Dale killed the engine. He stepped out of the stalled four-wheeler and, careful to avoid the wet canvas that lay under an overturned pizza box, fished around the open cargo bed for the little green army shovel.

As he dug under one of the rear tires, his knees sliding in mud, he thought more about money. If he could knock out two paintings a week and sell them for, say, two hundred each, then over the course of a month he could make $1,600. With that kind of income, he could extend his stay here, develop a cozy little retirement income in paradise, doing what he loved. He needed to live somewhere. Why not here?

Feeling a sudden rush of wind, he paused and looked up. A dark cloud was moving overhead, threatening rain. He'd already braved one fast-moving Pacific squall in his dawn climb up the mountain. He could sense another. He needed to hurry.

Rummaging in the backseat, he found the rusty machete he'd already used to clear his painting spot. He hiked a few feet into the bush to hack off a thick palm frond. After a few more minutes, he returned to the Jeep with a bundle of thatch for the ditch behind the rear tires. He hopped through the doorless entry, scooted behind the wheel, and fiddled with the choke.

Yes, he thought further, turning the key, hearing the old, touchy engine catch after ten cranks. If he could negotiate the odd little guesthouse to something like $1,000 for the month, that would leave Dale with $600—more than enough for groceries and a daily lunch at the bar with the outstanding fish tacos.

Success. The Jeep gained traction on the palm fronds and leapt out of the hole. Dale glimpsed his own grin in the rearview as he hurried down the road, ahead of the squall.

The trees hissed louder. The first few raindrops hit the Jeep's hood. Dale felt a shuddering chill on his sweaty neck. Looking through the windshield toward the white-whipped sea, he wondered what the weather was on the far side of the island.

And that made him think of Meth.

The grin faded.

The first two days of their Hawaiian vacation had gone surprisingly well. They'd spent them on the beach sipping tropical drinks, making suggestive comments to each other. It had been good to be with the original, relaxed Meth again—a person Dale sorely missed.

For a while during those forty-eight hours, Dale even thought they were headed back toward each other, which he found surprising, even a little unnerving. Perhaps sensing this, arriving from separate rooms on the third day, his ex-wife had initiated a serious talk over breakfast.

She wanted to analyze, she'd said, what had gone wrong between them. Over guava juice, she explained that she'd lain awake the prior night, thinking about their marriage. She'd come to an epiphany. She now believed that if they could just confront the old cracks, speak about them openly, they might, perhaps, have a chance to rebuild their relationship. Maybe, she'd said, John might even consider coming back to CIA, where they could patch together their old lives. It would all be as it had been in the early days, when they'd first started, when they were happy.

The relationship talk had all been a little uncomfortable for Dale, a little too much like new-age Oprah-speak. But Meth's expression had been so earnest, her linen shift dress over her bikini so fetching, her eyes so sparkling. She'd invited him to speak first. He'd cleared his throat, then offered his own explanations, a marital history of sorts, which started calmly enough.

Yet the longer he'd talked and the more she'd listened, the steeper her eyebrows had angled inward. Soon, every succeeding sentence of his seemed to further compress the lids around those formerly sparkling eyes.

Finally done with listening, Meth had rebutted. So had Dale. The debate became louder. Nearby couples made side glances. Dale had wondered what he was even doing there.

And then, Meredith had dropped the bomb: the old unproven accusation of an affair some seven years ago.

In that heated moment, it had suddenly occurred to Dale that the one glorious upside to divorce was the ability to choose one's battles. Or to simply duck them, which he considered the greatest perk of all. Exercising that ultimate option, he'd dropped his pressed napkin on the table, stood up, and left the sunny outdoor terrace without another word.

Then, striding with purpose to his room, he'd retrieved his trusty backpack and wandered into the valet's parking-lot breezeway. Without a plan going any further than avoidance of his ex-wife, he'd impulsively boarded a tour bus to Hana, a quirky remote town on the far side of the island. He'd thought it a good strategy at the time, since Meth could be tenacious in hunting him down. He'd even removed the SIM from his phone to prevent it.

One of the first stops in the remote village was an art gallery. There, Dale had struck up a conversation with the owner, an old down-and-outer named Dunphy who ran an Airbnb as a side hustle.

Kismet, Dale had thought. Together, they'd gone to check out the rental. To throw Meth off further, Dale had even given Dunphy a fake name.

Dunphy called it a *yurt*. Though rickety, it would serve as a roof over Dale's head, albeit a strange one. There was a bed, an easel, and a workbench for building frames. Dale had suggested the idea of selling him paintings to offset the rent. Dunphy validated the digital portfolio Dale carried on his phone and agreed, loaning the supplies. After dropping his backpack, Dale had soon found the local watering hole, sampled its fish tacos, and declared himself content.

Driving along the coast road now with his dawn painting in the back, the former CIA man found the passing squall violent but brief, replaced by rapidly building tropical heat. After another curving mile, he maneuvered the Jeep into the yurt's yard. There Dunphy waited with his thumbs hooked in the pockets of his cutoff shorts. The Jeep's blue paint was completely covered in oozing sludge, as was Dale himself.

Dale showed Dunphy the painting, which had been saved from the rain by the Jeep's canopy. The old gallery owner was impressed. He asked Dale to knock out a frame for it, which would earn him another twenty-five off the rent. They shook hands before Dunphy departed on the footpath to his art gallery.

Alone again, Dale stripped off his shirt, exposing his scarred, swarthy torso to a now powerful sun. He then dropped his shorts and hosed himself down in the crabgrass. Buck naked, he finally turned to the Jeep.

"I do *not* get this guy," Ari said into his microphone, speaking in his native Hebrew. Built like an NFL lineman, the Mossad *katsa* wiped a sheet of sweat from his forehead with a meaty forearm. He scratched at his beard and shifted his prone position, carefully shifting the slim, collapsible sniper rifle at this side. While most *katsas* on the American station would enjoy an op in Maui, Ari thought it miserable.

Eyes glued to the powerful spotting scope, a suppressed Sig Sauer strapped to his leg, Ari moved slowly sideways into the shade. He and his spotter, Nahshon, had lost the CIA man in the early morning hours when he'd driven the Jeep up the hill. The two *katsas* weren't about to take their eyes off Dale now.

"*Ben zona*," he said into the encrypted UHF mic at his mouth. "I think I figured it out. HVT just lifted what looks like a painting out of the Jeep and leaned it against the wall of that crappy little shack. Guess he's an artist or something. Maybe drying it in the sun."

Nahshon answered Ari from a quarter mile away, watching the corner where the footpath entered the town. He'd already watched Dunphy enter the art gallery. "I guess the old man made him a deal."

"Maybe we should pick up the old man?"

"Maybe so."

"Ach," Ari said disgustedly. "That *zayin* Dale is bare-ass naked now, hosing off the Jeep. Do I really have to watch this? Definitely not packing a weapon, is he?"

"Even CIA officers are hippies out here," said Nahshon.

"Now if Maya had let us surveil Dale's wife . . . But this fucking *gayaz* . . . Oh, hang on," said Ari. "Target just finished washing. Thank God he's put some shorts on."

"You *have* to come, Dad," Grace said to Dale some hours later, using the same tone of voice that had worked on her father since she was five. Dale was standing in the kitchen, leaning on the curved wall near the mounted phone, the cord stretching away behind his back. His cell phone was still pointedly disassembled in his bag.

He'd spent the remainder of the day building the frame. But before leaving for dinner, he'd decided to call Grace. It was late in Annapolis, but that was the only time his midshipman daughter ever had freedom at the United States Naval Academy.

"Two weeks?" Dale asked. "Really? I want to, Grace, I do. It's just that it'll be . . ." He paused. He was about to say *expensive* but checked himself. He'd called her to get some intel on how Meth was doing. Racked with guilt for leaving her on the morning of her triathlon, he'd been planning a grand reentrance at the resort in the morning. But he also wanted to make sure he wouldn't be landing in a hot LZ.

"Tell me again what the award is for?" he asked his daughter.

"A few days ago, I was in a sailing regatta on the Severn—winning, I might add. On my way toward the finish, I saw a sailboat capsize a couple hundred yards away. It was a civilian, just outside the marina, a little Sunfish. The wind was howling and the current was up. There was a woman struggling in the water, no life vest, splashing, panicking. I tacked over, jumped in, and swam her to shore."

"Grace, that's amazing," said Dale, smiling crookedly. "So proud of you. I'm sure all of Annapolis is proud of you."

"Yeah, thanks. So anyway, the superintendent wants to pull the whole Brigade of Midshipmen together to give me this Evans Valor Award. Not a lot of mids here in the summer, but Mom already said she'd come. Please, Dad, *please* come."

"Of course I'll be there," said Dale, mentally estimating airfares. "But Grace—you spoke to your mother? She okay?"

"Yeah, she's fine. I caught her in the airport on her way back to DC."

Surprised, Dale reconfirmed with Grace that Meth had already left Hawaii.

Wow, he thought. Meth was *really* pissed.

After saying goodbye, he took the overgrown footpath to Henry's, the local bar, restaurant, general store, and post office. The clouds were thickening again, forming purple furrows on the sea. Another squall loomed.

Under raindrops, Dale double-timed it from the path to the road. He noted a white rental car parked in a grassy lot. He paused, then dismissed it. Sad but inevitable, he thought, that tourists would ruin a place like Henry's. He stepped onto the warping porch.

Peering through the screen door, he saw a gap-toothed Samoan woman in the rear selling needlepoints. At the bar were three tattooed surfers with dreadlocks, using their hands to talk when they weren't eating their burritos. The screen door bounced after Dale walked through it.

He took a seat at the far end of the bar and asked for a beer. He kept an eye on the door in a window reflection as he made his dinner order. The barkeep went into the kitchen. Dale drank his beer and glanced at his watch.

It was six, midnight in DC. He'd meant to call Meth as soon as he'd hung up with Grace but had struggled to find the right approach. Now, with half an IPA's encouragement, he decided to give his ex-wife a jingle before she went to bed. It was late, but he knew she liked to stay up, usually reading. One of the reasons he liked Henry's was because it had a rare, old rusting pay phone.

He wandered back to the phone near the restroom, decided to go ahead and risk using a credit card to pay for the call, and dialed Meth's cell. Several rings. Voice mail. Tongue-tied at the beep, Dale hung up.

Returning to the bar, he stopped, looked down, and maneuvered behind a potted palm tree. There were two bearded men in their mid-thirties at one of the tables. One of them was enormous. Dale thought of the rental car.

But he stopped thinking of it when he noticed the backside of a good-looking redhead that had taken the barstool next to his warming beer. Her auburn hair was similar enough to Meth's Maggie O'Dea wig that for one fleeting moment, Dale's heart skipped. Maybe Grace had been wrong. Meth could be surprising as well as tenacious.

But, coming closer, he realized it wasn't his ex. *Just as well*, he thought.

From behind, he couldn't see the look-alike woman's face. *However*, he thought, regaining his footing. If the front side looked even remotely as good as the back, he was very much looking forward to making her acquaintance.

He sat down next to her and tried to catch her face in the mirror behind the bar. But she was looking down, shielded by her hair. Dale tipped the beer to his mouth, gaming out various openers.

But before he could say anything, the woman nudged him with the bare knee below her short skirt. She twirled her fingers through her hair and pulled a long curl behind her ear, revealing more of her face.

"Hello, John," she said.

Dale glanced up from his beer. Her reflection in the bar mirror was inescapable now. She was smiling widely into it.

It had been seven years since he'd seen that smile.

"Hello, Maya," he said.

CHAPTER 4

WERNER DAVIDAI ACCEPTED THE STRAIGHT VODKA ON ICE FROM THE
flight attendant. The leader of Mossad's Caesarea group was up front,
near the bulkhead, slouched in a large, padded seat. He looked out the
oval window of the Gulfstream G650, which idled on a taxiway at Andrews Air Force Base, just over the Potomac from DC. Across the red
and blue taxiway lights, through the open doors of a well-lit hangar,
Werner could see two shining green VH-3 Sea Kings—the old, modified
helicopters known as Marine One, famously used to fly the president of
the United States off the White House lawn.

Very old helicopters, Werner thought, thinking how he'd seen the image of those flying Sea Kings playing out on the evening news all the
way back to LBJ, when he was a kid in the sixties. Watching the president come and go from the White House had always seemed a powerful
symbol back then, a reassuring one. Werner missed that feeling.

That's what America is now, he thought. *Nostalgia.* He pulled his
focus closer to the dim taxiway. He watched a US Air Force airman
wave his glowing wands, directing the unmarked Israeli jet to the runway with crisp military gestures. The Gulfstream's engines whined somewhere near the tail. The jet turned and the airman slid by the window,
out of view.

As the plane gathered speed down the runway, Werner took another
sip of the vodka and reclined his seat. He felt the tarmac bumps shud-
der up through the aircraft's floor. The engines grew louder, the dishes
in the forward galley clinked. He closed his eyes. Whenever he left a

foreign country he felt an oozy calm, as though the danger were behind him, as though he could finally relax. *Sad*, he reflected, *that I should feel that way when leaving the United States.*

But fair, he thought.

The CIA director had given Werner a sound thrashing. The meeting had started heading south as soon as Werner began making the case for the Baramzedeh Red Page. Then it had turned into a lecture from the director about peace, diplomacy, Washington's new Iranian nuclear *containment* policy. Then the director got going on the dead civilians in Beirut, dead due to Mossad's recklessness. And then the demarche. The ridiculous demarche.

It was at that point that Werner knew he was no longer in the office of an ally. The drone strike on Baramzedeh was tragic, yes, but effective as an instrument of a war—a *real* war, where the survival of a nation was at stake. The Americans would never understand that. Certainly, this young CIA political *putz* would never understand that. As far as Werner was concerned, that official demarche may as well have been a legal decree of divorce.

Still. Tearing it up was probably going too far, Werner thought now, shuddering, sipping the booze, not quite smiling to himself. The demarche was an official diplomatic letter of the United States, delivered by a cabinet-level official. Werner thought he'd probably earned himself a lifelong enemy in that director.

But so what?

After the disastrous Langley meeting, the Caesarea boss had retreated to the embassy. He'd called his boss, the Mossad director, waking him early. First, Werner relayed the disappointing news that Dorsey had denied any knowledge of Lieutenant Colonel Kahlidi, the Quds man Mossad suspected was now an agent of CIA. And second—even worse—Werner had confessed to tearing up the DCIA's formal demarche. He warned the Mossad boss that an escalation was likely headed his way, maybe even going to the prime minister.

But by the time the call was over, Werner realized his boss would give him the air cover he needed. The Israeli PM would be handled. It was more important, the Mossad boss had said, to get to the bottom of *Taniyn*, the Arabic code name they'd picked up in Beirut COMINT intercepts that referred to this deadly new Hezbollah missile. It was far more important to round up the network of collaborators, killing the lot of them, destroying the stockpiles, rooting out the supply chain, exterminating the brainpower, ensuring this thing went nowhere, ever.

If the Americans didn't want to offer up their best assets—or worse, stood in the way to protect their precious Iran deal—then so be it. That's how war worked. Mossad's director had told Werner to do what he had to do. And if that involved crashing through a traditional taboo with the Americans, well, then that was just one more casualty.

Wilco, Werner had said in his old fighter-pilot jargon, relieved.

Now, hours later in the predawn, Werner tossed the rest of the vodka over his teeth as the jet shuddered through a layer of turbulence over the Chesapeake. Soon he was tilted comfortably back, enjoying the sense of speed, the warm salve of booze. To the former F-15 pilot, that feeling—speed—would always be a comfort.

There was just something peaceful about soaring over the Atlantic at night, something that allowed him to unwind. For those precious, isolated eleven hours, he could at least recline and think of other things, putting some altitude between himself and the problems of the world.

The cabin lights dimmed. He raised the footrest another few inches. The drone of the engines lulled him. Ten and a half hours to go. Maybe he could get some sleep . . .

"Boss," Mordechai said, interrupting as the plane nosed over to cruising altitude. The young adjutant was in the aisle, squatting on a knee.

Werner shot him his surliest look. But then he remembered—he'd asked Mordechai for an update as they were boarding. The Caesarea leader softened his face. "What?"

"Washington Station sent this over just before we took off," Mordechai said, leaning in close to be heard over the jet noise. "It's a new workup on the woman—like you asked. Came in from the Lexicon hit."

Lexicon was the spyware program Mossad had inserted at the US Passport Office, designed by the Israeli spyware software company NSO.

NSO had clandestinely installed it in a hack for Caesarea as a means to forge their own passports, using them as cover when conducting foreign ops, since American passports were widely accepted globally.

But an unintended side benefit of the simple little spyware op was that NSO could tap requests that came in from the Department of State's consular attaché section—the way CIA created their own manufactured legends.

Werner flicked on the reading light. He put Mordechai's iPad on his lap. He thumbed through several digitized passport versions created for the woman he'd seen in the lobby of the director's office: Meredith Morris-Dale.

There was the US Maggie O'Dea ID, her Canadian Marguerite Bouchon, three others from UAE, UK, and EU. After inspecting the aliases, Werner swiped to the next page.

Here he saw surveillance shots from Mossad archives. They showed Meredith exiting a car wearing a hijab, entering a building, hailing a taxi at the Dubai airport. The final photograph was of Meredith coming down the steps of her Dupont Circle brownstone in business attire. She was in profile, her hair down, a handbag over her shoulder as she stowed her keys. That photo had been taken at night. Meredith was under a porch light.

Werner used his fingers to zoom in on the photo of Meredith on the porch. "Yeah," he said. "That's the woman that was waiting outside the director's office. Interesting that they kept her out of the meeting. Is the team all set up now?"

Mordechai nodded. "Wiring the house up now. Eli has another squad on car surveillance."

Werner kept swiping. He came to digitized passports for John Richard Dale. First was a Canadian passport, an alias with the name Reza Shariati. Then Dale's US passport with his real name. Then a French passport calling him Etienne Crochet. Werner noted that all three passports were currently active, according to Lexicon.

"And him . . . *Mister* Dale?"

"Maya's still tracking him down. No report yet."

"Okay," said Werner, tapping the iPad screen, thinking. He swiped back to the photo of Meredith at her home. He looked at it again, zooming in tightly on her face. "And when did you say this shot was taken?" he asked.

Mordechai looked at his watch. "About two hours ago."

CHAPTER 5

"ENJOYING YOUR VACATION?" MAYA ASKED DALE. THE MOSSAD *KIDON*'S English had an accent, vaguely French, but muddled with the occasional hard consonants of Arabic. Dale remembered it well.

He took a gulp of his beer and ignored her question. She was just as he remembered: stunning. Maybe even more so in the redhead wig. He remembered her large white teeth, the long straight nose, the dark eyes. If she'd aged at all, he couldn't tell.

Conscious of the goons behind them, he lowered his voice. "Maya. What are you doing here?"

She leaned toward him, twirled a finger through her hair. "Isn't that obvious? Looking for you."

The auburn wig was good, but not that good up close.

A wig. Tradecraft. Dale thought again about the two men who sat behind him.

"And why's that?" he asked. He let his eyes wander back to hers. She'd flown to the other side of the world with a team, hunting him down. Senior *kidons* didn't do that to reminisce.

He ran quickly through escape options. No window in the bathroom, no back door. Two bearded goons blocking the front. They'd boxed him, waited until he'd had a pint of IPA in him. Of course they had. Tradecraft.

She smiled brilliantly. Her big white teeth shone like a sunrise. "We always said that if we could meet again in another life . . . another time . . . if things had been different . . ." She nudged him with her knee again.

The seductive sloe-eyed grin hadn't changed at all, Dale thought. Another bit of tradecraft. He asked himself if he really had said something corny about meeting her in another life one day. *Yeah*, he answered himself, thinking back on who he was then. *I probably did.*

"I'm actually in my other life now. Can't say the same about you." He nodded to her. "Nice wig."

"Third acts are overrated, no?" She slid her hand toward his, lifting it. She wore a lot of rings, he wore none. The most prominent of hers a big gem on her middle finger. The stone was yellow, like topaz. It reminded Dale of their time in Egypt.

Dale flinched, then let her have his hand. "Hawaii's made you dark again," she said, turning it over. "I always thought you could pass for a Jew. And look. No line where your wedding ring used to be."

Dale pulled his hand free. "I'm sure you know all about it." Had they followed Meth too? She was back in DC according to Grace. But still—they'd stayed here in Hana, on him. It was *him* they wanted. He ran through his egress options again, came up with nothing.

"No woman could keep *you*, John," she said, smiling, releasing his hand.

Dale grunted.

"Is that to be our fate, Dale? A couple of singular souls?" The smile softened, barely. It was different now—truer, almost rueful, a mild cant to the eyes. He remembered that about her—the occasional tell of some long-buried sadness.

He nodded, raised his beer to his mouth. There was something strangely cold at his core—nerves? It collided with the tingle of a pang—an impulse, a wish to be back in the snowy Cascades, his cabin in Washington State, Cle Elum. He had the urge to wriggle through the window, slide down the muddy bank, disappear in the dark. But there were those two big *katsas* behind him.

"Sorry," he said, eyes down, smelling her, remembering her. "Whatever you want from me—I won't be able to help you."

"But it's still good to see me, right?" Again, she tapped his leg with her knee. The soft smile was still there, the sad one.

Dale looked down, said nothing.

Into the void, she said, "Look at that. I can still make John Dale blush." A drink arrived in front of her, a club soda with lime.

This time Dale nudged her and smiled. "If you want to talk, I'm going to need you to have a real drink."

Dale watched as she stretched out, twisted to place the order, her skirt riding up on her thigh. He looked for a leg holster but saw only smooth, tanned flesh. In the mirror behind the bar, he stole a quick glimpse at her exposed shoulders. If she was armed, then it was on the bag by her stool on the floor.

But, of course, she didn't need a gun. Dale glanced at the table goons. He assessed their posture, looked for a telltale weapons bulge. Nothing. Her goons would be too good for something that obvious. *Of course they would.*

Dale wondered if there was a door hidden in the kitchen, wondered if he could knock through one of the thin bathroom walls with a shoulder. For a second, he questioned whether he could start a fire, throw some grease on a flame, yank a gas line out of the wall, blow the whole fucking place. Maya was looking at him, the sad smile.

A whiskey in her hand, neat. She handed a second one to Dale. "To old friends." She interlocked his elbow, pulled him close, tasted the whiskey.

"We need to talk," she said, staring frankly into his eyes.

"About?" He glanced away. He couldn't hold the stare with her. He knew he couldn't.

She pulled him even closer. He could feel her humid breath on his lips when she spoke. "It's been too long," she whispered. "Let's go."

It was after midnight in DC. Meredith had dashed home for a quick shower before heading straight back to the office, running on Clif Bars and Diet Coke. On her way back out the door she'd noted the incoming call from the 808 area code. Hawaii.

John, probably.

She let it ring, checked voice mail, got nothing. Typical. *Asshole.*

Hurtling in her Volvo down Virginia's Route 123 on her way into HQS, she summoned her team, pinging all of them on their emergency lines. It was a shitty thing to do in the middle of the night. But shittiness came with the job. There was new intel coming down the pike, an NIE to get done for the brass. Wake up and get dressed, she told each of the four analysts she'd dialed. And hey, look on the bright side—no traffic this time of night.

Once installed in a large SCIF on the second floor at HQS, Meredith directed her groggy subordinates to Americanize the Israeli intel. Even from a putative ally, their first job was to vet, to confirm. She made it clear to all of them that this was priority uno, to drop everything. An NIE was at stake—Dorsey needed this new information verified. Yesterday.

But while she whipped her team into action, she didn't mention the intelligence asset she hoped would really cover the NIE: Atlas, Kahlidi, the Quds man who would have all the answers. She didn't mention that if the solve came through Atlas, she'd look like a genius to the director. And if that happened . . .

She pictured the Paris chief of station job, walking around the banks of the Seine with Grace, showing off her French language skills. She could show her daughter what it meant to immerse oneself in another culture, to mingle with exotic people, to learn a new language, to . . .

"Here's everything we have off the shelf on Hezbollah smuggling through Syria," said one of her young female analysts, dropping a stack of reports in front of Meredith. "You want *all* of this?"

"Yes," said Meredith, grabbing the stack as she rose from the table. "And shipping too. Call ONI. Naval intelligence should have something on sea routes from Iran. That would be the easiest way to smuggle a nuke."

The girl, who quietly worshipped Meredith Morris-Dale, ran off, a ponytail swaying rapidly behind her.

In the solitude of her office Meredith pored over copies of the Mossad files in a small circle of lamplight, comparing the Israeli intelligence to what she'd assembled so far. It was immediately clear that Kahlidi should know all about this mystery missile. She recognized the IRGC front companies, even saw Kahlidi's Hezbollah cryptonym— AMIR—come up in reference to a meet with a front company importer. She also saw Mossad's Hezbollah COMINT intercepts, which the Israeli Unit 8200 analysts had tagged as the code name for the missile: "*Taniyn.*"

Meredith's father had been a Foreign Service Officer, and she'd spent much of her childhood overseas. Sixth through eighth grade had happened in Rabat, Morocco, where she'd attended the American School and honed her French. But along the way, she'd made several Moroccan friends and picked up a little Arabic. *Taniyn*— "dragon"—was an Arabic word that had struck her instantly back in Dorsey's SCIF, since she'd once been the only geeky girl in the Dungeons & Dragons club.

Taniyn—a winged Hezbollah weapon that breathed fire and flew at near hypersonic speeds. Though she'd been around the seedy world of WMD weapons procurement for years, the thought of the world's largest terrorist army holding a nuclear-capable hypersonic missile was especially chilling. She made a note reminding herself to draft an inquiry to NSA for a global search on the word "*Taniyn*" with Hezbollah overlaps and translations for the word "dragon" in French, Farsi, and Russian.

But that would take a day or two. For now, she closed the file and rubbed her temples, thinking in the lamplight. Even without a formal American vet, she thought, there was no question that Werner's intel was exceedingly thorough. She had a hard time imagining she'd be able to improve on it—were it not for her ace in the hole, Kahlidi.

Kahlidi. Atlas. She thought of the Quds man and the several rounds her assigned interrogators had already gone with him down at Camp Peary, where Meredith had him stashed. She shot off an appointment request, telling the Peary psychoanalysis team she wanted a personal meeting with Kahlidi in the next few days. It was time to really put the screws to her prospective agent. But not before she had this Israeli intel all squared away.

The key, she thought, would be to go at Kahlidi indirectly, already armed with as many facts as she could muster. Whatever *Taniyn* was, she knew Kahlidi wouldn't give it up easily. He'd want to try to improve the Agency deal he'd been cutting with her. He'd use this to reopen the whole negotiation for his spying contract with the Agency. That meant Meredith would need her own leverage. And the best leverage over Kahlidi was the woman he'd left behind in Iran, Kasra Khani.

Meredith fired up the intranet form to create a cable for London Station, asking for the latest status on Kahlidi's Iranian girlfriend. Meredith had received a report on the Khani woman's entrance to the UK weeks ago. Kahlidi had already admitted to Meredith that he'd told Kasra to get to the UK to avoid the MOIS people that would hunt her down to question her. As part of the Agency spying contract, Kahlidi wanted her brought to the US for safety.

But Meredith had claimed she couldn't find the woman—two could play the leverage game.

Besides—Meredith's claim had a kernel of truth. She *didn't* know exactly where Ms. Khani was, only that she was somewhere in the UK. Meredith had purposefully avoided direct MI-5 surveillance as a matter of fieldcraft, believing that too much Western intelligence attention would alert MOIS. If that happened, the opportunity to reinsert Kahlidi as an agent back into Iran would be lost forever.

But that was before Kahlidi had become the key to the NIE. Meredith's NIE. She thought she'd need to show Kahlidi some progress on the search for his woman.

She sighed and got to work.

After filling out the forms for the cables for London Station, Meredith moved down the dim hallways to the SCIF for the team's initial read-out at two a.m. She learned that the team had shipped the modified SA-5 specs off to DOD's Science and Tech group, asked NSA to verify the COMINT intercepts, tasked CIA's Iran country-desk watch officer with a biographical workup on Mohammed Baramzedeh, and requested DIA to analyze potential nuclear warhead smuggling routes between Iran and Lebanon. The team had also gotten in touch with

Beirut Station to request updated intel on a handful of agents CIA was running in Lebanon. After the briefing, even Meredith had to admit that the only thing left to do was wait.

But not wait long. She told her team she wanted to reconvene in six hours. They hurried out before she could change her mind.

Alone and spent, Meredith headed back to her office. She packed the Mossad files into an old battleship-gray safe. She clicked off her lamp and began packing a heavy sheaf of unclassified State Department Hezbollah reports into her bag, anxious to read them in bed.

But Rick Desmond, her HQS-based operations coordinator, surprised her at the threshold, a thick folder in his hands. Her deputy was the one person on her team who was read into the Atlas program, Kahlidi. He'd been running the counterintelligence work so Kahlidi could get back over the wire into Quds without suspicion.

Specifically, Desmond had already put out disinformation that Kahlidi had been wounded and recovered by the Iraqi Kurds on the night of the raid at the Iranian border, building up Kahlidi's cover. The plan was to have him "escape" Kurdish custody, then make his way back to Iran. Once reinstalled in Quds, Kahlidi would spy for CIA—in exchange for three million dollars, a guaranteed exfil in two years, and immediate safe harbor for Kasra Khani in the United States.

But Meredith didn't yet trust Kahlidi enough to go back into the wild—and she also didn't think his cover had had enough time to bake.

"Rick," she said, still packing her bag. "I've asked for an appointment with the shrinks to see Atlas in a few days. Have you heard anything from MI-5 about Kasra? I just filled the request for a new cable to Comms. Should go out in about thirty minutes."

"You didn't have to do that yourself," said Desmond.

Meredith zipped her bag closed with a nod, hoping Desmond would go away. He didn't.

"I have another Atlas thing for you," said Desmond.

She groaned.

"Fear not. You're going to like it."

Meredith clicked her desk lamp back on. She nodded.

Still standing, Desmond opened the folder on Meredith's desk, spinning it so she could read it in her circle of lamplight. "Turns out the Iran desk had already set up surveillance on all the Vienna scientists."

Meredith put a hand over her mouth, yawned, and slouched into her chair. "Please tell me they had something going on Baramzedeh."

"Yup. Baramzedeh made a quick trip to Vienna, which got him on the radar. He then landed in Charles de Gaulle, which tripped a flag with DGSE. The French alerted our Paris Station, who then set up surveillance on Baramzedeh."

She brightened at the mention of Paris Station. "I suppose Baramzedeh's commerce with Vienna strengthens Mossad's case about the nuke angle for this mystery missile."

"It does. But I'm thinking more about Paris," said Desmond. "Atlas has a place there. Right?"

"You showed me on Zillow. Flashy penthouse with a view of the Louvre. But you searched it, right? Couple weeks ago?"

"Yeah. It was clean, other than a machine pistol and a Lebanese passport. Not to mention a stocked wine cellar and a closet full of fancy suits."

"And? You're thinking Baramzedeh met directly with Atlas there in Paris?"

"That's what I thought at first," Desmond said, taking the chair across from her desk. "But somebody like Atlas wouldn't meet with one of these scientists directly in a neutral country like France, right? He'd probably use a cutout to keep his cover clean."

"I suppose."

"Well, check out this message." From the other side of the desk, Desmond flipped to a cable submitted by Nick Drault, the rumored-to-be-retiring Paris COS. It was a surveillance report of Baramzedeh meeting a woman at a hotel lobby bar.

"See how it says the woman pulled an SDR after the BREN?" A BREN was Agency shorthand for a brief encounter. "I called Nick about that to get a little more color. He thought the tradecraft interesting," Desmond said. "And, not surprisingly, the woman's a ghost. Came into the hotel bar and exited right after the meet. That makes her an ideal cutout for Atlas."

Meredith remembered what Dorsey had said. He'd mentioned that Mossad had stolen the missile schematics by luring Baramzedeh away from his room with a female Caesarea officer.

"Sorry, Rick," she said. "I think she's the Mossad honeytrap. We know they used a woman to lure Baramzedeh from his room to steal the missile schematics. We could compare her against our known Mossad operative files if we have a picture of her."

Desmond leafed through the folder. "We do. Here you go. Not a great shot, but at least we have something." He detached the photo from its binding and slid it across to Meredith. It had been taken from an odd angle, a CIA surveillant's cell phone. Most of the woman's face was obscured by hair, only one eye partially visible. Meredith studied it in the harsh glare of the lamp.

Desmond was saying something else now. But Meredith had completely tuned him out. The woman in the photo was sitting at a hotel lobby bar in Paris with her legs crossed, fingers wound in a curl of hair. Even in profile, there was something vaguely familiar about the curve of her smiling cheek. Vaguely familiar, but enough that Meredith was suddenly far away, lost in the accusation of an affair from seven years ago.

And from two days ago.

Goddamned John.

CHAPTER 6

THE TROPICAL SQUALL HAD STRENGTHENED SINCE THE SUN HAD GONE down. Dale and Maya walked in tandem down the narrow footpath back to Dunphy's guesthouse, dodging drips from the rustling overhang. A white moon backlit racing blue clouds.

Dale carried the food in a plastic sack, Maya walking in front of him, following his directions. Dale wasn't about to let Maya get behind him on that path.

The deal he'd made was that he'd meet with her, but only at his place, alone, away from her goons for his own safety. But he still assumed they were in the rental car, plotting a surveillance strategy, protecting Maya in case something went wrong.

"Welcome to Shangri-la," Dale said when they'd finally arrived at the yurt, motioning her inside and hitting the switch. The squall's wind rattled the windowpanes and swung a bare bulb that hung from the tin-sheeted ceiling. Closing the door, Dale took a long look toward the driveway. No sign of the goons—yet anyway. He threw the corroded deadbolt.

Three separate streams of water leaked through the rusty round ceiling, spattering the floor. Maya had been carrying her woven handbag, the one that had been at her feet in the bar. She now dropped it on a chair by the door.

Dale needed the food to get sharper, to mop up the booze. But there was the leaking ceiling to deal with first. He rummaged through the kitchen for pots to catch the falling water. Then he opened his Styrofoam container, sat at the little table across from her, and dug into the tacos. She picked at her dish.

"What?" he asked. "Not kosher?"

"Vegetarian," she said. She slid her tacos over to Dale.

"Oh yeah. You look a little thin, by the way," he said, swallowing. "Even for you. Maybe it's the wig. You just look a little different."

Her smile went to full wattage. She reached into her large woven purse and pulled a clear plastic bag from it, the kind used for airport security. Dale could see toiletries in the clear bag, a vial of perfume, toothbrush, toothpaste.

Maya removed a small mirror from the clear bag. She held it before her face and undid wig pins with her free hand. When finished, she ran her fingers through her hair, leaving the toiletry kit on the counter.

"How about now?" she asked, turning toward him.

"Better," said Dale. "But still a little too thin."

"Better than fat," she said, running her fingers through the strands.

Dale glanced at her from across the table. Her muslin dress was still wet, sticking to her. She'd placed one long shock of her natural hair to the side of her chin. The cold feeling in Dale's gut returned. Done eating, he stood and dropped the containers into a bin, then wiped up the counter, careful to keep her in his sight line, just in case.

"I'm soaked," she said, crossing her legs and looking around. "What the hell are you even doing here, John?" She grinned and shook her head slightly, a long, closed-mouth smile, as though sharing some old joke with him.

Dale returned the smile. For just a moment he even laughed at himself, at the ridiculous yurt, then shook it off.

From behind the counter he said, "I know. But it's just a shack for a couple nights to unwind. I'm working with the gallery owner to . . ." He looked at her. Her grin had opened, her eyes crinkled. It was a real grin. "Yeah," said Dale. "I guess a Mossad *kidon* on a mission would probably know *exactly* what I'm up to."

She nodded, still grinning. "I saw your sunset painting in that little gallery this afternoon. Your landlord tried to sell it to me, thought I was a tourist. But at least I finally got to see one of your actual paintings, more than just a sketch this time. It was *so* good, though I noticed you signed it 'Anonymous.'"

He nodded. "How much did he ask you for it?"

"Five hundred, US."

"Well," said Dale, running the sink water to rinse out a sponge. "Nice profit for him."

"It was *amazingly* good, John. I had no idea. Seriously."

"Then buy it. The government of Israel has the shekels." Dale killed the tap and glanced at her. "And I need the money."

She stood. Even in flats, she was an inch or two taller than him. She stepped toward the interior of the yurt. She stopped to flick a light at the workbench. The plywood surface was strewn with coils of wire, tape, a hammer, tacks. Dale had already built the frame for his new painting but hadn't yet cleaned up. The finished work was leaning against the wall.

"Wow," she said. "This sunrise painting's even better than the one in the gallery." She eyed the artwork closely in the light.

"Thanks," said Dale, admiring the shape of her legs, the curve of her hip. He'd often wondered if his memories of her had been blessed with his own artistic license. Looking at her now, he thought not.

The wind gusted. It sang through the cracks and rattled the roof savagely. They glanced at each other, marveling at the sound of it. A harder, extended gust shook the little round building. They heard a tree cracking somewhere outside, more roof clanks. The lights blinked once, twice, and then went out.

The yurt went dark.

"I'm assuming your *katsas* cut the line," said Dale. "They better not have done any permanent damage." Maya was still visible, traced by moonlit strobes behind her at the window. She had a hand over her mouth, an expression Dale couldn't quite read.

"Even Mossad couldn't have orchestrated this storm, Dale. Candles?"

"Yeah, right, good idea." Dale rattled around in the kitchen, making sure she stayed on the other side of the counter—he'd been half serious about the *katsas* cutting the line. But he also knew this little yurt had been a DIY wiring job. Dunphy had warned him.

Dale lit a match. "The gallery owner said the power goes out a lot. Guess he meant it. Here." He handed Maya the glowing candle. The door rattled with another gust.

Maya set the candle on the workbench and resumed her study of the painting, squinting in the dim light. "You know, you should come back to the Middle East. You could paint the Negev at sunset. Or the Red Sea. I remember that sketch you did of the mosque. Did you ever get around to painting it?"

Dale lit a second match for a second candle. "Negative. Not a scene I cared to relive."

Her eyes had narrowed, as though working through a misunderstood punchline. "If you came back, we'd treat you better than they treat you here. I can guarantee that."

Careful to keep her in view, Dale knelt to the floor to swap an overflowing pot. The drips banged loudly into the new one. She stood between the workbench and bed, watching him, still looking amused. The shadows put her features in stark relief.

"I was serious when I said I wanted you to paint me." She'd raised her voice to be heard over the leaks as Dale replaced another pot. "I was a model as a kid. Remember?"

"Your *cover* was as a model anyway," he responded from behind the sink. "But anyway, I don't really have the skills to do you in a portrait." He gave her his lopsided grin. "Of course, I suppose it'd be fun to try."

She replied with her big-toothed smile, a dimple forming to one side. "We need to talk first."

"Ah. So there *is* a catch," said Dale.

"Just talk." The smile transitioned to something softer.

"I'm retired."

"John . . ." She shook her head slowly, scoldingly.

"I know better than to lie to you, Maya."

She let fly a long, throaty laugh.

"Maya, goddamnit, I'm serious. I'm retired. Why don't you believe me?"

"You mean your *administrative leave* from last year?"

Dale said nothing.

"I hope your sabbatical wasn't somehow about me, John, was it?"

Dale shook his head. "No. Something else happened, a bunch of bullshit, really. But—how do you know about my status anyway?"

"Sources and methods."

"Within Langley?"

"Interested?"

"Ah," said Dale, crossing his arms, shaking his head. "I suppose if old Mr. Werner were going to send someone to recruit this disgruntled old has-been, it'd be you."

She paused and bit her lip. "It's only partly a recruitment mission for a disgruntled old has-been."

"And why would I spy for Mossad?"

The shadows lengthened her chin, outlined her cheekbones. Her skin looked dark. "Because we appreciate your talents more than your organization does. Because your leadership is soft and misguided. Because you know we're the last thing between a fanatical Islamic Iran and a nuclear weapon. Wait. John—come back into the light where I can see your face."

Dale had maneuvered around the counter toward the workbench. He waved a match out after lighting his third candle. "Soft and misguided leadership," he repeated, shaking his head.

"Your country's about to do a deal with the devil. You know Iran will abuse it, arm up anyway, hold the world hostage. And now you've pulled in Cerberus too, without even telling us. That was a stupid thing to do."

"I'm just a painter looking to get by."

"Cerberus was your best asset. With him out of the Iranian enrichment labs, this new deal's an even bigger mistake."

"As far as I know, Cerberus is still there. In Iran, Natanz. But you would know better than me."

"*Please*, John. You think our Unit 8200 just ignores IRGC comms when there's an incursion into Iranian airspace? We heard specific voices from that night. I *know* you were there for the Cerberus exfil, among other things. Just drop it."

Got me there, he thought. IDF's AMAN military intelligence wing had a long tradition of deciphering Iranian crypto. He thought it plausible that they'd also cracked US military codes. They were that good.

And if that was the case, Dale wondered, did Maya also know Meredith had been there on that exfil? And Kahlidi? "Well," he said, "whatever you heard, it doesn't matter. This is a problem for whoever's filling my shoes now."

"No one could fill your shoes. Exactly why I need you."

"I'm an American, loyal to my government."

"The same government that hasn't been loyal to you." She had her hands on her hips, her head canted to one side. Her eyes had leveled on him, unblinking. He'd never met anyone like her. Except Meth. He looked away.

"Fine," she said when he didn't reply. "You won't work for me. Then just tell me a few things. I just need some help filling in blanks. That's all. Some normal intelligence trading among allies. Like the old days."

Dale rubbed his chin whiskers. "I don't have anything to trade, Maya. I keep telling you . . ."

She watched his face for a moment. Then she looked toward the small circles of candlelight on the leaking ceiling, the rusted bed, the homemade workbench. Her hands slipped from her hips. She took a step toward him. "If you were my agent, I'd treat you better than . . . this."

"If you offer me money, Maya, I swear to God I'll throw you out."

She reached for his hand and held it between both of hers. "An ideological man, the perfect spy." Her hands crept up to his elbows, pulling him closer. Their bodies were nearly touching now. She was gazing at him, her eyes flickered with the candle flames.

Looking away, Dale glanced quickly toward the window over the bed, noted the bright moonlight outside.

"Draw the blinds if you think we're watched," she said, her gaze steady.

"Okay. I will."

Dale moved around her to lower the shade. In the flashing light outside he saw sheets of rain, swaying trees over an empty lawn, the Jeep. But that was all. "Aren't you breaking protocol by being alone in here with me?" he asked, coming back to her.

She grinned at him in a bittersweet way, her eyes still sad. It was the grin that had haunted Dale's memories. He wondered if she knew that. She'd always seemed to know everything.

She put her arms around his neck. "I gave my pitch," she said, putting her hand to his jawline, looking into his eyes. Her voice had mellowed as though exhausted. She sighed. "No sale. But at least it was an excuse to see you again. I couldn't say no to that, could I? Please . . . don't be angry with me. You understand, right?"

Dale pushed himself free of her, shaking his head in disbelief. All the old questions he'd asked himself then shot back into his mind.

She took a step back and sat on the bed, looking around at the curved walls, the tin ceiling. She crossed her legs. "This place . . . has its charms. If it doesn't blow over."

"It's just the first step. The painting business is going to be good in the Pacific," said Dale, backing toward the workbench. "After this, I'm thinking Polynesia, paint half-naked women there. Like Gauguin."

"I saw a blank canvas under that workbench behind you, didn't I? I meant it when I said I want you to paint me."

Dale leaned against the plywood top of the workbench. "Your *katsas* are expecting you outside, I'm sure."

She shrugged. "Those *katsas* take orders from me now. And you're single now. You can paint any naked woman you want. Including me."

Surprising him, she stood up, unzipped her muslin dress, and let it drop to the floor. Before him in her skimpy bra and panties, she stared unabashedly into his eyes. She wasn't smiling.

Dale blinked. Her gaze was so intense he thought he could feel it at the back of his head. He forced himself to turn around. Her *katsas* were probably out there somewhere. But they couldn't have ears inside the yurt. The leaking roof and howling wind made sure of that. Dale thought she might be genuine.

Might be.

"Okay," he said over his shoulder, mouth dry. "If we're going to do this, then I'll need to pose you." He turned back to her, took two steps forward, and put his hands on her bare shoulders, touching a bra strap. He'd forgotten how tall she was.

He tried to push her down on the bed. He felt her stiffen under his hands, a slight but certain resistance. He tried to push past it. She wouldn't let him.

"John," she said. "I've been traveling forever. Could I freshen up first?"

Dale lifted his hands from her shoulders. "Of course. Take the candle." He pointed toward the bathroom, just past the front door.

CHAPTER 7

DALE COULDN'T HELP BUT WATCH AS SHE WALKED AWAY. HE ALLOWED his mind to roam to the old places.

But then, just before she entered the bathroom, she reached down for her handbag on the chair and took it with her, throwing him one last grin. Her small toiletry kit with the toothbrush was still on the counter, there since she'd undone her wig.

Ah, Goddamnit, thought Dale.

After the bathroom door closed, he could hear the plumbing working as she ran the sink. Dale rushed to the window over the bed and raised the shade an inch. He scanned back and forth, seeing only dark foliage. But then, carefully watching the tree line, he saw what he'd hoped he wouldn't: a faint flicker of light, a flash of metal, a reflection.

It could have been something else, he thought. But then he saw it again. And based on the rhythm of the flashes, he guessed it was a car door's mirror opening and closing in the dark. And if so, the dome light had been disabled. Tradecraft. *Fuck*. Maya had contacted them from the bathroom, using the phone in her bag. They were coming for him now.

Fuck, Dale thought again, dropping the shade over the window. He turned to the workbench and hurriedly gathered a few things in his pockets. The bathroom door reopened. Maya walked toward him, hips swaying, a tiny triangle of fabric where her legs came together. She'd pulled and fluffed her hair before her shoulders. Dale wasn't sure he'd ever seen anyone look that good, except Meth.

They embraced by the bed. Maya was more aggressive now, one

hand moving toward his waist, the other pulling his mouth onto hers. Though Dale couldn't help but have the normal healthy male response, he thought her passion felt a little forced. He could picture the *katsas* outside, setting up.

"Wait," Dale said when her hand got near his loaded pocket. He backed up. "I was serious about wanting to paint you. Something to remember you by. Go ahead, lie back on the bed."

She sat, then stretched herself out as he'd asked.

"It'll be better if one knee comes forward a little, like this," he said, running his hand slowly over her bare thigh, her hip, the thin line of her panties. "Some draping fabric would also paint well in this light." He draped a sheet over her ribs, letting the bulk of it gather behind her. He bent forward and kissed her. He brushed his hand over hers, their fingers interlaced for a moment.

And that's when Dale knew.

With his hand running over hers, he'd noticed that the big topaz gem on her middle finger had been turned inward.

It was a spike stick, he thought now, the gem filled with a few milligrams of highly concentrated ketamine, enough to dull him in a fight. There could be no other plausible explanation, Dale thought, for that ring to have been turned inward.

"You're serious," she said playfully. "You're actually going to paint me."

"You thought it was a metaphor?" Dale shot her his lopsided grin and moved deliberately away from her. "I'm not going to pass the opportunity to paint this. Look at you."

She pouted at him.

"That's the pose, the look. I want to capture it. It's perfect. Hold it right there. Keep focusing up there at the ceiling. Perfect." He stepped toward the foot of the bed where she couldn't see him as she held her pose. Along the way, he picked something up on the workbench. She glanced at him, then went back to her pose.

"Now," he said softly, approaching her knee. He reached into his pocket. "Let me just adjust this . . ."

Dale sprung onto the bed.

He had a loop of wire in his hands, straddling her, seizing her arms, careful to stay free of the ring.

Without even yelping, Maya flipped instantly to her back, eyes wide, an arm springing up out of the wire. Dale caught her wrist, inverted it, twisted it painfully. She grunted and writhed sideways. Within a second, Dale had the wire around her elbows, avoiding her hand with the toxic ring.

She swung a wild knee at him, knocking him in the ribs. He cinched the wire tightly, joining her arms behind her. "*Ari! Ari!*" she cried.

Dale wrenched her arms, turning her, squashing her face into the pillow, putting his knee across her shoulder blades. Her legs jerked, her back bucked. Dale grabbed the length of duct tape that he'd stuck to the rear of his leg while she'd been in the bathroom. He pulled her hair, lifted her head. He put the tape over her mouth. She bucked again, but his weight held her down. He threw a length of tape around her hands, covering up her fingers, the ring.

The extra moment to tape her hands had been a mistake.

She twisted and bent at the waist, ducking under Dale's arm. With robotic speed, she hooked her right leg around his chest, surprising him with a strong kick as she twisted. He gasped. The force of it made him fall forward, smacking his head on the metal headboard. He felt something across his back. She was as fast as anyone he'd ever fought. And she had the lean brute strength of a young mare.

She suddenly had her naked legs around him, locked, her arms still pinned behind her by the wire. She turned her shoulders, sliding sideways off the bed, falling to the floor. With her elbows pinned awkwardly, she leveraged her knees into a vise around Dale's chest, crushing it by locking her ankles together.

Jesus, Dale thought, wheezing, pushing uselessly against her knees. On that last op in Iran, he'd taken a round that had been stopped by a Kevlar vest. The still sore rib was getting crushed.

He was shocked by her strength. Asphyxiated, he felt his chest compressing. It felt like a blade was going through him.

He clawed at her thighs, felt the narrow scrap of her laced panties. She twisted once more, throwing him to the floor, still entangled in her legs. As his hands worked at her ankles, the tight squeeze forced his head closer to her thighs. She tightened them around his neck, forcing her powerful quads into a vise. Pressed against the lace of her panties, Dale's vision dimmed. He knew he was just seconds from choke-out now. He could hardly believe it.

Desperate, nearing unconsciousness, clawing ineffectively, he turned his head and bit her inner thigh. He clenched down hard, feeling the soft flesh give. The disciplined *kidon* shrieked under the tape, holding the squeeze around Dale's neck, tightening it anyway.

Dale bit harder.

She shuddered, moving by reflex. But enough. Greased by blood, Dale wedged a hand between his face and her thigh. He jerked his head free and scrambled to his feet. She did the same. Her underwear was askew but intact, arms tied behind her, a smear of blood at her thigh, her hair wildly mussed. The look in her eyes was predatory. He remembered that too.

Dale dropped to a crouch and swept her ankles, knocking her to the floor. As he came back up, she managed a rising kick to his groin. He groaned hoarsely with the shock of pain, backing, struggling for air. She clambered to a knee, fighting to get back up.

Dale grabbed the remainder of the wire spool off the workbench. He tackled her as she stood, the momentum carrying her half under the bed. He pinned one of her ankles under his armpit, turned the spool around her kicking legs, binding her. Even now she flipped to her back and bucked at him with both feet, hitting him in the chin, making him taste blood as he bit down on his own tongue.

Dale cursed. He backed two steps, spat blood on the floor.

He grabbed her by her bound ankles, twisted her onto her stomach and dragged her facedown to the yurt's center post. Careful to stay behind her, he raised her to a seated position against the post and ran the wire spool around her torso as she struggled. He kept going, spiraling up until it was around her neck, snug against the post. She stopped moving. He loosened the wire slightly, twisted the ends to hold the loop in place with an inch's worth of leeway at her neck.

Pinned, she looked at him, beautiful eyes twitching with fury. She tried to scream.

He tore another length of duct tape and reinforced the gag, running it all the way around her head, sticking it across her hair. "There," he finally said, chest heaving. He rubbed his jaw. His tongue was thick and throbbing, his mouth filled with blood. "Come on, Maya, take it easy," he said with a lisp, panting, spitting, voice low. "You know I'd never really hurt you."

She made a warbling sound under the tape.

"I really do need to see what's in that bag of yours," Dale said, spitting again.

She tried to kick him as he stepped past her. She missed. He found her bag on the chair and opened it. He shoved her short-barreled .22-caliber Beretta LRS into his waistline. He felt something else sewn into the lining. He grabbed a knife off the counter, tore it open to discover a vial of syrupy liquid. A syringe still in its plastic wrapper. He guessed he only had a few seconds before her goons would come crashing through the flimsy door. Then they'd go to work on him for real.

He stepped forward, holding the bag open in front of her. She watched him, shaking her head in short, determined bursts. "I assume this is scopalamine," said Dale, dangling the bag in front her. "I guess you were going to spike me with your trick ring first, then really get me talking with this juice. Disappointed in you, Maya . . . thought maybe you'd really come because . . ." He didn't bother to finish.

She groaned beneath the tape. Dale ignored her, dropped her bag to the floor. He hurriedly threw his collection of T-shirts, shorts, and flip-flops into his backpack. He zipped up and moved toward the window, pausing now and then to spit more blood on the floor. It wouldn't stop coming. His tongue felt like it had a nail through it.

He took one last look at Maya in the narrow flicker of candlelight, sitting upright against the post. A circle of blood had formed under her leg.

"I'm sorry about all this, Maya," said Dale, slurring, raising his voice to be heard over the storm. "I am. I really do wish we'd met again in that other life, like we said we would. But you're still in your original one. When you're not—I mean really not—then find me in Polynesia. You'll know how."

She growled angrily and writhed.

Dale blew out the candles and moved to the window. The rain was hitting harder now, splashing on the Jeep's hood. He confirmed the keys were still in his pocket. He cranked the kitchen window open, climbed on the counter, shoved his backpack through. Swiveling his legs, he pushed himself through.

Outside, he landed in mud, nearly falling. The storm was loud. The wind whipped at his shirt. Warm rain stung his eyes. He shrugged into the backpack and crept to the side of the house with Maya's pistol in his hand.

He didn't know where the two Mossad goons would be. He guessed there'd be one man at the door, another somewhere in the tree line. He paused, flattened himself on the curved wall. He saw no movement, save for the gyrating foliage.

With the pistol in his right hand, he crept forward. It was about twenty-five yards to the Jeep. After one last pause to look for surveillants, he ran for it, flat out.

Halfway there, stupidly, he felt a foot give way in the mud. Trying to correct for it, his other foot slipped too. He skidded to his knees and scrambled to get up. But as he tried to rise, Ari tackled him.

The large Mossad man had him pinned, struggling for a chokehold on Dale's neck. With the mud acting as a lubricant, Dale ducked free, backed up, leveled a kick into the big man's knee. He raised the pistol to the Mossad man's head. "*Don't!*" Dale shouted over the wind, one hand raised. He spit more blood into the mud. "*Don't!* I don't want any of this! Neither do you!"

The big man paused, his beard covered in sludge, his chest heaving. Then the Mossad *katsa* glanced sideways once, barely. Dale followed the Israeli's eyes and saw a pistol with suppressor lying in the grass.

Crabbing sideways, Dale kept Maya's .22 leveled at the Mossad man's face. He bent at the knees to pick up the lengthened Sig Sauer. He ejected its mag with his thumb and threw the disarmed pistol into the bushes. "No trouble!" Dale roared over the wind. He held up his free hand. "*Allies!*" he shouted, backing toward the Jeep.

Since the Jeep had no doors, Dale knew he could slide behind the wheel quickly. He backed another few steps, still aiming the .22 at the bearded *katsa*. He rotated, threw the backpack on the floor, and pushed himself behind the wheel. He hastily inserted the key.

The engine cranked several times. It wouldn't fire.

Oh fuck, Dale thought.

He kept his left arm out to the side, still aiming at the *katsa*. But he needed to pull the choke on the old Jeep, which required him to pause, look down, and use his other hand. When he looked back up, the big man was gone.

A half second later, Dale felt his head being pulled. The *katsa* had come in through the backseat. He had Dale's neck in a tight grip on the inside of his elbow, pulling him against the backrest. Dale's arm flailed. He dropped the gun and twisted, sinking in the seat. The slippery mud saved him—again. Dale fell through the door, outside the Jeep, drooling more blood from his injured tongue.

Dale rolled to his stomach and crawled quickly under the vehicle, sliding through a puddle. The big *katsa* was two seconds behind him, reaching for him, grasping, yet too bulky to follow under the car. Feeling the big man's hands around an ankle, Dale made it to the other side of the Jeep, jerked himself free, sprung up, reached into the cargo area for the machete.

The *katsa* had run around the long way. The big man launched a haymaker with his right fist, hitting Dale in the side of the head. Dale's face bounced off the Jeep's top. Without aiming, he swung the machete wildly, blindly, angrily, catching the *katsa* just above his elbow with the unsharpened edge of the blade. The man screamed.

With his other hand, Dale punched him in the face, two quick blows. The *katsa* was off balance now. Dale raised a leg in a kick to the chest, sending him backward. The Mossad man fell to his butt and slid backward in the mud.

Free for the moment, Dale hurried behind the wheel and tossed the machete in the backseat. With the choke pulled, the engine caught. He threw the Jeep in gear, floored it, let out the clutch, fishtailed down the driveway.

A few seconds later, he was bouncing toward the road junction. He turned the wipers on. There, in the blurred watery light, he saw a white rental car, the one from Henry's. Dale could see the dark form of some-one behind the wheel. It was parked perpendicular to the driveway, parallel to the jungle, ready to speed off toward town. The car's lights came on, evidently starting up. Dale pulled the seat belt over his shoul-der and buckled it. He sped up, steered for the lights.

The heavy brush bar smashed into the car's side with a bang, push-ing it into a thicket of broad-leafed jungle plants.

Dale threw the Jeep in reverse. In the rearview he caught a moonlit flash of the large *katsa* running down the driveway after him. The rental was dented, shoved awkwardly, but still serviceable. The man behind the wheel struggled at the bent door, now jammed shut.

The *katsa* ducked into the interior when Dale raised Maya's pistol. Dale emptied the seven-shot mag into the car's tires before speeding away.

CHAPTER 8

MEREDITH HADN'T SLEPT. SHE'D GONE THROUGH THE MOTIONS—TOSSED, turned, knocked out fifty-two pages of *Anna Karenina* before sealing her eyes shut. But it hadn't worked. Around five, she'd given up and gotten out of bed.

Sucking down coffee and toast, she'd immediately logged into her secure tablet to catch up on the results of her team's intelligence tasking orders for the NIE. Since Dorsey had given her the job some five days back, the replies had been steadily trickling in through the cable traffic. Every morning seemed to offer something new—but nothing that shed any significant light on Hezbollah's *Taniyn*.

The key was still Kahlidi. And while Meredith didn't want to go after him half-cocked, Rance had kept reminding her that Dorsey needed things wrapped up quickly. Meredith had little choice but to prepare for Kahlidi with less-than-optimal information.

DIA had responded to Mossad's S&T analysis that the Hezbollah *Taniyn* warhead cavity *could* contain a fission bomb. But DIA also said it could just as likely be a conventional warhead. Or chemical. Or biological.

Comforting, Meredith had thought.

NSA had counted a dozen intercepts of the phrase "*Taniyn*" over the prior few months. One of them had included Kahlidi's Quds code name, AMIR, referencing a meeting. But it was the same intercept Israel's Unit 8200 had already uncovered. Clouding the picture, NSA noted there'd been thousands of hits from regular civilians talking about dragons. HBO was running *Game of Thrones* dubbed in Arabic across half the Middle East.

Meredith had been especially disappointed by the tepid response from CIA's Beirut Station. Cloaked in operational-speak, the chief of station Beirut had essentially copped to having very little actionable intelligence on Hezbollah missile activities, due to a lack of recruited foreign agents.

Beirut Station's specialty was sectarian political maneuverings in the Lebanese government, which often included Hezbollah. But when it came to weapons procurement by active terror cells, the Beirut COS deferred to an intelligence-sharing arrangement with Mossad. And Mossad had gone cold on them.

It was becoming clearer every hour that Kahlidi was Meredith's best opportunity to shed light on the missile.

But that didn't account for her insomnia.

For four nights, Meredith had struggled with the image of the suspected Mossad honeypot woman in Paris, occasionally revisiting the surveillance photo in secret. Invoking her own cool reason by the light of day, Meredith could allow that the Mossad honeypot only bore a *resemblance* to John's paramour on the Red Sea from seven years ago.

And, Meredith had allowed, it was *possible* that she was leaping to crazy conclusions, being the betrayed wife. Seven years was a long time. Old memories played tricks. Especially jealous ones.

But still.

To finally put her mind at rest, Meredith had reopened the old file about the incident on the Red Sea from seven years ago. She'd dug out the passport number of the woman who'd registered with John at the resort there. Meredith had come across their liaison by accident years ago, but John had never known that.

And then, yesterday, Meredith had pinged a contact at French DGSE and made a back-channel request for updated information on the French national with whom John had been staying. Meredith had given her French colleague a thin excuse as to why she needed the information of a French citizen. It had worked. Just a few hours later, Meredith had been confronted with the old passport photo and the old shock of betrayal.

Meredith had then allowed that the likeness to the Parisian bar photo of the suspected Mossad honeypot wasn't a slam dunk. The cold chill faded a bit. The woman in the passport photo had auburn hair with blue eyes. The Mossad honeypot had dark hair, brown eyes. Only the smiles seemed similar.

The rest of the DGSE message went on to say that the requested passport of this particular French citizen had been deactivated. An international exec with the Swedish telecom company Ericsson, the French national in its photo had been killed three years ago on a Normandy cycling trip. Meredith wondered if John knew that. She also went online to see if there was news reporting about this cycling accident. There was. It checked out. Meredith decided to let it all go.

Besides, she'd told herself. It was high time to compartmentalize this shit. Nothing mattered but *Taniyn*, the NIE.

But still.

The compartment had kept reopening in the middle of the night.

After a three-hour drive and a swing through HQS to pick up more files, Meredith stopped her Volvo at the heavily fortified gate at CIA's Camp Peary, just outside Williamsburg, Virginia. Two security men in unmarked black uniforms approached, checking her ID. It took them five full minutes to search her car with a bomb-sniffing beagle. Even after that, it took two more calls to the Langley ops desk before they finally let her through.

On the other side of the razored fences, her winding route took her past the tiny airfield where she'd once learned to jump out of a plane, the small simulated "Combat Town" where they'd taught her to shoot, the York River swamp where they'd honed her survival skills. She drove by the one-story inner compound that served as her "prison camp" during SERE—Survival, Evasion, Resistance, Escape training. She sped quickly past the low-slung iron shipping containers, avoiding the memory.

She hadn't been back to Camp Peary, home of the training grounds for the National Clandestine Service—affectionately known as "the Farm"—since they'd first installed Kahlidi there and christened him as Atlas. Until now, she'd been letting the Agency shrinks evaluate her recruit's verities as a spy. But that was before the Israelis had shown up with the *Taniyn* schematic.

"This is the latest report," Dr. Paul said. A fit fifty-something in his snug blue polo shirt, he had the crinkled eyes and erect bearing of a former military man. Meredith thought him the archetype of the ageless experts that had always populated the Farm's training ranks. "You can read the report if you want, ma'am—or I can just brief you before you go in to see him."

Meredith glanced at her watch. Rance was back in Vienna, saying that State was anxious for the NIE to get closed out so they could move forward with the Iran deal. Rance was in a hurry, as usual. He'd set up a videoconference with Dorsey for that afternoon where Meredith was sure to be in the hot seat. "Whatever's faster," she said to Dr. Paul.

The doctor flipped open the classified folder. "Okay. Let's start here, then. A record of all the polygraphs we've given him. Up to sixteen now."

"Sounds like a lot."

"You ordered us to evaluate him as a paid agent. That's the regimen."

"And?"

"Look here."

Meredith followed his pen, noting the dotted scatterplot of Kasem's answers arrayed across various shaded bands. "You're saying he's passed all sixteen polys?" she asked, looking up from the chart.

"Not only that, ma'am, but he's at least within the margin of error on ninety-six percent of the questions—even when we know he's lying. See this line? A standard deviation that barely departs the mean."

"So he's beating them."

"Understatement of the decade. He may be the most talented liar I've ever encountered. His Quds trainers would be proud."

"Then—his efficacy as a paid agent is still . . ."

"Indeterminate, ma'am. I don't know his real motivations . . . yet. So I can't sign off on the two-fourteen form just yet. But I'll get there. I just need a few more weeks . . ."

She rushed a sigh. "I'm going to need real intel from him. Soon. There must be other methods to get at him besides blood pressure and finger sweat."

"Physical polygraphs have their limits, true. We could maybe use a functional MRI, a brain scan," the psychiatrist said. "There's some clinical evidence that neural activity and blood flow are directly correlated to prevarication. Several papers have postulated that certain prefrontal and anterior cingulate regions are recruited to prevent a prepotent response."

Meredith nodded. *Whatever.* "Why wouldn't we do that, then?"

"The tech's new. We don't have it. And even if we did, it's not an approved method by the Standards Committee. I'd need you to write up a request. Legal would have to clear it. It might even have to go before the Standards board itself. There are moral, ethical issues at play here. Big debate in the scientific community. It would take months, hell, years sometimes."

Her knuckles turned white as she squeezed her pen. She made a note for something to do. "What about psychological manipulation— enhanced techniques?"

The doctor paused before answering. "Not an option . . . not here."

Enhanced interrogations—torture—had ended countless CIA careers in the late 2000s. "Of course," she said, exhaling raggedly. "I didn't mean to suggest it."

The doctor watched her. "If it makes you feel any better—my *clinical* opinion is that an enhanced protocol wouldn't be that effective. Kasem has an embedded psychological anomaly related to a previous capture from ISIS in Iraq, where he withstood some brutal tactics. You've seen the scar on his neck. Coming one whisker shy of an ISIS beheading is not something that goes away. The trauma's come up several times in the sessions. And something else too—something about being held with . . . your . . . husband, I believe, during the event."

"*Ex*-husband," she said. "Former case officer John Dale, yes." It had been a line of questioning in Kasem Kahlidi's polygraphs because the Agency had looked to verify John's old story about their joint escape from ISIS.

"If anything, you might consider using Mr. Dale as someone he could potentially trust. Building genuine trust-based rapport is essential. That's how we'll get to the real him. I've noted that in my two-fourteen evals."

"All right," she said. "I'll think about it."

"As I wrote in the debriefs, in my opinion, bringing in Mr. Dale would be a show of good faith. Shared trauma creates a bond. I'd suggest you might even have Mr. Dale act as Kasem's handler, ultimately. There's also the girlfriend, of course. Ms. Khani. You already saw that Kasem's very motivated to—"

"Thank you," said Meredith, cutting him off. "How about the rest of Kahlidi's psychology? Besides Ms. Khani or Mr. Dale, what else does Kasem want? What else could we do—today—to get some solid intel out of him?"

The doctor smiled for the first time. "Oh, he'll be very eager to give you his suggestions."

"Well, well," Lieutenant Colonel Kasem Kahlidi, Atlas, said, entering the painted cinder-block room. Meredith was already sitting at the stainless-steel table, waiting. "Here I was expecting the daily rectal probe. Instead, it's the great Meredith Morris-Dale herself, my protector. I feel so honored." He smiled broadly and tipped his well-groomed head.

She didn't rise from her metal chair. "I'd shake your hand, Kasem, but the security team wants us to stay five feet apart at all times."

The Iranian looked up at a security camera on the wall and waved to it with a smirk. "A shame. I'd have preferred to give you a hug, Meredith." He sat down.

It rankled her endlessly that Kahlidi knew her real name. In the euphoria of his initial defection, they'd all shared too much. One more thing she wished she could redo.

"Do I detect some sarcasm, Colonel?"

"Nonsense, Mrs. Dale. Frankly, seeing anyone besides taut old men in dark blue polos is a *very* welcome distraction these days."

"You look right at home in your own dark blue polo, Kasem."

He plucked at the fabric on his upper arm. "You know, for all you Americans harp about diversity, I do believe you're the first woman I've seen since I've been on this extended holiday. And I must say *you're* in high color. Were you somewhere sunny? Tropical vacation, I hope? I suppose not. You look tan, but tired. You sleeping all right?"

He raised a carefully plucked eyebrow.

Meredith shook her head. Some of the women at Langley who'd watched the Persian's debriefs had been quite taken with his angular jaw, narrow waist, upper-crust English accent. She looked at her watch again.

"Are you ready for your first real intelligence assignment?" she asked.

This time Meredith saw something in his eyes—a tiny speck of shadow. "Of course," he said, spreading his hands, palms up. "As long as you've shown me proof of funds—and Kasra."

"Soon," she said.

"Then let's talk. Why not?"

Meredith opened the first of a stack of folders that she'd picked up on her way down from Langley. Each had been stripped of information, ordered carefully. She slid the brown manila down the table's length.

He caught the folder and opened it. It was a photographic composite of Mohammed Baramzedeh, the assassinated aerodynamics specialist. "Who's this man?" Meredith asked, watching Kasem's eyes carefully.

He studied the photograph for ten seconds before looking up. The smile was gone. "Why do you want to know?"

"Do you know him or not?"

"Yes," he said. "I know him. Or rather *of* him. He's a physicist."

"Name?"

He shrugged.

"Kasem, you know he's a physicist, but you don't know his name?"

He looked at her again. "Meredith, I'm sure you already know this man's name. A junior analyst could figure that out."

"That's not how this works. Answer my question. Think of it as one of the control questions in your polygraphs."

He smirked. "All right. He's Mo Baramzedeh."

She took a note. "What does Baramzedeh do for Quds?"

The Iranian looked down at the picture of the physicist and then up again, hesitating. "You know, the wonderful thing about you being here, Meredith, is that I'm finally talking with someone who can actually get something done."

"What does Baramzedeh do, Kasem?"

"All the other junior field people you've sent in, all the psychiatrists, the trainee analysts, the phony tough guys—don't get me wrong, they're all lovely people. But not one of them has been able to respond to a single request of *mine*." He slid the closed folder back toward her, watching her face.

She stared back at him, blankly.

He said, "You must have Kasra back in the US by now. It's the one thing I've consistently asked for, the crucial part of our deal. Like I said before, I want to see her. Let's close *that*."

"Can't," said Meredith. "We don't know where she is yet. And our deal didn't stipulate that we get her to the US as a *precondition*."

Kasem looked toward a blank spot on the yellow-beige wall. "If you want something now, then I want to see her. Simple terms."

"I told you, I don't know where she is. You know that."

"Can I go back to my room now? I am really coming to enjoy the solitude."

"Give me something, Colonel. Then we'll talk about Kasra."

"I just did. Mo Baramzedeh. Physicist. Your turn. That's how this needs to work." He remained staring at the wall.

Meredith drummed her pen on the legal pad. "Kasem—look at me." He turned his head. He settled a cold stare on her, a different man now. *Good*, she thought. "I've been looking for Kasra. So far, we've got info from the UK Border Force that she entered with a visa. A few weeks ago. But after that, there's no record of her. She's hard to find."

"She's in the Queensway neighborhood of London. She knows enough to be in hiding. I told you about the doctor friend of hers. They were engaged once. She'll probably seek him out. She doesn't know anyone else there."

She glanced at a file. "Dr. Roger Gulrajani, her ex-fiancé. Yes, we've checked. No sign that he's been in contact with her," Meredith said, lying.

"Who do you have looking?" Kasem asked.

"Case officers."

"Your UK officers are clumsy. I've seen them. Classic G-men, barging in with boxy suits and American accents. The locals will all be worried about Gitmo. They'll hide her."

Meredith shrugged.

"You must surely have contacted MI-5 by now," he continued. "They run a surveillance state." He looked away from her, breathed deeply. "There isn't much *time*, Meredith. You're not the only intelligence service tracking her. MOIS will be after her. You realize that?"

Meredith didn't need Dr. Paul's fancy MRI equipment to see that she'd tapped an authentic nerve. "I'm using the resources I have at my disposal, MI-5 included."

"How's John?" Kahlidi said with a sudden smile.

The abrupt shift surprised her. It was her turn to glance at the cinder blocks.

"Oh . . . ," the Quds man said, the smile widening. "I'm *so* sorry."

Meredith opened her second folder, the photo of Baramzedeh with the Mossad honeytrap in the Paris bar. She slid it across the table to the Quds officer. "How about her? Who's she?"

Kasem studied the photo, shifting the angle. "I don't know. But . . . I very much wish I did. I'd say old Mo is punching well above his weight, wouldn't you?"

Below the table, Meredith formed a fist, squeezed her thumb. "So you recognize Baramzedeh in the background there."

"Yes."

"And you really don't know her?"

"No." The Quds man shut the folder, slid it back. "Your turn. Tell me about John. Where is he?"

"What would be the point of talking about John?"

"He's the only man you have that would be able to blend into Queensway." He stroked the scar on his neck. "He speaks the language, understands the culture, knows how to do an exfil without tipping MOIS. He could slip into London under MOIS's nose, find Kasra in two hours, and get her back here safe. *That's* when we'll have a deal."

Meredith knew John would be coming to Annapolis in a week for Grace's award. Though she didn't want to see him, she'd have no choice. "John's not active," she said. "I'll talk to him—but you understand he doesn't take orders from me."

"I understand that *very* well."

She stowed the urge to whip the legal pad at his head. "I mean it," she said, staying as impassive as she could. "I'll talk to him. I'll see him in a week or so. Who knows? Maybe he can help."

Kasem nodded. "All right. Thank you."

She returned the nod. Time for the big play. Staring straight into his eyes, she said one word: "*Taniyn.*"

Kasem's eyes were blank, expressionless. Small wonder he made a mockery of polygraphs, she thought.

"*Taniyn,*" she said again, louder. By now she knew Kasem had put together the photo of Baramzedeh and the code word.

"Have you been studying Arabic, Mrs. Dale? It means 'dragon.'"

"Morris-Dale. It means more than that, Kasem. Give me something."

"If you let me talk to John, maybe I will."

Bingo. She kept her eyes focused on her pad, taking a note. *Deal. A meeting with John for a lead on* Taniyn. *Easy.*

"Actually . . . ," he added. "I want something else too."

Fuck. "What?"

He looked at the camera on the ceiling, the two-way mirror along one wall. "I assume, based on the way you people pop in and out of my interrogations, that I'm somewhere in Virginia."

"How do you even know you're in the US?"

"I've been to DC and New York, Meredith. I know America."

"New York? FBI's been looking for IRGC since that botched kidnap attempt of an American journalist up there. Maybe I should ask them to join us." She glanced at the cameras, reminding Kasem that everything he'd said to this point had been recorded. They both knew he was at their mercy—CIA would forever be able to blackmail him with these tapes.

"That New York snatch was MOIS," he said. "I had nothing to do with it. And you already ID'd the suspects. It caused quite the stir back in Tehran before I . . . left."

"What then?" she asked. "You come over here for some weapons deals with one of the various Hamas or Hezbollah lobbying groups on K Street?"

He smiled. "Let's just say I think I'm not far from the sticky swamps of the Potomac. And judging by the gunfire I hear every now and then, probably a military base, maybe Quantico."

"I could have ordered much worse accommodations for you, Kasem."

"*Bah.* This place is insulting, Meredith. I'm a field-grade intelligence officer. You should treat me like one. We're on the same side now."

"Have you any idea, Lieutenant Colonel Kahlidi, how much worse we could have made things for you?"

He inspected his fingernails. "Maybe I should ask a lawyer to file a habeas writ." He glanced at the camera and smiled, waved. "Remember, Meredith, we're being recorded."

"Right," she said. "And I could send you back into Iran. Today. I could leak an edited tape that shows how cooperative you've been. Would that be better?"

He smiled again, shaking his head. "Meredith. That would blow your big nuclear deal, wouldn't it? My MOIS friends and I would tell the world how the Americans invaded our country, snatched one of our officers, played fast and loose with the international order. I confessed under torture . . . *torture*. Would that be good for you?"

Bastard. She took another note. "We have more to gain by helping each other."

"The smartest thing you've said to me today."

"All right. Besides John, what can I do to make your circumstance more comfortable?"

"I've toured Virginia's horse country. Acres on acres of rolling green, not unlike the downs of Suffolk. I so miss those downs, those horses."

She nodded. "True enough. You're near horse country. I can tell you that much."

"Then it should be very easy for you to get me what I want."

"Are you picking anything else up now?" Eli asked forty minutes later. The *katsa* team leader was behind the wheel of a rented Nissan Altima, twenty cars behind Meredith's silver Volvo SUV in the dense late-morning traffic of northbound I-64. An early-summer shower had crept in.

"No," said Rina in his earpiece. "She's riding in silence."

"No music or anything?"

"We could try another path-loss signal test, see if there's another frequency with less noise. But I can hear turn signals, the wipers. The phone rang a minute ago. I think she didn't answer."

"Huh," said Eli. "Second time she's done that. Either she's using tradecraft to avoid roving Bluetooth snoops or just blowing someone off. Alone at home, alone on the road. Lonely woman."

"Or just focused," the young *katsa* collection officer answered.

Eli clicked the mic twice. He'd made a pass at Rina on a previous Caesarea op in Toronto and gone down in flames. He watched a low helicopter over the traffic, skirting beneath the iron-gray overcast with its anti-collision lights blinking.

"Okay," he said, thinking about Meredith's reported patterns, the time of day. "HVT's Volvo is probably headed back to Langley now. But let's confirm. What's your pos, Mia?"

"Richmond. Just passed exit 193."

Rina came on the encrypted UHF net. "Wait one. She just made a call. Stand by."

Eli waited. The three Mossad operatives each carried a receiver capable of picking up the audio snoop, a thin wire heat-fused to the lower inside glass of the Volvo's windshield to pick up sound vibrations. The receiver had to be within seventy-five yards of the car to pick up the low-wattage transmitter. It was Rina's turn to close in for the take.

Thirty seconds later, Rina came back on. "She called someone named Ed—sounded to me like her boss. She said she's making progress with Atlas, whoever that is. She asked to delay a meeting at HQS until she can get him to a new location, it sounded like. That's it. Short call. I had to close to two car lengths for the gain to work. I'd better drop back and exit here."

Eli checked his speedometer. "Mia, slow down so she passes you. You can pick her up in case there's a follow-up call."

It was their first lead worth reporting since Eli had initiated surveillance a week ago. He'd need to get this to Washington Station ASAP. "I'll speed up in the left lane and make a pass. Rina, exit and report the take to the station. Oh—wait. Hang on. HVT's moving over now, slowing down. *Chara*. She's exiting—abruptly, too fast, feels like an SDR. I can't follow. Going to have to pass her too."

"What's the exit?" Rina asked.

Eli sped up, moving to the far-left lane, staying well clear of the Volvo. "Instead of merging to I-95, she's staying on I-64, westbound, toward Charlottesville. I don't like it. She might have made us."

"Copy," Rina answered. "I'll stay on her then but drop back. Losing audio. Exiting I-64."

"*Chara*," Eli said. "What's in Charlottesville? Is this just an SDR? Are we blown?"

"I don't know. Your orders?"

Eli wondered what his best move was. The rules for operating in the US were different. Word had come down that this woman was exceptionally important, that contact had to stay tight. But, he wondered, what would that mean if they backed her into a corner?

He supposed he'd find out soon enough.

CHAPTER 9

THE WARMTH CRAWLING ITS WAY UP HIS SOCKS MADE MAJOR SIAMAK Azad grateful to have landed late in the day. Though the sun had peaked a few hours earlier, the Iranian MOIS counterintelligence officer could still feel the hot sidewalk through the soles of his shoes. Walking to the curb, looking for his ride, he inhaled the polluted air with its ripe diesel stink and remembered just how much he disliked Tehran. Though he'd grown up here, once again, the major wished he hadn't been ordered to return.

But it was neither smog nor heat that accounted for the MOIS major's dread. It was, rather, the botched snatch of Kasem Kahlidi's woman, Kasra Khani, at Paddington Station some twenty hours earlier. What a clusterfuck.

That Siamak had even made it out of the country was a minor miracle, he thought as he watched the cars driving on the terminal loop road, picking up passengers. His trouble-free exit was a testament to the strength of his UK visa, which had declared him an employee of the National Iranian Oil Company, NIOC.

What with the expected thaw in sanctions from the emerging Vienna nuclear deal, BP had *leapt* at the opportunity to sponsor Siamak for a meeting to discuss drilling leases in Iran's South Pars field. Once in London, BP had driven him around like royalty, feted him. And when it was time to leave, they'd gotten him through the executive lines at Heathrow, made calls to the people that mattered to leave this Iranian alone. How shocked those BP execs would be to learn that Siamak had ordered a Hezbollah cell to abduct a poor, unsuspecting National Health Service nurse a few miles away while they were all lunching at the top of the tallest building in Square Mile.

Now, while standing on the curb, Siamak checked the news on his phone, fearful of what he might find. Sure enough, there were plenty of stories about the shootout in the alley just outside Paddington. But helpfully, BBC was calling it "gang activity," nothing related to politics or terrorism. The reporting was going the way of cultural commentary— screeds on the proliferation of weapons and drugs, just like in America. Nothing related to Iran or Hezbollah.

Siamak held the phone in his hands and looked around, wondering what he should do next. He'd already gotten the updates from his cell, and it was better to keep communications to a minimum. After thinking through his options, he sent a text to his wife back in Beirut, the meat of which was that he'd finally been able to find the *Star Wars* LEGO for his son, Ali. Siamak had even had it gift-wrapped right there at the LEGO store in Oxford Circus. He hated that his son wanted that LEGO, a symbol, he thought, of Western consumerism and overall cultural decay. But he was still a father and a husband, and the boy wanted what the boy wanted. In the end, Siamak had ridden the tube to Oxford Circus to find the godforsaken thing.

And *inshallah*, he'd added to his wife in a second message, he'd be flying home to Beirut in the morning, early enough to make it back for Ali's birthday.

He hoped so anyway as he watched a full-sized Range Rover pull to a stop at the curb in front of him. Tinted glass on the forward passenger's door lowered. A bearded, plainclothes man behind the wheel glanced at Siamak before the tinted window went back up.

The lack of greeting was typical of the culture at MOIS. Descended from the Shah's vicious SAVAK secret police, MOIS had maintained its foreign and domestic intelligence mission under the Islamic Republic. Among other duties, its officers operated clandestinely to affirm the loyalty of the *pasdaran*, the devout IRGC soldiers that preserved the spirit of the revolution. And for that reason, the men in the ranks often kept mum—just as they were doing now. They rode the half hour to MOIS headquarters in silence.

Once in the HQ building, an IRGC sergeant led Siamak to an airless anteroom. Another orderly let the MOIS major duck into a restroom to wipe the sweat from his face and freshen up.

Still clad in business attire, Siamak finally came to attention before the colonel on whose summons he had traveled. The roller bag that held his son's LEGO was propped near the door.

Colonel Naser Maloof, leader of MOIS counterintelligence operations, listened to Siamak's report as he scrolled through a Sky News site. The older man removed his Coke-bottle glasses and lit a Winston with an old-fashioned Zippo. He offered Siamak neither a Winston nor a seat. "Well, Major Azad. At least nothing's come out of Interpol so far. And the media seem to be calling it gang-related."

"Agree, sir," said Siamak. "I would also note that I didn't have any trouble with the UK Border Force. Made it through Heathrow without a second glance."

The colonel puckered his mouth and made a clucking sound. "So you're not quite blown . . . yet anyway. Sky is saying here that the dead man was an undercover cop. Hope he wasn't MI-5. That will set them to digging. And then what? Bloody fucking mess, that's what."

Siamak stayed silent.

Maloof adjusted the glasses on his nose and clicked the mouse. "*Kos nagu*," he said as he read. "When this is over, Major, I have half a mind to put your whole London Hezbollah cell on a real martyrdom op, just to get rid of the lot."

"They would be honored to become martyrs, sir."

The colonel tilted his chin to exhale vertically. "Yes. Well. UK foreign office has yet to say anything to our foreign ministry team in Vienna. So far, so good. But a gunfight in public . . . How?"

Siamak had posed the same question to his Hezbollah team about the chaotic snatch. The unsatisfying explanation had been the Arabic-UK version of *shit happens*. "The undercover cop came out of nowhere.

I know we hadn't seen that kind of surveillance at Paddington before—or the men just missed it."

Maloof was in his sixties, skin pitted, paunchy, a beard of gray strands spaced like dead trees. He puffed a growing ash to a fiery orange, then exhaled with the force of a bellows. "And you felt comfortable leaving these same jokers alone with the woman? Where are they now? I mean *exactly* where?"

"Safe house on Alexandra Road, sir, north of the river. At least until things cool down. It's good cover. I set it up myself."

The head of MOIS counterintelligence leaned back and folded his hands across his belly, staring at the young officer in front of him, thinking—and worrying.

Maloof couldn't afford to let Iran's involvement spill into the open. It was just the thing to screw up the nuclear negotiation, which, from the Supreme Council's perspective, had been going well. If the order for the snatch of an Iranian citizen in the middle of London was traced back to Maloof, he was a dead man.

Moreover, Maloof was already in the hot seat for his failure to prevent seven Mossad assassinations of Iranian nuclear scientists in the past year. And this last hit on Dr. Mo Baramzedeh in Beirut had been a doozy. Especially since Baramzedeh had been on the *Taniyn* initiative, the most sensitive operation of all.

"The girl's in custody anyway," Maloof said after more reading. Sky was already beginning to push the story further down the page. "Let's see if that brings Kahlidi out of hiding, shall we?"

Until recently, IRGC had thought the missing Quds officer dead, killed in the American exfil op that had brought out their spy. But a week ago, a Kurdish radio intercept suggested that a man who faintly resembled Kahlidi was alive, captured by one of the wilder Hanafi Kurd units that operated well beyond the grasp of Quds, friendly with the Americans. That intercept had breathed new life into Maloof's search for Kahlidi.

It had also breathed new life into Maloof's prospects for survival.

The wily old colonel could now pin the successful Mossad hits on a possibly traitorous Kasem Kahlidi, who, Maloof had been suggesting, might be supplying targeting intelligence through the Kurds. And by grabbing Kasra Khani first, Maloof had the leverage to force a confession out of Kahlidi, the ultimate prize.

"How badly wounded is she?" the colonel asked Siamak now. "When can we get her out?"

"I'd wait on the exfil," said Siamak. "Her leg was grazed by a bullet. We're working on getting that doctor again to patch her up. But with the police searching, we should probably lay low."

Maloof nodded and smoked. "Yes. You'd better get that doctor. But we *can't* have this traced to us, obviously."

"Won't happen, sir."

"What has she said about Kahlidi so far? Anything?"

"Says she doesn't know where Kahlidi is, sir. But she also says their last contact was exactly one day before Kahlidi disappeared during the night of the American raid. He'd told her to go to England. She didn't know why but listened to him. That's it—so far."

The colonel's eyes danced on hearing this unexpectedly good news. "Oh? She said that? You're sure Kahlidi ordered her there?"

"Yes, sir. I should be able to verify it. We have the phone records."

Alhamdulillah, thank God, thought Maloof. If spun with care into the higher halls of IRGC, it would suggest Kahlidi was definitely plotting something on his way out. And now that Kahlidi was in the wind, the old arms dealer could be selling details of the Iranian scientific staff to the Zionists. Even the hint of such treachery would be enough to cover Maloof's own security failures.

But that would be a balancing act too. Kasem Kahlidi had been well liked and respected, a former adjutant to Soleimani. Many officers didn't want to hear that the Quds man could betray the revolution so easily. Maloof knew that if he pushed too hard, he risked offending the new head of Quds himself.

Maloof settled his eyes on the young officer. "A gunfight in public . . . witnesses . . . news. This is—"

A bearded sergeant stuck his head through the door, interrupting. "Sir, the brigadier has moved the *Taniyn* meeting up. It's in an hour."

Maloof nodded. With the Israelis continuing their ruthless assassinations, the brigadier wanted *Taniyn* queued up as a real contingency, not just some far-off special weapons program. That meant building up the target packages, getting in the warhead, beefing up the counterintelligence in Beirut to keep all the operational planning safe. As the head of MOIS counterintelligence, keeping all *Taniyn* activities under wraps was Maloof's job—though the colonel had deftly delegated said duties to Major Siamak Azad.

"Major Azad," Maloof said when the sergeant had gone. "I'd ordered you back here for the brigadier's meeting tonight since it will be on Hezbollah countersurveillance. But Siamak-*jon*, I'm not going to let you come with me now."

Siamak stood stiffly and stared straight ahead.

"Do you know *why* I'm not going to do that, *baradar*?" rasped Maloof. "Can you guess?"

"I would not presume to guess, sir."

"It's because I'm going to give you time to clean up this mess of the abduction. You need to make sure your tracks are covered. This *cannot* become public." Maloof let the cigarette dangle from his lip, a tendril of ash growing dangerously longer. "You'll have a national search to find the killer of a British policeman. You'll need to lay *very* low. No leaks, no word of this—even internally. You continue to communicate only with me, and even that should only be in verbal form. Am I clear? We have no idea how far Kahlidi's spy network runs internally. Secrecy is everything. Clear?"

"Clear, sir."

"And I don't want you leaving town. Not now. In case the news gets worse on this abduction, I'll want you here to explain it. It was your mission, Major. You need to own up to it."

Siamak's eyes drifted toward his suitcase, the LEGO. He nodded once and held his tongue.

The colonel grimaced at his now cold tea. "Well. I suppose since you've come all this way, you may as well bring me up to speed on the rest of the Kahlidi search. Phone records? Other women? You must have some other lead by now."

Still thinking of his son's soon-to-be-missed birthday, Siamak cleared his throat. "Other than this Khani woman, I don't have anything new on the Kahlidi search, sir. We're checking his other women. He had a relationship in France, but it seemed brief. He also dated a Christian woman up in East Beirut. Nabil has her under surveillance now."

"What about Kahlidi's money?" asked the colonel. "Still no withdrawals?"

"Credit cards and bank accounts flagged, sir. If he accesses anything, we'll know."

The colonel shook his head. "A Quds weapons merchant, living in the shadows, by design. I doubt it. If he's on the loose, he must be using something. You just haven't found it yet. I can't imagine he'd just abandon his accounts. He must be funneling money through one of the front companies."

"There are thirteen front companies, sir, all funded by IRGC, all well documented. I've installed a MOIS forensic accountant in every one of them, working directly for us, combing through payrolls, accounts payable, vendors, everything. We haven't seen anything we couldn't explain, sir. All of his associates assume he's still alive, since they don't know about the American raid. But none of them have heard from him. We've tapped all their phones."

The colonel rocked in his chair, nodding. "And you have nothing else on Kahlidi's family? Extended relatives?"

"He was an only child, sir. His parents and grandparents are dead. We interviewed an aunt, but she hadn't seen him in years. We've tapped her phones too—just in case."

"What about his people? His father was rich, had a lot to lose in the revolution. Possible associations with guerilla groups? The Kurds? Have you looked?"

"His father was Turkomen, his mother Persian. They used to own a horse ranch in Golestan and the apartment in Elahiyeh. Kahlidi inherited them but rarely visited after he went to live in the UK. While in Tehran, working for you, sir, Kahlidi had been staying in the Elahiyeh place, living with the Khani woman. I've had men staking both locations. But it's been a dead end so far."

Maloof felt the urge for another cigarette. "This Kasra Khani woman is the key. I'd say the way he told her to flee to the UK proves it. He'll figure out a way to come in to get her. You watch. And when he does, we need to be ready."

"Sir."

"Make sure you get her healthy. And talking. But keep our involvement three steps removed, at least. You trust your Hezbollah martyrs there to handle her? Even after all this?"

"I do, sir. They're committed. But I'll stay close to them."

"And if this makes the news again, you'll be—"

The sergeant was back, opening the door after a knock. His eyes were wide this time, locked on the colonel's. "The brigadier wants to see you. *Now*, sir."

"What are you talking about?" Maloof glanced at the clock over the window. "You *just* said I have another hour."

"There's been another assassination. Here, in Iran, up near the Caspian."

"*Kos nagu*. Who?"

"Dr. Farzad," said the sergeant.

Maloof's mouth gaped. *Farzad*, a physicist who'd helped design the *Taniyn* warhead. Another counterintelligence failure on Maloof's watch.

CHAPTER 10

THE HOT DESERT WIND HAD SETTLED TO A MERE WARM WHISPER BY
the time it met Maya on the shore. There the beautiful Mossad *kidon*
stood in ankle-deep water, pants rolled to the knees. Her feet were
pleasantly warm in the Sea of Galilee, the ancient freshwater lake that
straddles the modern Israel-Jordan border.

In the darkening distance, Maya noted the rounded hills of Jordan,
the first few lights of the wind-scrubbed farms. Closer, under a pink
evening sky, she watched the spreading wake of a patrol boat that ran at
idle speed along the bank. The armed men in it, Mossad operatives from
the commando group called Bayonet, were aiming binoculars over her
head toward a house three hundred meters up the hill. It was the house
where Werner Davidai lived.

"*Doda*—should we go?" asked Dil, addressing Maya as her aunt, the
way the seven-year-old always had. Holding Maya's hand, she too had
her feet in the warm water, her pants rolled above her knees. "I hear
Saba's bell," added Dil, squeezing Maya's hand for emphasis. "*Saba*
hates it when I'm late for dinner."

Maya cocked an ear against the gentle breeze. She heard the bell too.
It was clanging away up the slope, near the house. But Maya also heard
something else—the thumping bass of a helicopter.

The *kidon* watched the black Eurocopter race in from the south, its
anti-collision lights blinking. It banked into a curve, slowed to a hover,
and landed in a grassy field. Maya knelt and held Dil in place, waiting.

"All right," the *kidon* said into the girl's ear when the engines had finally died down. "We can go to dinner now. Shall we do the race up the hill?"

Maya lost. The week-old bite wound on her thigh that Dale had inflicted had required five stitches, forcing her to shorten her barefoot stride up the hill. Once to the top she found herself twenty paces behind Dil, who was already celebrating, hair bouncing in a flurry of coppery curls.

Beyond Dil, through the pergola vines that bearded the house, Maya could see the visitors walking over from the helo. The *kidon* paused to ensure there were no surprise guests. As expected, she saw Galin, commander of AMAN's Unit 8200, and Mitz, leader of Junction, Mossad's ultra-secret embedded foreign agent group. Remembering her bare feet, Maya grabbed Dil's hand. Together they slipped into the far wing of the house.

Reemerging in fresh clothes, Maya found the outdoor table lit by a string of café bulbs draped among the vines. Both visitors were already seated, listening to Werner at the head of the table with polite attention. Rachel, Werner's wife, was busy at the far end with Dil, trying to settle the girl. When Rachel caught sight of Maya, the older woman pushed out a chair and patted it. Dil ran off, delighted with her escape from the adult dinner.

". . . and you *must* try this cabernet," Werner was saying to his guests, filling their glasses, going on about the sunny climate, its effects on viniculture, his own rows of vines. "Ah, there you are, Maya. You too. I know how you prefer the white. But try this. I was just telling them, it's from a vineyard to the northwest of Capernaum, not four clicks away. Incredible." He handed her a glass. "I insist."

"Tell him it's good," whispered Rachel to Maya. "Or I'll hear about it all night."

The next bottle was also Galilean, a Syrah. Werner spoke of deep roots, the snowmelt off Mount Lebanon, soil alkalinity. "I'm an investor in this one," he added, emptying the bottle in Maya's glass. "If you like it, let me know. I can show you how to buy it. In my opinion it's one of the best to come out of Israel."

Rachel rescued them all by asking the men about their families. Maya learned that Galin had a son in the IDF, that Mitz had an Air Force daughter. When Mitz politely asked Maya about her own family, Rachel deflected by serving up.

"You must try her *hamin*," Werner said, passing a bowl. "Rachel started the marinade yesterday. *Yesterday*. Maya, there's something vegetarian for you down here too. The *chraime* with the tofu instead of fish. It's better than it sounds, I promise . . ." He laughed.

"He's nervous about Mitz being here," Rachel whispered to Maya. "Look at those red cheeks. Make sure he eats something later tonight or he'll be very drunk."

Maya nodded. But she knew Werner wasn't in excess because of nerves at Mitz, a rival for the top spot at Mossad. The Caesarea chief's imbibing was, rather, a form of relief. The latest op—a Red Page near the Caspian in northern Iran—had been a smashing success. For this one, Mossad's Junction group had hired a group of Kurdish rebels. Their ruthless work had meant that another scientist within the Iranian nuclear hierarchy had been eliminated.

And not just any scientist. The Red Page had been for Farzad, the deputy chief of Iranian nuclear research. If anyone had been developing a *Taniyn* warhead, Werner had convinced himself, it would have been Farzad.

But that good news was not to be acknowledged until Rachel had disappeared into the kitchen and Dil had been put to bed. Only then did Werner invite his guests into the garden with a significant look in his eye. "Come," the Caesarea boss said, smiling, carrying four empty glasses in one hand, a new bottle of red in the other. "We have much to discuss."

Maya, Galin, and Mitz followed Werner to a small pagoda overlooking the lake. There, Werner flicked a match and lit two candles. Over his shoulder, Maya watched the navigation lights on the patrol boat as it maneuvered in the distance.

"Here," said Werner, sitting with a scrape of his chair. He opened the humidor that had been on the teak table. Mitz took a cigar then passed the box to his right. The men took turns leaning into the candle, lighting up. Maya declined.

Werner puffed. He looked at the sickle-moon that had risen over the dark Jordanian hills. He inhaled deeply and held his breath, listening to the screech of the crickets, ensuring they were alone. "What a day," he said finally, exhaling, smiling crookedly, one eye squinted. "Let us all drink to those brilliant, *brilliant* assassins, the Kurds." He passed the bottle. They murmured their approval of the Kurds and poured.

"And no one's been picked up?" Werner asked Mitz, the Junction leader, touching his glass with a wink.

"So far, so good," Mitz said, sipping. "But it's early . . ." While Mitz's Junction ops were normally obscured from the rest of Mossad, Werner had been appointed to oversee all offensive covert ops against the Iranian nuclear program. This dinner, tonight, was a meeting of his ad hoc intelligence committee.

"IRGC is already blaming us on their social media channels," noted Galin, the 8200 leader. "We're putting out disinformation through spoof Telegram accounts to counter it."

Werner nodded and smiled. "Let 'em blame us. This hit's going to scare the shit out of them."

It had been a particularly chilling Red Page. Weeks prior, Kurdish Junction agents had received a remote-controlled Belgian FN MAG machine gun smuggled through Turkey to a remote hide in the crease of two hills. The Kurds had mounted it to an Iranian Zamyad pickup bed, then prepositioned the truck on a scouted highway. When Dr. Farzad drove his Nissan to Tehran from his Caspian villa, an Israeli satellite had activated the gun's electric servos, spraying the physicist and his wife with a fusillade of 7.62 rounds from the bed of the pickup truck. Then a timer activated a bomb under the truck's chassis, destroying whatever evidence might have remained.

"Are we hearing anything else on the ground?" asked Werner.

Galin ran a hand through his thinning white hair. He squinted against the smoke. "Tasnim hasn't reported anything yet," he said.

"Well—I wouldn't expect IRGC's own propaganda TV station to

advertise a security failure. Not until they can firmly pin the blame on us."

"They'll be flogging us in the press soon enough," answered Mitz. "This may be the world's first remote robot hit."

"They'll sound crazy," said Werner. "Like they usually do. What about IRGC activity on the ground in Iran? Any mobilizations?" he asked Galin.

"The Mazandaran Provincial force has been activated. They're setting up roadblocks, checking vehicle traffic. Comm circuits between the Provincials and *Thar Allah* have been lighting up."

"I can't keep their Farsi names straight," said Werner, blowing smoke.

"*Thar Allah*'s the civil unrest division. They know we were behind this, but they'll take it out on whatever dissidents they can squeeze. That might threaten our ability to recruit."

"Or help it," said Werner, grinning. "Nothing like house-to-house IRGC searches to rile up the Kurds. What about the core force, the Imam Hussein battalions? Farzad's a very big get. They may step up their readiness stance."

"Not much activity yet," said Galin. "But we're listening."

The phone in Werner's pocket buzzed. He dug it out, looked at it. "It's him," he said, referring to his boss, the Mossad director. "Apologies. Enjoy the Cubans. I'll be right back."

Maya watched the glowing tip of the cigar as Werner paced near the shore, out of earshot. Beyond, the dark security boat traced another oval. Though she'd been left alone with Galin and Mitz, the three of them spoke of the food, the wine, the view—as if they hadn't just celebrated the annihilation of a middle-aged couple a thousand miles away.

Werner returned. "Well," he said, looking at Maya. "The Americans are already pissed."

"What? How?" asked Maya. She was genuinely surprised, a rare thing.

"Evidently, Akbari called them, got through to some deputy secretary of state named Hopkins. Within minutes, it made it all the way to the president's desk. Prime minister's already gotten a call."

"So—Iran's deputy foreign minister has a de facto hotline into the

White House. With friends like that . . . ," Galin said, shaking his head, smoking.

"Precisely. The Americans will do anything for that diplomatic deal . . . anything to maintain the farce of their containment strategy. I would have enjoyed seeing that idiot CIA director's face when the White House called to let him know." Werner laughed contentedly.

The smile faded when he noted Maya's long, straight face, her eyes staring off into the dark. The old man puffed his cigar, looking at her. "Maya—what?"

"Nothing," she said, her eyes still on the lake in the distance.

Werner shook his head and refilled his glass. "Well," he said. "Here's to you, Mitz. And Junction." Raising his glass, he spoke to the stars. "And here's to Professor Farzad of the Iranian Atomic Institute. May he enjoy his forty virgins in Paradise!"

Galin congratulated Mitz. Mitz congratulated Werner. The glasses clinked to either side of Maya.

"We should probably game out retaliation," Maya said. "Especially if the Iranians think they might have world opinion on their side. They're the ones looking reasonable in Vienna right now."

Werner's eyes narrowed over the glowing tip of his cigar. "Retaliation."

"Farzad was a big deal. They may go all out."

"By 'all out,' you mean *Taniyn*," said Werner.

She nodded. "We still don't know what its warhead is, and we don't know what they managed to export. We already said we're seeing Hezbollah beef up countersurveillance in Beirut. That could mean they're getting ready for another launch—and they might be mad enough to use it without a dummy this time. We're all playing for keeps here, are we not?"

"Maya . . . ," Werner said, shaking his head. "Always keeping me honest. We'll cut this *Taniyn* business off before it gets to that. You know we will. We'll figure that thing out." He winked.

Maya stayed focused on the lake, letting Werner's claim hang in the air.

"All right," the Caesarea boss conceded with a wave of his cigar, dissatisfied with her silence. "I get your point." He turned to Galin, the 8200 leader. "You picking up any Hezbollah chatter on that goddamned *Taniyn* missile, Noam?"

"No," said Galin. "No comm hits on *Taniyn* at all. But they may be using messengers now. I suppose that on its own could be a signal that they're getting closer to activating it. Then again, that might also just be confirmation bias on my part."

Werner grunted. Galin liked to hedge. "How about you, Mitz?"

The Junction commander looked down at the table. "We've got people in Hezbollah, of course. But I'm not hearing anything specific about *Taniyn*."

"And Quds? Have we seen any increased tempo out of them with Hezbollah in Beirut?"

"The usual people coming in and out of the Iranian embassy area in Jnah."

Werner looked at Maya. "Sounds like our signals intelligence is at its wit's end. We could use some HUMINT. Your department, my dear."

"Yes," Maya replied. "I have my Sparrow teams looking in the *dahiyeh*, conducting sorties out of the refugee camps. They may get something. But it's too bad we lost Mo Baramzedeh in that drone strike. He was our best lead. At least he was *my* best lead."

Werner exhaled a smoke ring. "Indeed. He was. But that couldn't be helped, could it? Time for a new HUMINT op, I think, my dear. You had another lead in Hawaii, I thought."

Maya stared into his face, saying nothing. Werner met her gaze over his cigar, equally silent. The other two men fell into a hushed sidebar, assessing Israeli ELINT capabilities for Hezbollah missile sites in Beirut. Finally, Werner joined them, refilling their glasses. Maya stood and excused herself. She went into the kitchen to help Rachel.

Later, when the moon was high and small, Werner and Maya watched the helo carrying Mitz and Galin ascend into the night, shattering the calm. With the roar fading off, Maya walked to her compact Fiat 500, carrying a gym bag.

"What, Maya? You're not staying now?" Werner called after her.

"No," she said, her feet crunching on the gravel. "Kiss Dil for me. Tell her I'll be back in a few days. I'm going back to Tel Aviv. Tonight."

"Hang on," Werner said, raising his voice. "Why? Talk to me."

Maya stood still on the driveway, waiting for Werner to get to her.

The Caesarea boss put his hand on her shoulder, turning her toward him. "Is this how you talk to me now? Is this your way of saying you don't approve of my next op? I'm doing it for all the right reasons."

"The right reasons," she said. "But in the wrong way."

Werner paused for a moment, looking down at his feet. "Well," he said. "You said we should be worried about the most severe kind of retaliation. If we're going to figure out if *Taniyn* is a real nuke, the easiest path is to get Kahlidi."

"I don't disagree with the *what*, Werner. I disagree with the *how*."

"Come, now. They were *your* American Station *katsas* who reported Kahlidi enjoying himself in Virginia, treated like royalty by the Americans. And if he's the fastest path to establishing what *Taniyn* is, then we have to act. We may not get another chance."

"Have you thought of the consequences if you're caught?" she asked, looking down. She was six inches taller than Werner.

"Of course I have. Rule number one. But I've also thought about the consequences if we don't act."

"I'm just going to say it. The op's a huge mistake."

Werner rubbed his knuckles on his bald head. He looked up at the crescent moon, clear and bright in the dry summer air of Galilee. "Well. Your op against Dale ended in disaster. If anything, it proved the Americans are deliberately holding us back. It's time to come at this another way."

"Maybe. But that shouldn't mean the *wrong* way."

"No. It shouldn't. It should mean *my* way."

CHAPTER 11

DALE SAT ON THE RUBBER BOAT'S TIGHTLY INFLATED SPONSON, GRIP-
ping the throttle of the straining three-horsepower engine. Now a half
mile from the anchored *Mollymawk*—a decaying thirty-foot Laguna
sloop he'd chartered—he struggled against the Severn River's current.

Just that morning he'd tested the approach with his own marine re-
con. He'd sailed *Molly* up College Creek, rounded the forbidding US
Naval Academy seawalls, passed below Decatur Road Bridge, then drifted
back out with the current. It had proved a promising landing spot.

Now, at three p.m., the sun was high, the heat strong, the tide low.
Dale found the beach empty, just as he'd hoped, since the Annapolis
crew team was off this time of year. He goosed the throttle for another
knot, pointed the blunt bow at the beach, and sputtered ashore on his
own modest wake.

The former naval officer had pinned his long hair up, hiding it under a khaki military-issue ball cap with Velcro where the American flag
had been. He wore his Ray-Bans, a chambray shirt, Levi's, and Blund-
stones. More than one stray midshipman cast this visitor a curious eye
when he asked for directions to Tecumseh Court, site of Grace's awards
ceremony.

There he found them gathered near the steps in front of Bancroft
Hall, residence of the Brigade of Midshipmen. Clad in a dazzling blue
dress, Meredith was bordered on all sides by starchy white uniforms.
She barely acknowledged Dale when he arrived.

"Dad!" Grace shouted, pushing past her mother, grinning, brilliant in her summer whites. She introduced her father to an admiral, the Naval Academy superintendent. Dale was soon making small talk with other officers, staking common ground through his own stint in the Naval Intelligence service, some years ago. A boatswain's pipe squealed. The assembly came to attention. All eyes were fixed on the podium that stood in front of the steps.

"Ernest E. Evans gained his commission here, at this hall, with the Academy class of 1927," said the superintendent from behind the microphone.

"Seventeen years later," the admiral continued, "Commander Evans earned the Medal of Honor when he sacrificed his ship, the destroyer *Johnston*, during the Battle of Leyte Gulf. With no regard for his personal safety, he sailed *Johnston* directly into a line of attacking Japanese battleships, deliberately drawing fire away from a vulnerable American troop convoy, changing the course of history. Here, today, we have created *this* award in Commander Evans's name for those midshipmen who show exemplary acts of faith, bravery, and sacrifice. Here, today, we come together to proudly bestow it on our own Midshipman Second Class Grace Dale, who, on the twenty-ninth of June did so admirably act to save a drowning civilian sailor . . ."

As the superintendent went on, Dale nudged Meredith in the elbow, leaning toward her. "Hey—I made different dinner plans. Hope that's okay."

Meredith kept her face forward in a look of frozen disavowal. Dale followed her eyes toward his daughter, who stood at attention next to the podium as rigidly as the court's namesake bronze Tecumseh figurehead. While the captain recounted her exploits, Grace's unshakable bearing twitched only once—a lightning-fast glance at her parents in the front row, whom she hadn't seen standing next to one another for nearly two years.

Amid the applause, a crush of mostly male officers surrounded Grace, shaking her hand, obscuring her in a phalanx of creased white. But she soon escaped and, grinning, raised her right arm in a fist bump to her father.

A yeoman stepped forward with his camera as the family held the award—a framed replica of the *Johnston*'s battle ensign. Hands were shaken, salutes exchanged, backs slapped, and before long John, Meredith, and Grace were walking by themselves along the shaded lanes named after naval heroes, toward the gate at King George Street in downtown Annapolis.

"Let's go this way," Dale said, turning them instead toward the boathouse where he'd beached the dinghy. "I have a special surprise."

"What the *hell* was that?" Meredith said over the *Mollymawk*'s side to John some three hours later. He'd just returned from shore in the rubber boat, where he'd deposited Grace at the Academy, barely in time for the evening mourn of taps.

Dale tied the dinghy to a cleat before answering. "Well . . . I think Grace enjoyed the boat." He killed the dinghy's engine. "It *is* the Navy after all."

Meredith stood barefoot by *Molly*'s helm, helping Dale up. Gaining the swim platform, he noted the cleared table, the swept deck. "Thanks for cleaning up, Meth."

"What else was I supposed to do out here? I'm trapped on this old bucket."

"'Old bucket'?" He looked at the teak, which had faded to three shades of tan. "You said we needed to talk privately. What could be more private than this?" Now fully aboard, Dale opened a cooler. The little sloop rode a swell and jerked on the anchor rode, pointing into the current.

Dale cracked open a beer. He offered another to Meredith, who turned him down. "Suit yourself," he said, dropping it back into the ice. Her foot fidgeted. She checked her watch. "Hey," said Dale. "I'll take you back as soon as you're ready. But Meth, as long as I have you here, let me start by saying what I did back in Maui . . . leaving like that . . . it was . . ."

She looked toward the shore. "Don't bother. I'm over it."

Dale arrested the bottle that had been on its way to his mouth. He set it down on the splintered cockpit table. "Okay. But I shouldn't've—"

"Can we just skip this?" She hugged her arms against a modest breeze, still looking toward land. "I wish you'd warned me I'd be on a goddamned boat."

"It was a spur-of-the-moment thing."

"What a surprise."

He gave her his lopsided grin. "Come on. You love that about me." He turned sideways to pass her, on his way down the steps into the cabin. He returned with a zippered wool sweater. "Here." He tossed it to her.

Meredith zipped the collar to her chin. "Why'd you buy a boat anyway, John?"

"A deal I couldn't refuse. Got it for a song."

"You overpaid."

"No way. I'm chartering her for three months, only two thousand bucks. If I end up wanting to buy, the rent counts toward the purchase. *Rent to own.* I'm going to paint seascapes."

"You do know a mollymawk is an albatross, don't you?"

"Is it?" Dale looked up the length of the bow and scratched his beard. "Well, I can change the name."

"And you're seriously sailing this thing to the Outer Banks? Or was that just bragging for Grace's benefit?"

"Of course I'm serious. I need someplace to stay. I'm still waiting for the Agency to finish fixing up my house in Cle Elum. And pay me. Remember?"

"You didn't even mention the idea of sailing to me in Maui. This just popped into your head in the last week or two?"

Dale nodded, slowly. He'd found *Mollymawk* on Craigslist, small enough to handle himself, he thought. And cheaper than renting someplace ashore. Not only that, but it would be impossible to trace and offered a good tactical hide against any Mossad incursions—just in case.

"I really am sorry about leaving you alone back in Maui," said Dale.

Meredith turned toward the lights of Annapolis, hugging herself. "It doesn't matter."

"Doesn't matter?" Dale stepped around the helm, touched her shoulder. "Yo. Meth. What's going on with you?"

"Nothing." She looked away. "Forget it. It doesn't matter. I mean it."

He lifted her hand, turning her toward him. "Hey—I'm trying here, man. I . . ."

She completed the turn and looked into his eyes. "Did you see the way Grace was looking at you tonight?"

"No. What do you mean?"

"Talking about her award. All that talk of *sacrifice* . . . honor, duty, courage blah blah *fucking* blah." She flung her hand toward the glowing buildings of the Academy. "I've committed my daughter to a goddamned cult. The way she was going on and on at dinner about her inspirations. She sees you as the model of sacrifice, the lone desperado, the misunderstood warrior—except by her."

"Meth—*you're* her inspiration, her role model. I'm just a washed-up bum."

"That's not even half right. I'm the one that drives her to Target, nags her to change her major to something useful, tells her to stay off Instagram, buy more practical underwear. And that's only when I'm in *town* for God's sake. When I'm not, it's a bunch of bitchy e-mails and text messages. *That's* what I am to her. But you're her . . . her . . ."

Dale stood there, waiting for the verdict, listening to the current running along the hull.

"What*ever* . . ." Meredith finally shuddered, dropping her arms, looking away from him. She glanced at her wrist, noted the time. "I need to get home. Early meeting tomorrow. The director's losing his mind since that Israeli hit a couple days ago on Farzad, the highest nuclear scientist in the country. Even you must have heard about it. The Iranians have walked from the Vienna negotiations. They're demanding we do something about Israel. We can't tell if they're bluffing. The president wants the deal. He's authorized concessions to lure them back."

"Yeah, I did hear something about that," Dale said, shaking his head. "But that's pretty much how it always goes, isn't it? Israel and Iran have been quietly at war for twenty years. Now you said you wanted to talk. Was it just this? Grace?"

"No." Meredith shut her eyes briefly, sighing. "Look, John," she said, opening them. "I need a favor. A *work* favor. It's related to this whole Vienna mess. I'm on the hook to complete the NIE to certify the Iran nuclear deal. But that Israeli hit on the Caspian last week fucked up the intelligence picture."

"You own the NIE? Wow. Congrats, Meth. I didn't realize that."

"Save the celebration. So far it's been a curse with Mossad running around like maniacs. But it's why I need your help."

It was Dale's turn to look away. At the mention of Mossad, he'd been tempted to tell her about his recruitment—but that would mean bringing up Maya. Since Dale had ultimately dodged Maya's approach, he concluded it shouldn't matter now.

"Relax, John. I'm not going to ask you to gear up for another mission. It's not like that. *Fuck*," she said, exhaling again. "I wish it were that simple. I am *so* screwed." She hugged her arms tightly, shivering.

"Okay," he said, relieved. "What, then?"

"Your old friend—Kahlidi."

Dale removed the beer from his mouth, shook his head. "No. You promised me, Meth. You promised I wouldn't have to handle Kahlidi. I don't want to be his case officer. I don't want a job. You promised."

"We've both made promises."

"Yeah, well . . . Is Kahlidi why you came back early? Is he why you have the NIE?"

"Sort of. He's in the middle of something related to it—something big. I need him to talk. And I can't get a goddamned thing out of him."

"He volunteered to spy for us," said Dale. "I was there in the back of that helo. My *last* mission."

"He's negotiating his agent deal."

"What's he want?"

"Besides a lifetime annuity and a safe exfil in a few years? Mostly he wants to see his woman. I think he mentioned her to you. He's annoyingly devoted to her."

"So go get her. What's the big deal? Can't you find her?"

"Oh, I've found her. I was having her tailed by MI-5, keeping the surveillance at arm's length to avoid tipping MOIS. But the Iranians got her anyway, killed our MI-5 watcher. Five fucking days ago." Meredith pushed her hands together, cracked her knuckles. "They took her right outside Paddington. The Brits are furious. Of course, we're all looking the other way, calling it a gang scuffle—scared it'll mess up the nuke deal if we publicly finger Iran."

"Does Kasem even know about this yet?"

"No. And the timing's terrible. That last Red Page was something right out of *Terminator*. We're hearing tremors about IRGC units activating. If the Iranians retaliate, it could be . . . well, you know, very bad. It's why I need him to talk. Now."

"Israel kills scientists all the time. What's different about this one?"

Her eyebrows slanted inward. The wind ruffled her hair. "*This* scientist happened to be close to something Kahlidi was working on . . . and the Israelis are saying that they might have the capability to . . ." She stopped talking when Dale held up a hand.

"Don't," he said. "I can't know anything about this. For both of our sakes."

"I'm sorry," she said. "But I may have to. We need Kahlidi talking."

"Leave me out of it."

"John," she said, sitting on a thwart's torn cushion, ignoring him. "Before Kasra got snatched, Kahlidi wanted *you* to go in after her, do a simple exfil out of London. He thinks you're the only one that could pull it off under MOIS's nose. And he's probably right. I'd been planning a big speech tonight to talk you into it. I was even going to lure you back to my place to soften you up. But then MOIS up and took her. And the Israelis whacked another scientist—and you showed up with this *fucking boat*." Meredith breathed sharply, almost like a gulp.

Dale put his arm on her shoulder. "Hey. I'm sorry I missed the softening up . . . But I don't want to be involved in this."

"You don't have to be involved in the big picture," she said. "It's just that the shrinks say Kasem might talk to you. He likes you. They think you could finally establish his trust as an agent. That's all I need. I promise. Just get him warmed up for me."

"He just likes me for his woman's exfil. He's playing you."

"It's more than that. You have a shared history. You saved his life. They say it matters."

"I'm out of practice on asset debriefs. And I'm out."

"Well. That's not exactly right."

"Come again?"

"John, you're technically still active, working for me until we clear up your pension. All I want is for you to tell him I *did* ask you to gear up to go get Kasra. Tell him you were working it, but this MOIS thing happened. I've got police surveillance photos of the abduction from Five. Tell Kasem what happened, break it to him, show him the pictures. Then leave. That's it. I've already got it all set up. Tomorrow afternoon. You'll only need to delay your departure a day or two."

"What good would me breaking the bad news to him do?"

"For one thing, if it comes from you, he'll believe it. He wouldn't if it came from me. For another, it'll flip the leverage. He'll be so worried about her fate that he'll be begging for our help. To get that, he'll need to give up the intel we need."

"That's pretty manipulative, Meth."

"I'm in a manipulative business. So are you."

"Don't I know it."

"Please, John. If I don't get him talking, it could be—"

He held up a hand. "Please don't. Tomorrow, you say?"

"Yeah . . . and maybe a few days after that for mop-up. You can give me that before you sail this tub over the horizon, can't you? I *am* your boss still, technically."

"I don't have a car. Or an interview protocol. You'd have to get the

Special Activities detail briefed, all of that. And I'm still no closer to getting my pension paid off."

"I'm working on that—I am. I can handle the other stuff. A car will get you, tomorrow. Let's say two o'clock, take you to his new safe house. Briefing prep will be waiting. *Please.*" She put her open hand on his chest. "Please," she said again, softer.

"*New* safe house?"

"Yeah. I got him set up in better digs a couple weeks back. They say he's been more cooperative—just not with me yet. It's a perfect time for you to go see him now."

"Where is this safe house? Over in Alexandria somewhere?"

Meredith closed her eyes and shook her head, looking down at his feet. "Just make sure you wear those boots. Trust me—it's rural."

CHAPTER 12

RURAL ENOUGH THAT THE SAFE HOUSE CREATED A VERY COMPLEX surveillance problem for the *katsa* team on the American Station.

At least that's what Eli was thinking as he slouched on the fiberglass white wall of the extended cherry picker bucket. Its boom had elevated him twenty-five feet above the rented van, where he now stood, facing the cross-arms of a wooden multipurpose utility pole. Graphics on the side of the van declared it part of Virginia's Dominion Cable fleet.

The *katsa* team leader had parked the service van a third of a mile from Cadberry Farm, across a field on a road that paralleled Highway 657, the main road that threaded between the pasturelands. From his elevated perch, the thirty-six-year-old tilted his hard hat and held the Zeiss spotting scope to his eye. He adjusted the zoom and focus until the wrought iron gates of the distant farm came into stark black relief.

Though surveilling the gate, he faced inward, toward the utility pole. The modified Zeiss made this possible by redirecting the magnified image through a U-shaped attachment. Refracted by a complicated array of mirrors, the main optical tube faced aft, resting on Eli's shoulder. The modified equipment was an invention of Mossad's R&D group. Eli had heard of it but had never used it before. It had arrived with the diplomatic pouch—a wrapped pallet securely offloaded from an El Al flight at National—thirty-six hours ago.

"Shift change complete," Eli reported in Hebrew into the mic that dangled near his mouth, fumbling with the awkward shape of the Zeiss. The Brooklyn-born Israeli émigré watched as the diesel pickup with the blacked-out windows exited the gate. "GMC pickup out. Turning southeast. Headed your pos, Ari."

"Roger," Ari said loudly from two miles away, rolling along Highway 657. He'd practically shouted to make his voice heard over the heavy truck's howling transmission. "Just arriving position Kilo." With a slight grind, he found second gear and downshifted the old Chevy flatbed to a moaning crawl, bouncing on the seat due to its shot suspension. The truck came to a stop near a cattle grate. With another grind Ari found reverse and backed toward a fence.

He killed the engine. Dust from the two tons of alfalfa bales behind him drifted through the window. He sneezed, then heard the approaching GMC pickup. Ari lowered his truck's visor and slouched. He sneezed again.

"GMC is clear," the *katsa* operative finally said into the UHF, watching the pickup's rear bumper in a side mirror, noting the Virginia plate. "Setting up."

"Copy," Eli answered from the elevated bucket.

Ari exited the truck, donned a pair of work gloves, and climbed to the top of the flatbed. After tossing a dozen sixty-pound alfalfa bales to the ground, he reported back in, sweating hard. His elbow still smarted from the glancing machete blow he'd taken during the Hawaiian surveillance op. "Ready," he said, wincing.

"Rina—say Rover status," said Eli. "Rover" was their name for the CIA guard that walked Cadberry Farm. Sometimes, Rover, a CIA Special Activities operative, was out in front of the main house. Other times, he circled the stables and its second-story living quarters.

"Condor has eyes on Rover," said Rina from her seat below the boom of the cherry-picker van. She was manipulating her laptop, using the computer's touch pad as a joystick. "I've got our HVT now. He just stopped his horse to chat with Rover." The HVT this time was Quds lieutenant colonel Kasem Kahlidi.

"Estimated two hundred meters bearing ninety off the barn. Caretaker is still inside the main house," Rina continued.

Listening from his high perch on the utility pole, Eli looked up from his scope, bending his neck for a view of the sky. Squinting against it he glimpsed Condor, a drone made by Priora Robotics, an American company. It too had come in the pouch from Tel Aviv, rolled into a tube. The drone had six-foot flexible wings, painted, arched, and angled to resemble those of a raptor. Its three-pound battery kept it aloft for two and a half hours, quiet as a kite.

"HVT's on horseback," said Rina. "Heading toward the stables. Walking pace."

Eli flicked the bucket's control lever, raising himself another two feet. He settled again behind the backward Zeiss, looking over the curve of the one hundred acres of knee-high corn that separated him from Cadberry. "Can't see him from here," he said. "Nahshon, you have eyes?"

Atop a short hill to the property's west, Nahshon shifted the Remington 700's twenty-four-inch barrel between the stalks of yellowed grass. The Bayonet sniper lay on his stomach, fully enveloped in an elaborately fringed ghillie suit. He'd been lying there since dawn, having crept up the creek that bordered the rear of the neighboring property.

He looked through the Leupold that he'd sighted two days prior at a local gun range. The off-the-shelf hunting rifle had been improved with a bipod and suppressor, courtesy of the pouch. With these mods, the hunting rifle approximated an M-24, used by the US Marines.

"Rover is good target," Nahshon whispered, his eye fused to the scope. Through the lens, he noted the distant heat vapors that blurred Rover's face. Slowly, the sniper clicked the windage and elevation turrets. "Low wind, four hundred yards," he added. "Good target."

Over at the hay truck, Ari clicked back onto the net. "Achilles is set. Moving to—wait, hang on. Another vehicle headed your pos, fast mover. Suburban, dark windows, fits official profile. Hold, hold, *hold.*"

"This is One," Eli said. "Confirm mission hold. Let's see what this is." He put the Zeiss back to his eye. "I've got it in sight," he said a moment later. "Black Suburban. Stopped at the main Cadberry gate entrance. Idling. Continue hold."

Off the net, Eli cursed at the black SUV. You never knew what might pop up on an op.

Across the wide fields that separated the two roads, the Suburban's window lowered at Cadberry's gate. The driver peeled off his sunglasses and looked into the blocky camera at the end of a thick metal post in front of the gate, speaking a few sentences of authentication. He then flashed his ID, holding it up for the cameras.

"Okay. You're cleared," blared the tinny speaker. "But say the visitor's name again, please?"

"Case Officer Dale," the Suburban driver from Langley's special security service said from behind the wheel. "That's D-A-L-E. John Richard." Dale leaned forward from the backseat, smiled at the camera, and held out his freshly reissued CIA ID. It had been in the satchel that Meredith had prepared for him and stowed in the SUV.

The iron gate buzzed and slid. Before it had fully opened, Dale exited from the rear of the Suburban, touched his toes, and twisted his torso. He removed the brown leather messenger bag from one of the rear captain's chairs and leaned over the still open driver's window. He pulled his ball cap low over his head and donned his sunglasses.

"Don't you want me to drive you up to the barn?" the driver asked him.

"Nah," said Dale. "A little walk around a horse farm sounds pretty good to me. Head on out, get something to eat. I'll call you when I'm ready to head back." Dale threw the rear door closed.

"This is One," said Eli. "Suburban backing into the road now." He watched the SUV's reverse lights through his refracted scope. It did a three-pointer and headed back down the highway. "Caretaker coming out to meet visitor. Visitor walking up driveway with bag over shoulder. Designate visitor as 'Walker.' Rover staying at position in field. Mia, remaining time on station for Condor?"

"About thirty minutes."

"Let's get an image capture of Walker. Do we recognize him? Is he a threat?"

From the passenger seat of the lift truck, Mia enlarged the laptop's drone video. "Capturing image. Male, forties, semi-formed beard. Khaki ball cap, dark hair sticking out, sunglasses, green T-shirt. I'll run a facial, but there's probably not enough of an image to get us anything concrete. He's wearing boots—just stopped to look out over the field at the horses. Appears unarmed. Dressed like a worker. Stable hand? Horse trainer?"

"Stable hands don't arrive by government chauffeur," said Eli. "Ari, the Suburban's back on 657, headed your way. Be ready."

Two clicks.

Rina leaned over from her position behind the wheel in the boom van to inspect the captured image of Dale in Mia's laptop. She tapped the transmit button wired to her wrist. "This is Two. Walker's face is hard to get, even enhanced." Looking again at the drone video, she added, "Whoever he is, HVT knows him. Assess as unarmed, no active threat."

They watched as Kahlidi rode through a pasture gate, dismounted, and walked toward the unknown visitor, leading his mount by the reins. Once on the ground, the Quds man extended a hand. The visitor, Walker, shook it in a two-handed clasp.

"Yeah," Rina said, relaying the scene. "They definitely know each other. But I'm still firm on non-threat assessment. Friendly visit, unarmed. Your call, One, on whether we continue mission."

"You say he's definitely unarmed?"

"Unarmed," confirmed Rina.

"Not a threat, then," said Eli.

CHAPTER 13

KAHLIDI TIED HIS MOUNT TO A POST IN FRONT OF THE STABLES. HE cupped a hand below the horse's soft muzzle, caressing it. The animal murmured and bared its teeth. "This fellow was a racer once," the Iranian said. "A Half-Arabian put out to stud. Possibly a bit beyond his prime, but—based on my ride this afternoon—he still has a few kicks left. A bit like you—eh, Dale?"

"Which part?" Dale answered. "The stud or the half-breed?"

Kahlidi caressed the horse's forelock. The Iranian brought his face close to the stallion's nose and exhaled. "If you breathe near their nostrils like this, it calms them down." The horse murmured.

Dale stood next to the towering animal. He ran his hand down the long snout. The horse jerked its head up powerfully and bared its teeth. Dale recoiled.

Kahlidi turned toward him. "Don't you know anything about horses?"

"I know not to get too close to them."

"I thought you lived in the mountains out west somewhere, like a cowboy."

"I prefer to ride things with engines, not minds of their own."

"Stable boy has this on so tight," Kahlidi said, adjusting the stallion's cheek piece, loosening the noseband.

Dale watched the Iranian's expert manner. "How'd you get so familiar with horses? I thought career Quds men spent their time teaching ignorant kids in madrassahs to blow themselves up."

Kasem looked sideways at Dale. The smile was still there but had dimmed a few watts. "We do have an actual country, you know," he said. "Families and farms. Mothers and fathers. Pets. My grandfather ranched on the Golestan plain—near the Caspian. We raised Bakhtiaris there. This fellow here," Kasem rubbed the Arabian, allowing the horse to lick his shoulder, "is much like a Bakhtiari. Tall, lanky, fast. Come on." He led the horse toward the stables.

"What about this one over here?" Dale asked, walking alongside. To the right was another horse, its large black eye blinking at them over the stable gate. "Is he an Arabian too?"

Kasem tied his stallion to an iron bar. He squatted and bundled some loose hay for the horse. "No, not that one," he said, feeding the mare. "See the yellow mane, golden forelock, mottled color? She's a Tennessee Walker. Fair racer, smooth gait. But she'd lose to my Half-Arabian, here—and definitely to one of my Bakhtiaris." Kasem turned to offer the Tennessee Walker some hay. The spotted horse ate from his hands.

Dale watched, shifting the bag on his shoulder, shuffling his feet. He looked up through the open trapdoor of a hayloft. "Seems like they're low on hay."

"Yes. Supposed to be a delivery today. Took too long. They're CIA security men. Not livestock managers."

Dale looked at his watch. He was hoping to set out on *Mollymawk* at dawn, which would mean getting to bed early. "Well—seems you like it here anyway."

"After two months in a cinder-block cell? Yes, the past weeks have been much, much better." He went farther into the stable. He moved to the side of the horse and reached for the leathers on its ribs.

"Meredith will be glad to hear that," Dale said.

Kahlidi looked up at Dale, pausing. "She's been here a few times, you know. Your wife shows up like a tornado, turning the place over with her army of shrinks and analysts."

"Ex-wife. And I guess I'm the storm's aftermath." Dale patted the side of the messenger bag, raising it slightly. "I'm here to talk about Kasra."

Kahlidi stood very still. He stopped adjusting the leathers. "Finally," he said.

Dale heard footsteps shuffling behind him. He turned to find a Special Activities man in the driveway, a guard with a walkie-talkie and a pistol on his hip. "I'll escort you up to Mr. Smith's residence," he said. "Just make sure I can see you in the cameras. I'll be monitoring."

Ten minutes later, up the stairs in the fortified living quarters over the stables, Kahlidi stood and paced, his face reddened, hair messed. "I must have told your wife a *thousand times*," he said with sharp, chopping hand gestures. "Why didn't she listen to me?"

The folders Dale had brought in the satchel lay scattered on the ground. Alongside them was a folded two-day-old copy of *The Times*, a London newspaper. Kasem had slapped the entire pile from the table in a rage.

The Iranian stepped over the mass of papers. He stood by the bulletproof polycarbonate window, looking over the fields. Two horses, a Morgan and a Thoroughbred, stood in the pasture, grazing, their shining coats reflecting the sun. He sighed. "Why didn't she listen?"

"She did," John replied.

Kasem squatted and picked up the photos. He looked again at the image of the abduction. He could see the top of Kasra's head, bundled under a man's arm.

"They're *Hezbollah*," said Kahlidi, disgusted, tapping the photo. "I know the MOIS colonel that would have sent them. Maloof. These men," he put his toe over a second photo, "are his cutouts. Dangerous zealots."

Dale listened. "I'm sorry, Kasem."

"I told you all to move faster."

"You did. But we had a hell of a time finding her."

"Do you know what's going to happen to her now?" His eyes were searching Dale's face, his fists clenched.

"No. They'll take her back to Iran?"

Kahlidi sat on the bed, dropping the photos beside him. He leaned forward and looked at the newspaper. It had been folded to the small quarter-column that reported the kidnapping. "With media," he said, tapping the paper, "probably not for a while. They probably have her in hiding in some safe house now—denying involvement. But eventually she'll be handed to MOIS. She'll go back to Iran. Evin Prison." The Quds officer sat on the bed opposite Dale. He dropped the paper to the floor. He held his head with his palms.

"You may not want to hear this right now, Kasem," Dale said. "But your best option is probably to go back into Quds. Quick. Meredith says your cover is about ready. They want to slip you in through Iraq, make it look like you'd escaped from Kurds. You'll be a hero."

"Oh, Meredith would love that, wouldn't she? As soon as I show up, the MOIS head of counterintelligence, Maloof, will frame me—blame me for missing your spy, Rahimi, probably blame me for whatever fall-out has happened since. He'll slap me in irons in Evin, have Kasra gang-raped in front of me, force me to *confess*. He has all the leverage now—thanks to your wife's delay. I'd told Meredith that she needed to take care of Maloof before I went back. This is bloody bullshit." He stared at the floor.

"There's still time to do a deal here, Kasem," Dale said. "You need to trust us. If you need us to get Maloof, we can."

"You mean trust *Meredith*," Kasem sneered. He started to say something else but took a look at Dale and stopped short. His shoulders hunched as he held his head in his hands. He spoke to the floor. "I had plenty of information to trade. But . . . with this . . . with Kasra . . ."

To give him some privacy, Dale walked to the window and stared out at the road. A quarter mile down the long-fenced driveway, he saw a large flatbed hay truck pulling up to the gate. The horses were running toward the fence. They seemed to be able to smell it.

"How long would it take them?" Kahlidi asked after a few seconds, still staring at the floor. "To activate this cover? It would have to be a few days of prep at least, wouldn't it? And I'd need proof that Maloof has been eliminated."

"I really don't know," said Dale, still looking out the window. To-ward the back of the hay truck, he saw something odd. A dark circle, a head. He wondered if workers typically rode in the back, like garbage men. Seemed unsafe. "Not my area of expertise. Maybe a week?"

"Whatever they've come up with . . . I'd need to be comfortable with it."

"You can probably drive the whole story," said Dale, watching the truck. The way the hay was stacked seemed strange. A gap in the middle, as though the load had been hollowed out. "Maybe there's some way to trap this Maloof guy at his own game. Think about that."

"Meredith's going to want something in return for this. Immediately."

"Yeah," said Dale. "She will." A guard had walked down from one of the hay fields and stood at the gate, keeping a safe distance from the truck. Dale saw the guard pull a walkie-talkie off his hip, move to the rear of the truck, looking up at the hay bales.

"But whatever you have to trade," Dale continued, "sounds to me like it's going to be worth it."

The gate began to slide open. The truck moved forward up the drive.

"There *is* something," Kahlidi said. "Can you call her? Get her here tonight? It's this initiative she's been after. Tell her I'm ready to talk about *Taniyn*."

Dale saw the guard reach for the weapon on his hip. But before drawing the pistol, the security man went suddenly limp, falling out of sight into the long grass. The tiniest mist of pink drifted in the air where the guard had just been standing.

Almost instantaneously, the hay truck's engine roared. A big man leapt off the back. His face was hidden by black cloth.

"*Get down!*" Dale shouted, dropping to the floor.

From his stomach, he turned to the surveillance camera at the ceiling, gesturing wildly, trying to get the attention of the Special Activities man who was supposed to be monitoring them in the main house. Kahlidi crept up next to him.

Dale heard a loud boom coming from the direction of the main house, then a muffled pop, followed by two more a few seconds later.

Dale reached for his cell phone, tried to hit the speed dial for his CIA driver. The call failed. He tried the same with Meth. There was no cell service. *Jammer in the truck*, he thought.

He looked at the structure of the secure room above the stables. It occupied half the second floor of the barn, alongside the hayloft. Other than the polycarbonate window that faced the driveway, there was only a dormer vent over their heads, too small to be of use. The only door was hardened metal, secured by a buzzing cypher lock. There was no other way out.

A large crash toward the main house vibrated the floor. Dale looked at Kahlidi. The Quds man's eyes were wide.

"There's a team assaulting the property," Dale said in rapid staccato, lying on his stomach. "I saw one male driving the hay truck, other assaulters on the back, using the hay for concealment. My cell phone's jammed, probably with a device on the truck, maybe a drone. Whoever they are, they took down a guard in the field—sniper, overwatch." Another explosion boomed. "*That*," Dale said, "is them breaching the main house, probably neutralizing the guard by now. They're going to be breaking in here next. Must be your people."

"*My people!*" Kahlidi shouted at him. "We couldn't mount an operation like this."

"You've been out of the loop. They could have figured something out by now."

Kahlidi crawled toward Dale. "Not like this. What are we going to do? There's no way out of here. I've looked before."

Dale's eyes searched the room. There were four metal twin beds with mattresses bolted to the floor. Only Kahlidi's was made up. There were no floor lamps, only overhead can lights. Two chairs around a small table. Even the picture frames were bolted, devoid of glass.

"You're right," said Dale. "We have to let them break in."

"*What?*" shrieked Kahlidi. "Are you armed?"

"No." Dale slid sideways, rose to a knee at the bed, pulled up one of the bare twin mattresses.

"What are you *doing*?" cried Kahlidi. Another loud boom.

Dale was pulling the mattress across the room. He turned his head toward Kahlidi. "Get up. Get another one. We need all four."

"Why?"

"That was a C-4 strip charge I just heard, designed for a breach. Those other pops are flash-bang grenades. They're clearing the house, probably setting up on the other side of this one right now. But it won't blow easy. Look at the hinges—blast resistant. Come on, pull them up. Drag them over here, under the door."

"What are we doing?" the Iranian said, pulling on a mattress.

"Based on that beast of a door, they're going to set up a shaped charge, here. A regular breaching charge wouldn't be enough. The door's going to fire in, blow right off the hinges. Then they'll throw flash-bangs before running in. *Come on!*"

"How do you know?" Kahlidi pulled a mattress toward the door.

"Feels like a snatch op. Otherwise, they'd have just bombed our whole building. Here. If we get under this mattress, the door's going to blow off or down. They'll run right over us."

"But who the hell are *they*?"

"If they're not your guys, then they have to be Mossad," said Dale, shuffling under the mattress, thinking of his Maui scrape. "They're the only ones this good—other than us—and they're very interested in whatever it is you have to say. Now get down under here. Be ready when I say to go."

"*Mossad . . . ,*" Kasem whispered under the confines of the mattresses, his voice hollow.

"Put it out of your head." Dale's voice was hot and muffled under the mattress. "After they run over us, we have one shot to hop up, drop to the stable and get the fuck out of here."

It was oddly quiet under the smothering weight of the bedding. Then a thump, vibrations coming through the floorboards. "They're here," Dale whispered.

"This is insane."

"They're at the door now. Setting up the breach charge. Be ready to run for it. And keep your mouth open to guard against the air concussion."

Boom.

Kasem started to rise, pushing against the mattress, scrambling up.

"*No!*" Dale rasped, pulling him back down, hard. "That's not it. It didn't go. They're going to try a stronger charge now. A big one that'll—"

Boom!

The explosion stole the air from his lungs, cutting him off. Even under the mattress the blast left his ears ringing. The heavy door fell, squashing them. Dale's hand had still been on Kahlidi's back, holding him down. The falling door overextended Dale's elbow, a sharp pain. He pulled it back under his chest, coiled himself in a flexed push-up position, and prepared to rise.

Loud pops, flash-bangs, suppressed pistols, ears ringing. Footsteps, running over the door—over them.

Go.

Dale sprang up, flinging off the heap of bedding, yanking Kahlidi with him, rolling from under the heavy door. Dale pushed Kahlidi into the hallway, toward the loft. The Iranian went forward on his hands and knees first and then made it to his feet, stumbling forward. Dale was right behind him, hurling himself across the splintered threshold. Blinded and choked by smoke, he lost sight of the Iranian.

He tripped on an iron bar lying on the floor—a dynamic entry breacher, a cross between sledgehammer, spade, and twin-bladed crowbar. Dale picked it up as he came to his feet. He saw Kahlidi ahead, dropping through the hayloft.

Dale felt a hard tug at his arm, a hand, yanking him. Someone was shouting. A big man faced him. The man was thick, head wrapped in a balaclava, beard visible on the neckline. Dale dropped to the ground, slipping the man's grip. He rolled, reaching for the breaching tool, angling it up, struggling to swing the heavy bar up. The big man was already diving for Dale, falling fast, preparing to pin him down.

Dale angled the sharp end of the tool upward, bracing. The man's thick stomach met with the double-bladed crowbar, falling forward, pushing the butt end of the tool out of Dale's hand, slamming against the floor. Impaled, the assaulter fell to the side, screaming, flailing at the tool with both hands. A pistol with suppressor dropped to the floor. Dale took it, aimed, pulled the trigger three times, the rounds suppressed. *Phht, phht, phht.*

At least one hit the man just above the ear, tearing away a chunk of skull. The man thudded to the floor planks, the iron bar still sticking from his gut. Dale rolled away, scrambled to his feet. He raised the barrel into the gray smoke of Kasem's quarters and fired twice more before leaping through the open door. He turned and ran for the trapdoor.

He landed hard in the stable below, rolling in loose alfalfa to absorb the fall's energy. He coughed—ribs hurting, knees stinging. He ignored the pain and limped forward toward the light. He still had the pistol in his hand—a Sig Sauer nine-mil P365, he realized with a glance at it. He'd last seen one in Maui. The big man he'd just killed . . . *Five rounds left.*

Another assaulter was at the hay truck, a black cloth on his face, something hanging from his back. *No,* Dale thought. *Too short. Ponytail. Woman.* She saw Dale's pistol and rolled to the ground, raising her own pistol. Dale shot her in the shoulder. She returned fire, her aim off. Dale took a knee and shot her again, hitting the top of her head. *Phht. Three rounds left.*

He heard footsteps on the floor above. They'd be on him now. He heard a horse bray, saw Kahlidi climbing onto it. He ran for the stallion and grabbed the Iranian's kicking leg. He shoved the pistol in his leather belt and clawed at the Iranian's arms, pulling himself up on the horse's back. One, two, three running steps before he levered his leg far enough to swing his weight upward. The Iranian tugged at Dale but was also struggling to get control of the Arabian. Dale finally managed to throw a leg over the horse, straddling it behind Kahlidi's saddle.

The horse pivoted, facing back toward the stables. Another assaulter was coming out, small. Another woman, Dale thought, a black assault rifle in her hands, suppressed. There was a larger man behind her, same weapon. Dale emptied his mag. A ragged volley, he was sure he missed.

But the assaulters took cover, dove to the floor. "I'm Winchester, empty!" He shouted at Kahlidi, showing the open slide as the horse rounded the barn, galloping down the slope. Dale dropped the pistol to the ground and used his free hand to get a better grip.

"*Heeya, heeya!*" Kasem was yelling, kicking the Arabian hard. Dale hugged the Iranian's waist, struggling to stay on the horse's back, everything moving beneath him. The horse's coal-black coat was slick. Dale hooked a leg around Kahlidi's, clawing at him, struggling to stay on.

He was finally able to look forward, over the Iranian's shoulder. He felt a buzz like a passing insect, a rush of air. It zoomed by his head, back to front. He ducked, nearly falling again. *Overwatch.*

"That way," Dale shouted into Kasem's ear, hugging him tightly, risking a free hand to point toward the woods. "Down there. Get in that tree line, now, *now!*" Dale ducked low.

The Iranian hunched forward, kicking the horse furiously. *Unbelievably fast,* Dale thought uselessly, worried about falling off the wildly galloping animal.

He stayed low, thinking the sniper would have a decent shot, waiting for it, cringing. But they were farther down the slope now. The tree line was getting closer. Over Kahlidi's shoulder, Dale saw a fence before the trees, a tall one, the horse running straight for it. Dale hugged Kahlidi tightly, holding on, squeezing his own legs around the horse's haunches. "You see that?" he shouted.

"*Quiet!*" cried Kasem, spurring the horse on, the fence right in front of them, then disappearing under the stallion. The horse leapt.

Silence. A full second that felt like five or ten. Dale wasn't sure what had happened. Then the hoofs slammed down on the other side, jarring him, nearly making him fall off. He squeezed Kahlidi tighter, flailed his legs to get a better grip. More furious galloping. Dale glimpsed a second fence, a second jump. He held on, bracing for the landing.

The hoofs thumped dirt. They were suddenly in shade. Dale scrunched lower, avoiding a tree branch. The horse had barely slowed, despite the brush. Dale heard a splash. They were crossing a creek, then up the far bank, then breaking free into another field, another jump. They galloped across a pasture, down another slope. They were safer now—unless the assaulters had air support. Dale looked up. Nothing.

He felt Kahlidi's shoulders shift. The Iranian was pulling hard on the reins. The horse suddenly stopped. It reared on its hind legs—higher, higher still, whinnying fiercely. Dale saw only sky, felt his thighs losing grip on the slick fur. He clutched Kasem desperately, tearing at his shirt. The horse went impossibly higher. The stallion let out an angry, piercing neigh. Dale thought it was going to collapse back, crush them both.

The CIA man felt a sharp elbow in his sore rib. Another, another, a shove against his hips. Kahlidi was kicking Dale's leg free, jerking him loose. Dale clawed madly at the Iranian's back, shouted, "*Hey!*" Another elbow struck him at the shoulder.

Dale's hands grasped air. He was falling. He hit with a jarring thud to his back that stole his breath. Stunned, struck dumb, lungs paralyzed, he stared up at the clear blue sky for a moment, trying to make sense of what had happened. He rolled to his stomach, gasping in the dust, still unable to breathe. Ahead, he could see the dirt flying up from behind the horse, Kahlidi bent over the animal, racing away, the sound of hoofbeats fading.

PART TWO

FIRE

CHAPTER 14

"SPECIAL ACTIVITIES HAS SECURED THE SITE," SAID MEREDITH. "THEY have a team doing a full forensic workup now, but since the assaulters left no dead or wounded behind, the early findings are inconclusive."

"*Inconclusive*," Rance repeated through the flat screen at the far end of the room. His expression of pinched distaste was obvious, despite the 4,400 miles between Langley and Vienna. "How's that even possible?"

Dorsey was pacing. Meredith sat at a long conference table in the room's center.

She opened a red folder. "I'm going off SAC's report. The nine-mils are Magtechs, available in any sporting-goods store. The stun grenades were from Securitech, a police outfitter in Pennsylvania. The hay truck was reported stolen in Owensville three days ago. It was torched. Blood residue has been sent to FBI for DNA analysis." She closed the folder. "That's how."

Dorsey circled the room like a caged animal. He occasionally passed behind Meredith, putting her on edge. "Ed," he said to the screen. "What's going on back there in Vienna? How are the Iranians behaving?"

"Nothing new here," said Rance. He was in a suit and tie, sitting in a conference room somewhere in the bowels of the US embassy to Austria. "We had an IAEA meeting on Anarak spent fuel reprocessing. The usual grind—hung up on camera placement and resolution. The main delegation's gone back to Tehran in protest after that last Mossad Red Page on Farzad."

"What about the MOIS probables?" Dorsey asked, pushing at his sleeves.

"They're still here too. Business as usual, in the back benches, taking notes. I've had case officers from Vienna Station surveilling them. We have voice intercepts here and there. Nothing out of the ordinary."

Still pacing, Dorsey looked down at the top of Meredith's head. "John *must* have something else. He must have heard a voice, a language, an accent . . . something at that ranch."

She looked up, twisting her neck to keep up with the spy chief. "John said it all happened too fast, his Mossad assessment is purely based on their tactics. He wasn't there long. As you saw on the tape, whoever they were, they breached with a big charge and tossed in flash-bangs. John and Atlas were out the next second, escaping."

"Together," Rance noted through the monitor. "On a horse . . ."

"Yes—until Atlas pushed John off, damn near breaking his back," added Meredith.

Rance nodded. "Right. And—whoever they were—we don't know if they ultimately recovered Atlas or not. John said he lost sight of everyone while he was evading in the woods. But he thinks Kahlidi *probably* got away."

"Right," said Meredith.

"Christ . . . ," said Dorsey, still circling, eyes pivoting around Meredith. "Has John come in for a formal AAR yet?"

"No. Not yet."

Dorsey stopped pacing. He shoved his hands in his pockets. "And did you say something about John being on a *boat*?"

"A boat," repeated Rance, nodding. "That's what you said earlier, right, Meredith?"

Meredith shifted in her seat. "Yes. John happens to have chartered a sailboat that he's keeping over in Annapolis. He hasn't come in for the full after-action review yet, but he did give me a quick tactical synopsis. He's only on a boat because he'd already been planning on sailing down to the Outer Banks when—" Mercifully, Dorsey looked away toward the ringing phone on his desk. He answered while standing, said "yes" into the receiver four times, then hung up.

"Well . . . ," Dorsey said, sighing, leaning on his fists. "The director wants us to keep the Atlas loss quiet for fear of throwing yet another wrench into the nuke deal. But he also wants me up there in ten minutes with answers." He looked up. "So give me some. Who the fuck hit us?"

"I think John's assessment is probably right," said Rance. "Has to be Mossad. IRGC couldn't pull this off. And the mullahs want the deal—their economy's getting worse by the day. This is Werner."

"That's quite an accusation," said Dorsey. "The Israelis may have spied on us here and there—but they've never gone kinetic before."

"Oh yeah?" Rance raised an eyebrow. "Remember the *Liberty*, our intel ship that they bombed in their Six-Day War? And FBI's tracked Mossad recruitment reports as recently as six months ago."

"You think one of those recruits came through?" asked Dorsey, looking over Meredith's head toward the video monitor. "You think Mossad has someone in our squad?"

"Werner was sniffing around for a take on Kahlidi in that meeting with the director," said Rance. "Like he already knew something. I wouldn't put it past him to go kinetic after we didn't take his bait to offer up Atlas intel. You saw what he was like when he got that demarche."

"But what if this is IRGC or MOIS?" asked Dorsey. "How much exposure would we have if Kahlidi's back with them?" He looked at Meredith. "How much does Kahlidi know?"

Meredith took a long breath. It felt like a moment where thinking came before speaking. "Kahlidi knows we want info on *Taniyn*. He knows we have some clues on what it is, but not the whole story. But that's about all he knows."

"No," said Dorsey. "He knows you. He knows John. He knows Cerberus and how we penetrated Iran's information systems in the first place. If he makes it back to Iran unscathed, this may turn out to be the intelligence failure of the century."

"You could even wonder," said Rance from Vienna, "if Kahlidi was a dangle. Maybe MOIS set up this whole thing to get inside our tent. 'Course, Meredith, you couldn't have seen around that corner when you made your call to take Kahlidi that night."

While quietly entertaining a fantasy of garroting Ed Rance to death with his own tie, Meredith tensed her calf muscles. "I don't think he's a dangle," she said as calmly as she could manage. "This couldn't have been IRGC."

Dorsey stopped pacing to look at her. "No? Your take, then?"

She cleared her throat. "Mossad. We saw women on the tape. IRGC would never do that."

"So you're with Ed," said Dorsey, pacing again.

Meredith nodded. "Based on Werner's reaction, I'd say Mossad knew about Atlas and didn't trust us with him. The tactics smell like Caesarea to me."

"Fuck," said Dorsey. "The Atlas op is supposed to be a code word access program, eyes only. How could we have a Mossad mole?"

"We should recommend the director initiate a full CI rundown ASAP," said Meredith. "I think it plausible that Mossad has some kind of mole. We need to protect ourselves."

"Concur with that," added Rance. "I'd also add that John Dale may be the place to start looking."

"*Ed*," Meredith said, exhaling, flattening her hands on the table. "Please tell me you're not suggesting my own husband has been a Mossad mole all this time."

"Ex-husband, now. No—I'm *not* saying that. But Mossad worked with him on Cerberus, early on. He got to know them. And I'm just saying John was at the safe house. It stands to reason that Mossad tracked him there . . . that they found the site through John. At least at this point, that's as far as I'll go."

Meredith shook her head, looking down. "I don't see it. It was John's first visit to the safe house—at my direction. And all we have to do is look at the two dead assaulters John took out to show he's not a mole.

Besides, I don't know anything about John having a lot of prior Mossad contacts. Most of his ops were paramilitary, Iraq."

"Well, you wouldn't know about his Mossad contacts," said Rance. "They were Cerberus related—before we brought you in on that."

"To Ed's point," said Dorsey, "don't assume you know everything about John's past operations, Meredith." The spy chief rummaged through a drawer and found a pen that made its way to his mouth. "Let's move on. Forget how Mossad knew John for a second. How do I even begin to explain Dale even being *involved* in this thing? I thought you said you weren't going to use him, Meredith. How did he end up in the middle of a Mossad assault on a black site?"

Meredith searched for the right way to answer. Two seconds became three. Then five. "Technically, sir . . . John's off suspension—since you reactivated him for the Cerberus exfil. And until his retirement comes through, he's still a case officer . . . reporting to me." When Dorsey failed to respond she added, "And, like you said, sir, the psych team thought John could get Atlas talking."

The spy boss looked down at his desk blotter, pen twitching in his mouth as he chewed. "Right. But you said you wouldn't need John. I never got around to signing the appropriate forms."

"I said I'd do whatever it takes to get Atlas talking," said Meredith. "In the end, I thought John might help."

Dorsey nodded without conviction. "Okay. Back to our situation. Since Atlas is likely in the wind . . . how do we get him back?"

"I met with Special Agent Maddox from the FBI liaison team this morning," said Meredith. "He's activating their Facial Recognition Database and has placed some generic suspect info in NCIC in case Atlas turns up in police custody. FBI said it would all be online within the next few hours. Nothing public—you can assure the director of that."

"Well, that's a relief," grumbled Dorsey, shaking his head. He tightened his tie. "So, before I head upstairs—let me see if I have this straight." The pen angled up as he struggled with his collar's top button. "Just as soon as I finish explaining that we let a case officer with *questionable* status into a secure safe house, I tell the director we lost the only Iranian asset that could have given us the intel we need to avert the next Middle Eastern war."

Meredith looked back at him, forcing herself not to blink.

Dorsey unrolled his sleeves, focused on the cuff buttons. "I'll also remind the boss," he went on, "that this is the *same* Iranian asset that had a suspicious history with said questionable case officer, who—by the way—just happened to show up a mere fifteen minutes before a raid that allowed our prospective asset to escape."

Meredith looked down, studying the wood grain of the table.

The spy chief removed his suit coat from a hanger and slid into it. He went on. "*And*—this may be my favorite part—I'll mention that this asset is *also* the Quds colonel we illegally snatched in an op the director feared would jeopardize the new nuclear deal, if *ever*, God forbid, discovered by the Iranians. An outcome we *guaranteed* to the director would never happen. Or he might have been a dangle all along. Oh, and by the way, we probably have a Mossad mole in our midst. Does that about sum things up?"

It took a few seconds for Meredith to realize it wasn't a rhetorical question. "Look, sir. It's my mess. I'll clean it up. I'll take care of it."

Dorsey nodded, leaned on his knuckles, and stared down the length of his tie.

"You know, Meredith," Rance said through the video screen. "At some point I'm going to have to warn State. What if Atlas turns up back in Iran? That might kill the deal right there. Mossad would love that."

"Thank you, Ed. I realize that."

"Not yet, Ed," Dorsey said, raising a finger toward the monitor. "Not *fucking* yet."

The silence held as Dorsey kept his finger extended. Meredith was looking down, ducking it. Dorsey's assistant knocked and stuck her head through. She told the spy boss the director was ready, waiting upstairs. Meredith could have kissed her for it.

"Stay right here," Dorsey said to them, hurrying to the door. "I'm only getting fifteen minutes with him. We resume as soon as I'm back."

Meredith spent the interlude answering questions from Rance as he prepared the request for the official CI investigation. Cringing, she had to give Rance details about her Hawaii trip so he could get going on the CI internals. She found herself relieved when Dorsey came back in.

"Well, that was fun . . . ," the spy boss said, walking straight to his desk. He stood behind it and looked down for a moment, composing his thoughts. Meredith noted the bare patch of pink at the top of his head. "All right," he said, finally looking up. "The director's on board with our Mossad assessment. And he's made a few things very clear to us. We've got a play."

Meredith sat up straight, pen in hand, determined to salvage something.

"We all think Mossad probably found a way to round up Atlas," Dorsey began. "But we can't be sure. Since Atlas *might* be in the wind somewhere here in the US, we're going to hand the search over to FBI. Meredith, as soon as we're done here, we're going to call in their big guns, make sure this Agent Maddox has what he needs. I have Janine setting up a call now."

She nodded. "Yes, sir."

"I happen to know the deputy director over there from the counterterrorism task force," Dorsey continued. "I'll give her my version of context, tell her it's a Pri-One. But I may need your help explaining John's involvement."

"Of course, sir." Meredith scribbled furiously, looking down.

"If Atlas is in the wind," Dorsey added, "the director doesn't even care if FBI brings him in alive—as long as they keep it black. And all this bullshit about enlisting him as an agent is over. His deal is done, can't be trusted. If we get him here in the US, I want him offshored the moment we cuff him. Rendition his ass to Camp Delta, Djibouti, wherever. I'll even authorize enhanced techniques to get him talking about Hezbollah, figure out what the fuck they're up to with this *Taniyn* thing." He glanced up, looking at Meredith.

"Yes, sir, understood. I'll take care of all of it. Personally."

Dorsey raised a finger, stabbed the air as he spoke. "And obviously—this doesn't leak. None of it—the takedown of our site, Atlas, John . . . fucking none of it. State can't know about it. The director doesn't want this thing to jeopardize the deal. I told him it wouldn't."

Dorsey came out from behind his desk, glowering. His eyes shifted between Meredith at the table and Rance on the screen.

"Now. Speaking of Mossad," he continued, "the director wants CI all over this, figure out where we fucked up, find our mole. I agree with that. I want a max intensity counter-package set up ASAP. I want them looking into everything, everyone, deep. Eyes only, this stays within the family. We can't let anyone realize how badly Werner has fucked us here. Clear?"

"Yes, sir," said Meredith, taking another note.

"I was talking to Ed," answered Dorsey. "You and John are *way* too close to this to be involved in the CI workup."

She nodded and looked away.

"As for you, Meredith." He turned toward her. "You were right about one thing. This *is* your mess. You *are* going to clean it up. The director even wanted to yank the NIE from you. I talked him into giving you another chance."

She swallowed. "Yes, sir. I'll spin up my team to get FBI whatever they need for the recovery op. And I'll get to the bottom of *Taniyn* for the NIE ASAP—with or without Atlas. I've got this. I'll—"

"Save your breath," said Dorsey. "You can brief me on your revised NIE strategy on the plane—now that we've lost your best lead."

"Plane?"

"Meredith, you and I are wheels up at Andrews for Tel Aviv at fourteen hundred today. We've got a meeting with Mossad leadership booked for the morning. If Mossad does in fact have Atlas, we're bringing his ass back—dead or alive."

CHAPTER 15

BUT ATLAS WAS NOT IN THE CUSTODY OF MOSSAD. LIEUTENANT COLO-
nel Kasem Kahlidi of the elite Iranian Quds Force was, rather, standing
at the corner of L Street and Pennsylvania Avenue a mere ten miles
away from Langley's HQS.

Waiting for the Trader Joe's on that corner to open, the Quds man
stood watching the door, rocking on his feet. Having been awake for
more than thirty hours, he wanted desperately to sit—but he thought
that might attract the wrong kind of attention.

Instead, the Iranian pulled the flat brim of a green John Deere ball
cap over his eyes and tapped his foot to stay awake. Despite the balmy
morning temperature, he'd already zipped the oily Carhartt jacket he
wore up to his sternum. Now he raised the collar to cover his neck and
watched the doors from behind a shrub, looking out for security cameras.

Mercifully, the bells at St. Anthony's began to chime a half block
away, marking the top of the hour. Just as the eighth gong faded, the
bright lights blinked on at the Trader Joe's. The electric doors hummed
and opened. A worker pushed a train of shopping carts to the sidewalk.
Revived, Kahlidi made his way through them.

Once inside, he moved immediately to the right, toward the produce department since it offered the best view of the entrance. He
picked up a cantaloupe and held it near his face. He watched a slow
dribble of customers from beyond the rind.

He moved on to a bin of cucumbers. Holding one, he glanced up and scanned the aisles. He then looked up at the long stretch of two-way mirrors where the walls met the ceiling. In doing so, he caught a glimpse of himself, meeting his own eyes. Among the early morning joggers and health-conscious professionals, the Quds officer realized he looked ridiculous. He turned the collar back down. Despite everything he'd been through, he thought, he'd probably made it. America wasn't a tough place to hide in, even when escaping on something as obvious as a horse.

The Half-Arabian racer had been loyal, right up to the end. Exactly on cue, with a hard yank on the bit, the high-spirited animal had risen on its massive hind legs, flailed its front hoofs, and let out an angry cry while Kahlidi nearly strangled the beast with the reins.

From there, elevated, it hadn't taken much to shake Dale loose. And then, as soon as the CIA man was on the ground, the Arabian had leaped forward with little more than a sturdy kick in the ribs and a whipping crack of the reins. The horse had bucked like a raw mustang before bolting downhill to a rushing creek.

Kahlidi had accepted his mount's intuition to run upstream since they'd been, in a way, partners in the escape. He'd kept the horse in the water, staying below the banks, moving as fast as the terrain would allow. After twenty minutes, perhaps a mile of sloshing, he'd let the animal slow to a walk. It had been just the respite needed to stretch his back, catch his breath, and knock the mud off his pants. But then, still holding the reins, his hands had started shaking.

Mossad.

Fucking Mossad.

The Quds man had been battling the Zionist intelligence force for years—in Beirut, Damascus, Gaza. He'd had several near misses as they'd renditioned his Hezbollah, Hamas, and Fatemiyoun agents into their fabled prisons, rumored to exist in the catacombs below Jerusalem. While he knew they'd tracked him before, he couldn't believe the ruthless *kidon* killers would go to such lengths as to attempt a snatch on

American soil. It meant they knew what *Taniyn* really was all about—even if his CIA hosts didn't.

And if Mossad knew that, then they'd probably already infiltrated his Hezbollah weapons-import network in Beirut. It must've been why Meredith Morris-Dale had been asking about Baramzedeh, he'd thought. He guessed that Mossad had probably already taken out the scientist. And if that were true, then by now the MOIS counterintelligence teams would be blaming Kasem for the leak, saying he'd tipped the Americans and Mossad. It had to have been the reason behind Kasra's reckless London snatch.

Horrid images of Kasra's suffering had held him in thrall, until, sloshing in the creek around midnight, he'd been jerked back to reality with a near collision into a low rail bridge. He'd been looking for those rails. While confined at the CIA ranch, at least twice every night he'd heard a train's long horn, seemingly headed east. East meant the Atlantic, ports, cities, escape.

Riding east along the graveled tracks, it wasn't long before Kahlidi had heard the distant horn and kicked the beast into the woods, hiding. Soon the freight cars were passing in a maelstrom of wind, squeals, and clanks. The noise had made the Arabian jumpy. The freight cars had seemed to go on forever—but were impossible to board.

It wasn't until later that Kahlidi had seen his salvation through the trees—landscape lights along a driveway, a pickup truck, a darkened farmhouse with a wide porch and a barn. The pickup had been locked. The barn doors had been wide open.

On a wall hook he'd discovered the Deere hat and Carhartt, which he'd bundled in his arms. Farther into the dark interior he'd almost run into a refrigerator, opened it, found a case of beer. He'd taken the clothes and left, planning to get back to the horse. But then he'd seen the other roof. It was smaller, a shed, right at the wood's edge. It contained an old Kawasaki dirt bike.

At first Kasem had thought he'd found his new means of escape. But there were no keys in the ignition. And he had no clue how to hot-wire a motorcycle. Other ideas had come to mind. Pointing the handlebars at the shed's interior, he'd tested the headlight, which didn't require keys. He'd thrown the hat and coveralls over the seat and rolled the bike to the edge of the tracks.

Grunting, he'd shoved the bike between the rails. He'd turned it so it faced west, propped it on its kickstand, and waited.

This time when the whistle sounded in the distance, Kahlidi flicked on the motorcycle's headlight, mounted the horse, and galloped at full speed toward the oncoming train. After a few hundred yards, he veered the horse into the woods and dismounted, trying to catch his breath. As before, the train had clanked by. But on this pass, there'd been a sudden screech of the brake, sparks on grinding wheels. When it had finally come to a stop, Kahlidi smacked the Arabian on the ass and climbed a ladder to the edge of a tanker car.

The freight train had finally slowed as it entered Alexandria's suburban sprawl, making the jump-off easy. From there, Kasem had walked into the DC Metro without a ticket and watched how the early morning commuters behaved. There'd been a turnstile with a card, a man standing on the curb playing sax for handouts whenever the crowd picked up. When the sax had fallen silent, Kahlidi had hopped the turnstile.

Now at a DC Trader Joe's on a fresh summer morning, the Quds colonel wandered down a second aisle, toward the back. The store was almost empty, too early for many customers. At the back of the frozen section, he went through double doors, hopped off an elevated loading bay, crossed the alley, and entered the building next door.

On the third floor of this building, he opened the door to the offices for Project Jerusalem, a group that lobbied for the establishment of a Palestinian state to govern the old city. It had been founded by an expat Saudi billionaire with a bone to pick against the House of Sa'ud. The construction magnate had turned religious in his old age, giving himself the title of Sheikh, though his group had no official religious sanction. It was, rather, a money-laundering front for Hamas that used the Saudi's money to buy weapons—through Kahlidi's network.

It was a relationship Kahlidi had kept secret from the meddling counterintelligence spies at MOIS. Kahlidi had operated the partnership with the Sheikh himself, personally. Both Soleimani and the Sheikh had insisted it work that way to preserve Iranian innocence for their rebellions around the world. Soleimani's vision had been to keep the Sheikh's budget off the books to finance truly black operations—Quds only, away from prying eyes. But he couldn't know if Mossad had figured out the Sheikh's relationship to Iran. He'd find out soon enough.

The young woman in a headscarf manning the fancy corporate lobby desk looked horrified when Kasem approached. But removing his ball cap and zipping his jacket down to a genteel level, the Quds man gave a broad, disarming smile. He addressed her in his royal Oxford English. "Good morning," he said. "It's imperative that I speak with the Sheikh."

The girl looked apologetic. "I'm sorry, sir, but the Sheikh is—"

"I know exactly where the Sheikh is," said Kahlidi, his voice gaining an edge. "Asleep in his bed on Battery Park Road with his American girlfriend, Charlene. Call him anyway. You may tell him that General Soleimani's old friend from Beirut is here to see him."

CHAPTER 16

"HAVE YOU CONNECTED KAHLIDI TO THE MOSSAD HIT ON FARZAD?"
Major Siamak Azad of MOIS counterintelligence said into his encrypted
cell phone.

The MOIS major was sitting behind the wheel of an old Peugeot,
one car among a hundred in line at the Syrian-Lebanese border.

"Maybe," said Siamak's lieutenant from the MOIS HQ in Tehran.

The MOIS major gripped the phone tightly. "*Maybe? Please don't
tell me you called with a maybe.* It's a simple question. Do we see any
direct Kahlidi connection or not?"

The lieutenant hurried through a crisper explanation, summarizing
the take from the suspects in the Farzad hit that they'd rounded up so
far. There were more than ten now, stuffed into the underground Evin
Prison chamber known as the "room without light."

Among them, said the lieutenant, were a Kurdish pickup-truck
owner and a Turkish smuggler who'd brought the truck used for the
robotic machine gun across the border. IRGC had intercepted their call
to get payment for the vehicle. The smuggler had wanted to use PayPal.
The Kurd needed a new bank account to link to the app. When he'd
gone to open one, MOIS had been waiting.

"And the Kahlidi connection?" asked Siamak.

"The trucker confessed to knowing the Kurdish fighter we recovered
when Kahlidi disappeared. The truck owner said he'd served with the
Kurd together in the PKK. He's even related to him, by marriage." PKK

was the Kurdistan Workers Party, a rebel group that had long been at odds with Tehran.

"What Kurd?" asked Siamak.

"The dead one we recovered in Alut. In April. Killed during the American raid to extract Rahimi. The Kurd's name was Zoran Karimi. He was the city commander for PKK in Alut, though his unit had disbanded a few years ago. I'm saying that one of the men from the Farzad hit knew Karimi and that Karimi knew Kahlidi."

Months ago, initiating his assignment to find Kahlidi, Siamak had discovered the nearly headless corpse of the old Kurd PKK fighter, splayed with an AK-47 at its side. "Ah yes. Zoran Karimi. The Kurdish jute farmer," he said.

"Him, sir."

"But we rounded up that farmer's family weeks ago. They knew nothing. What's one dead Kurd rebel in Alut and another live one in Evin Prison got to do with Kahlidi?"

"Actually, sir, the Kurd we picked up yesterday for the Farzad hit died this morning in Evin under . . . procedures."

"I'll amend, then. What do two dead Kurdish rebels have to do with Kahlidi?"

"Communications records confirm Kahlidi was on his way to intercept the American raid that night. No one disputes that. And a Kurdish militia leader was *also* there—who happens to be related to one of the men who was in on the Farzad hit. The Kurd happened to have been killed, lost in the op. But Kahlidi disappeared. You see, sir?"

"Could just be a coincidence."

"How else could Farzad's Kurd assassins have gotten such good intelligence on one of our most protected scientists? They knew the doctor's patterns, the address of his summer home, the car he drove. The Kurds had that information. It had to have been Kahlidi. Either he went over the border with the Kurds or he left with the Americans that night."

"Or maybe the Kurds captured Kahlidi and tortured that information out of him."

"It's still a connection. You could use that for your brief to Colonel Maloof."

Siamak bit the inside of his cheek and said nothing. It wasn't a bad idea, he thought.

"I know it's not much," the lieutenant stammered, filling the void.

"Keep working this Kurd angle," Siamak said while looking through the windshield, growing depressed at the long line of cars in front of him. He hung up and watched a bored truck driver who'd climbed down from his rig, trying to gauge the remaining distance before the Syrian Army checkpoint.

Seeing a sudden gap develop between cars, the MOIS major leaned out the window and shouted at the truck driver. "*Adhab!*" He honked his horn and waved.

Other border-crossers suddenly joined in. The long line of cars sounded off like a flock of geese—until a Syrian soldier fired off his AK into the air, shutting them all up.

Hopelessly stuck, Siamak switched on the old Peugeot's AM radio for something to do. He found one music station and tried to get into the beat. But the bouncy Azerbaijani folk tune only reminded him of the Kurds. And Kahlidi.

Spinning the dial further, he found three talk stations. Two were propaganda outlets for the Assad government. The third, Al Manar, was the Hezbollah news channel in Beirut. Siamak kept it tuned there, listening to the host interview a Hezbollah member of Lebanese Parliament. The dialog was about the dire national economy, the devalued currency, the crushing unemployment rate, the usual.

"How do we turn this around?" the reporter got around to asking the MP. "How do we get back to a place where every Lebanese Shia has a job, a family, a life?"

"By breaking the American sanctions," answered the Hezbollah MP. "By ending our foolish and weak dependence on the decadent infidels who would sell us like livestock. And that means building a trading bloc of our own, leaning on our Shia brothers from the East, doing what we have to do. We need to make our *own* rules, *baradar.*"

Siamak had a quick thought that the Quds political officer he knew in the Beirut embassy had really gotten his money's worth out of this MP.

Over the airwaves, the Hezbollah MP went on to laughably compare the American designation of Hezbollah as a terrorist organization to the Israeli Farzad assassination—the latest Zionist crime against Iran's nuclear ambitions. *That* was true terrorism, the MP said—more evidence of the global conspiracy to keep the Shias as a permanent underclass.

"A tragic irony," agreed the reporter.

"*More* than a tragedy," moaned the MP. "A willful Sunni-Western-Zionist plan to repress us, to exploit our riches, to undermine us, to . . ."

The politician ticked off the long litany of offenses committed by Sunnis against Shias, glossing over the fourteen centuries since the Shia-Sunni split over the rightful prophetic heir as if the dispute had happened last week. *That's* when the Sunni conspiracy had begun, the MP reminded his listeners.

Siamak switched off the radio. He already knew all this. And believed it.

He tapped his fingers on the Peugeot's wheel. The line of vehicles hadn't moved much as Syrian soldiers accosted one driver after another, shaking them down for bribes. So much *baksheesh* was required to make it through these random stops that travelers had taken to calling them the "Marlboro Checkpoints." Even now, just three cars ahead, Siamak could see a brown bottle of whiskey passing through a car window to a grinning guard while another guard searched the car's trunk.

Try that with me, he thought. In Siamak's trunk lay a set of hand-carved, colorfully painted mujahidin fighters he'd bought for his son at a Damascene market one evening after a long *Taniyn* counterintelligence briefing.

Siamak had laid out a stack of Syrian pounds for the toy soldiers. The MOIS major was hoping he could convince Ali that they were at least as interesting as his LEGOs. But what if the Syrian border guards took them? He supposed he could give up the gift to the Syrians just to stay in cover. *But what a . . .* Siamak sighed, checked his watch, and cursed this stupid waste of time.

At least, he thought now, the relief convoy trucks in front of him would get through quickly. The Syrians wouldn't mess with those.

With goods shipped from Tehran to Damascus, the trucks were an ongoing lifeline that supplied commodities to the poor Shias, especially diesel. Hezbollah politicians like the radio's MP had been flogging these convoys as a great success in the international media, a way to thwart American sanctions. And there they were, just ahead of him, queued up to cross the border.

Siamak looked at the curving line of the big vehicles from his Peugeot. Towering above the waiting cars, the five three-axle Scania tankers were colorfully decked in yellow flags, red beads, white taffeta flowers, and the ubiquitous posters of politicians and martyrs, one solemn face after another.

Some were images of Ali Mansour, the general secretary of Hezbollah's putative political wing. Others were of Khamenei, the current supreme leader of Iran. Another was of Mugniyeh, the warrior who'd blown up the US Marine barracks in 1983, only to be murdered by a joint Mossad-CIA car bomb in Damascus decades later. But most posters were of the original revolutionary: Ruhollah Khomeini, revolutionary founder of the Islamic Republic of Iran.

And above that famously stern face with its black eyebrows and white beard snapped the yellow flags of Hezbollah—*Hizb' Allah*, the Party of God—each emblazoned with a green AK-47 and a Quran quote in Kufric script: *Then surely the party of God are they that shall be triumphant.* Siamak looked again at the image of the old Ayatollah, coldly incongruent with the gaily snapping flags.

"*Salam alaikam,*" the corporal at Siamak's door said when he made it to the barrier after another twenty minutes. "Where are you going?" the guard added in Arabic.

"I'm returning to Beirut from a business trip to Damascus," Siamak answered in the same language, his voice even, staying in his cover.

The corporal looked sideways at the MOIS man, uneasy at this border-crosser in civilian clothes who spoke Arabic with a Farsi accent. "What do you have with you?" the soldier asked, disappointed to see that the passenger seat next to Siamak was empty of *baksheesh*. The barrel of the guard's AK poked rudely through Siamak's window.

"Apologies, sir. But I don't have anything to give you."

The guard laughed at that answer. "Open the trunk," he said, waving the AK.

"No need for that," said Siamak, bristling. "I think I *do* have something I can give you, Sergeant." Siamak reached into his pocket and retrieved his wallet.

"How much have you got?" asked the Syrian sergeant.

"Just this. Siamak held up the plastic window that contained his IRGC identity card.

The Syrian sergeant paled, nodded, and waved the MOIS major through.

It had been worth breaking cover for that, Siamak thought as he drove away to the west.

After a two-hour descent from Lebanon's higher mountain altitudes, Siamak pulled over a dozen kilometers shy of Beirut. He removed his circular clay *mohr* from his trunk and faced east. When finished praying, the MOIS man dusted his knees, climbed back in the car, and continued the drive toward the city on the sea, admiring the view.

Though an ascetic by nature, Siamak had long ago allowed himself to like Beirut. For one thing, he thought the sea and mountain air so much fresher than smog-choked Tehran. And looking at the distant city now, framed as it was by this charming cobalt sea, Siamak could still believe in Beirut's oft-repeated reputation as the crossroads of empires, "the Paris of the Middle East."

Beirut was where Siamak wanted to raise Ali—to expose his son to the world, to gain the advantages that were denied most Shias. One such manifestation was Siamak's fine old apartment building up in the Sunni area, nestled on a boulevard where Christians and Sunnis sipped coffee on sidewalk cafés under elegant colonnades, an echo of empires from both East and West.

But Siamak was driving the Peugeot south now, into the Shia area, the *dahiyeh*. Soon any trace of Beirut's imperial past—Phoenician, Roman, Ottoman, or French—was displaced by an endless tapestry of leaning shanties, crumbling alleyways, wandering dogs, leaping children, and collapsing walls seemingly held together by tangled laundry lines. Far from the frequent comparisons to the French capital, this part of Beirut was more aptly reminiscent of a Brazilian favela.

He arrived at Nabil's second-floor apartment at six p.m., just as the streets were growing dark. Leaning over a narrow alley, the building's stucco facade had begun to crumble, flaking away like dead skin. A large fabric banner with another martyr's face swayed under a cracked window. That martyr had been one of Nabil's cousins—sacrificed in a suicide bomb in Haifa during the 2006 Israeli war.

After Siamak compensated each of Nabil's Hezbollah men with a four-inch stack of ever-devaluing Lebanese pounds, the cell members sat on Nabil's floor around an array of tea and sweets. Four AK-47s were propped against a sofa, canted as casually as umbrellas. The men wore mostly black in the Shia warrior tradition. They'd unwound their turbans, letting their long black hair dangle. Before Siamak had arrived, Nabil had chased his five nattering children and protesting wife away. The smell of cardamom from the family dinner was still strong.

"Do you have any other photos of these people?" Siamak asked Nabil after the cell leader's update on local activity. "I need more to go on than just chatter. A photo of their vehicle would have been good. Video would be even better."

"We have these," said Nabil, handing over a stack of ID cards. "We confiscated them."

Siamak thumbed through the ID cards. They identified the visitors as workers from Save the Children, an NGO that had long been active in Beirut, headquartered in Mar Elias, a sprawling Palestinian refugee camp that bordered the port. Two blond women, one sandy-haired man, all Dutch nationals, according to the IDs.

Siamak thought of the Damascus meeting he'd just attended with its emphasis on *Taniyn* security. This would be something to sort through back at the Iranian embassy. He pocketed the ID cards.

"And you're saying these potential spies were in a white Land Cruiser? Aid workers? You think they were aiming for the convoy routes?"

"Yes, *Effendi*. It was strange. They went to the port first, but only stayed for a few minutes. Then they suddenly turned back east, toward the truck routes, just as they were coming down. Some of the boys watching at the port noticed the fast exit and called us. We stopped them at the last checkpoint before the camp. Fortunately, we'd beefed up personnel, as you suggested."

"Where did they go when you let them go?"

"To the airport, directly. They said that's what they'd been looking for. They said they'd gotten lost."

Siamak nodded and thought. Up in Damascus, the *Taniyn* planning group—a coterie of anti-Zionist Hezbollah, Quds, MOIS, Syrian, and foreign technical leaders—had debated how to get additional components into the areas where they assembled the missiles. Now that another test launch had shown the missile's guidance system was solid, the group believed it was time to plan on transiting warheads into the assembly sites. One proposal had been to use the trucks in the relief convoys. The Iranian foreign ministry thought they could even codify a supply route into the Vienna nuclear deal for safe passage. Could these convoys already be compromised?

"So these aid workers got close to the convoy. Did they also approach the Laylaki building?" *Taniyn* guidance system assembly happened under a seven-story residential tower in the Laylaki neighborhood. It was where they would eventually have to deliver the warheads, should the order come down from Tehran.

"Almost, *Effendi*. We stopped them a half kilometer short."

Siamak grunted. If these blond aid workers were American or Israeli spies, then their information was eerily good. Perhaps Kahlidi really was out there selling secrets. Colonel Maloof would certainly love to hear that.

"Nabil," said Siamak. "In addition to beefing up our monitoring pickets, we need at least a dozen men to step up surveillance of Westerners entering the country." With the economy in freefall, Western visits to Lebanon had dropped dramatically, which should make the task a little easier, Siamak thought. And because Hezbollah sympathizers infiltrated every area of Lebanese government, especially law enforcement, gaining access to incoming passports and travel records wasn't difficult.

"Yes, *Effendi*," said Nabil.

"Our Hezbollah immigration officers will alert the Iranian embassy for any suspicious travelers. I need to make sure we have someone ready to follow suspects coming into the airport on a moment's notice. A lot of them will go immediately up toward the Corniche, near the American embassy."

"Understood, *Effendi*. I will get twenty more men on this. We will follow whoever you say."

"Good—and tell your men not to be surprised if they're women. CIA and Mossad use a lot of clever women as spies."

CHAPTER 17

"WHICH ONE OF YOU HAS IT?" MAYA SHAHEEN ASKED WITHOUT PRE-amble. She breezed into the Mossad HQ room and sat across from the reconnaissance team that had just returned from Beirut.

By now the *katsas* had disassembled their covert equipment bags and slouched in their chairs, relaxing after the long, complicated travel routes they'd taken out of Lebanon to avoid detection. They considered it a blessing to be back in Tel Aviv. For three weeks they'd been living undercover in a Palestinian Beirut refugee camp where they conducted reconnaissance.

The sandy-haired man dug through his bag and laid what looked like an Android phone on the table. But it wasn't an Android phone. It was a device that had been modified to sniff radioactive alpha particles when plugged into a hidden sensor on the modified Land Cruiser they'd been using. "Here," he said, sliding it over. "This is the one that was closest to the convoy route. You'll tell us, won't you, if we need to take our iodine pills?" He grinned.

Maya's mouth stayed flat. She tucked the device into the pre-cut foam core of the lead-lined case she'd brought with her. She had four separate Sparrow teams roaming around Beirut with similar devices and varying cover stories to look for the suspected *Taniyn* nuclear warhead, if such a warhead indeed existed. A new team rotated in every two or three days. "I'll get it down to the lab right now. Now who has the other special phone?"

One of the women put another Android phone on the table. This one could make phone calls. But it had also been enhanced with extra circuitry to make survey-quality geographic measurements, accurate within two centimeters. "You had geofencing turned on?" Maya asked, turning it over in her hand, inspecting it.

"Of course," said the woman, by now knowing better than to smile. The young *katsa* stood in awe of Maya Shaheen, a legend in the Caesarea ranks.

"Okay," said Maya, checking her watch. "We'll sync it up with yesterday's drone pass. Now, tell me. What happened on the run?"

It had been a week since the last *Taniyn* launch into the sea. The following day, a Unit 8200 intercept between Syria and Moscow suggested that another Iranian nuclear scientist had traveled to Damascus. Such commerce between a Tehran nuclear scientist and a *Taniyn* meeting in Damascus had ramped up suspicion that the missile might have a radiological warhead.

But they lacked confirmation. And having lost Kasem Kahlidi for good in the Virginia raid, Maya thought that pushing her Sparrow teams to look for radioactive dust and provoke a Hezbollah reaction was her next best option. Especially since Mossad couldn't count on the Americans for any further intelligence sharing, not after the disastrous Virginia raid.

Jeff Dorsey himself had flown over for a meeting with the Mossad director to make it clear he knew who'd been behind it. Though Maya hadn't attended the meeting personally, she wasn't surprised to learn later that John Dale's ex-wife, Meredith Morris-Dale, had accompanied Dorsey. To Werner and Maya, it only confirmed their suspicions that Meredith Morris-Dale was ultimately the leader of whatever intelligence operation they were running with Kahlidi.

And it had also set Maya to wondering about John Dale's ex-wife. Eventually, Maya had even checked out the CIA woman's dossier from the Mossad central records bureau. The record had been significantly strengthened by Maya's America Station team, including reams of surveillance transcripts. But after studying them, after looking at photos of

Meredith at home, in the car, with John and their daughter in an Annapolis marina—Maya felt like a voyeur. She replaced the dossier, guiltily.

"We went into the port to check the aid shipment," the woman in front of Maya said now. "Security was definitely stepped up—way more Abu militia than usual. They guarded us the whole way, only let us near the one container, which they'd separated along with the other NGO supplies."

Maya took a note. The surge in Hezbollah militia forces in the *dahiyeh* was concerning. She hadn't seen that for several years, not since the last war. And now it was on top of a new *Taniyn* test firing—just a week after Mossad had hit Iran's most revered nuclear scientist.

"There was a lot of positive chatter among the Palestinians about the aid convoys," said the first woman. "Hezbollah politicians are milking it. Tons of rallies happening. Usual hatemongering against us Zionists."

"Yeah," added the man. "But the Abu militia guys got nervous when we headed east toward the souq, getting up close to a convoy truck. You'd think as aid workers, they'd go easy on us. But . . ."

Maya typed rapidly on her laptop, using the letters AL for "Arab Lebanese" in place of Abu, the racial slur favored by Israeli security forces.

"And there was something extra intense about the crew that stopped us," the man continued. "It seemed a little more squared away than your typical Abu team."

"How so?" asked Maya.

"They were asking very direct questions, really diving into our covers. Seemed to suspect us. Even took our IDs. I'd wager they had some IRGC counterintel training, maybe Syrian Mukhabarat. They were pros."

Maya took another note. "You get photos of them? Can we get them in the database?"

"Too hot. I thought there was going to be a gunfight for a minute there." The Mossad *katsa* recounted how he'd quietly lowered his hand to the grip of the Jericho pistol stuck to the underside of his seat.

In which case you might have sparked the next Lebanese war, thought Maya. "Glad you didn't," she said, eyes down. The team finished their reporting. Maya dismissed them.

Now, canted over her notepad, she reread the part of her notes where she'd underlined and bolded the passage about the counter-intelligence activity near the aid convoy. That was new behavior, she thought. She'd need to check that out, maybe double up the Sparrow teams to see what these Hezbollah militiamen were up to—especially near Laylaki, a residential neighborhood where they'd assembled missiles for years.

Responding to that latest hit on Farzad, these fanatics were capable of anything now. Anything. The only way to prevent the next war would be a sharp intelligence posture.

Or maybe, she thought, they were already too late for that.

CHAPTER 18

DARK CLOUDS OVER THE SEVERN RIVER THREATENED A MORNING RAIN.
The heated squalls had been drifting over the Maryland shore for three
solid days, soaking the grounds, canceling countless summer outings.
But the weather had done little to diminish the spirits of Midshipman
Second Class Grace Dale, USNA, who'd been having a hell of a summer.

In addition to her award for rescuing a drowning civilian, Grace had
been selected by her company cadre for a coveted leadership position.
Soon, when the next school year started in earnest, she'd have the additional honor of leading a platoon. And with the busy fall now bearing
down on her, that meant she wanted to take advantage of these fleeting
summer days while her father was still in town. Despite the rain.

Naturally, then, when he'd called on Friday to say he could meet
Grace for brunch that Sunday, she'd made reservations at her favorite
restaurant, Café Normandie, and worn her new pink-and-white printed
summer dress. It was only later that she'd learned that her father insisted
on meeting on his decrepit old boat again—the dread sloop *Mollymawk*.

The driving rain had forced them below the deck into the mildewy
cabin. "Grilled cheese is my specialty," Dale said over his shoulder, raising his voice to be heard over the drumming rain. "I use Gruyère. And
I'm telling you, it should be Michelin-starred."

Stuffed uncomfortably into the salon's U-shaped settee, her hair still
damp from the long walk across campus, Grace nodded. Dale was stand-

ing at the gimballed range, adjusting a blue flame. Black smoke rose from the pan. He opened a porthole over the sink to let it out. It barely helped. Grace thought the boat smelled like it was engulfed in an oil fire. "Voilà," Dale said as he placed the plate on the table.

Grace eyed the dark sandwich and potato chips. She'd long ago accepted that her father was not a rich man. And a terrible cook. With a stoicism acquired through two years of military drill, the twenty-year-old midshipman bit into the burned bread and smiled.

Dale sat across from her, eating his own sandwich. Behind him were piled an array of groceries pinned to the bulkhead by elastic netting: cereal, crackers, fruit cans, protein bars. He'd stocked up for the sail south. It had left him barely enough room for them to sit together.

"What time are you setting out?" Grace asked. She shifted slightly in the banquette, hoping to avoid staining her dress.

"Flood tide starts at four," Dale said. "I intend to be out of the Chesapeake by six. And the weather's looking good on the Atlantic tomorrow. Should be a smooth sail."

The young midshipman noted the flakes of rust at the open porthole over the galley, still carrying away the smoke. She caught the shadow of a brown water stain in the headliner above the table. Had it grown darker with the rain? "Dad," she asked, "how are you outfitted for safety equipment? Have you been inspected by the Coast Guard?"

Dale looked up from his sandwich, chewing, eyes narrowed. "Coast Guard. Uh, no, I'll be fine."

"We're in July now," she said. "Tropical storms come up the coast. Based on the rain we're already getting, I'm just saying . . . this . . ." She touched the stain with her finger, testing whether it was wet.

"Relax, Grace. This boat's tight as a teacup," Dale said. "I'll be fine. Eat up."

"I mean, do you even have a working radio? The one over there looks ancient."

"Of course I have a working radio." It was true—in a way, Dale thought. Yes, the radio that had come with *Mollymawk* was broken. But

Dale had bought a new one, still in its box, stuffed in a locker above the head.

"But what if I need to get in touch with you? What if Mom does? Do you have a sat phone? Shouldn't you?"

"No, I don't have a sat phone. But I'm hitting marinas on the way down. I'll call when I can. You don't need to worry about me. I won't even be out of sight of land." He gave her his lopsided grin.

"Speaking of phones . . . ," Grace said, abandoning her sandwich. She scrambled through her handbag, searching for the ringing device. Dale smiled at the frantic way his normally poised daughter had abandoned all composure.

He stopped smiling when he heard her answer the phone.

"Hi, Mom," Grace said. "Yeah, we're on Dad's boat. Sure, it's no problem, you're not interrupting. It's okay—I don't mind, really. Yeah, Dad's right here."

Dale had failed to anticipate this move on the part of his ex-wife. It was a good one.

He held out his hand for the phone, clenching his jaw.

"*Don't hang up!*" Meredith said just as soon as he'd pressed Grace's phone to his ear. "Hear me out."

"Oh, *hi*, Meth," Dale said, leaning back into the boat's settee, ignoring the rest of his sandwich. "Nice to hear your voice. What luck you should call Grace's phone and get me too. Lucky."

"You know I had no choice. You keep ducking my calls. And we really need to talk. Can you get somewhere private . . . away from Grace?"

"The boat's thirty feet long. And it's Grace's phone. So . . ."

"Grace said you guys are in the marina. Send her on an errand or something."

"*Dad*," Grace stage whispered, poking Dale's shoulder.

Dale put his hand over the phone and looked at her.

"I'll go walking around the docks," said Grace. "It's okay. I have an umbrella. Really. I understand."

Dale shook his head slowly. "Fine. But, hey—Grace? Hit that shop on C dock and get me a Diet Coke." He scrambled in the pocket of his shorts and came up with a grimy five-dollar bill. Grace snatched it and left the boat.

"All right, Meth," Dale said when alone. "Nice move. Good fieldcraft."

"Why haven't you taken my calls?" Meredith shot instantly.

"Well, let's see. The *last* time we spoke, a team of Mossad *kidons* dropped out of the hills and—"

"Stop right there," Meredith said sternly, cutting him off. Dale knew the tone, knew not to mess with it.

"What?"

"I need you to go secure on Grace's phone."

"What are you talking about? That's not a thing."

"Yes, it is," said Meredith. "Grace carries a secure phone just in case I need to get in touch with her with operational details. There's an app . . ." Meredith went on to explain how Dale could enact the encryption protocol on Grace's otherwise ordinary Android phone.

"All right," she said when they were both secure. Her voice sounded suddenly compressed by the encryption algorithm—distant, ethereal. "You just mentioned *kidons*. When you called me right after the raid, you said you couldn't be sure the assaulters were Mossad. Now you're saying you're sure? Do you know something else? Something new?"

Dale bit his lip. He still hadn't copped to his attempted recruitment in Maui. Nor had he admitted that he recognized the *katsa* he'd stabbed with the breaching tool in the hayloft. He knew that doing so would only sink him deeper into the CIA swamp.

And worse, he'd have to give details about Maya to Meth—another kind of swamp.

"So, this is another debrief?" Dale asked. "That's why you needed the secure circuit? I already gave the AAR at Langley. I'm not going back in there. You promised."

After a full second's silence, Dale heard Meth sighing on the other end of the line. Or maybe not sighing—there was a distorted hash of interference, a delay. The secure circuit must be bouncing off a satellite, he thought. He thought she must be overseas somewhere.

"Look," he said into the interference. "I've met with the FBI goons, like you asked me to. I gave them everything on Kahlidi I could think of as well as the assault. Same story I gave you. I'd just as soon not relive it if that's okay."

After Kahlidi had dumped him on his ass at the horse farm, Dale had crawled into the brush to evade the Mossad raiders. Then he'd tried to gain some reconnaissance on them. But by then, the assaulters had been pulling out, collecting their casualties, roaring away in the hay truck. All in all, Dale wasn't too proud of his performance.

"Is that why you skipped out on your last FBI meeting?" asked Meredith.

"*No*. The FBI guy in charge is an idiot. He doesn't want me around anyway. And the whole thing's pointless."

"What do you mean 'pointless'?"

"I mean the FBI guy won't listen to me," said Dale. "He and his team are dumbasses."

Dale heard a rasping sound through the phone. He wasn't sure if it was a gasp, a laugh, or just more machine noise caused by the delayed encryption protocol. "Those dumbasses are the best we've got," she replied. "And I need you to keep talking to them. Dorsey's set you up with them as *the* key witness. Whenever you duck out, it's my ass. *Please*, John. Just do it. For me."

Dale sighed. "It's been almost two weeks. He's a goner now."

"The last report *I* got said they caught a facial of Kahlidi at a Metro station in the city the morning after the raid. That confirmed Mossad doesn't have him. But . . . why am I telling you all this? You're supposed to be part of the search team."

Dale waited out the brief satellite delay, then added another of his own for emphasis. "Meth, I told you. The FBI guy's a prick, so I'm not playing along. And besides, he's looking in the wrong place. I haven't been able to talk him out of it."

"What do you mean?"

"I mean Kahlidi's going to get to the UK. I'd bet you anything he'll find a way to get to his girl. FBI should already be looking for him over there, but they're not. A guy I spoke to at MI-5 thought the same thing, told me all about Hezbollah hotbeds back there. But apparently, no one wants to freak out the Brits or whatever for fear it will somehow leak to the Iranians and screw up the nuke deal. And there's political sensitivity about shaking down Hezbollah types."

"You broke up there a little bit," said Meth after a two-second delay. "I'm on a sat phone. The encryption can't handle all the switching between low earth orbit birds."

"Right. I know. Maybe you should use a regular phone when you call me."

"Can't. But John, our only real lead would suggest that Kahlidi is still in the US. It makes sense to concentrate there. And his girl is probably in Iran by now—she got snatched by MOIS and Kahlidi knows as much."

"You sound like the FBI agents. Kahlidi told me personally he thought they'd keep her in the UK until the police heat died down."

"If you feel so strongly like you know what should be—"

"Sorry, Meth, you broke up there," Dale lied, interrupting her. "You know how shitty the encryption is on these low earth orbit sat phones. Anyway, I can't go to Langley. I'm going sailing, leaving tomorrow—us retired guys do stuff like that."

"You're not retired."

"I've done everything you asked of me on this thing. Right?" His voice had risen to make up for the poor connection and the driving rain.

"John," said Meredith. "You're *not* going sailing tomorrow. You're technically still active, working for me until I can at least unfuck your pension. And it would be a hell of a lot easier to do that for you if you'd cooperate. Why don't you . . ." A burst of encryption-driven machine noise overrode her last sentence.

Dale looked around at the provisions stacked on the bulkheads, listening to the noise, waiting for it to clear.

"Where are you?" he finally asked.

"On an op," said Meredith. "I've got that NIE. And I've got to get the goddamned thing done."

"I know you've got the NIE. But why a remote op? Most department heads would run an NIE from a desk at HQS. Be like them."

The encrypted satellite delay garbled the first few words of her answer, giving her voice an otherworldly, detached quality. "I can't say—and it's why I really called. I needed to tell you I'm going to be out of the office on this thing for a while."

"Where?"

"Can't say."

A metallic quality to her voice indicated a problem, Dale thought. It betrayed a lack of confidence, a bit of fear. He'd heard it in her before in the very rare moments when she'd confessed her vulnerabilities to him. "Meth," he said. "Tell me what's really going on. I'll do your FBI thing. Just tell me what's up. For real. I mean it."

"Can't," she said.

"I'm not doing anything unless you tell me, then. *I* mean it."

She said no again. He repeated his threat. It went back and forth three more times.

"All *right*," she finally relented. "But this goes in your mental SCIF. I'm serious. And you *have* to go back to the FBI tonight. Deal?"

Dale gripped the phone hard, straining to hear her over the weird encryption noises. "Fine. Deal. It's in my mental SCIF. Now tell me where you are. Hurry up. This connection's shit. Not sure how long it will hold."

"I'm in France, leaving a safe house."

"Where in France?"

"Paris. Well, Sartrouville. Not a nice neighborhood, but a good place to disappear. I'm in a car."

"But why a safe house? Why disappear?"

"Why do you think? I'm getting into cover."

"As in *nonofficial* cover?"

"Yes. And that's all I'd like to say about it."

Shit, thought Dale. "Meth, you aren't going into Israel, are you?"

"Israel? No. Already been. Dorsey and I met with the Mossad director—wanted to clear the air after their hit on us. They denied everything, of course . . . kept circling back to the Iranian deal. Dorsey was furious." She stopped there—or so Dale thought. There was another long burst of machine-generated noise.

"Okay," said Dale. "Meth—I have to ask this. Did the Mossad people say anything . . . about me?" Dale was mortified at the prospect that Maya might have been at that same meeting with Meth.

"There was no mention of you, John. Why would there be? Like I said, they're denying everything. And we know Mossad's got us all bugged. The CI people don't even want you and I to speak for a while, if we can help it."

Suddenly the connection became clearer, as though a new satellite had taken up the circuit. Meth's voice close now, right in his ear, loud. She continued, "Dorsey didn't want to raise their safe house hit on us directly, but they knew he knew. Honestly, it was like watching two serial adulterers in marriage counseling. Total bullshit."

Dale held the phone an inch from his ear. If Dorsey was directly in Mossad's face at this point, Mossad would probably abandon their effort to recruit Dale, he thought. He'd become an insignificant detail. Thank God.

"But John," said Meredith, her voice loud and jarring now. "The FBI meetings aren't the only reason I need you to hang around DC for a while. It would be good if you were near Grace. She'll need some support once school gets going in September. Did she tell you she got picked to be a platoon commander?"

"Yeah . . . But did you just say you might not be back until September? Why?"

"I told you. I need to finish that NIE. And to do that, I need to keep Mossad interference to a minimum. Not sure when I'll be able to come up for air again."

There was that fragile quality to her voice again. "But why aren't you working it from back here?" asked Dale.

"Because this Mossad thing is *delicate*. It's better if I'm vetting sources myself, so they can't manipulate me. I can't rely on other people."

"Vetting what? Where? Dubai? Your usual haunt?"

Dale heard a hiss on the line as she hesitated. "No," she said. "I'm going to Beirut."

Dale took another glimpse through the hatch to make sure Grace was still gone. "*Beirut!*" he rasped through his cupped fist.

"Yes. Take it easy, John. The NIE needs to vet the Iranian weapons connection with Hezbollah. They're in Beirut. I have to go."

Now he knew why she sounded as she did. "No fucking way, Meth. Uh-uh. I'm not letting you do a solo NOC in that shithole. It's where intelligence services go to war. *I* wouldn't go in alone against Hezbollah— and I'm trained for it. I forbid you to go."

"You *forbid* me to go? Did you just say that?"

"You know what I mean. You can't do this."

"It's my NIE. I need to get it done—quietly. I think I can judge the risks."

"Meth," said Dale. "We haven't sent NOCs into Beirut since the eighties, let alone singletons. I heard Beirut Station officers never go past the old Green Line. Mossad does all the dirty work over there."

"Exactly. Mossad's just going to feed us the info they want so we won't go through with the Iran deal. I need to get to ground truth myself. That means going to Beirut. And they seem to have a mole in our shop. We think they tracked one of us to the safe house."

Dale winced.

Meth continued. "I *have* to crush this NIE, John. The entire State Department's waiting on me. And it's the biggest career moment of my life. I'll keep it low intensity."

"Fuck career. Screw the State Department," said Dale. "There's no such thing as low intensity in *Bay-fucking-root*. Hezbollah *killed* our Beirut chief of station in the eighties, right? And your Arabic's for shit. You can't blend in."

"My Arabic's not for shit. Besides, I'm going in with a solid French cover. It will be backstopped all the way. And the Beirut chief of station will be briefed, embassy security will know I'm in the city."

"Who's the chief of station in Beirut these days?"

"David Cowles."

"He's a pussy."

"You think they're all pussies."

"They are."

"Look, John. Don't go sailing. For me, do the FBI meetings, keep up the Kahlidi search, stay near Grace, and try not to call me. Just know that I may be off the grid for quite a while."

"Fuck that, Meth. Manage your NIE from here. Use the people in the field."

"The Kahlidi thing's a disaster. It's on me to fix it. It's all me."

The faint quaver in her voice chilled him. "There's another way," said Dale suddenly. "Just resign. You have enough pension built up. You've seen me get by. It's not so bad. Hell—maybe we could hang out a little bit. You could give my boat a second chance."

"Are you fucking nuts?"

"What's so crazy?"

"Resign? Just because I . . ." The machine noise was back. Dale only made out a few words, which, strung together, made no coherent sense. He tried to clarify, asked her to repeat.

But by then, the encrypted circuit had dropped. And Meredith didn't call back.

CHAPTER 19

"*ENTREPRISE OU PLAISIR?*" THE INSPECTOR ASKED AS MEREDITH stared into an iris scanner at the Beirut airport. He'd already taken a long, hard look at her French passport with the alias name of Margot Henri.

"*Entreprise,*" Meredith replied. To make sure she was black, free of surveillance, she'd avoided any trips to CIA Paris Station. But she managed a good bit of old-fashioned sightseeing on the Seine as a portion of an SDR for a few days. That had been something, at least.

"*Pour quelle entreprise?*" asked the immigration officer.

"*Journaliste—pour Le Monde.*" Specifically, as her visa spelled out, a *Le Monde* reporter who was there to write a story about the devastating 2020 port explosion that had left two hundred Beirutis dead. Meredith produced the letter and slid it under the heavy plexiglass.

After a careful study, the inspector looked up. "*Journaliste? Très bien . . . La catastrophe du port est une tragédie, tragédie.*" He forced Meredith to leave a fingerprint.

Though officially illegal for CIA officers to use journalist covers, Meredith had found a loophole. As she'd pointed out to the Counterproliferation general counsel, Sheffield, the law applied only to *American* journalists covered by US passports. *Foreign* governments could still legally approve them. And since France had long shared intel with CIA about Lebanon, a former French colony, Meredith had been able to wheedle a DGSE colleague into a clean French passport.

"*Bonne journée, Margot Henri,*" the officer finally said, handing her the passport.

Once Meredith had walked away, the inspector made a note on her file.

He then lifted his phone to make a call.

Meredith hurried to the Europcar counter, got behind the wheel of her rented Mini Cooper Countryman, and headed north on Général de Gaulle Avenue. It was her first time in Beirut.

Now she wondered why John had been so worried about her. *Like Santa Monica*, she thought when she got to the northern coast, noticing the palm trees on both sides of the road, the crowded beaches, the arches at the foot of colonial buildings. She checked her GPS and drove on to the Corniche, the northern edge of the ring road, which overlooked a spritely marina, the boats white in the sun. It made her think of John's crappy little boat. She downshifted into a curve and kept an eye on the rearview to watch for a tail. Then she took three random SDR turns to make sure she was clear. If she was honest with herself, she would have said she wasn't sure. But that was okay. Her appointment site should be clean.

Her visa application had required her to submit a list of interview targets. The first on the list—a fake appointment set up with a professor who was on CIA payroll—was at the American University of Beirut, AUB. After verifying the appointment at the university's entry gate, she drove through to the big white administration building, entered its underground parking garage, and waited in a stall.

Soon after, her Surface tablet buzzed in her hands. She went through the complicated set of swipes and gestures required to turn the tablet into an official Agency covcom, encrypted covert-communications device. Once authenticated, she opened the message waiting for her: *Welcome Ms. Henri. Third floor, A-15.*

A junior CIA case officer was waiting in the otherwise empty office with a Department of State Security (DSS) special agent with a big bulge under his jacket. *Machine pistol*, she guessed, judging by the size—not the kind of thing you usually see in urban civilian settings.

They were there to transfer her via covert route to the embassy, secretly, since Meredith was now in Lebanon as a NOC, without the benefit of an American black passport, diplomatic cover.

"Meredith Morris-Dale," said a smiling David Cowles, shaking her hand. "What's it been? A couple years?" The Beirut Station chief slouched into the wing chair in front of his desk and crossed his legs. His office was on the sixth story of the building. Behind him, she had a view of the cool blue Med fading to a blur at the horizon.

"At least five years," she said, running her fingers through her hair, shaking it loose. "Congrats on Beirut, David. You made chief early."

She'd gone through the Farm with Cowles, twenty years back. She'd thought him a bit of a lightweight then, more suited to the diplomatic track. But here he was on the sixth floor of the embassy, looking out over the sea like an Ottoman pasha.

"Thanks, Meredith. That's kind of you to say." Cowles looked out the window, then back at her. "I'm sure your shot's coming soon, by the way. I heard you're even running this big Iranian deal NIE now—congratulations. Can I assume that's why you're here?"

Meredith had kept the contours of her mission at the 50,000-foot level—Cowles wasn't privy to the Atlas mess or the Israeli *Taniyn* intel. Like everyone else, he thought the last missile launch was a benign test-firing of an anti-ship weapon.

When she stopped answering Cowles's operational questions, he turned to small talk. She learned of his obsession with tennis and his surfing lessons, both of which helped explain his ruddy tan. After a few more sentences, she put a hand over her mouth to stifle a yawn.

"And you?" he asked, missing the hint. "How's John?"

She held up a ringless finger.

"Ah." He nodded, shifted, smiled awkwardly. "I guess I did hear that. Sorry."

"It's all right," she said. "Would you mind if I get on to my setup? It's been a long day and I need to get back to AUB to maintain my French journo cover."

"Of course, of course. Your team sent a huge set of files," he said.

"I've set you up at a workstation in the bullpen. If there's anything else you need, just say the word."

"Thank you, David." She stood up and smoothed out her skirt. "Oh—there is one thing. I'd like to set up a surveillance op whenever the next Hezbollah aid convoy comes down from Damascus. Did you see my cable on that?"

"Of course," he said from behind his desk. "I mean of course I saw the cable."

"Can I get a ground team set up, ready to go on short notice? I need better intel than what we've been getting from NSA. The Iranians have figured out how to go dark on us—they must be using one-time pads or messengers or something."

"Well . . . ," said Cowles, darting a look at some papers on his blotter. "With the disastrous economy here, the ambassador doesn't want us to look like we're disrupting the flow of aid into the poor neighborhoods. Shitty optics."

"*Optics?*"

Cowles smiled. "Things are delicate here. Especially since the Israelis have managed to whip Hezbollah into a frenzy again by firing a missile into a neighborhood."

"But those trucks from Damascus are Iranian convoys going into Hezbollahland," Meredith countered. "What if they're planning some kind of retaliation into Tel Aviv?"

"Like what? Look, Meredith, you have to understand that Hezbollah has a legitimate political side. They're in the Lebanese Parliament. We don't just ride herd on them day and night. It would set back diplomatic efforts months, years even."

John was right, Meredith thought later as she settled into her desk in the bullpen. *Cowles is a pussy.*

She removed her reading glasses and rubbed her temples, having just digested a new CIA S&T tear-down analysis of Werner's *Taniyn* schematic, now appended with details of the second missile launch. For the most part, S&T concurred with Mossad's intelligence on the aerodynamic capabilities. The thing could maneuver at high speed and had a range of a few hundred miles. It really was like a poor man's hypersonic. But the payload, according to the assessment, appeared designed to carry "any number of potentialities."

Potentialities, Meredith had thought. *Classic weasel word.*

One of these potentialities, the paper disclosed among its three-thousand-word discourse, *could* be radiological. But the warhead cavity could also house something else on the doomsday spectrum—chemical, biological, or just plain old high-explosive. The second test launch of the modified SA-5 had gone into the sea after maneuvering in horizontal S-turns. CIA S&T's most likely final assessment: anti-ship, conventional.

Meredith slammed the folder shut and called her operations coordinator back in Langley, Rick Desmond. "So it *could* be radiological," she said as soon as he answered. "That could mean just about anything, couldn't it? Maybe it's not even a classic fission warhead. Maybe it's something cruder, like a dirty bomb made of nuclear waste or Low Enriched Uranium or—"

"Usually people start with small talk," interrupted Desmond from his desk in Langley. "Not *dirty bomb*. How's Beirut?"

She ignored him. "S&T is basically saying that Mossad could be right. This thing could really fly hypersonic, low altitude, evade Iron Dome, all of that. We saw that from the second launch ourselves. And the operational intel suggests it could be a nuke. Why else would Hezbollah and Iranian comms have shut down like this? Quds has gone utterly silent in Beirut, probably using messengers. They have to be worried that we're listening."

"They worry *Israel's* listening," said Desmond. "Israel's always listening. But you saw the official assessment. Anti-ship missile. Why else would Hezbollah fire that thing into the sea every time?"

"So no one can inspect it. That's why."

"Not what our guys are saying."

"Exactly why I'm here."

"Well," said Desmond after a cough. "Does Cowles have any good agents close to Hezbollah that you could use for HUMINT?"

"No. It's just like we thought. Beirut Station has left everything up to Mossad. As far as I can tell, Cowles has no worthwhile agents on the ground."

"But you still have Atlas. He should be about ready to go in now. I've been working that Kurdish disinformation hard, just beginning to leak evidence that Kahlidi's still alive, but held in Iraq. Before we fake his escape, why not lean on him harder?"

Per Dorsey's direction, the disastrous Atlas loss had been so closely held that even Meredith's own deputy didn't know about it. "I'll try. But I don't think he was as close to the *Taniyn* strategy as we might have thought," she lied. How quaint her idea to lodge Kahlidi back into Quds as a prized American agent now seemed.

"What do you mean?" asked Desmond. "Kahlidi's name is all over the front companies that provided the *Taniyn* guidance. He was clearly involved in the importation of—"

"*Rick*," Meredith said, cutting him off. "Just assume that Atlas won't talk about it yet. He's holding out. What's another way to get to ground truth on this warhead for the NIE?"

Desmond took two beats to respond. "Well," he said. "I suppose that whatever potential doomsday warhead this could be, it would have to be smuggled in. The opium trade sets up tons of overland smuggling routes between Syria and Lebanon through the Beqaa. For ships, they'd still land in Syria, since sanctions keep IRISL ships out of Beirut." IRISL was the Iranian national shipping line. IRGC had taken to using them to smuggle weapons to various hotspots.

"Then that leaves the aid convoys," said Meredith. "Bringing stuff in right under our noses. With our own fucking permission, I might add."

"True. But I'm not sure they're that important. Like the DIA report said, there are SA-5 launchers all over the Beqaa that could handle a *Taniyn* launch. I'd think that if they were smuggling a warhead, it would be a quiet route through the mountains, out to those remote sites."

"But we'd be ignoring the obvious," said Meredith. "The convoys. Cowles is holding up approvals on my surveillance plan on them."

"Why?"

"Political."

"Oh."

"Cowles is about to learn that I'm not going to lay down on this."

"Be careful, Meredith. Cowles is connected. Even I know that."

"I've at least met some decent case officers here. And I've got a good cover. My intent is to hunt up agents we can use in the airports, ports, and at points along smuggling routes to see if we can set up an op. One of the CO's is setting up a meet for me in the city as we speak."

"Be careful," Desmond said again. "Going NOC in Beirut is pretty hard core."

"Thanks, Mom."

"I don't get why you don't stay focused on plan A. The Kurdish ab- duction legend I'm brewing is working. IRGC has been arresting Kurds left and right after the Farzad hit. They're even reopening their purges of the Kurds down in Alut, arresting dozens of them. You *know* that's because they think they're on to Kahlidi."

"Nice," said Meredith, squeezing her forehead and frowning. At least her instincts had been right. Reinserting Kahlidi as her own spy would have solved every problem in front of them with respect to *Taniyn*.

"And just think what it will be like when we get Kahlidi back into Quds," continued Desmond, unwittingly preaching to a very large choir. "He'll be the agent of the century, an intel coup, you'll be a leg- end, you'll be . . ." Desmond went on with all the things Meredith knew she would never be now, since she'd bungled the op. "But maybe you think the loss of his woman has clammed Atlas up," concluded Des- mond.

"Exactly," Meredith said, having finally found an off-ramp. "Without Kasra, Kahlidi's a dead end. For now."

"Kasra's the key," echoed Desmond. "Do we know what happened to her after the MOIS people grabbed her in the UK?"

"If she's alive at all, she's probably rotting away in Evin Prison by now," said Meredith.

CHAPTER 20

BUT KASRA KAHNI WAS NOT ROTTING AWAY IN AN IRANIAN PRISON. She was in a London Hezbollah safe house. And she certainly could have died there—had her erstwhile fiancé, Dr. Roger Gulrajani, not been taken to treat her.

Literally taken. It had been ten days since the wild-eyed Hezbollah terrorists had kidnapped the Iranian expat NHS physician to examine Kasra. They'd forced him to bring a trauma kit along. In a decaying apartment on London's north side, Gulrajani had found his former lover Kasra on the floor, her leg striped and swollen as a gourd, shaking with fever, fully delirious, not even aware her past lover was standing over her.

Small wonder she was delirious, Gulrajani had immediately thought. One look at the pink stripes extending to the thigh beneath the scissored jeans had told Gulrajani everything he needed to know. Kasra's gunshot wound had become infected. Those pink stripes indicated lymphangitis. The septic wound was leaking deadly bacteria into her bloodstream, on its way to her chest, where it would snuff out one vital organ after another. The ER doc guessed she'd been hours from death.

But reversing course for an infection like that was simple. He'd saved her life with a solid wound cleaning and a syringe of amoxycillin. Then he'd given one of the terrorists instructions on keeping the wound clean and left them with the vial of antibiotic.

And for that reason, Gulrajani's conscience was now clear again, thankfully. Though he thought she was still in a world of hurt as a captive, that couldn't be his concern. Expat Iranians knew the government could come after you. And Gulrajani knew she'd dated a high-flying Quds man. That was on her. No, Dr. Roger Gulrajani would worry no more about Ms. Kasra Khani.

But he would worry about himself.

And that's just what he was doing as he walked now among a large crowd of hospital commuters outside the old black Victorian St. Mary's Hospital gate. Hiding among the herd, Gulrajani moved quickly, eyes darting, trying to spot any of the scary men that had been coming in and out of his life, using him, threatening him, on behalf of the revolution.

To check his six, the doctor bent to tie his shoe and looked through the crook of his armpit. People streamed past him like river rapids around a rock. That was good, he thought. After retying his other shoe and taking one more look around, he hurried along.

While he maintained his security practices, he thought he might be out of the fray now. After all, he'd done what the terrorists had asked. He'd saved poor Kasra, who'd evidently gotten herself mixed up in some terrible thing that had nothing to do with him. And despite the risks to his personal safety, Roger had done his primal duty as a physician.

Now the doctor stopped on the curb, waiting to cross a street with a crowd of fellow pedestrians. Looking around a dozen walkers, he craned his neck to study the streets. He waited out the traffic until it was safe to cross.

Finally free of the immediate hospital area where someone might know him, he ducked into an alcove to stow his white lab coat and ratchet a dark ball cap over his hair. He donned big sunglasses and a surgical mask over his mouth. The masks had largely gone by the board in the UK, but they were still handy for disguise. He watched the crowd from behind the arch. Still no followers as far as he could tell. He hurried on his way, cautiously relieved.

Out of it now. Probably.

The doctor's meandering route took him past the Paddington Quay Post Office. There he turned left down an alley toward the Fan Pedestrian Bridge. Once across that, he walked through a park and found his way to a pier, where huddled a small flotilla of long, low, canal-bound houseboats. Ungainly and rounded, each looked like a scale model of Noah's ark.

The doctor took one final look from the pier. He stepped onto his boat and fumbled through his pockets for his keys.

His actual home was a few miles away in Queensway, where he lived with his wife of ten years and his six-year-old twin girls.

This houseboat was just a little lodging on the side, a place for Roger to take his girlfriends. An ideal escape, really—cash-based, close to the hospital, quiet, discreet. Gulrajani had had it for years. Cheekily, he'd privately named it *The Love Boat*. He'd even tried to bed Kasra here when she'd gotten in touch with him a few months ago. She'd wanted no part of it.

And after all he'd done to help her get established here in the UK when she'd come in from Tehran. He'd even gotten her a job as an NHS nurse, triaging poor immigrants. He'd loaned her money. But then, even after he'd turned on the charm, she'd turned down his advances. She'd failed to feel the old spark they used to have together. The nerve.

Looking left and right, Gulrajani finally grabbed the knob to insert the key to the boat's interior. But just as he did so, the door flew inward on its own, taking him with it.

Two sets of hands tugged him by the collar and pulled him down the steps. And before he knew what the hell was even happening, a plastic bag had gone over his head. Suffocating, his instinct was to clutch at the bag—but he couldn't. They'd already zip-tied his wrists.

Something kicked the backs of his legs. The doctor was thrust to the boat's deck, on his side, flailing and gasping like a landed trout. Then the bag was ripped from his head. He lay flat on his stomach, chest heaving. A nasty set of knuckles caught him on the cheekbone. "*Stop!*" he cried, knowing now that Hezbollah had found the boat too. "I already did what you wanted!"

A foot had landed on the back of his neck, pressing hard, pinning him. He couldn't see their faces, only the occasional shoe.

"Stay quiet," a voice from above said. "Or *die*."

Gulrajani shriveled. But somewhere within his cold core of fear he thought, *This is a new voice*. It wasn't the same man who'd snatched him the last two times.

"What do you want?" the doctor managed through rapid breaths.

"Quiet," the voice said.

A kick landed in Gulrajani's ribs. The doctor wanted to curl into a ball, but the foot that held his neck in place hadn't moved. He coughed furiously.

"Where is Kasra Khani?" the voice said.

Gulrajani tried to get his breathing under control. He coughed again. The voice was English, but he still recognized a very slight Farsi lilt. Even the Farsi had an upper-class tinge. That meant this was an Iranian government man. "How would I know? They blindfolded me!" shrieked the doctor.

Gulrajani absorbed another viciously swift kick to his abdomen. "You need to take us wherever they took you."

"Me take you . . . ?" he moaned as he writhed. "I thought they were with you?"

Another kick.

"*Stop!* I treated her somewhere. I don't know where. They took me to her. I just did what they asked."

The voice delayed its reply. "What do you mean you *treated her*? Tell me exactly where she is. Or I'll have my friend Hassan here cut your throat."

"No. *No!* I'm just a patriot, a *fedayee*." Gulrajani gasped, now sure they were from IRGC, maybe even MOIS. *Goddamned Kasra*. "I'm a *pasdar*," he wheezed. "I thought I'd helped already. I just want to help."

"You mean help the mujahidin? Hezbollah?" the voice asked.

Gulrajani nodded. "Yes. I thought I was supposed to. I didn't know who they were. But I knew they were Khomeinists. They seemed . . . committed to the revolution."

"They're sadistic animals. You gave Kasra up to sadistic animals, you bastard. Again, Hassan."

"*Stop!*" Gulrajani screamed after a blow that bounced his head on the wooden planks. "I'll tell you everything I know! Give me a chance!"

"Pull him up," said Kasem Kahlidi.

His route to the UK, to this simpering ex-fiancé of Kasra's, had been easier than he thought it would be. After accosting the Sheikh in his Chevy Chase mansion and threatening to expose his sins to the polite society in which the Sheikh traveled, the billionaire dealmaker had come up with a proposition. He'd hire Kahlidi.

Kahlidi had instantly seen the wisdom of that. It was a much better deal than the American witness protection program and mediocre annuity he'd get for spying for CIA. Moreover, it was less dangerous. With the Sheikh's resources, Kahlidi could do whatever it took to remove himself from the CIA-Mossad crossfire. He'd also be able to duck those who wished him harm back in Iran—especially Colonel Naser Maloof.

After a deal was struck, the Sheikh had given Kahlidi a passport, a wardrobe, and a private jet flight to Farnborough. Kahlidi's former agent also lent him the use of Hassan, a personal bodyguard with a thick beard and a bald head. All he needed now was Kasra.

Hassan had dutifully thrown Gulrajani into a little padded chair now. The doctor's face was swelling, bruised, his black hair a mess. Kahlidi had never met Gulrajani before, only knew about him because he'd broken Kasra's heart a long time ago. This next blow would be for her. "Hassan, again."

The big man launched a haymaker at the doctor's temple that landed with a crunch. Gulrajani's head snapped sideways. "*Please!*" he screamed. "*Please*—I told you. I'll give you whatever you want. There's no need to hit me. Kasra should be fine. I did everything I could for her. When I left last time she was fine."

Kahlidi had found Gulrajani through social media. The doctor had posted a picture of his work staff on LinkedIn a month ago. Kasra had been plainly visible in the background. There'd been another pretty young nurse in the shot, Angie, her St. Mary's name tag easy to read. For a hundred quid and a smile, Angie had given up Gulrajani's houseboat in a matter of minutes. She shyly admitted she'd visited the doctor's boat once . . .

"When did you see her?" shouted Kahlidi. "Tell me—or Hassan goes again."

The big man cocked his arm. Gulrajani cowered, tilting his bruised head away.

"Ten days ago, eleven. I don't know what you want," the doctor blubbered, slobbering down his cheek. "I'll tell you whatever, whatever . . ."

"Let's have it, then. Tell me everything."

Gulrajani breathed hard for ten seconds, attempting to compose himself. "The . . . Hezbollahi," he finally said. "They found me—a week and a half ago, at the tube stop at my neighborhood. They threw me in a van and took me to her."

"Why?"

"To treat her. I thought I was working for you . . . for the government . . . for the revolution."

"You weren't. How is she?"

"She'd been wounded, shot in the leg. The wound had become septic. They were worried about it. I took care of it. I swear to you."

"She'd better be all right, *Roger.*"

"She is!" the doctor insisted. "I swear it. She is, she is! The infection was bad, but I caught it in time. I opened the wound to clean it out, dressed it, sutured it. I brought her amoxycillin and left them instructions. It'll heal. I mean it—it was just a flesh wound. Medically, she'll be fine."

"*Medically.* Where is she?" Kahlidi pressed.

"I swear to God I don't know. I was blindfolded."

"Hassan. Again."

Gulrajani caught a fist to the mouth. "*Goddamn it!*" he screamed. He took a rushed breath, ran his tongue over his bleeding lip. "Sorry," he said with a lisp, trying to get his breathing under control. "I *do* mean to cooperate. Just . . . please stop hitting me. There's no point to it. I'll tell you anything. Just ask me."

"Where is she?"

"*Mate*, I don't fucking know. They put a sack over my head. A tenement. Maybe Tottenham, Yeading, someplace like that. There were a bunch of concrete steps. I remember that. But they kept me blindfolded except when I was treating her. I've given you all I have."

Kahlidi couldn't keep still. He paced, looked out one of the little portholes at the empty pier. Though worried about her wound, he thought the news better than expected. Kasra was still in the UK. And once he found her, he'd get her out of this for good. As the Sheikh's head of security, he and Kasra could live anywhere in comfort now. It would be a much sweeter deal than what he'd negotiated with Ms. Morris-Dale. He'd already begun thinking of faraway Brunei . . .

"Tell me how to find her," Kahlidi said. "You must have something."

"I can tell you about the building they took me to. It was unique."

CHAPTER 21

MEREDITH HAD MANAGED A MERE TWO HOURS OF SLEEP IN THE NOISY
budget hotel in Beirut's northeastern Christian neighborhood. Though
she'd already spent a few days there, she still wasn't used to the honking
horns on the street ten floors below.

But she'd had to spend much of the night working anyway. Now she
was paying for it. Sitting in the conference room with Cowles and one
of the Agency communications techs, she was on her fourth cup of coffee. The tech, who went by Robert, was across the table from her.
Cowles sat at the head of it as though in charge, though he wasn't.

"More coffee?" Cowles asked her, forming a finger steeple before his
chin.

"No, thanks," she said. "I think my head's about to pop off from
this sludge."

"Right. Turkish. You should eat something." The tented fingers
bounced off each other as Cowles spoke. "There's a patisserie off the
lobby that's really good. The *pain au chocolat* is—"

The Beirut Station chief stopped talking when the drone video lit up.

Cowles took the speakerphone off mute. "Hello, Creech," he said,
looking at the wide-scale image of a city grid now forming on the TV.
The big flat-screen sat on a cart near the table. "We've got our first video
here."

"Roger that," said the pilot from distant Creech Air Force Base,
Nevada.

Everyone liked to say "roger that," Meredith thought. When she'd asked Robert, the communications tech, whether they would be able to communicate in real time with the ground team, the tech had replied, "Roger that." Even Steve Chadwick had said "roger that" when she'd spoken to him a few hours earlier.

And thank God for Chadwick. Getting the RQ-170 Sentinel drone sortied out of Incirlik AFB, Turkey, wouldn't have happened without him, she thought.

After running into one wall after another, Meredith had finally relented and called Chadwick, her occasional boyfriend who served as chief of base in Istanbul.

It had been an awkward call, at first. The last time she'd spoken to him, it'd been to throw him over the side so John could make the trip to Hawaii—though, of course, Chadwick didn't know that.

But none of that mattered now. What mattered was that he'd delivered for her. Around six a.m. Turkish time, he'd twisted the arm of the Air Force attaché in Ankara, who'd been away in Dubai perfecting his golf game. Chadwick had made some calls and eventually dispatched a local Dubai case officer to pull the Air Force colonel off the first tee box at Dubai Hills.

When Chadwick had finally recounted the episode to Meredith around two a.m., it had come along with a dinner invitation the next time he was in Langley. Meredith had been so grateful, she'd said yes on the spot. She'd already acknowledged to herself that she should have invited Chadwick on that stupid Hawaii trip. Not John.

"Can we get a check on the Special Activities ground team?" she asked Robert, the commo.

"Roger that."

Arranging the ground team to surveil the convoy had been dicey too. The US ambassador to Lebanon, Marlene Hendricks, had objected to the idea of using the Beirut detachment in an active op. But after Meredith had escalated, Rance had calmed Hendricks down—telling her it was all about keeping the nuclear deal solid. No one wanted Israel in Lebanon mucking about, like they'd done weeks earlier with a drone strike in a neighborhood, Rance had said. And in that way, this was like a peacekeeping surveillance op, an opportunity to keep the Israelis in line, Rance had said. Ms. Hendricks had backed off. Meredith had been pleasantly surprised at Rance's rare bout of utility.

"Ground guys in position yet?" Meredith asked Robert.

Slamming away at his laptop with his headphones on, the commo could have passed for a millennial on a Zoom call. "Yeah," he said. "They're saying they're in the parking lot at the Coral Beach Hotel in Jnah. It's our best position for a Quds comms intercept. Let me link the team's grid coordinates with Creech so we get them on the drone."

The Iranian embassy was where Quds tended to hole up. If there was something afoot with this convoy, then the ground team would be in position to do a close-range intercept, possibly solving for the Iranians' new comms discipline, which had eluded NSA intercepts.

"Ground team just got an Iranian signal," Robert said a few minutes later, his hand pressed to his ear. "A car just came out of the embassy. Three bearded men. Fit. Two of them on cell phones, right now. Ground says they've ID'd that car before as suspected Quds."

Meredith asked if they could get a facial hit on one of them to run it through their known Quds database. Robert relayed the message. The ground team said they'd try.

For now, they'd have to settle for the bird's-eye view from the drone. Now that the team's data link had gone through, the drone pilot asked for another comms check to make sure the real-time voice communications were working between the ground team, the embassy in Beirut, and the drone pilots in Creech. Anything short of instantaneous, clear comms could lead to a disastrous blue-on-blue friendly-fire risk, he reminded them all.

Cowles punched the speakerphone off mute. "Creech, we have you *five by five.*"

Meredith forced her eyes to keep from rolling.

The drone video zoomed out, then back in. Meredith was suddenly looking at the Beirut-Saida Highway, a stream of cars, a big building with a pool. In the parking lot, the cursors zoomed in on an aged, tan Mazda minivan. It was the CIA ground team, on station at the Coral

Beach Hotel in their armored embassy vehicle. The Mazda was optically fingerprinted by the RQ-170's system now. The drone would automatically keep surveillance lock on the vehicle.

"Ask them if they're getting any comms out of that Quds car," Meredith said to Robert. In the armored, overweight CIA Special Activities Mazda, they had a variety of tactical, short-range SIGINT sensors.

"RF freqs are showing data comms. Hitting an IP server owned by Touch," Robert said. "Touch" was the local wireless provider in Beirut. "Data's encrypted," the commo continued. "IP address relates to a Discord server."

"*Discord*," Meredith repeated. "As in the instant messaging app?" Grace had used Discord when she was in high school.

"Yeah," said Robert. "Same one."

For fuck's sake, thought Meredith. *Half a trillion's worth of American defense spending beat by a chat app for fourteen-year-old gamers.*

"Wait. Hang on—I have a fix on the possible Quds data traffic termination now," said Robert.

"Let's have it," replied Meredith. "Who are they talking to?"

"I only have geocoords, but with a radius. Bringing up a plot now . . ."

Two full minutes passed. Meredith watched the drone video and the plot of the Iranians on their cell phones somewhere within a shaded one-kilometer circle. She yawned. It had become boring, circling the Mazda in long, lazy ovals. Her stomach growled.

"I have a better fix," Robert said. He twisted his laptop to show her a map. "The Iranians are right here. That roundabout, there, down in the *dahiyeh*. I was able to tighten it up because they're getting a bunch of calls from their embassy terminating at that spot, right now. Ground team might be able to get some good intercepts if they can get close to that spot."

Cowles raised his eyes over his steepled fingers.

"Ground could get actual clear voice intercepts?" Meredith asked. "How?"

"All digital cell phones use the same voice encoding standards," explained Robert. "Those kick in before encryption algorithms. If the team could get close enough to the Touch mobiles the Iranians are using, we could capture encoding RF signals and use them to decode it into clear voice later."

"*Great* idea," Meredith said, without really understanding any of it. "Let's do it. Get the team near that corner. And I want video, see who's doing the talking down there. Let's see if we can contribute anything to our known Quds database."

"Shall I clear it with the ambassador?" asked Cowles.

"Negative," said Meredith. "No time. Let's just get the team close. We can always pull them back."

Cowles relayed the instructions to Creech. But he was also taking darting glances at Meredith.

The video shifted, tightened again.

Meredith was looking down on a checkpoint with tanker trucks, surrounded by black-clad militiamen and mobs of civilians. Through the drone's HD video, she saw posters of martyrs' faces on the streets, yellow-green Hezbollah flags, a long row of decorated trucks in convoy.

With communications flying between the suspected Quds people in the car out of Jnah and the Hezbollah militia in the *dahiyeh*, a communications intercept might finally give her some insight as to what Quds was doing. She asked Robert to tell the ground team to hustle up.

"Hang on," Creech said, interrupting her. "You may want to hold on that order. We have another aircraft loitering on-site. Just checked with ATC—the bogey has no flight plan, no squawk, angels twenty. Sensors are indicating it's the radar signature of a . . . wait one."

Meredith looked at Cowles. He was back to tenting his fingers.

"Radar signature of an Israeli Heron drone," Creech said. "Whoa— just caught another bogey, five miles south. Yup, another bogey, two miles beyond that. That's three Israeli Herons, orbiting same vicinity, lower altitude. Heat signatures confirm ID. Say again, *three* Herons. Getting a radar cross section now. Confirm they're armed up with missiles."

"Well, well," said Meredith. "Hello, Mossad."

CHAPTER 22

IT WAS NEARLY THREE P.M. BY THE TIME MAYA FOUND WERNER IN THE large Heron drone surveillance bay in the bunker below Matcal Tower.

Stretching thirty feet to the ceiling were six large monitors, each showing distinct angles of video or telemetry data. Compared to the bright Tel Aviv sunshine, she found the space dim and cold, lit by low-wattage path lamps and glowing scopes. After her eyes adjusted to the dark, she saw Werner weaving between the desks, a young adjutant trailing him with a phone to his ear. The Caesarea boss was looking up at the displays, mumbling commands.

Maya approached, a padded overnight bag at her side. She put her hand on Werner's shoulder, landing on an epaulet. He was wearing a green commando sweater to ward off the relentless air-conditioning. "Got here as fast as I could."

"Good," said Werner. He glanced at her bag then went back to staring at the big screen. "Glad to see you packed something. I already promised Dil you'd stay tonight, after the committee meeting. I'm looking forward to it. I haven't been home in a while."

Maya nodded. "So I've heard. But—what is this? They didn't give me much when they called." She followed his eyes to the video screens.

"Something hot came in from Mitz," said Werner. "One of his Hez-bollah Junction teams got word that at least one of these trucks would be heading into Laylaki on a special mission. It couldn't wait." The video the Caesarea boss was studying rotated around a block of low roofs in the *dahiyeh*. He asked the Heron operator to tighten up on the building.

Maya watched as the roof grew larger.

Werner angled his head toward her to speak in a low voice. "That building, right there. It's near where your team got that sensor hit for radioactivity." He pointed. "We picked up strong thermals on satellite too. This may be the *Taniyn* development site we've been looking for. The convoy route will go right past it. See all those militia people setting up? Will be interesting to see if any vehicles head in there."

It was the same building her Dutch Sparrows had been driving near, testing Hezbollah's defenses. One of the sensors had come back with a positive alpha particle hit. But the radioactivity level was low-level enough to be determined inconclusive. "You read my brief," said Maya. "The alpha hit was too small for us to think that's really a nuclear weapons site."

"Yes," said Werner. "But the radioactivity reading wasn't zero, was it? And now there's this convoy rolling west from Damascus, heavy with militia guards. I ordered Sparrow L to get ready, just in case this is really a warhead smuggling op." He looked up at the monitors and pointed. "Wait—what's that? Tighten up on the northwest corner of the building. Is that a ventilation shaft? Is that steam? We should get an analysis on what's coming out of there." The adjutant scribbled notes.

"Wait," said Maya. "That stray alpha reading could have come from just about anywhere down there. I don't know that it fingers *that* building. The geofence didn't indicate that."

The Caesarea chief grunted. "But it's a piece of the puzzle, isn't it? And you heard what 8200 was saying. The new Quds brigadier—what's his name?"

"Sharifi."

"Sharifi. He's been to Damascus a few times now. So have the Russian technical people. Seems like a pretty big coincidence to me. Or just good intel."

"Fair enough," said Maya. "But if Mitz has someone inside, we should wait."

"Can we afford that luxury?" The Caesarea boss turned his head to bark at the Air Force officer in charge of the drones. "See that fuel tanker there?" He pointed a finger toward the monitor. "Yeah, that one. Oh *ho*—there's another one. That's two trucks breaking off toward Laylaki. Tighten up on them. Really tight, all the way in. That's it."

"They need fuel in the *dahiyeh* too," said Maya, watching the rounded trucks. She noted clumps of black-clad Hezbollah militiamen loitering nearby. The two big tanker trucks were threading between them. "If all we've got is some vague inference from Mitz, then I'd say it's not enough to . . ."

She stopped speaking because Werner wasn't listening. He was shooting a half dozen commands at the drone crews. She knew his moods. She took a step back. She put her bag on a table and watched the God's eye view of the scene playing out two hundred kilometers to the north.

The daylight high-def color video was eerily good. She watched as the two trucks neared a checkpoint. A dozen militiamen surrounded it. Nearby, the haunting martyr posters hung on buildings and lampposts. Werner made sure the 8200 techs were trying to intercept communications to the trucks.

"Trying, sir," said an 8200 sergeant. "No clear voice. Encrypted. Trace is . . ."

"I have the other end. Getting towers," said another 8200 tech. "Looks to be coming from the Iranian embassy at Jnah. Got vectors on two towers . . . now three. Vectors are moving. There's a car coming out of Jnah. Signals are still moving . . ."

Werner turned to catch Maya's eye, one end of his mouth curling in a smile. "*Jnah*," he repeated, louder.

Maya nodded.

Quds operated from Jnah, they both knew, site of the Iranian embassy. If Quds was clearing a highly secured path for this truck to the Laylaki building—Werner's hunch could be right.

"Get Sparrow L ready," he said, leaning into her. "We're going to blow those two trucks."

———

"Marlene wants us to pull the ground team out," Cowles said, entering the conference room in a huff. "Lebanese intelligence called. They're hearing chatter about us—they think our ground team's at risk at those militia checkpoints—and I agree. This could get ugly."

Cowles had stepped away for a quick tête-à-tête with the ambassador, Marlene Hendricks. Meredith had stayed behind in the conference room, pressing the ground team to get closer. Robert, the comms tech, had said they were still too distant for clear voice intercepts.

"Can't," Meredith said without even looking at Cowles. She was desperate to get that close-in voice intercept. Meredith stayed focused on the monitor, watching the ground team's Mazda, wondering where best to direct them. "Creech, can you get tighter video on that building fifty meters to the south of the roundabout? I thought I saw movement down there."

"Roger that," said Creech.

"But this is clearly some kind of Mossad op," said Cowles to Meredith, putting Creech on mute. "We can't be seen to be in sync with it—not right now. The optics would be *terrible*. Especially with the Vienna deal so—"

"We're *not* in sync with it," shot Meredith. "We're just observing."

"Observing . . . what, exactly?" asked Cowles.

"What Mossad is doing, for starters. And that convoy. I need better Quds comms intel. I need that ground team in there."

"You're sending a ground team into a terrorist threat environment to surveil an aid convoy. And doing it in the middle of an active Mossad op. Do I have that right?"

"Yup. I need to get a read on those comms. It's part of my mission here, part of the NIE. Maybe if we had an agent in there, this would be easy. But we don't." She immediately regretted poking him over his failure to get a good agent in Hezbollah.

"I'm chief of station," said Cowles. "This is my AOR. I call the shots."

"I'm running an NIE," Meredith said. "For the director of National Intelligence, by way of Jeff Dorsey. And I'm in tactical command of this op."

Cowles looked at her. His hand had crept a little closer to the speakerphone, readying to take them off mute with a scrub order to Creech. If he pulled that when she was this close, she wasn't sure what she'd do. *Fling his hand off the phone? Coldcock him?* She stared back at him. Robert, the young commo, shifted his eyes between them like a kid watching fighting parents.

Cowles's cell phone buzzed. He answered. "Yes, Ambassador. Yes, ma'am, I told her. No, ma'am, it's still happening. She's assumed tactical control. She's saying it's on her, her orders. Uh-huh. Yes, I understand. And I'd suggest you take that up with Langley, ma'am. Meredith won't budge on this."

"I want them to deploy a road mine," Werner said to Maya. "If Sparrow L sets up at this corner, right here, we can see how they react. The Iranian comm circuits will really light up then."

"*What?*" Maya blurted. She could hardly believe her ears. "We can't plant a bomb in the middle of that. What if it's really diesel fuel in those trucks? We could take out the whole neighborhood."

Werner didn't bother to acknowledge her. He stared up at the video. The two trucks were nearing the militia checkpoint. "Look," he said, pointing. There were men on scooters riding in front of the lead truck now. A few more trailed the second vehicle, AK-47s slung over their backs. "They've set up an armed picket line. And the trucks are still heading toward the target building. We're going to take them out."

"They *seem* to be heading to the target building," said Maya. "They're always armed around there. What if they're just touting the amazing work of the Iranian Shia brothers in delivering fuel to this poor neighborhood? Look at the damn things—they're covered with flowers and Ayatollah posters. And worse, what if they're stuffed with radioactive material? You'd be setting off your own dirty bomb."

"Yeah, maybe. But it would be up *there*."

"With the population density in the *dahiyeh*, it would kill thousands, more than that. For years."

"Of *them*."

She took a step back from him.

"*Maya*," he said, his voice lower. "Are we just supposed to wait for the same weapon to come to us? You saw they launched that second *Taniyn* test flight. Even though it was a dummy, another dead drop into the sea, we all saw its maneuvering capabilities. We could never shoot that thing down. Would you rather we launch an air strike on this building? That would be just as bad—only everyone would know we did it."

"It doesn't have to be an air strike. We could send Bayonet into that Laylaki building. If it's the missile factory, they could kill the lot of the Hezbollah workers there and capture whatever's going on. Get real intel. Come back for a real strike on launchers out in the Beqaa."

"We'd get caught with a raid like that. The political blowback would be devastating. They'd never approve a secondary strike. But if those trucks are blown by a road mine . . . we'll have plausible deniability. They have untraceable construction Semtex from Amman, right?"

She stared at him.

"I want a road mine after that roundabout on Hadath," said Werner. "Those trucks are never going to reach that Laylaki building. Do you understand me, Maya?"

She still hadn't moved.

Werner looked into her dark eyes and exhaled raggedly. He knew her so well it was like arguing with his wife. "Listen. Maya. I know you didn't approve of the Virginia raid on the horse farm. But had it not been for that fucking John Dale showing up—"

An Israeli Air Force major interrupted, words sharp and fast from behind his console. "Hold on. Suspect vehicle coming down the Salideh Highway in Jnah. Mazda minivan."

"What do you mean 'suspect vehicle'? Suspect how?" Werner asked immediately.

"Hostile SIGINT profile, bursting, frequency hopping. Van's on monitor two. Assess UHF frequency hopping profile as US military."

Werner looked up at monitor two. He saw the Mazda minivan—a far cry from a US military vehicle. That meant it was CIA.

The meddling bastards, Werner thought, rubbing his head with his knuckles.

"How long before that Mazda's in the area of the fuel truck?" he asked.

"Ten minutes, maybe. No, wait. They just got stopped at a Hezbollah militia checkpoint. Probably longer."

"Then they're not a factor," Werner said, eyes glued to the monitor.

And even if that CIA van stumbled into the middle of his op, he was thinking, he didn't much care. If CIA wanted to come play referee and try to break up this fight, then let them bleed.

It was the American agenda that was enabling these maniacs. Let them suffer their own blowback.

Welcome to my war.

CHAPTER 23

MEREDITH WATCHED THE ARMORED MAZDA SPEEDING SOUTH ON THE Salideh Highway. The RQ-170's myriad lenses had provided a three-way-split view. The TV in front of her showed the Iranian embassy at Jnah, her ground team on the highway, and two fuel trucks headed toward Laylaki.

She watched the trucks. There were three black-clad militia fighters on scooters riding in front of them, clearing a path through the traffic. The various flags and martyr posters were fluttering in the wind. She noticed how the small cars pulled to the side to let the trucks through. *Nobody fucks with Hezbollah in the* dahiyeh, she thought.

"Ground team says they're about to be stopped at a Hezbollah militia checkpoint," said the commo, Robert.

Meredith glanced at the Mazda on the screen. Just like that, the street had closed off with people, led up front by militiamen in black, surrounding the vehicle. A few of the men were carrying their AKs in front of their chests now.

"Fuck," said Cowles. "We have no protocol to get our team out if they're picked up. Unless you've got something up your sleeve?" He looked at Meredith.

"The ground team's got good cover," she said. "That checkpoint there leads to the airport—and that matches up to their story. Just like we talked about. Plan A should be good enough."

"Unless they search the van," said Cowles.

"In which case they'll find luggage," said Meredith. "Let's just see what happens. Worst case, if they have to fight it out, they've got a clear path back on the Salideh Highway. And if the shooting starts, the Mazda's armored."

Cowles stared at her, saying nothing.

"Look," she went on. "I have to take this risk. I really need those voice intercepts for the NIE. Our team needs to get in there. It's what they do."

The commo glanced at Meredith, then at Cowles, who said nothing. "The team's on radio silence now, gone dark, per protocol," the commo said, indicating the team had stashed their equipment, acting out their cover story as lost travelers trying to get to the airport.

Meredith nodded. She knew she was relying on little more than the guts and wits of the three-man CIA Special Activities Center ground team down there. She thought briefly of John, what he'd do. SAC people were chosen because they had blood pressure that barely kept them upright. *If it were John*, she thought, *he'd be able to talk his way out of it.*

She watched as Hezbollah fighters stood to either side of the Mazda, looking in the windows. A lead militiaman was saying something to the team's driver, through a half-rolled window. God only knew what. The video quality was so good Meredith could see the ends of the fighters' turbans lifting in the wind.

She said a silent prayer that the van would get through without trouble.

I should pray more often, she thought a moment later. The van rolled forward. Cowles, Meredith, and Robert looked at each other.

"They're back up on comms," the junior man said. "I just got a Charlie Mike."

Meredith's breath returned to normal. *Charlie Mike*, continue mission. She watched the Hezbollah militiamen backing off, slinging their AKs over their backs. The van continued on its way.

The sluggish Mazda pressed on, slower now, snaking through the twisted alleys of the slums while Robert directed them toward the convoy. First, they'd hit the roundabout and get their intercepts. Then they'd drive toward the airport, to safety. If it all went according to plan, Meredith would have her comms intel by nightfall.

"How close does ground team need to get to the physical phone talkers near the trucks in order to get to the voice intercepts?"

The commo thought about it for a second. "About a hundred yards. Once they're in that roundabout, we should at least get a snippet. The suspected Quds callers are still active. I can tell our team to take a couple laps around the roundabout to stall while we wait for those trucks to advance."

"Perfect," said Meredith. "Send them."

"The bomb's set up," Maya said to Werner. She kept her eyes down, her voice low. "A Sparrow got a pinger stuck to the bumper of one of the trailing vehicles. But with all those buildings, we had a hard time getting clear line of sight for the radio trigger. It's going to be danger-close." She'd done as ordered, but had avoided looking directly into Werner's eyes.

The Israeli Sparrow team had put the sticky bomb on the inside of a thin wall at a turning circle where the street narrowed, just ahead of a roundabout. A ten-kilo satchel of high explosive plastique would create the equivalent of a hundred pounds of TNT, enough to take out both trucks and then some. The bomb was explosive in nature only, no fragments—the flying masonry would take care of that. It was critical to leave no fingerprints, none of the telltale tungsten cubes typical of an IDF warhead.

As much as Werner wanted to blow the trucks, he really wanted to monitor the Iranian reaction, to see what the Quds communications out of the Jnah embassy sounded like. *That* would really tell him if he'd struck something strategic.

"Werner," Maya said now, looking at the suspected American vehicle. "The CIA van is getting close to our projected blast radius. Look. *Look.*"

Werner recognized the strain in Maya's voice. He ignored it. The

Mazda was still a half city block away. The convoy wasn't yet to the roundabout. He only needed a few more seconds. The convoy would make it to the turning circle before the American vehicle. "I see it," he said to her. "Your team is clear? We confirmed? Pinger active?"

"Pinging," she said flatly after checking a message on her phone. The pinger was a transponder the size of a key fob, stuck to a vehicle bumper. With the appropriate signal, it could activate the bomb's detonator when in range. "We've got a man on overwatch too, two hundred yards off."

Good. Overwatch would cover the Sparrow team's retreat. It was as good a tactical picture as Werner could have asked for. The Sparrow operatives had been moving slowly, in disguise, blending with the population.

"Another thirty seconds," said Maya after trading a text with the Sparrow team's leader.

Werner glanced at the Mazda again. "All right. Then we're a go."

Maya touched Werner's arm with two fingers. He looked at her. For the first time in the past ten minutes, their eyes met. She shook her head slowly at him and backed three paces, leaving him alone. He let her go and looked back to the TV screens. The convoy was now entering the roundabout.

"Command, we have another drone in the area!" an Air Force major at a scope shouted suddenly.

"*What drone?*" Werner shouted back. "Iranian? Syrian?"

"Phalcon has a midsize turbine-powered aircraft loitering angels twenty, no clearance on file with air traffic control, no squawk." Phalcon was the Israeli AWACS on patrol over the Med. "There's more. Phalcon now assesses the aircraft as American Air Force . . . profile of a US Sentinel drone."

Werner didn't respond. Maya hurried to his side. "*Werner!*" she whispered hoarsely. "You know we can't go through with this . . . The Americans are watching us."

He glanced at her, noted her open mouth.

"I'm pulling the Sparrows out," she said.

"No, you're not," he retorted, looking away. "I don't care if they're watching us. Have the Sparrows blow those trucks. Now."

Maya didn't move. Her thumb hovered over her phone screen as if it were the plunger for the TNT fuse itself.

"*Blow the trucks!*" Werner shouted at her, loud enough that one of the comm techs looked at him.

Maya finally dropped her thumb to the screen, sending the fatal message to Sparrow L's leader to arm the detonator, awaiting the pinger's signal. Seconds later, the drone video whited out in the JWR. The view in the monitors then changed to eerily quiet billowing black smoke, obscuring everything.

Including the CIA ground team.

CHAPTER 24

THOUGH THE SUMMER SUN WAS STILL HIGH ABOVE THE VIENNESE streets, the Grand Hotel's grandest ballroom had the golden glow of an autumn sunset. Spotlights hidden among the thick, molded baseboards cast long shadows on the high buttery walls. Below, the oaken floor could pass for a carpet of fallen leaves, a pattern of interlocking fleurs-de-lis. Above, a massive nineteenth-century chandelier cast dappled jags like sunlight filtered through tree canopy. And at the edge of the large, well-dressed crowd stood Ed Rance, head of the CIA Counterproliferation group, all by himself.

Rance was watching the crowd with a champagne flute held between the two longest fingers of his upturned left hand. Left, since he liked to keep his right poised for a quick handshake. But for the moment, his right hand was idle, restless, plucking at the gabardine along his trouser leg.

His fellow conferees were all busy now, leaving him there, standing uncomfortably alone. He checked his watch and estimated the length of time he'd been standing this way. Two—no, three minutes now. *No good.*

He sipped the champagne, studied his phone, and retreated toward a wall so he'd be less conspicuous. Now and then he looked up and nodded, miming a fake exchange or a glance at someone. As another two slow minutes ticked by, he wished one of his State Department colleagues would come along. But they were all hard at work, doing what they did.

The American State team was gathered in knots on the other side of the ballroom near the fireplace. There, Rance had noticed, they were either intensely conferring with the members of the EU delegation, or exchanging a quiet word with Hopkins, their leader.

Over the course of the meetings, Rance had grown envious of the State people, their mission, their sense of purpose, their hands overtly driving what would one day be history. He envied the way they were able to live in the open, dress well, stay in the finest places, attend dinners, get actual media coverage.

By contrast, while he'd always loved his own life in government service, Rance had come to loathe the secrecy that hid his professional accomplishments. *How much better it would be*, he'd mused over the past few weeks, *to be one of these State people*.

Standing awkwardly along the wall, that sense of envy had boiled down to one simple thing. Right now, more than anything, Rance wished that he too had earned the right to approach Hopkins, the US Chief of Mission for the Vienna nuclear talks with Iran. Rance wanted to build a relationship with the important man, to engage directly with him on historic matters of state the way most of his colleagues did. And to also engage him in a discussion of Rance's next career step.

But not yet. Timing, Rance had long thought, was everything.

He took a tiny sip of his champagne, careful to avoid a conspicuously empty glass. Growing bored of his phone, he covertly watched one of his favorite young female waitresses. He admired her long legs, her elegant gait, the graceful nods of her head as she doled out goat cheese on folded cucumber slices. Her hair was up tonight.

That was new, the hair. Once, a few days ago, Rance had seen her looking over German books in the library alcove with her hair down, framing her face. Even though his German was rudimentary at best, he'd considered taking a run at her in that library. Now, he studied the curve of her hip under her long black skirt, wondering how he might go about it. But then she disappeared into the crowd.

He stole another glance at Hopkins, the patrician, leonine career diplomat who led the American delegation. As a career minister, the

Foreign Service man was two rungs higher than Rance on the US government career ladder. And he was busy now, his coiffed head bowed in conversation with the deputy Russian foreign minister.

Russian foreign minister, thought Rance. Perhaps he could approach Hopkins after all. Russia was a legitimate CIA party of interest. Rance could conceivably saunter up to join in the conversation under the guise of doing his actual job, which was to establish contact with potential diplomatic spies from Iran, China, and Russia. *Yes*, Rance thought. *Maybe I should saunter over.*

But no, he reversed himself. Hopkins looked too serious, too intense. Whatever was going on, Rance at least had the emotional IQ to understand that breaking it up could be intrusive—a disastrous setback in the relationship he'd been building with the senior State man.

The waitress reappeared, distracting him again. She was getting closer, headed his way. Rance smiled at her, beckoned her toward him with a small hand gesture. He watched as she came, his mouth curving in a smile. He was thrilled by the appearance of a leg through the skirt's long slit as she walked.

The waitress dipped her tray near him. Rance was about to say something, mustering his best German. But before he could, he was cut off by Miles Vorhees, one of the State men.

Vorhees had approached from the left, surprising Rance. The Foreign Service Officer took an hors d'oeuvre from the waitress's tray and purred out a smooth flow of rapid-fire German, of which Rance caught every fifth word. The girl laughed at whatever Vorhees had said and went off into the crowd, smiling gaily.

"She's not bad," said Vorhees, chewing, noticing the direction of Rance's eye. Vorhees was fifteen years younger than Rance, taller, blessed with a lordly square jaw.

The CIA man immediately colored. "She's all right. I thought her teeth looked a little crooked. Anyway—progress today, Miles? We getting closer to a deal on missiles?"

"Closer," said Vorhees, chewing, sipping, scanning the crowd. "Thank God we're done with isotope lectures from foreign eggheads. *Gad*, what a bore." Vorhees turned to look at Hopkins, who was now deeply engaged in a conversation with a white-haired African man across the room. "See that? The *real* work's starting now. Pay attention, Eddie, pay attention."

"Right," said Rance. "I saw Hopkins talking to the Russian a minute ago. Now who's the white-haired guy?"

"Nigerian minister," said Vorhees. "On the IAEA board now, as of a few months ago. Someone else we need to win over if we're going to get missile concessions." IAEA, the UN's nuclear regulatory body, had sent half its board of thirty-five governors to this hotel for the negotiation.

"Really? I can't think it'd be too hard to lean on the Nigerians."

"Now, now, Eddie. If you're an oil exporter, like Nigeria, you want sanctions to continue—to lessen the Iranian petro-competition. If you're an oil importer, like India and China, you'd argue that Iran has signed the NPT, that they're being treated unfairly regardless of weapons status . . . defensive . . . blah, blah, and so forth. That's what the Russian was doing to Hopkins a minute ago." Vorhees sipped his champagne and nodded his head. "And now, of course, the Chinese are promising military supplies to the Nigerians so they can get cheap oil *and* foreign military basing rights in Africa. The dance goes on." The State man rotated his shoulders to mime a waltz.

"Yes," said Rance. "I suppose—"

"Oh hello," Vorhees interrupted, taking a fluted piece of zucchini from the silver tray offered by another pretty young woman. "*Danke schoen*, darling, *danke schoen*."

"*Bitte*," the woman said, smiling, moving on. Rance noticed she hadn't even glanced toward him.

"Just once," Vorhees said, popping the zucchini in his mouth. "I'd like a dinner that wasn't served on toothpicks. You follow?"

Rance followed. They traded small talk for a while. Rance tried to score a point or two by offering up his views on the Russians. But Vorhees had a maddening way of sweeping the crowd with his eyes, throwing Rance off. He couldn't be sure if Vorhees was even listening.

Rance changed tack to talk about the Iranians. "I suppose you'd say it's good to have the Iranian foreign minister back, wouldn't you? I'd imagine you all chalk that up as a win after he left in such a huff."

"Well," Vorhees said, continuing to scan the crowd, "it's good to have him back, yes, of course. Otherwise, Eddie, what would be the point of all this? The food? I think not. I don't think I could eat another vegetable after this. No. Going strictly carnivore from here on out. Mark my words, if not my deeds." He chewed. "But, yes, as long as your Israeli friends can keep from murdering more Lebanese civilians as seems to be their habit, then yes, we'll keep talking. That *is* progress. Hopkins is happy. But I suspect the Israelis won't be able to stop the killing for long, will they?"

More than a week had passed since the fuel convoy explosion in Beirut had roiled the conference. An Israeli soldier had been wounded in the raid, captured, and paraded in front of the TV cameras by Hezbollah. Worldwide condemnation of Israel had been swift.

"Hopkins's censure letter of the Israelis was a brilliant idea," said Rance. Rance wondered if he might say something else about how he'd been stumping within CIA to keep Mossad on a tighter leash. He kiboshed the thought. *Probably can't trust Vorhees.*

"Do you think she's German?" Vorhees asked, watching the same blond waitress that Rance had been admiring. "I didn't get that much out of her with my German joke. Usually I get *something*. They almost always come back for more."

"I don't know . . . I would imagine she's . . ."

"Well," said Vorhees, looking around. "I need to go find the Swiss energy minister. He wants us to get on board with their centrifuge maintenance proposal. Let's just see what the cheddar-churners will take in trade. *Ta ta.*"

Rance glanced toward the fireplace. One of the Foreign Service men had finished his piece with Hopkins and was stepping away. Rance had suddenly seen his opening—then lost it just as quickly. The South Korean IAEA governor had stepped in front of the lead US diplomat.

Just as well, Rance told himself, staying still, waiting, plucking at the seam of his trousers, still thrown off by Vorhees.

Patience, he said to himself. A professional reputation with Hopkins was a meticulous job. It had to be done slowly, carefully. *Rome wasn't built in a . . .* He sipped his champagne and looked again. *Fucking Koreans still there . . .*

Rance turned and pretended to see someone across the crowd. At least he'd made progress, he told himself, sweeping the faces with his eyes. Over his weeks in Vienna, he'd found subtle ways to show he wasn't the crude CIA-neocon-Luddite they'd originally assumed him to be.

Yes, thought Rance. His forced exile to Vienna *hadn't* all been for naught, not by a long shot. Far from it—it would be Rance's bridge to the next step in his career. At State—where the real work of the world was happening.

He'd found the odd moment here or there to build that bridge. He'd quietly voice his opinion to whoever at State would listen that all the world really needed to do was wait the Iranian revolutionary regime out, contain them. This, Rance had told them, is simply the new Cold War. *And for every hotheaded Lenin*, he'd said to Collins in one of the pre-meeting briefings, *there awaits a Gorbachev.*

That, Rance thought now, had been a good line. And Collins was close to Hopkins. It seemed likely Collins would have repeated it. But just in case Collins had failed him, Rance was anxious to use it *directly* on Hopkins now, score dozens of points, hundreds even.

And if that could just happen . . . , he thought, noting that the Korean diplomat was still there.

The crowd shifted. Rance saw Vorhees's tall, well-groomed head. He watched the State man as he spoke effortless German with a silver-headed Swiss government minister. Rance tossed off the rest of his champagne, swallowing hard.

Carrying his empty glass, the CIA man wandered toward the bar, wondering whether he should have another.

He'd been like Vorhees once, he thought to himself. A young Turk, going somewhere. But then he'd fucked it all up, stumbled into the affair with the Russian SVR woman, the honeytrap, the whole goddamned sordid mess. Even his wife had somehow figured it out—the clandestine CIA spousal network, home to a million heartbreaks. She'd filed for divorce. Not that Rance loved her anymore—but he *did* have a career to think about. What if she made waves?

And that wasn't the only woman in his life that gave him heartburn. There was also Meredith Morris-Dale. She'd exposed the whole honey-trap, putting Rance in this purgatory.

But at least Meredith was finally getting hers now.

As if losing Atlas weren't enough, Morris-Dale had gone and ordered a SAC ground team into the breach in Beirut, a crazy risk, directly contravening the ambassador. It'd taken a whole State-led hullabaloo with the Lebanese government to get the wounded CIA ground team back out after the massive explosion. Only their armored vehicle had saved them. But their covers had been blown.

That had led to angry denunciations from the Lebanese government, saber rattling from Hezbollah, accusations from Iran. It had taken that hastily arranged censure letter to put the pieces back together, prove to the world that it was a Mossad issue, not a CIA issue. Everyone knew we'd lost some leverage now and the Iranians were playing that up, winning concessions left and right. Things were going in the wrong direction. All because of Meredith.

Karma, thought Rance.

Out of the corner of his eye, he could see the Korean had departed. Rance was about to saunter over to Hopkins to congratulate him on the censure letter and the return of the Iranians.

"Pardon," a man said, stepping in front of Rance. He was a little shorter than the CIA man, bearded, wearing a white Nehru shirt and a silvery suit. His hair was black, his beard gray, about fifty, a smile with small white teeth.

Rance was caught off guard. But as a career spy, he recovered with a modest smile of his own. "Hello. May I help you?"

"You were at the meeting on fuel rod storage today, I believe," said the man in accented English.

"Yes," Rance replied, fighting through the rush of champagne that had now made its way to his head. "And you are . . . ?"

"Walid Zafir, deputy second secretary to the foreign minister." The Iranian held out his hand and modestly bowed.

"Very good," said Rance, taking the soft handshake, a show of respect in the Middle East. Rance returned the bow and summoned his own diplomatic cover alias. "I'm Edward Pine. Assistant fourth secretary deputy liaison for science and technical affairs." Rance handed over a US Department of State business card.

"Yes," said the Iranian, pocketing the card. "I know who you are."

Rance was completely sober now. *You know who I am?*

"I just came over to say *moteshakaram*," the man continued.

"I'm sorry?"

"It means 'thank you.' In Farsi." The man smiled and held out his hand again.

"Oh? And why would you do that?" asked Rance, instinctively shaking the hand for a second time.

"For the censure of the Zionists. I'm told you were a champion of the letter, of the need to expose them. We are grateful. It is one of the reasons we returned. An important symbol of trust."

"Well," said Rance. "What happened was . . . was . . ."

"Pardon me, Mr. Pine," the man said. "I must go. But perhaps we could pick this up later? Perhaps we could meet somewhere more discreet, away from all this . . . finery? I'm sure we could have many things to discuss."

Well, thought Rance five minutes later, fingering Walid Zafir's card in his trouser pocket. Alone again, he'd picked up another champagne flute and debated whether he should send a report of the encounter with the Iranian back to Langley. Normally he would. But maybe he shouldn't. Maybe he should think about doing things differently for a change.

Zafir seemed like an approach from someone in Iranian MOIS. It seemed to Rance that whoever the man really was, he was looking to set up a back-channel relationship among senior spies. That's what that invitation to talk had been all about, Rance was sure.

That had never happened with the Iranians before. *Imagine the pos-*

siblities! he thought, his face warm from the bubbling wine. He'd have his own back-channel source, special grounded insight into Iranian intentions. That could make him a star in front of the director . . . and Hopkins. And it would all flow through him.

On impulse, Rance turned to look toward Hopkins. The chief of mission was alone now, looking at his phone. The Koreans had cleared off. But the Japanese delegation now had Hopkins in sight.

Rance had a small window to head off the Japanese. Fresh with the notion of his improving prospects, he made his move.

CHAPTER 25

JOHN DALE WANDERED INTO THE LITTLE THRIFT STORE CALLED TRAID just after nine-thirty in the morning, Greenwich Mean Time. He walked with a slight limp, his nearly empty backpack slung over one shoulder, banging the bell when the shop door snapped closed behind him.

"You need to leave it 'ere, luv," said the girl at the counter. Dale dutifully dropped the pack on the counter and shuffled down an aisle, fingering faded shirts on hangers in the otherwise empty London dump.

Jesus, thought Dale, rotating his torso, trying to shake the stiffness. The cramped middle seat's armrest in the back row of the transatlantic flight had dug into his sore rib for six straight hours. It had made him sit awkwardly, cramping his hip flexors. He raised a knee up and down, loosening up.

"All right there, luv?" asked the pierced, tattooed twenty-something at the till. She was leaning over the counter. The messy wad of jewelry around her neck banged on the glass.

"All good," said Dale, looking down at the shirts to avoid eye contact. He knew his British accent sucked, so he hadn't bothered. He kept his head down, hoping his stringy hair would obscure his face from whatever security cameras were lurking in the corners.

The tattooed clerk went back to reading a smudged paperback. Dale looped a few shirts over his forearm. He tried on a chambray overshirt, lightweight, but long enough to hide a weapon. He spotted another

T-shirt on the rack and was surprised at his own excitement. It was a souvenir from a Radiohead concert at Wembley in 2013.

Damn, he thought. *Keeper.* He threw the shirt over his arm.

"Hey," Dale said a few minutes later as she rung him up. "Is there a place around here where I can get some underwear?"

"Wut—you mean you don't want to buy them used knickers over there?" The bracelets jangled as she worked the register.

"Uh, no." His strategy was always to go native—but not *that* native.

"Tesco, luv. Just 'round the corner." To Dale, it sounded like she said *cawnuh*. She threw his four shirts in a plastic bag. He paid in cash.

He'd found long ago that it made more sense on an op like this to buy old clothes in the field. Instant authenticity, no luggage to be searched. But it always led to some shitty little rummage shop.

Outside, he stuffed his "new" clothes into his small backpack, then tossed the plastic bag and receipt in a public bin, shoving them deep. He looked up and down the street. All he needed now were a few minutes of alone time with his new burner phone and a decent bite to eat.

And a weapon. They were impossible to get in the UK, legally.

He saw a low-rent pub with a hundred sandwich pictures in the window. He walked toward it, trying to hide the limp.

After downing a sausage and using the bathroom, he passed an open kitchen door. A Slavic cook faced away, arranging plates under a heat lamp, barking at someone Dale couldn't see. Another kid was banging pots in a scullery, headphones on, tuned out from the world. No one noticed Dale.

With one quick movement, Dale snagged a sticking knife from a cutting board and shoved it up his sleeve. It was an eight-incher, blue rubber handle, double edged. It was illegal to buy a decent knife in the UK. This one was a rare find. *Lucky.*

Dale paid up, cash again, and stood on the sidewalk, firing up his phone. He was still feeling stiff, weighed down by the jet lag. He knew he couldn't allow that. He needed to get sharp. *Okay to be lucky*, he thought. *Not dumb.*

He fished a tin of Altoids from his backpack and snagged three pink Adderalls, swallowing them without water. He wasn't too proud of using those pills. But whatever, they were easy to get—and they worked. A mission was a mission.

Almost instantly perking up, he followed Google Maps to the closest tube station, descended the long steps, and stood on the platform. It was the middle of a weekday and foot traffic in this stop was light. He checked his phone again. Still no calls. Nothing from Meth.

Dale, you magnificent bastard, he thought.

Then he cursed himself. The Addies were kicking in. They tended to make *everything* seem easy.

Still. He couldn't help feeling good, proud that he'd eluded the people who'd been running him, freeing himself up. He guessed he had about a week or two before they figured out where he'd gone and started to demand his return. But surely by then, he thought, he'd be waltzing into CIA's London Station with Lieutenant Colonel Kasem Kahlidi in custody.

All would be forgiven.

Well, maybe not *all*, he corrected himself on the tube platform, thinking with drug-fueled clarity of the uptight FBI special agent. He could picture the agent's face, hear his voice.

He also thought of the blowback Meth would probably get for John going AWOL . . . again—especially after this latest cock-up in Beirut. They'd traded a quick message the day after he'd heard about her disastrous decision, the explosion, the injured Special Activities operators, the protesting Hezbollah mobs. She'd said she couldn't talk about it—but that she was okay.

No, Dale had thought, *she wasn't okay*. All hell was breaking loose in Beirut. Rioters were starting to blame CIA along with the Zionists. They were out for blood. Meth, Dale thought, needed to get the fuck out of there, whether she knew it or not.

And it wasn't lost on Dale that the only reason Meth was in Beirut was because *he* had led Mossad to the horse farm where Kahlidi escaped. He'd even failed to hang on to the asset during the raid. He'd done this to her. Time to make that right, he'd decided three nights ago.

That epiphany was when Dale had cooked up his little plan to simply fall through the cracks, free himself up to do something useful. He'd come round to thinking about it as Operation Crack Fall. Now, hopped up on Addies, he smiled again at the name, his own cleverness: *Crack Fall.*

Great fucking name.

Not just a great fucking name, he thought, but a great fucking plan. The way the Agency had set him up had almost *demanded* he pull off something like this.

For the past couple weeks, he'd been reporting into the FBI liaison office in Langley, driving Meredith's Volvo over from the Annapolis marina for an hour a day to answer questions for the special agent in charge, Lew Maddox.

Maddox . . . idiot, Dale thought now, stepping backward on the tube platform as a stream of silver subway cars squealed by on the inside track. *Maddox,* a class A douchebag if ever there was one. A dyed-in-the-wool G-man, the kind that bought suits at T.J. Maxx, shoes at an orthopedic shop, and flattops at Supercuts.

Dale wondered how long it would be until Maddox realized he'd been duped. Would the class A douchebag put two and two together? *Nah,* thought Dale, grinning. He'd found long ago that most people were absorbed in their own little worlds. Especially big-ego types like Maddox, whose world was very, very little. *Douchebag.*

Dale traced his finger down the Paddington line, then checked his phone again, ensuring he was headed to the right place. He felt a surge of positive energy, the effusion of his Adderall-adrenaline cocktail. Even his hip felt better.

Do NOT take these at home, he warned himself.

He turned again, waited for the train, his foot tapping feverishly. *No way,* he thought. Maddox wouldn't be thinking too much about Dale, simply because the cop didn't much like the CIA man. The FBI special agent had taken one look at Dale's retreating dark eyes, overgrown beard, stained T-shirt, and immediately classified the CIA man as shifty, unreliable . . . a scumbag spook, a professional liar. That was pretty much the opinion most FBI men had of low-level CIA case officers. But Maddox seemed especially wary of Dale. There was a raw negative vibe clanking between them. Dale could feel it.

It hadn't helped that Dale had griped about having to come into HQS by Uber, paying out of his own pocket. The overheated CI goons had confiscated Meredith's Volvo in the search for the Mossad leak. Dale had asked Maddox to provide him with a car if Dale was going to keep coming in. *Figure it out*, Maddox had said dismissively, barely moving his eyes from the monitor on his huge gray desk.

And that was when Operation Crack Fall had been born.

First, Dale had told Maddox that Dorsey was redirecting him to work on some new hush-hush initiative, highest national priority, couldn't even disclose the code word. On uneven ground, the G-man had simply nodded his big douchey head—clearly nervous to question an Agency he'd never understood.

Then Dale had left a message with Dorsey's office saying Maddox had released Dale from the FBI search team. "Special Agent Maddox is cutting me loose. He says I'm only getting in the way," Dale had said into Dorsey's overstuffed voice-mail box. And surprise, surprise—as one of the busiest men in the building, Dorsey hadn't bothered to respond.

But the coup de grâce, Dale thought now, almost laughing to himself as he watched his train slow, was the text to Meth. In that pseudo-Shakespearean verse of fifteen words, Dale had confirmed to his ex-wife that Dorsey had asked Dale to minimize contact with her—since they were still *very* nervous about having a Mossad mole in their midst. They'd even confiscated Meth's Volvo, Dale had added, truthfully. He knew she'd respect that.

Consequently, Dale and Meth had agreed they'd only send each other "keep alive" texts—a *1* for *all good*, a *2* for *find a way to talk*.

Now Dale looked at the time on his phone—it would be late afternoon in Beirut, so he sent Meth a text: *1?*

The reply came seconds later: *1*.

No smiley face, no little thumbs-up icon, no adornment at all. Just a *1*. But that was Meth in business mode. And it was all Dale needed to hear.

And the beauty of this, Dale thought as he stepped onto the train, relieved by Meth's quick status message, was that he was still—technically—an active case officer. At least until they finished processing his retirement paperwork.

And by dint of that simple *1*, Dale had just officially checked in with his boss. Meth was helping him without even realizing it.

Yeah, he thought. She'd get over the blowback. As soon as he nailed Kahlidi.

For Crack Fall, Dale had selected his EU/French passport with the Etienne Crochet legend. Years ago, when he'd been working European field ops, Dale had paid $15,000 for a one-bedroom cottage in central France. It didn't even have running water. But he'd always thought of it as his "oh-shit" escape hatch, just in case he needed someplace black to go. He'd never even told Meth about it.

Now he figured he'd finally get over to his French hide once he deposited Kahlidi back in the glossy new US embassy in Westminster—after Dale was done beating the living shit out of the double-crossing Quds man.

In the meantime, Etienne Crochet was a perfectly clean, perfectly solid alias, courtesy of the CIA legend factory. It was the best of both worlds. Dale wasn't persona non grata for once. And he didn't have anyone crawling up his ass at HQS. High speed, low drag. Without interference, he'd walk right into the US embassy with Kahlidi and nip this whole stupid problem in the bud. And then, Meth could get the hell out of Beirut.

But that also meant he had to deal with his own logistics—which always took a measure of creativity. If he was going to be bumping up against Hezbollah scumbags in his search for Kahlidi, he'd need a gun for his own safety. Having fallen through the cracks, he couldn't just wander into London Station and ask for a Glock. They'd check with Meth—and that would be that.

He'd have to figure that out. At least he had that nasty little sticking knife in his backpack now, wrapped in one of the crappy T-shirts from the rummage shop. Better than nothing, he thought.

Mind your own goddamned gap, he said inwardly in response to the PA, hyperalert to the passengers next to him as he exited the train at Paddington. Walking past the hissing train, he caught sight of his own reflection—hair long, beard crawling down his neck. He was all slopped up in his old chambray shirt, looking just as he'd hoped.

He spent twenty minutes checking out the area where Kasra Khani had been abducted. He stayed to the corners, careful to avoid notice. But he recognized the spot. He recognized the photos MI-5 had provided that showed her being bundled up by some Hezbollah scumbags and, in the background, the man Kasem said had been her ex-fiancé, Dr. Roger Gulrajani.

Maybe it was the drugs, he thought now, still surfing the warm waters of the Adderall wave, but the limp was almost nonexistent by the time he was passing the main gate at St. Mary's Hospital, having finished with Paddington. Dale skulked smoothly past the gate, keeping to the opposite curb, taking side-glances at the security guards that stood by the entrance. He checked his watch and slowed. He noted the people coming through the exit. They tended to have that unsmiling, glass-half-empty English look to them. Judging by the rush, Dale guessed that it was shift change.

Just in time, then. Perfect.

Dale found a gift shop across the street full of mylar get-well balloons, flowers, stuffed animals. He thumbed through a rack of gift cards, one eye on the street, watching people exit the gate. Dozens of people.

But Dale knew who to look for. In addition to the MI-5 surveillance photo of Kasra's abduction that he'd shared with Kahlidi at the safe house, Dale also had social media as a source. He'd seen a recent picture of the doctor on Instagram, another on LinkedIn. The Adderall brought it all into sharp focus for him. His mind could reproduce every detail of the headshot on the hospital staff website . . . *Roger Gulrajani, M.D., Trauma Specialist, E.R.*

And there you are, Doctor.

Gulrajani's shift had ended, according to Dale's call to the switchboard. And right on cue, there was the doctor walking through the gate, removing his lab coat, stuffing it into a messenger bag that lay across his torso. The doctor then put on sunglasses, ratcheted a ball cap down on his head, donned a surgical mask, and moved with the crowd.

With his backpack over his shoulders, Dale entered the flow of pedestrians on the cobblestones, staying a few feet behind the doctor. After a long shift, Gulrajani should be tired, anxious to get home, maybe grab a bite to eat, Dale thought. Hospital food the world over was atrocious—a universal truth, right?

Dale fell back to avoid detection.

After three blocks, Gulrajani reached Paddington Station. Worried he might lose the doc in the thickening crowd, Dale closed the distance and ducked into a newsstand. He watched Gulrajani wait on the platform.

He'd already noticed Gulrajani tended to look around, staying to the outskirts, in the shadows. He wasn't exactly a trained operator doing an SDR, but he was twitchy—and that seemed strange. With his hat low, dark glasses, mask over his mouth, the doc moved like a criminal, thought Dale. If an upscale one.

When Dale was sure the doctor was looking away, he came forward to take a spot on the tube platform, twenty feet down. A train pulled up. Dale and Gulrajani stepped on at the same time. Dale tried to maneuver himself so he could keep an eye on Gulrajani's hat, if nothing else. The CIA man stood near the door, leaning on a vertical rail, unsure where they'd be getting off. Soon the train was whining and screaming its way under busy London streets.

The doctor hopped off at Edgware Road. There, he hurried through the lunch crowd and threaded his way up the steps. Dale followed, staying laser focused on that black ball cap.

Soon they were walking down a residential side street, nearly empty in the midday commuting lull. Dale had noticed a few signs indicating the area was called Queensway. He remembered Kahlidi saying it was a neighborhood with a lot of Persians, so he wasn't surprised.

The street was crowded with three-story row houses—like Meth's brownstone in Dupont Circle, thought Dale. At the bottom of each row house was a black iron railing and steps down to a separate entrance, a basement apartment.

The doctor was slowing. Dale was worried he was nearing his residence. Time to move. He wanted to get to Gulrajani alone, someplace he couldn't just lock Dale out. So Dale hurried forward, quietly, approaching the doc from behind.

"Excuse me," Dale said when he was only a few feet away.

Gulrajani turned, startled. Dale instantly noticed the man's stance. Knees and arms bent, eyes wide. He seemed to be shifting his messenger bag across his chest.

"*Whoa*—" said Dale, showing both his hands as he approached. "I'm just looking for Kasra. I'm a friend." Dale attempted a smile, attempted to put the man at ease. "*Hal-e shoma chetore?*" he added in Farsi, thinking it would help.

Wrong.

On hearing Farsi, Gulrajani pulled something from a side pocket of the bag. Dale shot his hand forward by instinct, trying to grab the doc's wrist. Too late. The doc was already spraying.

"What the *fuck*!" Dale shouted as the pepper spray misted into his left eye, his cheek, his ear. By pure instinct Dale had raised and crossed his arms, blocking his face. But he still managed to throw out a leg to knock Gulrajani down, hooking him behind a knee, an old judo move. The doc stumbled backward, then recovered. He started running.

Dale ran after him, coughing, spitting, but making reasonable speed thanks to the drug fuel. After a bleary-eyed 100-meter dash, Dale tackled Gulrajani on the pavement, then threw him down five concrete steps to the entry to some other random basement apartment.

It was the middle of the day—Dale hoped no one would be home at the place. On the damp concrete at the door stoop, Dale leaned over the doc, eyes swollen, half shut. "*What the fuck's wrong with you?*" Dale shouted, coughing, spitting. "I just want to talk!"

The doc writhed sideways, trying to reach into his bag. The tears welled so fully in Dale's swollen eyes that it was like fighting under water.

Frustrated, Dale jammed the doc's head down on the doorstep. He jerked the messenger bag from around Gulrajani's shoulder, threw the flap back, and looked inside.

"*No!*" the doctor was shrieking, his face sideways on the concrete. The surgical mask had twisted halfway down his neck. "*Please, no!*" He started flailing in terror. With one hand still in the bag, Dale clapped his hand over Gulrajani's mouth, then slammed his head off the pavement again.

The doc's sunglasses fell off. Dale noticed the black eye then. Somebody had already beaten the crap out of this guy. Dale felt something hard and heavy in the bottom of the bag. His fingers touched cold metal.

Gun.

Dale pulled out the little Beretta. He noted the weight of the full mag. He shoved the gun in his belt.

"Jesus!" seethed Dale. "I just want to talk. What the fuck's wrong with you?"

"Don't hit me!" Gulrajani whimpered, shrinking, curling on his side, scrunched into a fetal. "I'm a *fedayee*! A loyal *pasdar*, like you! *Please!* I'll tell you anything you want!"

CHAPTER 26

WHEN THE PHONE HAD RUNG WITH THE DREADED SUMMONS BACK TO
Tehran, Major Siamak Azad of MOIS counterintelligence had assumed
he'd be going on a one-way trip.

The Zionists had attacked the high-profile relief convoy in Beirut's
dahiyeh, right under Siamak's nose. The Jews had hit the Laylaki missile
assembly building, which represented a complete and utter failure of
Siamak's mission, he thought.

And it wasn't just the Jews. There was no denying that CIA had
been involved too. The Lebanese intelligence service had had to rescue
three of the wounded American operatives who'd been down there—
another sign of Siamak's failure.

And, given the accuracy of the intelligence, Maloof had resumed his
careful accusations that Kahlidi must surely be out there somewhere,
feeding information to the Jews and Americans. A few of the higher-
ups in IRGC had begun to believe him. Which meant that the compass
arrow of blame was swinging ever closer to Siamak, for it was *his* job to
find Kahlidi too.

Take it like a man, Siamak had thought when the watch officer from
MOIS HQ had finally called.

That evening, with a knotted stomach, the MOIS major had arranged for a final quiet dinner with his wife and son in their tenth-floor
Beirut apartment. The boy hadn't taken to the hand-carved Syrian soldiers. He still preferred his *Star Wars* LEGO. But Siamak let the boy
play.

From the lofty perch of their apartment balcony, they enjoyed the Mediterranean sunset and knelt for the evening Maghrib prayer. Siamak held his family's hands as they knelt, clutching them in a way he'd never done before. And then the e-mail with the itinerary to Tehran had come to his secure in-box. As expected, it was a one-way ticket.

The Turkish Airlines flight had touched down at Tehran's Imam Khomeini International Airport in the gleaming dawn. Siamak hadn't even bothered to travel under a fake name on this trip. There'd be no point to that, he'd thought, since he wouldn't be going back.

He was therefore shocked when he saw Maloof enter with a waxen smile on his face.

"Well—are you going to keep standing there, Major? Or would you prefer to sit down?" The MOIS counterintelligence colonel grinned and waved an arm. "Stand at ease, boy. You're making me nervous. Come, sit at the table, here."

Wary, Siamak sat across from Maloof while the colonel lit a cigarette. His orderly, an IRGC sergeant, entered with a tea service and spread it between them. Thinking about poison, Siamak took a wary sip.

Maloof stoked the cigarette's end to a molten orange. "So," he said. "Bring me up to date on the Khani woman." Smoke hung over his desk like diesel exhaust.

"Since the doctor's visit, her health's improved," said Siamak, squinting against the fetid air. "The swelling in her leg is down. The safe house is holding. No chatter about her that we've heard. But no sign of Kahlidi either, unfortunately. If he is still out there somewhere, he must not be as concerned about her as we'd thought."

"Not surprising, I suppose. Kasem Kahlidi is rarely concerned about anyone . . . except Kasem Kahlidi. But you never know. And she's still a criminal. Can she travel soon? You think the police heat has died down enough to bring her back here?"

Siamak wasn't sure what to share. All this civility had confused him.

"I believe so," he began tentatively. "It should be safe to bring her back to Iran now. As long as we use a small airport in the UK—and a jet from a front company."

"Good." Maloof grinned. "Then it's time to go get her. I'm going to get you clearance for the jet. We need to get her back here, fast."

"That's . . . kind of you to assist, sir," Siamak said carefully.

"There was another *Taniyn* meeting in Damascus. With the Vienna negotiations back on track we think we're going to get a secure transit route into Lebanon for the warheads. The Supreme Council has asked us to look at targeting plans now. And with it all coming together, Brigadier Sharifi agrees with me that uncovering Kahlidi's spy ring should be our highest priority now," Maloof said, smoking.

So that's it, thought Siamak. The old fox has finally sold the new Quds leader on the concept that Kahlidi is the source of all counter-intelligence problems, a de facto acquittal of Maloof himself. But not an acquittal for Siamak, who was the one who'd yet to find Kahlidi.

"It may take a few days, maybe a week to get at Kahlidi's network," Maloof went on. "And—obviously—the need for secrecy is higher than ever. We don't know what other spies Kahlidi's recruited—and, of course, I'll want you to keep your Beirut surveillance up. But I do believe we may have his treachery boxed in now, Major."

"I'm . . . pleased to hear it, sir," Siamak said, watching Maloof's eyes.

Maloof put the cigarette back in his mouth, nodding, leaning back. "How *is* Beirut anyway? Any new incursions since the Zionist bombing? I've read the reports. But I'd like to know what you really *think*. Have you seen anything unusual? You can tell me."

Siamak kept his answer as close to his reports as possible, just in case. He explained that Nabil, his Beirut Hezbollah cell leader, had surged his men to look for potential spies up in West Beirut where the CIA case officers tended to operate. Nabil had young boys with cheap prepaid camera phones on nearly every street corner, watching, waiting. They had set up a half dozen picket points for surveillance around the American University of Beirut.

"And you're keeping their work separate from the rest of the Quds people at the embassy . . . as we've previously discussed?"

"Of course, sir, completely contained. No one knows about the search except me and my men."

"And—still no Kahlidi chatter on the radio nets between the Kurds and the Americans? Nothing?"

"No COMINT, sir. And I assess that the Kurdish suspects we picked up from the Farzad hit have given us everything we're going to get. Since then, the trail's gone cold."

Maloof nodded. "But you still think the Kurds could have been informed by Kahlidi." The colonel was smiling now, stirring more sugar into a fresh cup of tea.

Why smiling? "I don't think we should discount that possibility, sir," said Siamak.

"Precisely. Neither can the Russians." Maloof smiled again.

Siamak thought he understood now. The old man had lucked out, had wheedled something out of the Russians. The men at MOIS considered SVR information the intelligence coin of the realm, rarely shared, never questioned.

"At the Damascus *Taniyn* meeting I met with SVR's Middle Eastern section leader in Damascus," said Maloof. "A Colonel Niskorov. Brigadier Sharifi was there too. We were discussing *Taniyn* targeting options, among other things . . ."

Of course, thought Siamak. He knew the Russians were close to the Vienna deal. They were part of the multinational agreement. They also maintained the "bank" for supplies of Low Enriched Uranium, LEU, which was the *permitted* non-weapons-grade stockpile to be used in Iranian nuclear reactors. That was part of the deal too.

"It turns out that the brigadier worked with Colonel Niskorov in Aleppo, years ago when Quds and SVR were training a Syrian unit," said Maloof. "I believe, Major, that you were also stationed in Aleppo?"

"Yes, sir. But I was IRGC. Infantry."

Maloof grunted. "Well, you'll be very interested at what I learned from our Russian friends."

Siamak nodded, kept his face neutral.

Maloof smiled. "It's why I brought you back, Major. I had to tell you this face-to-face. This is sensitive, not to be discussed on the phone or in communications traffic, even over our encrypted circuit. And it has to be kept between the two of us. Us only."

"Of course, sir."

Siamak watched as the old potbellied colonel went behind his desk and rummaged through a document safe. He returned to the table and sat down in a heap.

"Colonel Niskorov was kind enough to give me this," said Maloof, opening the folder. The colonel chuckled hoarsely. "I asked the Russians to translate it for us; but, of course, they didn't have a Farsi-speaking clerk. We settled on English, believe it or not." He chuckled again.

Siamak looked at the file. It consisted of a few cardstock pages with color photographs and descriptions. He'd never seen an SVR dossier before. Maloof unclipped four of the stiff pages and spread them on the table.

"This man runs CIA's Counterproliferation center, the people vetting the nuclear deal for their government." Siamak saw several candid photos of the CIA man—walking on the street, eating at a European street café, talking on the phone. "His name is Rance. Edward Ronald Rance."

Siamak nodded, studying the blond-haired man in the dossier photo. He looked like a typical American businessman. Well-dressed, well-fed. He didn't really look the part of a spy to Siamak. But then he'd never really known any Americans.

"Rance," continued Maloof, "is currently in Vienna at the nuclear negotiations, posing as a diplomat. It seems that Niskorov has some history with him. They say this Rance is . . . vulnerable, made a mess of his career, fell for a Russian honeytrap. Niskorov thought he might be a target for blackmail. We'll see."

"Yes, sir."

"The brigadier already approved an initial approach at Rance, a friendly one from Colonel Walid Zafir, who's leading MOIS collection in Vienna."

Siamak studied the picture of Edward Rance and nodded cautiously—still unsure what this senior CIA man had to do with him.

"Now," said Maloof. "As much as I'd like to think we could turn someone in Vienna, I doubt we will. That would be too easy." The colonel put Rance's file back in the folder.

He spread two additional cardstock dossier pages on the table. "Instead, we need to focus on *these* two spies." The card at the top of the stack had John Dale's picture in the upper right corner. "Niskorov said that *this* is the man who entered Iran to exfil Rahimi out of Alut back in April."

Siamak nodded, taking in the picture of Dale. It looked like a surveillance photo from a crowded street. Somewhere in Asia—India?

"Now," continued Maloof. "This spy, John Richard Dale, is the one who slipped NAJA on the train from Turkey, killing an officer." NAJA was the Iranian National Police Force. The colonel clucked his tongue and shook his head. "And do you know who was supposed to have been leading the search for this man Dale?"

"No, sir."

"Our very own Lieutenant Colonel Kahlidi. But, of course, instead of apprehending Dale, Kahlidi disappeared right along with him. At Alut. And I can tell you, Major, that Kahlidi never shared any of this with me while he was here. He kept any knowledge of Dale a secret."

"That's . . . significant, sir," said Siamak. "A good lead."

"Yes. Dale was using the alias Reza Shariati, posing as an Iranian, as it notes there. He entered Iran via rail through Turkey." Maloof tapped the page. "But, unfortunately, the Russians don't have much else on him. We know now, however, that Dale was present during the April raid. Probably leading the exfil. He must have been Kahlidi's handler. You see?"

Siamak studied the photo. The CIA man looked Persian, a dark beard streaked with gray. But it was hard to see his face under the sunglasses and ball cap. "Kahlidi's handler . . ."

"Yes. Now," Maloof tapped the second card, "this woman, here, is John Richard Dale's wife. Her name is Meredith Morris-Dale. She's also a CIA spy and works for the man in Vienna, Edward Rance. According to SVR, *she* was the mastermind behind getting Rahimi out. Niskorov said *she* even killed one of his officers in coordinating the exfil. The Russians had this surveillance photo of her from an old operation in Dubai."

Siamak nodded. He looked at the surveillance photo of a fit, dark-haired woman leaving a taxi, a phone pressed to her head.

"Now, Major, think about this. The Americans have suddenly become more active in Beirut, buzzing drones around the *Taniyn* assembly sites in Laylaki. And here we have a file on the two very people that took Dr. Rahimi. Rahimi knew nothing about *Taniyn*. So they're almost certainly getting this new intelligence from Kahlidi, who at least knew about the *Taniyn* warhead, if not the latest target proposals."

"Yes, sir."

"You see?" Maloof tapped the table. "We find Mr. and Mrs. Dale, we find Kahlidi. He's not with the Kurds. He's with these *Americans*."

Aware of self-incrimination, Siamak merely blinked.

"And now for the best part," said Maloof, exposing a wide span of eroded, yellowed teeth. "I initiated a facial-recognition search with the Hezbollah Port Police, just to see if the Dales were involved in the last Zionist bombing in the *dahiyeh* in Beirut. And guess what? I got a *positive hit* on a French passport at the Beirut airport."

Siamak tapped the card. "You're saying this man, John Dale, is in Beirut?"

"No," said Maloof, grinning widely, his finger tapping on Meredith's photo. "His *wife* is."

CHAPTER 27

THIS TIME, THERE'D BEEN NO WINE SERVED WHEN THE SPECIAL INTELligence committee gathered along the Sea of Galilee. Nor had there been a helicopter. Instead, to maintain secrecy, Mitz, Galin, and Maya had each driven the 150 kilometers from Tel Aviv separately, taking their personal cars on that Friday morning, the first day of an otherwise glorious Israeli summer weekend.

"Listen, Werner," Mitz said as they walked along the vineyard path, "you know we're all sick about . . . sick about . . ." The Junction leader's voice died off. After the enormous political outcry from the horrific attack on the convoy fuel trucks—including the damning Hezbollah capture of a burned Sparrow *katsa*—Werner had avoided going into Tel Aviv. He was, rather, working on the irrigation system in his vineyard when they'd arrived.

The Caesarea boss waved them through and closed the gate behind Mitz with a length of wire.

"It's all right, Mitz," Werner said on the other side of the gate as sprinklers clicked away behind him. "There will always be a natural conflict between politics and intelligence. I propose we stay focused on the latter." The Caesarea boss removed his straw hat. He brushed the sweat from his reddened forehead, then put the hat back on his head. "It's hotter than *sheol* out here. Let's go in. Rachel left a cold platter for us up at the house, in case you haven't eaten." He attempted a small smile. "And if I haven't mentioned it yet, thank you for visiting me here in my pariah kingdom. *Toda, toda*."

They walked on in silence to the one-story home, seeing but not enjoying the view of the Sea of Galilee, just down the hill from the vineyards, shimmering under a pellucid sky. The visitors had assumed this would be their final meeting. Each tended to their own funereal thoughts.

Finally, pausing at the driveway gate a few meters shy of the house, Werner stopped to let them pass. Maya came through last. Werner shut the metal gate with a rusty squeak.

"Look," Werner said, addressing the three of them. "Before we go in for our formal meeting, I have something I want to say to you all."

He had their attention now. They stopped on the stony path and turned toward him.

He knew they'd been waiting for him to say something. The popular backlash against the Israeli security establishment for the horrific bombing on the aid convoy in Beirut had been swift and devastating. It had sucked even formerly sympathetic politicians into a shared condemnation of Mossad's overreach. Werner's thought had been to address it head-on, outside, in the hot sun's glare, so they could see he was not deterred.

"I know it feels like we're finished," he began, stating the obvious. "I realize we have perhaps moved back a step, that we're all under political scrutiny now."

The old man paused. The wind rattled the leaves on the nearby arbor while sprinklers clicked. "But hear me on this," said Werner. "I offered my resignation yesterday. And I need you all to know—the director didn't accept it. Nor did the prime minister. Not yet anyway." Werner looked up at them from under the brim of his hat, waiting to hear what they'd say, looking, for once, like he was a little nervous.

"Good," said Galin.

"Absolutely," said Mitz.

Werner carefully eyed each of them in turn, still peeking from beneath the hat. "Well. I guess we'll see if it's good. I'm a target for the Knesset now. The weaker members will make a career of coming after me. You may yet come to regret having me around. You know that, of course."

"Nonsense," said Mitz.

"Crazy," said Galin.

Werner nodded. He glanced briefly at Maya, who had yet to say anything. Then he raised his head and fanned himself with his hat. "Well. Since I'm still here, still leading Caesarea, then this committee still operates."

"Amen," said Mitz.

"And I need it to develop a new op, something that can get us *real* intelligence. Last night we picked up a mention of *Taniyn* from a Hezbollah man who'd been at a meeting in Damascus. We assess it to have been some sort of operational planning meeting. It seems that whatever *Taniyn* really is, they may be preparing to use it again. It could be another test launch or it could be something else. But given the state of things, we need to understand what they're doing. We simply *must* go on with aggressive operations. As before. Even bolder, before it's too late."

"Hear, hear," said Galin.

"Without a doubt," said Mitz.

"Thank you, gentlemen," said Werner with a nod to each of them, still fanning himself. "That is all I really wanted to say before we head in. That we continue with our work. That we go on as before. That we're not finished. There is still much work to do and we must get creative. But first, come in, come in. Eat, eat." He pulled his hat onto his bald head and waved them toward the shade of the arbor, the patio.

"Hold on," Maya finally said, standing on the flagstones, one hand affixed to her hip, a leg cocked forward. "What do you mean we go on as before?"

"Was I not clear, Maya?"

"Not entirely, no. What do you mean we need to be *bolder*?" Mitz and Galin turned uncertainly to look at her.

A hot gust of wind ruffled Maya's blouse. She stayed very still, refusing to acknowledge it. "What do you *mean*, Werner?" she repeated. "How can you say we will go on as though nothing has changed? How can that be?"

Werner stopped and turned. He removed his hat, turned it in his hands, and seemed to study its straw weave. "What, exactly, is confusing, my dear? I *meant* just what I *said*. We're not dissolving the special intelligence committee. We haven't solved what we set out to do—stopping the Iranian nuclear program and, by extension, Hezbollah. This *Taniyn* represents a clear and present danger. Of course we have to keep operating."

"But surely we need to change the *nature* of how we're operating. Our active raids have done more harm than good. Even *you* must see that."

Werner's shaking head remained bowed toward the hat in his hands. After a few seconds, he raised his wrinkled eyes toward her. "Maya. Don't be naïve. You heard what Galin said on the walk up here from the field. Any of the SA-5 sites across the Beqaa could handle a modified *Taniyn* variant. And since the Sparrow strike in the *dahiyeh*, things are escalating quickly now. Who knows what that Damascus planning meeting was about? I certainly don't. And that's on us. We *should* know. That's why this committee will go on as before, with active covert intelligence operations. Now more than ever, as they say, my dear."

Mitz and Galin turned toward the patio. Maya stayed where she was, blocking Werner. Her cocked leg hadn't moved. "But *we're* the ones that caused the escalation," she said. "We don't even look at our mistakes? We just go on like nothing happened at all? Like we were right all along? Shouldn't we try to learn? To adjust our tactics?"

"What's to learn, my dear? We did nothing wrong." Werner's face had grown pink.

"Nothing *wrong*?" Her voice had risen in volume, if not octave.

The Caesarea leader concentrated on the hat brim that he twisted in his thick hands. The other two spy bosses were looking uncomfortably away. "Look, Maya," said Werner. "Sometimes . . . in the heat of battle, you have to take your shots. And sometimes . . . you miss. But you still shoot. It doesn't make it wrong. The cost of a miss can be—"

"You *don't* always shoot," she interrupted loudly. "I've never confused good aim with good judgment. There was a time when you didn't either."

Werner recognized the look in her eye, her stance. He turned fully to face her, still holding the hat before him. "Maya—a warrior can't hesitate, can't wallow."

"Is that what you think I'm doing, Werner? Wallowing?"

"No—I didn't mean it like that. I'm just saying—I'm a bomb dropper, a trigger puller, a *warrior*. And this is *war*. I don't regret the shots I've taken. I regret the ones I haven't."

"Even after what's happened? You don't regret *any* of those shots?"

"No. On balance, I'd do everything I've done to this point all over again." He turned toward the house, took a step. "Come, my dear."

But Maya hadn't moved, still blocking him. "Do it *again*?" she said. "*All* of it, Werner? Really? Even that disastrous declaration of war you made on the American CIA?"

"Yes," said Werner, meeting her eye. "The Americans happen to be against us this time. I'll acknowledge that we're usually on the same side. This time we aren't. And this time, it's war. So no. I don't regret a thing."

"I'm surprised to hear that," she said. "I, for one, happen to agree with the people in Rabin Square who marched last night in protest of our bombing, who say we're walking ourselves into the next war. I went there myself. I marched *with* them."

"That's good," said Werner. "You *should* do that. They're your countrymen—and you protect them. I only ask that you never confuse the popular cause of the day with real morality, with the founding of who we are as a *people*. Have you forgotten that? We," he rotated his finger in a circle, "can *never* afford to do that. We do God's work."

"*That's right*," said Maya, the breeze ruffling her dark hair. "But don't we all do that? *Allahu Akbar. Salaam alaikum.*"

"And *habah l'hargecha hashkem l'hargo*," Werner snapped rapidly, a fire lighting in his eye.

"*What?*" she said.

"That's from a Talmud tractate. I bet you know the one, Mitz."

Maya turned toward the shimmering waters of the Galilee, then back at him. "What are you even *talking* about?"

"How 'bout it, Mitz?" asked Werner. "You know that tractate? You've studied the Talmud more than any of us. You want to enlighten her?"

"Well . . . ," the Junction boss said. "As it happens, yes, I do know it. Sanhedrin seventy-two. 'When a man comes to kill you, rise and kill him first.' It's also in Deuteronomy, by the way. But . . . now I'm just showing off." He attempted a weak smile at Maya.

But Maya hadn't looked at Mitz. She remained staring at Werner, her face rigid.

"'When a man comes to kill you, *rise and kill him first*,'" Werner repeated archly. "And make no mistake about it. They're coming to kill *us*, my dear. And *we* are going to follow that tractate. *We* are going to rise and kill them . . . *first*." He threw the hat back on his head.

"And what about the fifth commandment, then?" said Maya, her jaw set, her hair moving in the warm wind. "*Thou shalt not kill.* How do you square that contradiction, Werner, since you've embraced Talmudic teachings so thoroughly now in your old age?"

"Old age." He laughed, rolling his eyes at Mitz and Galin. "You see how they turn on us?"

"Tell me," Maya said, her head thrust forward on her neck. She took an uneven breath. Mitz and Galin had both taken a step back from her. The sun, the breeze, the unwavering gleam in her eye had molded her into a creature of devastating beauty and power. "Tell me how you square that, Werner. I want to understand."

Werner licked his lips and glanced down at the flagstones. After three or four seconds he looked up, squinting against the mirrored shine of the lake. "You know, Maya, I think it's pretty simple."

"Enlighten me, then."

"Because God teaches us that life is sacred, as you note, in that fifth commandment. But to destroy an *anti-life* is to preserve another sacred one, is it not? *They*—" he pointed to the east, across the Sea of Galilee, "are the anti-life. And *they* are coming to kill us. All of us. That's what their hypersonic dragon, their *Taniyn*, is meant to do. And because of *them*, we're not violating the fifth commandment, Maya. We're affirming it. And if they're going to act at hypersonic speed, then so are we."

"Your latest action proved nothing, except to provoke them to use it. We still don't know if *Taniyn* is nuclear."

"We know enough. We know it can penetrate every defense we have. And the nuclear threat is too high to discount. We know they're up to something. Right now. You've seen the communications intercepts about the high-level meetings in Damascus. The Russians, the Syrians, Quds."

"There's a big gap between information and intelligence."

"That's true. And whose fault is it that we have a gap between the two?"

Mine, she thought—for failing to recruit Dale in the first place, failing to get Kahlidi. She took another uneven breath.

Werner sensed the opening. He charged through it. "We still have our orders, my dear. They may not be popular with the marchers in Rabin Square. But we're still here. And we're the ones who do what the politicians *need* but can't say they *want*. And if done right, no one will ever know we were there. If anything, this time, we'll—*Maya!*" he called to her as she rushed past him, through the gate. She was headed toward the driveway, toward her parked car.

"Where the hell are you going?" Werner shouted through hands cupped around his mouth. "We have more work to do!"

"Oh yeah?" she shouted back at him, pivoting on a heel without slowing her pace. "Then you can do it without me. I'm *out*!" She marched to her car without looking back again.

Werner watched as she got behind the wheel, slammed her car door shut, and started the engine.

Mitz put a hand on Werner's shoulder, slowly shaking his head.

Together, the two men watched the cloud of dust fly sideways as the car drove off. "That's that red-hot half-Lebanese blood of hers, you know. But she's still family. She'll be back."

"Of course, of course," said Werner, irritably shaking off Mitz's hand. "She's probably going back to Tel Aviv to be with Dil and Rachel right now. Just as well. Maya's in no shape to help us with this meeting today."

"Agreed. I'd say it's even fortuitous that she left," said Mitz after the car's noise had died off.

"What?" asked Werner, turning. "Why?"

"You said Maya had some kind of relationship with the American we targeted for recruitment—John Dale. Right?"

"Of course. It's why I sent her. She failed."

"But you'd still like to get at Dale, I assume."

"I want to get at Kahlidi. Dale is Kahlidi's handler, that's all."

"Yes. And what about Dale's wife? She was here, with Dorsey. They met with the director. She must be all over Kahlidi."

Werner knuckled his head. "Yes. We think she runs the program they call Atlas. And whatever that program is, they're denying us the intelligence take because they want the deal with the Iranians. Or Kahlidi is simply lying to them."

"And you said Maya may have failed in getting intel out of Dale . . . maybe because she's a little too soft on the man. Maybe a relationship beyond the professional."

"Maybe. But it's water under the bridge. What are you getting at?"

"I think it's better that Maya not hear what I have for you on Dale, that's all. Maybe it's good she's off the op. Her judgment might be compromised for what I have to tell you." Mitz raised an eyebrow and looked at Werner significantly.

Galin had been standing out of earshot, respectfully letting the two men speak privately. Now Werner called to Galin and told him to go inside the house.

When alone, Mitz leaned into Werner's ear. "This morning I got a Lexicon hit on the flagged passports of both John Dale and his wife,

Meredith. They're traveling under nonofficial covers, illegals, unprotected by diplomatic status. They're traveling separately."

Werner stared at him.

"Which means," said Mitz, "that if you want, you can take another shot at them."

CHAPTER 28

ON THE TENTH FLOOR OF HER BEIRUT BUDGET HOTEL, MEREDITH TRIED to face the lunch that sat on her hotel room desk. Her knees scooted below it, she was sitting in a rolling chair, sucking on a warm bottle of water, looking at the wrapped Quest bar with disdain. *Cookies and Cream.*

She guessed she'd eaten fifteen of them over the past few days. The only upside to this diet was that the bars had become aversion therapy to actual cookies. Having lost her appetite, she shoved the execrable thing aside.

But it wasn't just the food. It was this miserable, low-budget room with its relentlessly unforgiving fluorescent light and its cheap, scratchy sheets. Who'd have ever guessed, she'd said to herself more than once, that her cover, the romantic French journalist Margot Henri, should have to endure such banalities?

Though she'd had the shades drawn, she'd grown sick of the bright white lights. She walked to the window, parted the curtains an inch, and looked down to the street at the happily striped café umbrellas. She was *dying* to try that café—but she wasn't sure it was worth the risk. But, she reasoned, shouldn't Margot Henri be allowed the occasional luxury?

After gifting herself ten seconds of self-pity, she got her head back in the game.

She rolled the chair back under the desk and caught her own eye in the mirror. She thought she looked a little pale—but then, who wouldn't? The lighting was awful. Besides, it wasn't a beauty contest. She propped up the Surface tablet, went through the voodoo of gestures to unlock its capabilities, and opened the secure videoconference system back to Langley.

In the app's self-view box on the lower right, she saw her own face, washed out in the fluorescence. Her Glock was on the desk next to the table, never out of arm's reach. Behind her she could see her unmade bed. On John's advice about how to survive as a NOC, Meredith had dragged the bedding into the closet to sleep, just in case there might be a security breach.

Doing office-level videoconference meetings was not something typically allowed of case officers in the field. But Meredith was not a typical case officer. She had an NIE to complete. And she was on a NOC assignment. This entire op had required her to make her own rules along the way.

But admittedly, it would have been much easier to do this videoconference from the embassy SCIF. She'd avoided it because she didn't much like the looks she'd been getting over there.

Gone were Cowles's folksy stories about tennis and surfing. The station chief was clearly dissing Meredith now, ensuring the ambassador understood that Cowles was *not* on the same page as the visiting department head from HQS who'd pushed for the disastrous convoy surveillance op that nearly scotched the all-important Iran-Vienna-nuke deal.

As for the ambassador herself, Meredith had hoped the two of them could make common cause. After all, were they not two senior women cast adrift on the Testosterone Sea? Shouldn't they be on the same team?

Apparently not. Marlene Hendricks had formally complained to her boss about Meredith. Then she'd riled up a State Department diplomat, a chief of mission in Vienna named Hopkins, who'd complained to SecState himself.

Well, Meredith had thought while getting the beatdown from Rance. *At least they all know who you are now . . .*

Now she cleared her throat and sipped more water. A small hourglass in the videoconferencing app told her the other two attendees for the conference—Rance and Dorsey—had yet to sign in. Meredith tapped her fingers, checking her makeup again in the self-view camera. *Maybe*, she thought, *John was right. Maybe I should just quit, resign, whatever it is they would call it when you're only forty-effing-four years old.*

As though on cue, Meredith's secure cell phone buzzed. She looked at it. It was a message from John—his usual daily check-in on her status. The message was his regular coded question: *1?*

Meredith wondered how to respond to him. Yes, she thought, physically she was fine, a 1. *But spiritually I'm a . . .*

Another message came in on top of John's before she could finish the thought. This one was from her boss. *Prior meeting running late. Need 15 minutes. Stand by. Rance.*

Meredith acknowledged Rance, then considered how to answer John. Finally she sent: *1 . . . U?*

X, he sent back immediately.

X? she thought. Was that a kiss? She felt slightly better. But then John sent a second message, a few seconds later. *Butt-dial, sorry. 1* ☺

Goddamned John.

"Hey, Meredith, we can see you, but we can't hear you," said Rance, his voice tinny through the speaker. She threw her cell phone down and faced the tiny web camera on her tablet.

"Sorry," she said, "I was on mute. Give me one second while I come up with a little more audio concealment."

She went into the bathroom and threw the shower on. Then, after checking the dead bolt for the fiftieth time, she attached her earbuds. "Okay," she said. "Sorry about that. I'm ready."

"You're not in the embassy," said Dorsey. Rance and Dorsey were split-screened in front of her. Both men wore suits and ties. It was very early morning in Langley, about ten in Vienna. "You sure you're secure?"

"Yes, I'm sorry about that, gentlemen. But my circuit's showing end-to-end green—secure radio patch set up to Beirut Station. I know you said it was urgent that the three of us talk, so the hotel room was my best option."

"All right," said Dorsey. "Got it. Before we get going—anything new from your end, Meredith? I may as well hear it from you live, rather than wait for another cable."

"Not much new, no, sir. I've asked all the case officers here to report in any suspected Mossad contacts that their agents might be getting with associations to *Taniyn*. I'm culling through their agent lists too, seeing if Cowles's people have anyone in Lebanese government who might tip me to some smuggling routes. I might poke around with some interviews myself, going with my journalist cover."

"So your cover's holding, I take it?" asked Dorsey.

"Until the end of the week when my visa dries up, yes."

"Okay. What about Mossad? Anything new I should be worrying about?"

"We've been watching known Mossad agent behavior. Nothing significant to report. But I'm sure they have spies everywhere. I can't imagine we're seeing everything."

"As long as they're not doing offensive ops. We really don't need that screwing the Iran deal up again," said Dorsey. "Tip me if you see anything."

"Will do. But Jeff, while I have you—if I'm going to finish up the NIE, I should really get a NEST team in here for radiological monitoring on the *Taniyn* warhead possibilities. I'm still worried we're—"

Dorsey waved her away. "No," he said. "Forget the NIE. You've done enough. The official assessment on *Taniyn* can't wait any longer now that the Iranians have come back to the negotiating table. And you've got too much on your plate."

Meredith winced. *Too much on my plate?*

Dorsey continued. "So, *ah*, Meredith, I'm going to pass the NIE vetting back to the Iran desk for completion. We're going to call that *Taniyn* missile a poor man's hypersonic experiment designed for anti-ship warfare, since we have no new intel. That's no reflection on you, you understand. In fact, you've . . ."

As Dorsey went on with all the reasons that the NIE-firing was no reflection on her, Meredith froze every muscle in her face, absorbing the blows, secretly checking her own eyes in the self-view camera to make sure she showed nothing.

"But thanks for everything you've done up to this point," Dorsey finished, inadequately, his pallor nearly as wan as hers. "You know how much I appreciate it."

Meredith mumbled the most gracious reply she could muster. But as the hollow syllables slid off her tongue, she wondered why she was bothering. No officer ever fumbled an NIE on the five-yard line and survived. And that was on top of her losing Kahlidi, who was the original reason she'd been given the highly coveted role. So this was it. The end. Kaput. At forty-effing-four years old. Now what?

"Well . . . now that we have that cleared up," Rance said brightly, as though Meredith's most ardent dreams hadn't just burned to the ground. "Jeff and I have to bring you up to speed on the Mossad CI investigation. We just got the debrief from the counterintel folks on the Mossad leak. It's why we were late. There's something in here you need to hear. Okay?"

"Yes," she said, her face locked in a mask of indifference. "Of course. Glad they're finally done. Just realize I need to go soon. I'd like to get back over to the embassy. Like I said—I'm still hoping to pull that smuggling thread to look for potential warhead routes. Even if not for the NIE, the case officers here think I could help. We might still get to the bottom of *Taniyn*."

"Okay. Understood. I'll keep the CI findings quick," said Rance. "Let's start with what I think you already know about the Mossad incursion—starting with your car. The CI technical team found a passive audio enhancer on the windscreen of your Volvo."

"Yes. I know about that," she said despondently. "But like I told the CIs, I don't think I had any Mossad- or Atlas-related conversations in there. Or if I did, they were minimal. I try to stay quiet when driving."

"Good," said Rance. "And . . . we also wanted you to know that the CI team went over your house very carefully. It came up clean. So— we're thinking the take they had from you is non-material."

Meredith cringed inwardly. She was picturing the CI snoops combing through her underwear drawer. But what did it matter now? "All right, good," she said, anxious to get off the call, planning a vicious attack on the mini-fridge bar. "Glad to hear it."

"But this next bit," said Dorsey, seeming to pause, "may come as a bit of a shock."

"Okay . . ." Meredith tightened her abdomen, waiting. How could this possibly get worse?

"Let me start by saying, Meredith, that you know how these things go," said Dorsey, his face even whiter than before. "The CI spooks have to go through everything you've done, look at all the places you've been. It's very invasive. We all hate it—if it's any comfort."

She could see her own eyebrows contracting down in the self-view. She forced them back up.

"Anyway," said Rance, resuming. "CI took our known Mossad case files and looked for any possible ports of entry into the US."

"Makes sense they'd start there," she said.

"Uh-huh. And then the CIs compare matches to places we've all been, looking for overlaps. That kind of analysis."

"Of course," she said.

"Well, we did a passport facial search on our known Mossad operatives. Naturally, a bunch of them popped up in DC. We know they come in and out of the embassy. Werner's whole entourage, for example. CI is following up on all of them—as you'd expect."

"Okay, yes, sure."

"But one of the Mossad file faces popped up as entering the US through Honolulu under an alias. The ticket then connected to Maui. And . . . since CI knew you and John were in Maui, they dug further into this suspect passport."

Oh dear God, she thought. *Am I going to have to tell them about our Maui fight too?* She held her face very still. "All right . . ."

"Now, the CI officers reported that you flew out of Maui on the thirteenth. That makes sense. That's when I called you back," said Rance. "You were in Langley the next day, right?"

"Right."

"But, *ah*, John stayed on in Maui for a while. So the CIs followed up on him too. And, as it turns out . . . he stayed on in Maui for another few days after you'd left . . . out in that town on the tip of the island, Hana. Were you aware of that?"

"Not really," she said. "I . . . I don't really keep tabs on him like that . . . as I'm sure you understand." They both nodded. She shifted in her chair. "Look, gentlemen, John and I had a big fight in Maui. I'd hoped we might reconcile, but in the end, after our fight, John took off. I don't even know where he went. And I never asked, since that would just piss him off. Nor did he volunteer it. That's how he is. And that's the whole story. Just what are you getting at?"

"Just that John stayed behind after you left. And a day after John left, the Mossad people left too. Their timelines sync up. You see?"

"I see, but so what? Mossad went there to follow *me*, missed *me*, and then kept on following John, since I left. It doesn't really mean anything. That's probably what our case officers would do too, right?"

"Well," said Rance after a brief pause. "There's something else. One of the Mossad operatives in Hawaii happened to be someone John worked with on a prior op. So . . . there's at least a connection there."

"Yeah," said Dorsey, finishing. "The optics are that John was with a Mossad operative he *knows*, in Hawaii . . . and then, just a few weeks later, Mossad does this raid on Kahlidi—while John's there, at the safe house. And Kahlidi escapes. You can . . . well . . . you can see how this looks."

"I can see how it *looks*, Jeff. But like I said before, *I* was the one who wanted John to go to the safe house. I *begged* him to go. He didn't want to do it. He's not our Mossad mole."

"Yes, well, however it works, Meredith, *you* told John where Kahlidi was. And Mossad showed up while he was on his visit. We can't exactly ignore that connection."

She shook her head. "Okay, fine. It's a coincidence, I get it. But who is this operative John knew? What's his name? Maybe there's another coincidence there."

"Not a *he*," Dorsey said, looking down. Even the bald spot at his crown was pale.

"Let me share my screen so you can see her," said Rance. The image on Meredith's surface changed to an enlarged passport photo. "Here, that's her. Her name's Maya Shaheen. She's a Mossad *kidon*, a fairly senior one, very close to Werner himself."

Meredith's heart stopped as she stared into the eyes of the woman. *Goddamned John.*

"*Oui*," Meredith said to the French-Lebanese waiter exactly two hours later. "*Apportez-moi la bouteille entière de vin.*"

Screw it, she thought as the man went through the swinging door, hurrying away from her sidewalk table. Margot Henri, her debonair journalist alias, would *certainly* get to drink from the whole bottle of French burgundy. She *certainly* wouldn't just sit in her room eating protein bars. Especially if the Frenchwoman had just learned that her husband was a lying, cheating scumbag. And that her career was over.

Meredith raised the glass, drinking it to the bottom.

By the time she'd polished off her full plate of coq au vin—sufficiently enhanced with an entire bottle of *vin*—her senses were at least dulled.

She dug through her purse and left a huge stack of Lebanese pounds by her plate. She scraped her sidewalk chair back with an effort. Once standing, she kept a steadying hand on the table for a few seconds. She picked up her heavy handbag and the reassuring weight of the Glock. Then she got on her way back across the street, back to the miserable hotel room and the partially made bed.

Her eyes fixed on the hotel door, concentrating hard so as not to stumble, Meredith never saw the young man in the black polo shirt, watching her from behind the wheel of an '88 Volkswagen Scirocco.

PART THREE

AIM

CHAPTER 29

Six years earlier

THERE WAS JUST NO MISTAKING THE SOUND OF TACTICAL JET NOISE, Dale thought. The son of an aviator, he'd grown up in Oak Harbor, Washington, just outside the gates of Naval Air Station Whidbey Island. Back there, back then, they'd called it *the sound of freedom.* But here, now, in Syria's Mozelan creek valley, he suspected he should give it another name.

It had first rolled in like distant summer thunder, a far-off desert squall. For about ten seconds, he'd clung to the hope that it was just weather. But closer now, there was no mistaking that rising roar, bouncing off shallow canyon walls like the growl of an irascible god.

Fuck, Dale thought, running through the possibilities as he lay in his sleeping bag. American air support wouldn't venture this far west into Syria. The whole point of this op, Timber Sycamore, had been to fight Assad's Syrian Arab Army without directly implicating the US. That meant no friendly air. So, he wondered, whose jets were those roaring up the valley right now?

"*Athbut makanak!*" Dale cried over the rumbling echo, commanding the team to stay still. The sun had only just set on this cloudy day, already obscured by the slopes on either side of the creek. Dale's team had been about to break camp and set out for a road junction on the Riya Kengelo where they'd planned to ambush a tank platoon with Javelin missiles. But he'd ordered them to freeze now. They had good concealment in this narrow creek valley—as long as they stayed very still.

Turkish Air Force? he wondered, listening. Ever fearful of separatist rebels, the Turks would use just about any excuse to launch an attack on the Kurds. Dale pulled back just enough of the scratchy netting over his eyes. If TAF, then they'd be American-made F-16s. But these seemed too loud to be single-engine aircraft.

There, he thought a second later, turning his head ten degrees to look back toward the flat of the creek. *Gotcha.* Two dots on a south-westerly course, dim against the darkening sky, a blurry exhaust plume floating off behind them. Whatever they were, they'd be overflying his position in five, four, three, two . . .

"*Athbut makanak!*" Dale cried again, putting the netting back over his camo-painted face. Through the net, he watched the two planes roar overhead. Now he recognized the triangular sweep of the wings. Russians, SU-24 Fencers, racing below the overcast on burner, about 500 feet, two short blue flames sprouting out the tailpipes. Once they'd passed, Dale scrambled to his stomach and reached for his binoculars.

Fencers, he confirmed, staring through the big lenses. Bombers. *What the fuck?*

He studied the wing pylons. Each bird carried two sets of three bombs, outboard of the extra fuel tanks. *Not guided missiles. Cluster bombs.* That meant they were dropping on troops as opposed to a hardened target. He watched until the dark jets with the flickering blue flames disappeared over a western ridgeline.

Mustafah elbowed Dale. "Sahib," he said. Dale lowered the binos. The old rebel's eyes were starkly white against his black face paint. "Is safe to move, Sahib? Dark enough?"

The tough old Kurd, the only English speaker on the team, didn't even ask about the jets. Dale looked up at the purple sky above the canyon wall. He canted his head to listen. The jet noise had finally faded. "I need to call those in first," he said, waving toward the ridge. "But yeah. Get 'em up."

While the team stirred, Dale unfolded a small hexagonal antenna and aimed it to the south, aiming for the comms satellite.

"Alpha Bravo, this is Whiskey Six Actual," he said into the little handset, after the tracking light went green.

"Go, Whiskey Six," said an ethereal voice from the ops center in Jordan.

Wait till they get a load of this, thought Dale. If he had to bet, he'd say the roar of those Russian Fencers was the death knell for this op, Timber Sycamore. He spat out a summary of the enemy ground assault aircraft, estimating altitude, course, and speed. "Rapiers," he said, using the code word for Russian air. "Repeat, Rapiers, estimated course two-six-zero."

"Roger, Whiskey Six. Stand by." For five full minutes, the line stayed quiet. *That's it*, Dale was thinking as the time mounted. *Go ahead and pull that plug, boys . . .*

"Whiskey Six Actual, this is Alpha Bravo," the watch officer finally said into Dale's ear. "We want you to proceed point X-Ray for air evac to Charlie Papa. Extract, twenty-three-hundred Zulu. Your team proceeds to objective Cobalt without you. Your relief will join the team en route. Copy?"

Relief? thought Dale. The op was still on—but without him? Dale held the mic near his mouth for a moment, wondering if he could ask questions. Probably not, he thought.

"Copy all . . . ," said Dale. Mustafa was back at his side now, holding a marked-up terrain map. The team was loaded up for the hike over the hill. Dale looked into Mustafa's darkly lined face, wondering how to explain something he couldn't comprehend himself.

And it was Mustafa's face that was still on Dale's mind when the US Air Force C-130 finally touched down at King Hussein International in Jordan's southwestern corner some thirty-nine hours later. Exhausted, bearded, stinking, Dale was wondering whether his team had gone on with that tank assault at objective Cobalt. He was also wondering what on earth he was doing down here, 600 miles below his operating area.

Maybe it's not that weird, he'd been telling himself for the past droning hour in the cargo bay, *that I'm not the only one on this flight to Aqaba.* After all, the US Air Force had been flying crates of weapons in for the Syrian rebels. Those planes must surely head back empty somewhere. Maybe they just wanted Dale's advice on the next weapons load.

Or am I just going home?

That would be nice. Though he still had ten months on his tour, getting back to Virginia early would certainly be good for his marriage. That last conversation he'd had with Meth had been a real barn burner. She'd been going on and on about a fight with Grace, who'd been struggling to fit in with wealthy teenage-girl cliques in the new school district they'd carefully selected.

Dale had already checked on Grace, had already texted her his fatherly advice. But when he interrupted Meth's rapid recounting flow to share as much, his wife had taken it as a snub. He didn't understand, she'd accused, had oversimplified, countered her own parental guidance. How dare he. Dale hadn't been in the mood to be accused of anything. He'd let her know that—until she'd hung up on him.

Through the oval window now, he saw a Jordanian Air Force SUV speeding across the tarmac. As the truck got closer, he noticed a blond-haired civilian in the backseat. *Dear Lord, no,* Dale thought. *Rance.*

"Has Cerberus checked in since your last cable?" Rance asked when they were finally alone in a nondescript office in the air-ops building some fifteen minutes later.

"Not sure," said Dale. *Because I was eating snakes in the bush until a few hours ago.* "I can look now if you want." Dale withdrew the ruggedized covcom tablet from his backpack.

He was still wearing heavy twill cargo pants and desert combat boots. But he'd cleaned his face with water from his canteen on the plane. And Rance had supplied him with a new madras shirt so as not to panic the civilians in the air traffic control building.

Dale went through the sequence to get online, then checked the Google Drive file he used to communicate with Cerberus, the Iranian scientist embedded in a covert Iranian uranium enrichment lab. "Nothing new," he said, looking up from the tablet. "Sorry."

"Then we have no counterfactual," said Rance. "It's still our assessment that the Iranians are going to replace those Siemens controllers in Natanz. That's your official assessment?"

"That's what Cerberus said last time. And there's nothing new. So yes."

"And you still think they're expecting a delivery from the Pakis? Nothing new there either, I assume?"

"Correct. New Siemens controllers, new chips, new software. That's all I got. Same as what's in the cable."

"But do you really think Cerberus will be there to meet the Pakis for the pickup of the updated tech?"

"He's been close enough to the installation in the Tabriz pilot-lab that I think they'd want him there to verify the equipment. He indicated something to that effect but, as usual, kept it blurry. That's why I marked it as unverified in the cable—but probable. If I had to guess, I'd say Cerberus will be there. But I don't know for sure."

Rance nodded and reached for his phone. "Right. Close enough. Wait here." Left alone, Dale stood up and walked to a window. He squinted at the dusty sky, the blazing white tarmac, the peekaboo view of the flat Red Sea between the buildings.

"Pack your shit," Rance said when he came back a few minutes later. "We've got a meet to get to. I'll get you caught up on the way."

On the way turned out to be a ride in the same Jordanian Air Force SUV down a wide four-lane highway to the town of Aqaba. Since Dale and Rance had never clicked at small talk and since there was a foreign driver behind the wheel, they stayed silent. Far from getting caught up, Dale was left to wonder where the hell they were going.

The answer arrived in the form of the Moon Beach Hotel, a shabby little seaside tourist inn smack on the Gulf of Aqaba. But it didn't seem like the kind of place Rance would stay. *And that's because*, Dale thought a few seconds later, *Rance isn't staying here.* It was just a stop on the SDR, apparently.

Into the Moon Beach Hotel lobby and out a side exit, Rance led Dale to a nondescript Toyota Land Cruiser with dark windows on the far side of the parking lot. The Toyota's driver hopped out and opened the rear cargo door as Rance approached. The new man said nothing as Dale and Rance stowed their luggage and climbed into the backseat. Rance stayed quiet too, evidently thinking this kid wasn't cleared either. Or just to annoy Dale.

Dale looked the young driver over: short dark hair, smooth cheeks, black short-sleeved shirt, creased khakis. *Creased. Military. Ours?*

Whoever he was, the kid soon parked the Land Cruiser at a restaurant just outside a marina. Rance and Dale followed through a security gate, then down toward the docks. At the last berth, tucked just inside a sloshing breakwater, the kid waved them toward a yellow forty-one-foot Apache offshore speedboat with a blazing white interior and three massive outboards.

Well, Dale thought, as he helped the kid untie the lines. *Things are looking up* . . . He stood with the rope in his hands, squinting, almost smiling.

"Don't get too excited," Rance said from the boat, watching him. "You don't know where you're going yet." But even Rance allowed a grin when Dale finally hopped aboard.

Once the boat had slipped its moorings and passed the breakwater, the kid hammered the throttles down. The three hulking Evinrudes howled angrily. The driver propped himself with both hands on the helm while Rance and Dale held on to his left, watching the long, heaving bow break wave after wave. Still having no idea what was happening, Dale finally allowed himself to relax, smiling for real. Refreshing sea air inflated his cheeks.

But after another roaring minute, his lips compressed into a flat line. There, up ahead through the windscreen, he saw the angular mast of a gray warship in the offing. Ugly and black, it sprouted from the hazy horizon like a rising weed. *Oh fuck*, the former naval officer in Dale thought. He steadied himself with a tight grip on the chrome rail. Sea duty.

"Meet Mr. Werner," Rance said once they'd finally settled in the wardroom of the Israeli Navy corvette *Eilat*. Mr. Werner was in his mid- to late fifties, balding, short. His civilian polo shirt was tucked into his pants, old-man-military style. Dale had already noticed that the regular Israeli naval officers had been shooed away.

"Mr. Werner's team," Rance said, "has led the Mossad side of the code development for Stuxnet."

"Yes," the Mossad man said, rubbing his close-cropped hair with the knuckles of his right hand. "The joint Stux op has been one of our best collaborations ever. And, as I understand it, that's largely thanks to you, Mr. John." The older man held his hand over his heart and looked embarrassingly earnest for a moment. "On behalf of the nation of Israel, may I express our most heartfelt gratitude."

Dale nodded. His windburned face felt raw and hot.

"You must be wondering what the hell we're all doing here on this tin can," Mr. Werner added after an awkward pause. "But then I also understand you're a sailor. I should think you like being back at sea . . ."

"Well," said Dale, "I certainly liked the way I got here, since I—"

The door cracked. A woman stepped through. Dale stopped talking.

"Ah, there you are, my dear. Come in, come in." Mr. Werner's eyes darted between John and the woman. "Mr. John, meet Ms. Maya. She's from our Iran nuclear desk, one of the . . ."

Dale stood. He tried to listen to the rest of the introduction but lost the thread. His mind had already wandered into a secret appraisal: long brown legs, thick dark hair, wide Eastern eyes, halter top with bared brown shoulders. It was as though a mermaid had sprung from the dull gray bulkheads.

He shook her hand from across the table, suddenly aware of his own elbows. Sitting back down, he stole a glance at Rance to see if his boss knew she'd be here. But Rance was mumbling something incoherent by way of his own greeting, adrift in the same idiotic fog.

Mr. Werner then introduced another man, Yosef, who was from the Mossad science and tech group. Still stuck in the Maya haze, Dale barely noticed that Yosef had started the briefing. He was already rat-holing on uranium enrichment.

"With our alpha five-five capsule," Yosef was saying, "we've managed to slow down centrifuge speed from the necessary 100,000 RPMs to approximately 80,000."

Pay attention, Dale said to himself, forcing his eyes on the little science man.

"Our metallurgists are saying that at best, isotope separation and secondary cascade refinement will get them to twenty-three percent," continued Yosef. "Far short, of course, of what they'll need to create a fissile uranium disc. Now, as some of you know, our five-five digital capsule gives commands from the Windows PCs on the Iranian network to the Siemens controllers that manage the IR-2 cascades, spoofing the real speeds . . ."

As Yosef went on about Stuxnet, the computer virus they'd installed on the Iranian network, Dale noticed that Mr. Werner and the beautiful Ms. Maya nodded in sync.

Dale wondered at the nature of their relationship.

"Now," Yosef was saying, "the virus 'phones-home' whenever it penetrates one of the Windows machines in the lab. Since we've now got more than a hundred machines infected, we believe we're covering the majority of the cascades. Why, even yesterday, we received a phone-home on a new section . . ."

The S&T man droned on. Out of the corner of his eye, Dale stole another look at Maya. He hadn't seen an attractive woman in weeks. *Certainly not like . . . oh goddamnit.* She'd caught him looking. He faked a yawn and stretch.

". . . and so," Yosef was wrapping, "we thought we had it all solved. Until Langley shared your cable last week, Mr. John. And *that*, of course, was very unsettling to us."

Hearing his name brought Dale back to the present. The cable. The new Siemens controllers coming in from Pakistan as reported by Cerberus. Right.

But Yosef was starting up again, "You see, once they swap out the existing controllers for the new ones, we won't be able to manipulate centrifuge performance because we . . ." He continued with a lengthy technical explanation until Mr. Werner shut him down.

"Suffice to say," the elder Israeli said, holding up an imperious hand, "these new controllers are a disaster. Before, we had someone inside Baramar, the equipment reseller in Dubai. We had a way to design the malware. But now, based on what your man Cerberus is saying, we'll need to get these new motherboards with the customized chips directly from the Pakistanis. And it would be a lot easier if we got them *before* they were installed."

"Yes," added Yosef, nodding energetically. "Based on what we can see, the *only* thing holding up enrichment right now is our virus. As soon as they put the new Siemens controllers in—we lose it."

Rance, who'd been quiet for the past fifteen minutes, finally turned to Dale. "Mr. Werner, here, has some intel on how the transfer of the chips is going to go down. It gives us a rare opportunity to pull a swap. Since Cerberus should be at the meet with the Pakis, he can swap out the real ones, give them to us, and take our dummies back to Tehran, where he'll say they're faulty."

"Yes," added Mr. Werner. "The swap won't be easy. But it's probably our only chance to get these new controllers so we can redesign the virus."

Rance looked at Dale. "Welcome to your new op, *Mr. John.*"

"Put more sunscreen on my back," Maya said, rolling over. The hotel was called the Rixos, which advertised itself as "adults-only five-star luxury." At $1,200 per night, most guests—predominantly rich Europeans and Emiratis—arrived in big black German sedans. Conversely, Dale and Maya had swum ashore from the speedboat before sunrise, trailing waterproof parcels with doctored French passports.

The poolside waiter arrived with the drinks and deposited them on the small table by the chaise lounge. "*Ach, madame et monsieur. Voulez-vous que j'ajoute la note à votre compte?*"

"*Oui*," Maya said, looking up at the waiter through large, dark sunglasses. She'd ditched the green contacts she'd been wearing when they checked in, having worn them to match her fake French passport photo, just in case. But she'd opted for the sunglasses now. She twisted to her side to sign the check to their room, then adjusted the wire-thin strip of fabric on her hip that passed for a bikini bottom.

Rolling over again, she pulled Dale in close, touching her lips to his cheek, then his ear. She smelled like a piña colada—partly from the lotion, partly from her breath. "If I lean up," she whispered in her accented English, "can you get a photo of him?"

Wearing nothing but his Israeli-supplied board shorts, Dale backed up until his heels touched the red-hot beach sand. Behind him, he heard the occasional crash and hiss of a wave from the Gulf of Aqaba. They were only fifteen nautical miles from where they'd met on the Israeli corvette, which was still on patrol somewhere out there, over the horizon. If things should go south, they'd been told, the speedboat would be back for exfil.

The CIA man knelt and aimed the lens as Maya smiled brilliantly. She bent a knee and tilted her shoulders in a pose worthy of *Vogue*. Dale tried to ignore her to take the picture of the suspected target of their surveillance over her shoulder. But it wasn't easy. He reluctantly focused on a Middle Eastern man who seemed to be vacationing by himself.

Yet the fat Arab with the hairy gray chest on the other side of the pool was probably *not* the targeted go-between from A. Q. Khan's nuclear-know-how business. According to Mossad's intel, a Pakistani member of Khan's team would be delivering a set of six new Siemens controllers for the Iranian centrifuge arrays. He was supposed to stay here, at the Rixos. That made sense since it was Khan who'd sold Iran the original equipment.

The problem John and Maya had was that they didn't know who, exactly, the Pakistani courier would be. Nor did they know when, exactly, the exchange was to take place. Cerberus had only said "later this September," and the Mossad intel had suggested it would take place at this resort. The idea was to get an update from Cerberus to zero in on the meet. A Caesarea team would coordinate the intercept. But, as often happened, Cerberus had gone frustratingly dark. They still weren't sure whether the American agent would even be at the meet.

Dale finished taking the picture. He sat on the chaise next to her and blew it up with his thumbs. She looked at the man's face and took her phone back. "I'm sending it in to HQ to see if he's a probable. Who knows? Maybe the eighth time is the charm." She rolled to her stomach, typing. "John, rub my lower back. We need to keep up appearances."

Yes ma'am, Dale thought.

Rance had made it clear that Mossad had tactical control of the op. *They* were the ones who'd be developing the code for the new controllers. They also happened to be much better at industrial interdiction, having conducted dozens of such ops over the years. And they had tighter intel on the A. Q. Khan network. On Mossad's insistence, Dale's TDY assignment to them would only be known by Rance, Dorsey, and the director. That was it.

But even with that kind of senior attention, Dale didn't like being a straphanger on a foreign agency's op. "Vacationing" with the lovely Ms. Maya had taken out some of the sting.

"Do you think Cerberus will actually be here for the meet?" she whispered to him over wine at the hotel restaurant two nights later, once they were sure they were alone. Despite sending off nearly twenty probable mug shots, they had yet to get a positive affirmation of an A. Q. Khan courier. Dale thought the op was beginning to feel like a well-orchestrated bust. But he'd decided to make the best of it.

He'd even persuaded Maya to walk with him up the beach that day on the pretense that they could check other resorts for Pakistani agents. The real reason was that Dale wanted to sketch a big white mosque a half mile south. He always traveled with a sketchbook, even in the Syrian bush. She'd been surprised to learn that but had agreed to come along.

While Maya looked around the neighboring hotels, Dale had struggled to capture the mosque's unusual shape. The Moorish curves made it hard to get the perspective right. But worth it. He was convinced the cool green of the water against the desert's warm yellow would make a good painting when he finally got home.

Every now and then, Maya had watched while he sketched, holding out her shawl to make shade for him. When he'd finished the drawing, she'd studied it closely, nodding in appreciation. Then she'd smiled at Dale in a way he hadn't seen before—warmly, genuinely. Now he was having dinner with her. Again. And that warm smile had fleeted in and out. She'd turned to talking about the op, keeping the language vague.

"Maybe your man isn't even here," she was saying over the table, leaning back, her legs crossed. "Maybe that's why he's gone dark."

"I don't know," answered Dale, scanning for eavesdroppers, seeing none. A warm evening sea breeze stirred the linen. "Could be. He likes to protect himself. How long before we call this thing a bust?"

"Three more days," she said. Then, surprising Dale, her warm smile reappeared. "Do you think you could sketch me? Not my face, of course. I like to protect myself."

"Sure," said Dale, smiling crookedly, thinking he wouldn't need a drawing to remember that face. "Maybe an over-the-shoulder pose, contemplative. Girl on balcony. A wistful kind of thing."

"Exactly what I had in mind," she said.

And two evenings after that, as Dale was preparing to crash on the couch for the sixth straight night, he heard Maya making calls on the seaside verandah with the door shut, her regular midnight routine. She'd propped the sketch he'd made for her—a view of the sea from over her shoulder—by the lamp on the desk. When she was finished with her call, she came back from the terrace and stood on the inside of the doors wearing a T-shirt and shorts.

By now, they'd developed a comfortable, almost domestic familiarity. Perhaps *too* familiar, he'd begun to think. Just the night before, over one too many cocktails at the rooftop bar, he'd finally admitted to being married. Until then, he'd gone to great lengths to cloak details of his identity. But when Maya had asked him point-blank, he'd confirmed it—thinking himself noble.

But that's where his nobility had crumbled. He'd gone on to say that being married to a fellow intelligence officer hadn't been easy. He'd admitted to frustrations with the Agency in general. Covering his mouth with his hand then, he'd wanted to immediately shut himself up. But the quality of the second bottle, the sea breeze, the warm smile—had all argued otherwise. He'd kept on talking. The dam had burst.

She's a goddamned good one, he'd thought later that night on his couch, smothering his head under a pillow.

But she'd opened up too. Unless, Dale had considered, it was all a well-constructed legend. She'd said she was an orphan, raised by Mr. Werner. That clicked, Dale thought, since he'd seen their close interaction on the ship. Maya had also shared that her biological father had been a military pilot, like Dale's. He'd flown for the IAF, been shot down over Lebanon in a dogfight with Syrians. Werner had been his wingman, had witnessed it, had failed to fight off the Syrian plane. Captured in enemy territory, Maya's father had ultimately been tortured to death by Hezbollah.

Not long after, her Christian Lebanese mother had tragically died in her sleep. She'd been just three. Pills, Maya told Dale now. He understood that. His own mother had struggled with substance abuse after his dad's untimely death.

Orphaned, Maya had grown up in the Galilee hills under Mr. Werner's watchful eye. But anxious for independence, she'd moved to France when she was only eighteen to try her hand at modeling. But they wanted blondes in Paris back then, and her career never really got going. By twenty-three, Mr. Werner had recruited her home. An easy pitch. She'd get to avenge her parents. *Not a legend*, Dale had concluded. Too much sadness lurking in those Eastern eyes.

"It's happening tomorrow," Maya said to Dale now, coming in through the sliding glass doors as she put the phone in her hip pocket.

"What?" He sat up on an elbow. "I've got nothing from Cerberus. How do you know?"

"I can only tell you it's happening tomorrow. You have to take my word for it."

He kept his face as still as he could. *They get to know my source, but*

I don't get to know theirs. "Well—can you give me any details on the op?"

"Sort of. They're going to meet with their Iranian contacts in an office on the other side of town, leased by an IRGC front company. Since we never ID'd a contact here, I suppose we won't know who's who until they get to the office. We're getting things set up now."

"Okay—then what should I be doing tomorrow? You guys want me to wait here or . . . ?"

"It's probably not going to be safe here," she said.

Not safe?

"You and I will be in a car, near the meet," she continued. "Our intel says they're going to review technical documentation. Your job will be to communicate with Cerberus, assuming he establishes communications with you tomorrow. Hopefully he will. If so, he can help us with the switch. I'm afraid I can't tell you anything else. Sorry."

"That's all right," Dale said, lying back on the sofa. "I get it."

Still standing by the door, Maya nodded once at him. She then approached the couch, smiling sweetly, as though in apology. Dale had previously noticed that she could go from Mossad *kidon* to girl next door in under a second—a skill displayed during their fake dates. Or maybe not so fake.

Either way, there was no point to faking now. They were alone.

She sat on the sofa, placed his feet across her bare lap, and rubbed them. At first, he didn't find this unnerving. They'd been playing at affection with each other to reinforce their coupling ruse for a week. But they were alone now.

She massaged a foot and played up her sweet smile, looking sideways at him in the moonlight. "I really am sorry, John. I wish things were different. I mean . . . *really* different . . ."

"Yeah, I know. It's okay . . ." *We're just working,* he thought.

"You and I make a good team, don't we? I think we operate well together."

"Maybe. I guess we'll know for sure tomorrow."

She nodded. "But, John, whatever happens tomorrow . . . What we're doing here, this is big. Think about it—no one else in the world could do this—except you and me. We're the last line of defense. It's a big deal. You and me."

"I guess so," said Dale. "Until we report it all and our bosses tell us we're a couple of dumbasses for not finding the A. Q. Khan guy."

"*Your* bosses might do that. Not mine. We're more like a family in Caesarea."

"Consider yourself lucky, then."

"When this is all over, do you think we could . . . keep in touch? I know spies don't usually do that—but we're not spies to each other. You know me. The real me. Not many people do."

Do I? "I'm not sure we should do that, Maya."

"I'll give you a protocol. You'll be able to find me. You might regret it if you don't."

Holy shit, Dale thought. *Did she just recruit me?*

"How 'bout I give *you* a protocol," Dale said with a slanted smile.

She returned it, unblinking, staring straight down his pupils. *Jesus*, Dale thought, looking away with a chill. *It's like looking at the sun.* Even in public, deliberately faking affection, she hadn't been this good.

"I was thinking," she added, stroking his other foot. "This is probably our last night together. I'll give you that comms protocol tomorrow; but before everything falls apart . . ." While keeping her eyes locked on his, she nodded toward the open doors of the master bedroom where she slept. Lacy white curtains wafted on either side of the threshold, as though beckoning.

Frozen with a thousand conflicting feelings, Dale stared back into her Eastern eyes and said nothing. He was too busy groping for an answer.

By eleven the next morning, it was already nearing a hundred degrees.

Maya sat behind the wheel in a black linen pantsuit, her hair tied in a scarf, her eyes changed by the fake blue contacts. Dale was in the passenger's seat checking his phone, refreshing the Google Drive file every few minutes, looking for an update from Cerberus. They were cruising around the block in a Renault sedan in the busy section of the resort town, a few miles south of where they'd been staying.

"Hey—I've got something," Dale suddenly said, almost shocked to see the new file on G: drive. "Cerberus just confirmed the meet's today. He's given me the address." Dale read it off.

"You think Cerberus is here, then?" she asked.

"I still don't know. The fucker always stays shadowy on me. Does that address check out?"

"Yes. Our asset confirmed the same address."

"Maya," Dale said, reacting to the use of the word *asset*. "Are you saying we potentially have *two* agents at the same meet?"

She hit her turn signal and took a left, completing another lap around the one-mile square block. "Looks that way. And a few other scientists too. I'd say we have the all-stars of the Iranian nuclear program assembled here."

Fuck, thought Dale. He didn't like the idea of Mossad having a competing asset. He was worried that one day in the future when the Iranians went mole hunting, Mossad's man would have an ace up his sleeve by giving up Cerberus.

"I need to take a call," Maya said suddenly, pulling to the curb and parking. "Wait here." She killed the engine and grabbed the handbag that never left her side, even when they'd been at the pool. Dale hadn't ever minded that—one of them needed to be armed. But it bothered him now. She'd even taken the car keys.

"Someone's coming by," she said when she returned. She got behind the wheel and rummaged through her bag, pulling out a length of black fabric. "I'm sorry, John, but I need you to put this on." It was a silky black sack, a hooded blindfold.

Dale batted her hand away. "Are you kidding? No fucking way."

"We can't let you see our other *kidons*. You understand. It's for your own protection."

"The fuck I understand. Your operatives have probably seen me. They know who *I* am."

"Yes, but this is our op, our rules. You know that. You're temporarily with us."

"Well, this is a rule we're not following. No." He pushed her arm away.

She grabbed his hand quickly, a little too tightly. There were no smiles now. "John—would you rather I forced you into the trunk?" Letting go of his hand, she pressed the cloth onto his lap. She tilted her head to one side. "Please."

"Fine," Dale said tersely, putting the sack on. Maya lowered the car's rear windows on the driver's side. A minute later, a motorcycle sputtered by. A two-cycle engine, it seemed louder than the rest of the traffic. Dale heard something land in the backseat as it passed.

"Got it," Maya said, turning to retrieve the object. "Almost done. Hang on." Whatever it was, it had just made it into her purse. Dale supposed it was either a weapon, a communications device, or the dummy Siemens controller they were supposed to swap. "Okay, you can take off the blindfold."

Dale whipped the sack off his head and looked around. "What was that?" he asked.

"We need to go," she said. She threw the car in gear.

Without saying much to each other, they drove five more blocks to a five-story, glassy office building. She found a spot in the office parking lot with a view of the southwest corner.

"How are you going to do the swap of the controllers?" Dale asked. "Brush pass? Swapping briefcases in the bathroom? What?"

Before she could answer, her phone buzzed with an incoming message. She tried to hide it from him, but Dale could see the Hebrew script. "They're up there," she said, pointing to the second floor of the building. "The meet's already happening."

Dale looked up, watching the reflective glass. He wondered if Cerberus, whom he'd never met, was up there right now. *And if he is,* Dale was thinking, *then I'm going to need to . . .*

The glass on the fourth floor suddenly shattered, exploding outward.

Dale saw a man among the shards, his arms and legs waving as he soared backward toward the ground. He bounced like a mannequin off the pavement while a shower of sparkling glass rained over him. Above the dead man, Dale saw another flash in the jagged gash of the building. More gunshots.

Stunned, he was pressed hard into the seat back as Maya floored the Renault before the last fragments even hit the ground. *"What the fuck was that?"* Dale was yelling, steadying himself with the grab-bar on the dash.

She didn't answer. She maneuvered the car to the parking area in front of a fountain, slammed on the breaks, and hopped out.

"Stay here!" she shouted. She'd set the car up at a diagonal. She got out behind the open door, removed a Masada 9mm from her purse, and cocked the slide. She ran to the side behind a car, out of sight. Unarmed, Dale felt helpless. She'd even taken the keys. He had one hand on the door handle now, ready to bolt. But unarmed, he wasn't sure if that was the smartest move.

A black Mercedes S500 pulled up to the entrance and screeched to a stop. Two men leapt out. They were big, bearded, suit jackets, open shirts. And packing. They were drawing MP-5s, long-clipped machine pistols, running toward the building entrance. Until they saw the Renault.

Dale ducked, stole a glance over the dash. One of the men came toward him, the MP-5 rising. He fired a short burst. Dale shrank to the floor, taking shelter as glass splintered above him. Dale was unarmed, no chance to get away. The only move would be to throw open the door, stay low, throw out a leg. The man would be right in front of the car now. *This is it*, thought Dale, flickering through images of Meth and Grace. *This is how it ends.* He waited for the next shot.

Bang. Bang.

Two quick, singular shots, a different pitch than the machine pistol. Dale heard the hood thump. He glimpsed the edge of the windshield to see it splattered with bloody gray globs. Machine pistol man was down, the top quarter of his head gone, nailed by Maya from twenty meters back. He could see her near the fountain now, running, shifting her pistol's aim toward the Mercedes.

She was running, going for a better angle on the second man, who'd dived under the Mercedes for cover. Maya extended her arms as she ran, raising the pistol but holding off on the shot. She then rolled to her stomach and fired three times. A half second later, she was rolling back to her feet, sprinting toward the Renault.

"You get him?" asked Dale.

"Yes. But the op's off," she said quickly, breathing hard as she got in. She cranked the engine. "We're blown. They were IRGC. Our guys are coming out now. Make sure the backseat's clear."

Blown?

"I need to get my asset," Dale said. "I should exfil him. He's my—"

"I thought you don't know what he looks like."

"I don't, but if all hell's breaking loose up there, then I should—"

"*No.*" She glanced at the phone again. "Our guys are coming out. Right now. You're not getting out of this car." She backed the car with a harsh jerk so that the dead Iranian would slide off the hood. She turned on the wipers to clear the bloody chunks that had been his head. But the windshield had been strafed. The wipers just made a mess. "They're coming out!" she shouted at Dale.

Dale looked toward the building entrance, through the red-smeared glass. Two men carrying pistols were running toward him. Both were in suits, sprinting like the building behind them was on fire. Halfway to the car, one of them stopped, turned, raised his arms, and shot five rounds back into the lobby. Maya had her gun cocked outside her window, covering them. They both ran forward, diving into the Renault.

Before the rear doors had even closed, Maya was fishtailing into the street as the newcomers screamed at her in Hebrew from the backseat. The wipers were still going, windshield fluid spurting, trying to see through the bloody mess. Some of the fluid leaked through the window cracks onto the dash. In the back the two Mossad men were yelling at Maya, screaming, crazed. Dale guessed they were talking about him, an unmasked *nakhriy*, a foreigner, a risk.

"*Zem zechel, zem zechel!*" one of the men was shouting. He grabbed Dale's collar, pulled a Masada, and stuck the cold metal barrel against Dale's neck.

Dale snapped. He was willing to endure a lot for this op, but he'd already been a whisker away from death and the adrenaline was still flowing. He'd had enough.

He launched himself into the backseat, going for the pistol, driving the heel of his hand in an uppercut to the man's jaw with one hand, wrenching for a wrist lock on the shooting hand with the other. The other man in the backseat had pulled his pistol now, waving it at Dale, screaming. Dale went for the man's gun.

Maya was pulling on Dale's belt, shouting, telling him to stop as the car lurched with the windshield wipers scraping. Then she screeched to a stop on the side of the road. She twisted in her seat, leveling her own pistol at both backseat men now, screaming at them in guttural Hebrew. This was a Maya that Dale hadn't met before.

The man behind her shouted something back, then lowered his weapon, screaming back at her, eyes bulging, spit flying. She pulled the hammer back on the Masada, aiming at the Mossad man's head.

While operative one was frozen by Maya, Dale hit operative two in the jaw with a quick jab. Maya jerked Dale back into front seat, screaming at him now, telling him to settle the fuck down. She floored the Renault.

It bounced over a curb, then another, squealing. Dale saw that Maya was looking back at the building. He could see in the mirror that the two nutjobs behind him were doing the same thing, their chests heaving.

Maya shifted on her hip and picked up a device that had been trapped under her leg. She held it up, eyes focused on the rearview. *Oh no*, Dale thought, looking back.

Close to his ear he could hear a tiny, plastic click. Maya had pressed a button.

Dale watched as the building exploded, hollowing out the first two floors, collapsing half the structure in a billowing cloud of debris.

These people are insane, he thought. With his agent Cerberus in mind, Dale pulled the door handle and rolled out onto the street. He tumbled painfully into a curb, smacked his head.

Ignoring the ringing bell, he jumped up from the pavement and sprinted toward a narrow alley. He could hear the Renault screeching to a stop behind him. But there was traffic. He heard honking horns. Running, he snatched a quick look over his shoulder and saw that one of the goons in the backseat had hopped out, looking for him.

But by then it didn't matter. Dale had gained the alley. And he knew they wouldn't pursue him. They had their own getaway to think about.

In the Dales' Arlington, Virginia, condo, the secure phone by Meredith's bed started to ring. Springing upright at that odd hour, she hoped it'd be John. They hadn't spoken in three weeks.

But she quickly saw it was a 757 area code. Langley.

After authenticating, Meredith, a midlevel analyst with the Near East Division, reached for the notepad on her nightstand. It was Rudman, her section chief, apologizing for the late hour, telling her to get her ass into Langley. There'd been an incident—a bombing at a suspected IRGC office in the central business district of Sharm el-Sheikh. Rudman said he needed a report by close of business. Then he apologized again for the late hour. But by then Meredith was already slipping into her heels.

She left a note on the counter, telling Grace to take the bus.

Once in the office, Meredith canceled all the rest of her meetings and zeroed in on the bombing. Chatter had sprung up in Iran, according to NSA. Meredith burned up the phone lines, calling contacts, other agencies, trying to get to the bottom of it. *The director wants answers*, Rudman said in an e-mail. She was determined to give him some.

Over the next several hours, Meredith quickly learned that Cairo Station officer had an agent who'd reported that a Pakistani with ties to the A. Q. Khan network had been staying in one of the flashy beach resorts in Sharm el-Sheikh. Word had trickled in through a half dozen Egyptian Mukhabarat assets that were run by the agent.

Given the seaside location, Meredith had even made a quick call to DIA's Navy desk and learned that an Israeli corvette had been loitering off the coast. *Holy shit*, she'd thought. That was a mighty big coincidence. Something big must have gone down.

By noon that day, following hurried escalations through the US ambassador to the Egyptian Foreign Ministry, the Egyptian Mukhabarat agreed to help with the investigation by providing foreign passport registrations at the five best resort hotels in Sharm el-Sheikh. They sent her a comma-delimited text database file stuffed with info that was all gobbledygook. Annoyingly, she'd had to call the IT geeks to decipher it.

But once she had the Excel file set up, Meredith was sifting through 735 foreign passport entries. The IT guys had done a bang-up job. If she double-clicked a name, she even got the passport headshot on another Excel tab.

She was comparing the list to known contacts from the A. Q. Khan network, which an agent in Pakistan had filched at great personal peril. She spent hours running through the list, fighting off calls from Rudman, who'd kept asking when she'd be done.

But there were no known A. Q. Khan aliases at any of the hotels. She gave Rudman the bad news.

But she didn't share with Rudman her concerns about the two French passports of guests staying at the Rixos. One of them belonged to a Frenchwoman named Beauchamps, registered to Suite 811. The other belonged to a Frenchman named Crochet, also registered to Suite 811. They'd spent the week together, apparently. Crochet, Meredith knew, was the surname John used for his French legend.

Double-clicking on the line item to get the photo image, she was sure it would simply be a coincidence. Crochet was a relatively common French name. *Has to be a coincidence*, she repeated to herself, tapping her fingers as the passport image finally came up.

Then she realized it wasn't.

Goddamned John.

CHAPTER 30

Present day

ANOTHER DAY OF CONTRASTS HAD PRESIDED OVER BEIRUT, MEREDITH thought. The push and pull of opposing forces were everywhere, starkly adjacent yet worlds apart. Sea breeze, land breeze. Pine tree, palm tree. Gleaming high-rise, fetid slum. American University, vast illiteracy. Morning church bells, evening *adhan* calls. Yin-yang, tick-tock.

Just as some considered Beirut to be Europe's eastern outpost while others saw it as the Orient's farthest western reach, Meredith had found that everything in Beirut was a matter of perspective. It was a city precariously balanced on a razor's edge, ready to tip in either direction—or get sliced right down the middle.

Cowles had softened somewhat. Though artfully ducking the blowback from Meredith's disastrous convoy bombing, he'd at least continued to let her have access to his case officers, letting her submit queries of their agents. While the consensus had settled in Langley that the last *Taniyn* missile launch had been an anti-ship missile, she still disagreed—though that barely mattered now. What she wouldn't have given, she'd thought at least a thousand times, to have inserted Kahlidi back in Quds, as she'd originally intended. Instead, Kahlidi had ended her career.

Still, she thought she might try one last play, hoping to find an asset in the Lebanese government who might give her a little intel on Iranian smuggling activities. She may have been relieved of the NIE, she'd coached herself, but she still had a duty to head off a possible hypersonic *Taniyn* nuke if she could. And it was the least she could do after botching the Kahlidi recruit.

Having arisen early with a scratchy throat, Meredith had dutifully trooped into the embassy in her NOC disguise, going through the tiresome rigmarole of SDRs and security checks. Then, finally installed on the embassy's sixth floor, she'd hit the cables again.

To her, the operational security of the Iranians and Hezbollah was a problem, a tell of something troubling. Iranian and Hezbollah comms in Beirut had gone completely dark, using messengers. Ominous. She just couldn't let that go.

And even if the Iranians *weren't* up to something, she said to herself as she read, why go to all that operational trouble for a conventional anti-ship missile? Hezbollah had never really gone to war with the Israeli navy. Why go to so much trouble developing a maneuverable design for a relatively undefended ship at sea?

To no avail, she'd even called Rance, who was now back in Vienna with the reassembled State delegation. Meredith knew that Rance, as the head of Counterproliferation, had the juice to stop the deal on intelligence concerns—if he wanted. "Hezbollah is the largest organized terror force in the world, an Iranian shadow state, a country within a country," she'd said to him from the secure embassy videoconference room. "And now they've built a missile with deadly strike capability, maybe a radiological warhead, a WMD. And Counterproliferation is going to say it's not a *strategic* threat in the NIE? Are you *really* sure about this, Ed?"

Rance had countered that HUMINT was the only thing that could disprove the observable data they had. And the observable data indicated they were looking at an anti-ship missile. If only they hadn't lost Atlas, he'd added. What an indispensable HUMINT source Kahlidi might have been. What a shame.

Now at six p.m., her face sizzling, her throat swollen to futility, Meredith put two Tylenol pills on her tongue and swallowed painfully. At once hot and cold, she clutched at her arms to ward off a bone-shaking chill. She stood over the sink and judged her own glassy eyes.

After a brief internal debate, she decided to go ahead with the meeting she'd arranged.

Whether Cowles was aware of it or not, a few of his case officers still had a clue. And one of them had cultivated an agent called Cassius within the Lebanese port authority who said he had some information on clandestine Iranian shipments. Proving out a *smuggling* route had been the key from the beginning, Meredith had thought. Now it was probably her last chance before they signed the Vienna deal.

But Cassius was skittish, the case officer had warned Meredith a few days back. The agent would *only* talk to a senior CIA officer, someone direct from Langley. He didn't trust Cowles, who seemed too cozy with the Lebanese Directorate of Intelligence. It was common knowledge that many Lebanese intel officers were on the payroll of Mossad, Quds, or Syrian Mukhabarat. It was the Beirut business model.

Meredith had suggested she could pose as the senior officer from Langley, someone who didn't regularly lurk in the Lebanese swamps. There was even a grain of truth to that. She was relatively high up in Counterproliferation. Sort of.

The case officer sold the idea to Cassius. The agent was up for it—as long as he got paid. If he offered Meredith something worthwhile, he'd pocket ten grand, USD.

It would be a long drive, but she was itching to get away from her miserable hotel anyway. And the case officer had even said there would be a catered dinner waiting for her at the safe house. But he'd also told Meredith to wear something . . . *alluring*, as he'd put it. He said Cassius had an eye for the ladies. Of course he did.

Now wearing her snuggest dress, having labored over her makeup, she threw five drops of Visine in each pink eye and wondered just how alluring she looked. She gripped her arms and shivered.

And then, driving down the coast, she suffered through dizzying intervals of flaming heat and crippling chills. With her nose stuffed, she was forced to breathe through her mouth. The air stung her windpipe.

A few kilometers south of the city she considered calling off the meet. She knew full well what she really needed: two solid days in bed, reading a novel. She'd brought *Anna Karenina* to kill time during the flight over the Atlantic with Dorsey. She was about two-thirds into the book, anxious to keep going. But on that flight, she'd been scared to crack it for fear he'd think she didn't have her head in the game.

His impression didn't matter as much now, she thought.

Maybe she should just turn around, she said to herself as she shivered. Let Cassius meet with some other officer. This wasn't really her fight anymore. She didn't have the NIE. She didn't really need to do this.

Then she forced herself back to reality. Cassius was expecting her. And he might be the key to finding out what Hezbollah was up to with *Taniyn*.

Knowing she was south of the city now, closer to the Shia neighborhoods, Meredith wrapped her hijab over her mouth. The fabric almost felt good, like an air filter. Spend an hour making yourself beautiful and then cover yourself with a scarf. How Beirut, she thought.

According to Google Maps, the route to the safe house would take her along the coastal road, away from traffic, into a wealthy area. She raced by the old Ottoman Sidon Sea Castle, caught a pleasant view of the fishing boats riding the swell beyond the rocks, and thought of John's miserable sailboat. Suddenly cold, she blasted the car's heat. But neither the hijab, the setting sun, nor the car's climate control could keep her from shivering.

Her small Longchamp purse was in the valley of skirt fabric between her legs. It stayed there steadily, weighed down by the Glock 17 she'd checked out at the embassy. Cowles's approval had been required for the weapons requisition. He'd noted that few of his case officers ever carried.

Which explains a lot, she'd thought at the time.

Now she felt her phone buzzing inside the purse. It made a clacking sound as it vibrated against the gun.

Traffic was light and fast along this rural highway. She was doing ninety kph. The road was curving with the coast, and she was busily shifting—but she very much wanted to see who was calling her.

Grace, she hoped, coughing painfully into her shoulder. John had sent his usual keep alive messages a few hours back. But Meredith hadn't sent the one-character response she knew he'd be looking for. Let the cheating bastard stew over *that*. Asshole.

Instead, she'd called her daughter and left a voice mail. Meredith had never done that on a mission before, but she needed to hear a friendly voice. *Please be Grace*, she thought as she felt the phone's insistent vibration now. Knowing she shouldn't, she reached into her bag, taking her eyes off the road as she veered around a curve. She leaned into the motion and balanced the glassy Android in her fingers.

With her eyes darting between the windshield and the phone, she authenticated with her thumb. She looked down to see that it was another message from John: *1???*

Three question marks. She spent an extra second looking at the message, wondering if she should respond to him now, just to let him know she was safe. Maybe she owed him that much. But nothing more. She hit the number keypad and typed a one. Then she glanced up through the windshield before hitting the send button.

She saw that she was about to crash.

She jammed her foot on the brakes. The Mini's wheels locked, laying a long streak of black across faded asphalt. A dump truck was backing from a driveway, blocking the road in front of her. It had come out of nowhere, a blind curve. The Mini's abrupt stop had caused her purse to tumble forward, landing near her feet, taking her phone with it. And her gun.

Her heart was pounding, her breath fast. She coughed furiously. Her eyes watered, blurring her vision.

Still coughing, she noticed a red-and-black BMW with flashing lights speeding up behind her. Beirut City cop. She instantly wondered if the embassy would be able to fix up a speeding ticket as she moved over to the curb. *Diplomatic immunity*, she thought, trying to calm her stuttering heart. Then she remembered how careful she'd been *not* to travel with a black diplomatic passport. She was a NOC, on her own. *Fuck.*

"*Sortez de la voiture!*" a male voice rasped through the car's PA system after it had parked behind her. "*Montrez vos mains!*"

Fuck, Meredith thought again. Beirut cops were understandably paranoid—and she'd been driving like an idiot. Now they not only wanted her to get out of the car, but they also wanted her hands up. An outrageous thought for an American, de rigueur in Lebanon. She thought of the purse lying near the brake pedal. The gun.

If she got out with it, they'd search her, find the weapon, blow her cover completely. She could almost picture the pinched look on the ambassador's face when she learned that Meredith Morris-Dale had once again shattered diplomatic relations with the host government.

The PA from the BMW boomed again. Same command, this time in Arabic. A uniformed officer was walking toward her car now. Another waited by the vehicle. She didn't want to lean forward for her purse, knowing that would only make the officer panic, possibly shoot.

Instead, she got out of the car, keeping her hands visible at her side. But she kept the driver's door open, just in case, the purse just a quick dash away. Standing up from the low car without her hands for balance was something of a struggle in heels.

But she made it upright, hands out in front of her, a gust of ocean wind loosening her hijab. She wanted to reach for it, fix it back in place. But she didn't want to scare the cops with a sudden move. To keep it from flying off, she turned slightly, into the wind. From this new angle, she was watching the dump truck backing in the street, blocking it.

Two men were running from the side of the truck, pistols at their sides. They wore black.

No.

Meredith dropped instantly to a knee. She thrust herself into the car, lunging for the gun, fumbling with the purse clasp. With the door half open, she thought she might have good cover. She might be able to squeeze off a few delaying shots as she got behind the wheel. The purse was open now, the gun in her hand. She was swinging out, getting up. But she was off, dizzy with fever, slow.

Two strong hands were already grabbing her by the elbows, pulling them back painfully.

Meredith slammed her back against the man behind her and kicked at the other assailant, spiking him in the chest with her heeled shoe. The sudden jerk had loosened the first man's grip on her arms. She pulled free and spun on her assailant, smashing his chin with the point of her elbow, then raised a knee to his groin.

Without thinking, she noted the black cloth across his face, the dark beard that stretched to his collar. The man was reaching for her, but she was faster now. She jabbed upward at his chin with the heel of her hand. His head snapped back.

She felt a tremendous force at her side. Her knees buckled. She was on the ground, her face shoved into gravel on the road's shoulder. She caught a disorienting blow to her cheek. She tried to wriggle free, squirming under her assailant's weight. But the other man had her by the ankles now. She gave it everything she had.

It wasn't enough. The fever had robbed her of her strength. She felt a plastic cord going around her ankles. She yelled, grunted, kicked, but he had her knees wedged in his armpit and was tightening the cord painfully.

Her assailant was struggling to keep her under control. But she knew she was losing.

She bit his hand. He raised it and slapped her, hard. Then he did it again. Open-handed slaps, the condescending kind men reserve for women. Now the other man was working on her hands, jerking them down. She felt the plastic cord go around them.

Working together, her attackers flipped her to her back. Fully bound, she tried one last lunge, an attempt to raise her ankles, to use her body weight to knock one of them over. She contracted, grunting.

But while she pulled her knees up, she felt a sudden sting in her thigh. The man near her face looked at her, calmly—too calmly, she thought weakly. He knew he'd plunged the syringe.

And then he was gone.

The darkness closed in.

CHAPTER 31

FOR AN EVEN SIX HUNDRED POUNDS OF HIS OWN TRAVEL MONEY, DALE had purchased the '86 Triumph Bonneville bike, helmet, leather jacket, and tools. He'd also made sure to get a bill of sale. The Agency would be getting his expense report as soon as he was finally back on the map.

But not until then. Now, squatting with a wrench in his hand, he looked through the cracks of the bike's engine compartment at the tube station beyond, harmlessly moving a bolt back and forth, wondering why Meredith hadn't responded to his last series of texts, thinking through various explanations to stem the worry. But the thought was interrupted when Dale saw the first signs of the crowd coming up the street.

There. Over the greasy engine manifold, Dale watched a steady stream of walkers emerging from the tube station across the street. With the leather jacket rolled and bungeed to the rear passenger bump, wearing only his new/old Radiohead T-shirt, Dale stood up for a better view. He donned the helmet, straddled the seat, and started the engine.

He'd selected this corner for surveillance based on intel he'd gleaned from Dr. Gulrajani's quickie street interrogation. Though the doc had been blindfolded when the Hezbollah people had forced him at gunpoint to treat Kasra, he'd spilled a few useful tidbits: twenty-minute drive from Westminster, the sound of trains at the apartment, stacks on stacks of outdoor concrete steps. *Steps almost like a football stadium,* the doc had blubbered.

How hard could all that be to find? Dale had thought then, letting the simpering fool go. With information that precise mated to what he already knew, Dale figured he'd find Kahlidi's destination in no time at all.

Before bailing on his CIA-FBI task force hosts as part of his Crack Fall op, Dale had read up on likely Hezbollah hangouts in London. He'd spoken with FBI's MI-5 liaison, Jason Spring. Dale had learned that the British internal security agency had busted Hezbollah a few years earlier for stashing bomb-making ammonium nitrate in nearby West Hampstead.

But Spring had gone on to say that they needed very crisp intelligence before they could get approval for monitoring known Hezbollah areas. "Bleedin' MP thinks the Hezzies are a political party, if you can cop it, mate." Even the investigation of Kasra's kidnapping had been officially handed over to the Metropolitan Police—and they were jumpy at the politics too.

But Dale had very crisp intelligence now. He'd looked at Google Maps driving estimates for twenty minutes from the doc's place. *Yup.* There was West Hampstead, right at edge of the range, right where MI-5 had first looked. But across the rest of the routes, Dale knew to search for housing complexes that butted up against overland trains.

There'd been four built along the main rail lines that ran to Victoria Station. But only one of them had rows of outdoor steps—a place in Camden, south of West Hampstead, a huge complex called Alexandra Road.

And on Google satellite view, it looked weird.

Weird in person too. Dale had first visited via tube, exiting at a stop called Swiss Cottage. Walking only two hundred yards from Finchley Road, he'd looked up at a bizarre public housing estate that rose from the ground in terraces, leaning back like an Incan pyramid. Its five hundred apartments ran horizontally along three layered rows of either four or eight stories. A quarter mile in width, its decaying concrete looked like something out of a dystopian sci-fi flick. The architectural style, Dale had read, was called *brutalism*.

An apt name, he'd thought, walking around its driveways. The steps matched Dr. Gulrajani's description. And it was quiet, not a lot of cops, generally considered a respectable place to live—not a likely hangout for terrorists. After checking out public police reports, Dale had found that there'd been no reports of violence in the past week. That meant it had been overlooked by the cops.

And it probably also meant Kahlidi, the little shit, hadn't yet found it—unless he was here somewhere too, hiding and biding.

Well. Either way, Dale was going to beat the living shit out of the Quds man for dumping him off the back of that goddamned racehorse, making him look like an idiot. Then and only then would Dale make the call to the FBI legal attaché team in the London embassy, leaving Kahlidi bound to a lamppost, discarded like so much public housing trash.

Once FBI was on the way, Dale would ride through the Chunnel to his hovel in France and let Meth know that her prized would-be agent was back in custody. She'd be able to get the hell out of Beirut. The Agency could get busy finishing up Dale's retirement paperwork. Maybe hers too, he thought.

Dale had ridden around the block at sunset, casing the place from behind his handlebars, looking for the minivan that Gulrajani had described. From the back, the housing estate looked like the view from the parking of the LA Coliseum. From the front, it could pass for a minimum-security prison. Spilling out like open concrete drawers, its rows of open terraces would make entry surveillance difficult. And spotting the right apartment among five hundred would be nearly impossible. The silver minivan Gulrajani had described was nowhere in sight.

Fortunately, social media, that ever-undervalued intelligence tool, had provided an answer. Searching hashtags, Dale had meandered his way toward a sprawling digital forum for the Arab community that lived around these parts. While he hadn't come across any of the faces he'd seen in the MI-5 photos of Kasra's snatch, he *had* come across a post about an anti-Israel mob gathering tonight, a protest over the latest Israeli bombing in Beirut.

Specifically, the tweet had said the Israeli ambassador to the UK would be on the dais at an event at the London School of Economics.

According to the hundreds of comments beneath it, the plan would be to surround her, jeer her, shame her for the murder of innocents in the attack on a civilian aid convoy.

Fucking perfect, Dale had thought.

A bunch of hopped-up Hezbollah terrorists wouldn't be able to resist the opportunity to gather in the street and scream *Death to Israel*. And the LSE was in Westminster, a short tube ride from here—accessed via the Swiss Cottage station, which Dale was watching from the seat on his bike with his helmet visor down, right now. He might not see the exact Hezbollah terrorist he was looking for—but he'd probably get to see some of his friends.

And, here, right in view, was Superdrug, the closest pharmacy to the massive Alexandra Estate. Gulrajani had mentioned that Kasra's wounds would require constant irrigation and regular rebandaging. That meant the kidnappers would need to resupply too. Even hate-blind terrorists, Dale knew, had to shop in regular retail stores for the basics, just like everyone else. And who could resist the wide selection and low prices at Superdrug?

Watching now, he evaluated the stream of people coming out of the underground station. Though not so obvious as to be waving yellow-and-green Hezbollah flags, some of the walkers were of Middle Eastern ethnicity. A few carried rolled placards. One, Dale saw, had a crudely drawn Star of David wrapping around the cylinder.

A MAM—military-aged male—said something to one of the placard bearers before peeling off, heading into Superdrug. The MAM had short black hair, a dark beard, and seemed relatively fit. That matched the profile. And why go to Superdrug right after a rally late on a hot Saturday night?

For any of a thousand legitimate reasons, Dale told himself then, biting his lip, feeling the hum of the engine between his legs. But a lead was a lead. He shut off the bike.

After stashing his helmet, he donned the moto jacket and snugged down his backpack. He shoved his hands in the front pocket of his jeans to feel the reassuring barrel tip of the Beretta he'd stolen from the doctor. He'd developed a trick over the years where he could shove the barrel of the gun up from inside his pocket, then whip it free with his other hand. He'd been lightning fast with it. Once.

Under the reinforced leather of the jacket's forearm patch, Dale felt the hard, reassuring bump of the kitchen sticking knife he'd stolen at the sandwich joint, snugged between the layers of leather in a slot he'd created. But if it came to using either of these weapons, then he knew he'd really fucked up. He dug out his tin of Altoids and threw down an Addie.

Wired up, he stayed focused on the MAM entering Superdrug. He remembered to look right for traffic on the street, then stepped off the high curb. He trotted across Finchley Road.

Dale was already half across the street when the small Vauxhall carpenter's van passed behind him. But by then, Dale was too laser focused on the pharmacy to notice the van had its front sun visors down, hiding its occupants. They were watching him.

CHAPTER 32

DORSEY AND RANCE WALKED BRISKLY OVER THE TERRAZZO FLOOR, keeping to the far edge of the hall, faces down, saying little. With one DSS security man in front and another bringing up the rear, they walked like vehicles in a convoy, single file, in a hurry, shoes echoing.

State's Harry S Truman Building was a sprawling stone edifice, stuffed with summer tourists, visiting delegations, lobbyists, media. At Dorsey's insistence, State's resident deputy secretary had made a few calls to clear a path toward a side door on C Street so the two men could exit in stealth.

"Well, that wasn't as bad as I thought it'd be," Dorsey said, crossing his leg in one of the Suburban's rear captain's seats after the security people had cleared the path for them into the vehicle. The spy boss had thrown off his suit jacket and rolled up his shirt-sleeves, even though the vehicle's air-conditioning nearly frosted the windows.

Rance had kept his suit jacket on to ward off the chill. The heavy SUV was about to enter traffic. But now it waited out a chaperoned line of children crossing the street. Rance watched the children through bulletproof glass, thinking of his son, his pending divorce, his soon-to-be ex. His chill got worse.

"Agreed," said Rance as the Suburban chugged at idle. "I think State's just happy to have the NIE over and done with. Finally."

"Sure. But I *thought* Hopkins would ream me out after that fuckup on the aid convoy in Beirut," Dorsey continued.

"Right," said Rance. "And then to have to fess up to him that Atlas might spring up out of the woodwork and mess up the whole deal."

"Right," said Dorsey. "But he didn't go there, thank God. You seem to have some rapport with him. Probably helped my case. I'm glad you were there."

"Of course," said Rance, warming.

Rance had snagged a direct meeting with Hopkins back in Vienna, just before the entire delegation had decamped for a break to wait out the NIE conclusion. Hopkins had appreciated Rance's encouragement of the censure letter and his active support in managing that overexuberant officer, Meredith Morris-Dale, the one who'd been deservedly fired from the NIE.

Now the NIE was moving again. But there was still the Atlas problem—also courtesy of Meredith Morris-Dale. Hopkins felt the deal could probably get done in a hurry—before Kahlidi popped up on the radar. They all hoped so. There'd been a lot of deal momentum since the world had found its villain in Israel.

"Why was Morris-Dale assigned to the NIE in the first place?" Hopkins had asked Rance in an aside when Dorsey had gone to make a phone call. Hopkins had held a china cup in one hand, a saucer in the other. He'd looked down at Rance with Olympian authority. "It should have been *you* from the beginning, Edward."

Edward. Rance would dine out on that for a week.

"Well," Rance had answered. "She'd been the one to snatch Atlas. It was all on her. Given the unique opportunity to mine specific intelligence on a new type of missile, we thought she was in the best position to manage it."

"Whose call was that?" Hopkins had asked.

"Dorsey's," Rance had answered, just as Dorsey came back in the room.

"You heard from Meredith?" Dorsey asked now, slouched in his Suburban seat, reading his phone with glasses at the end of his nose.

The Suburban hit a pothole. Rance steadied himself, then nodded.

"Yesterday. She's still thinking that *Taniyn* missile's more of a problem than it is. Same story, though, nothing new. The damn thing's an anti-ship missile. Hezbollah is probably just tired of the Israelis inserting commandos on their beaches whenever they want."

Dorsey grunted. "You know, Meredith's taken a few knocks—losing Atlas, that shit about her ex-husband and the Israeli woman. Probably best if we get her out for some R&R. She should go see the sights if she wants, enjoy the damned beach."

"Good idea," said Rance. He pulled his phone from his breast pocket and shot a message to Meredith's phone, letting her know she could take as much time as she needed. He sweetened the message with authorization for VIP travel, first class, British Airways, the full treatment. He added a gratuitous sentence noting that she deserved it. His own private joke.

He put the phone back in his pocket. "Done. She has the message now."

"Good," said Dorsey. The spy chief was already on to other things, thumbing through his phone's in-box, glasses nearly falling from the tip of his nose. His remit covered the world. There was always something going on, somewhere.

"She'll check messages," added Rance, making sure he'd been heard. "But it might be better if I draft up an eyes-only cable for Beirut Station. Knowing her, she'll only go off the clock with official orders."

"Uh-huh," muttered Dorsey, still immersed in his phone. "Probably right."

"David Cowles won't be sorry to see her leave Beirut," continued Rance. "She's made no friends over there. And you heard Hopkins telling us what Marlene Hendricks thinks. The ambassador can't stand her."

"Right," said Dorsey, thumbing through an e-mail. "Meredith ruffles feathers sometimes, that's true. But that's okay. I still think her call to take Kahlidi and reinsert as a double took guts. Even if it didn't pay off."

"Guts . . . as in it involved risk."

"Reward involves risk. Having Kahlidi as an agent in Quds would have been the success of the decade for us."

"Big reward, big risk. Especially with this Mossad mole issue . . . and her call in Beirut."

"Yeah. But at least Meredith kept a lid on more Red Pages by having a drone in the air to witness what the Israelis had done. The Knesset's going to keep Werner out of the assassination game for a while. She deserves a bit of credit for that."

"Oh, I don't know," said Rance. They were stopped at a red light now. Lunch-hour pedestrians swarmed around their darkened windows. "I'd say Werner took *himself* out of the game when he killed that aid convoy. Dale may have let him in the door to run that op on us. But Werner ended up burning himself."

The SUV accelerated.

Dorsey looked up from his phone as though hearing Rance for the first time. He looked at Rance over the rims of his glasses. "I don't know if John Dale let Werner in the door. You saw the CI report. All the evidence showed Dale fought it out with the Caesarea team up there in Maui. That looked like a recruitment gone bad to me."

"Sure—if it was real evidence. You know how good Caesarea is at deception. They could have staged that whole thing—the wrecked Jeep, the crazy art dealer guy. Out there in the middle of nowhere, who would know the difference? And Dale didn't tell us about it did, he? Course not. Nice place to shack up with that girl Maya. Dale didn't exactly tell Meredith about that, did he?" Rance grinned.

"Would *you*?" said Dorsey, whipping off the glasses, looking directly at Rance now. "Dale knew Maya from the Stuxnet. It was a legit pairing back then. I think Maya went to Maui to recruit Dale. It's not like she just showed up at his feet like a random honeypot . . ."

Honeypot. Anxious not to remind Dorsey of his own tango with an SVR Directorate S illegal a few months earlier, Rance spoke quickly. "Well, anyway, such as it is, let's see what FBI has on Atlas, right? Let's not forget, Atlas could blow up the whole Iran deal."

Dorsey was staring straight ahead now, eyes compressed in a thousand-yard stare. "Yeah," the spy boss said. "Fucking Kahlidi . . ."

Seeing that his boss was in no mood, Rance retrieved his phone from his suit jacket and checked his e-mail. His heart thudded when he saw the sender in his in-box: *hopkins@secstate.state.gov.*

Nice job getting that NIE over the line, Edward. And also for generally keeping the more reactionary elements in your organization in check.

Thank you for supporting our mission.

—Richard

Richard. Rance's heart was still at three-quarter speed when the Suburban swung down the drive of the J. Edgar Hoover Building.

The Suburban parked underneath in the VIP lane, instantly indistinguishable from the long row of other government bigwig SUVs. An FBI man was waiting near the elevator to escort them up.

"Well," Lew Maddox said, greeting Dorsey and Rance in the conference room. "Thanks for meeting me over here. Emily sends her regrets. Couldn't be helped." They were in an FBI SCIF, just the three of them. Rance knew Dorsey was annoyed that the assistant FBI director, Emily Laird, hadn't shown up for the meeting. They were left with this blockhead, Maddox, who'd been leading the search for Atlas.

"So what have you got?" Rance asked. He wasn't going to put his boss in a position to have to ask for anything, especially after Ms. Laird's slight.

"Not much," said Maddox. He was looking down at a file. "Since your man, Kahlidi—*er*, Atlas as you guys call him—showed his face at the Metro station, we haven't come up with another contact. He's gone deep. Must have some friends helping him."

"Remember that attempted kidnapping of an American journo in New York?" Rance asked. "Might be some MOIS cell in the US."

"I've had counterespionage agents all over the New York thing, following through on those same suspects," said Maddox. "The search might even lead us to a new cell. That would be *some* good that might come of this. It's all documented here, in this summary. Here you go."

"This is fucked up," Dorsey said after a half minute of reading the typed one-pager in his hands. He looked up, removed his glasses, and rubbed at the bags under his eyes with one hand. "FBI seemed pretty confident you'd get him when we first got going. But it's been a couple of weeks now and you've got nothing."

Maddox's face flushed below his flattop. "Let me take you through everything we've done so far . . ." He turned his attention to a thick folder and spent ten minutes presenting an elaborate—yet ultimately frothy—investigative case.

"What about international?" Dorsey asked dryly.

Maddox closed the folder. "Like I said—we assess a border crossing as unlikely. We've had watch lists up at every airport in the country, facial recognition suites, NCIC alerts, the works. We've looked through the manifests of every port of US exit. Your man *has* to be in CONUS still."

"He's a foreign intelligence officer," said Dorsey. "A weapons dealer for terrorists in the Quds Force. I don't think you can dismiss that he might have a few friends here and there that could have helped him out."

"Well," said Maddox, "I've had agents looking internationally too. And they're also coming up empty. But based on what your man Dale had been saying, I suppose we could kick it up a notch in the UK—except that it might make some political sparks fly. Dale said he knows Kahlidi well and expected him to go to the UK."

"Yeah. Dale definitely knows Kahlidi. And—where is Dale anyway? We need to talk to him about the CI reports we got." Dorsey looked around the SCIF as though Dale might be hiding in a corner. "Why isn't he here? I thought he was assigned to your team."

Maddox squinted, quietly swirling the coffee in his mouth. "Just to be clear," he responded after an audible swallow, "you think John Dale is still assigned to me?"

"Of course that's what I think. Because he is." Dorsey folded up FBI's one-pager in half, then quarters, then eighths.

"But you reassigned Dale to another project," said Maddox. "Right? Didn't you?"

"*Who* reassigned him?" asked Rance, sensing his boss's sudden unease.

"I wouldn't know how you fellows detail your officers," said Maddox. "And Dale certainly wouldn't tell *me* of all people. But he told me he was going to work on some hush-hush thing of yours . . . Hasn't been around for at least two weeks. You guys saying I should be looking for John fucking Dale now too?"

The Suburban weaved down Virginia Route 123 without any regard for the slower traffic in front of it. The trip to Langley normally took about forty-five minutes. Dorsey had ordered the drivers to cut that time in half.

"Got it," Rance said over the humming transmission. He looked at his phone, then glanced at Dorsey. The spy boss was sitting quietly, staring out the window, the jaw muscles under his perennial five-o'clock shadow pulsing.

"Okay," Rance said to his boss. "CI ran a search of Dale's known legends and passports. State's passport tracker says Dale entered Heathrow using his French passport. Didn't bother with the approval paperwork to go into a foreign operating area. None of us knew."

Dorsey swore at the window. "Should have *never* taken my eye off Dale. Probably acting out his own hunch. God knows what trouble that'll cause."

"Well," said Rance, studying a message on his phone. "CI is saying something else. I don't think you're going to . . ."

Rance stopped talking when Dorsey's eyes turned toward him. "Just tell me, Ed," said the spy boss.

"Okay." Rance cleared his throat. "I think you know, Jeff, that our

CI spooks still have the Mossad search running, still looking for the leak."

"Yeah. No shit."

"Well—CI said they got a hit on Dale's old Mossad contact, Maya Shaheen. Facial recognition. Heathrow." Rance paused to let that sink in. "Looks like she landed there twelve hours ago on a French passport . . . just like Dale." Rance referenced his phone again. "They just now confirmed it. Looks like Maya and Dale are together again." Rance shook his head with an *I-told-you-so* cast.

Dorsey looked out the window at the blurring guardrail, working his jaw. Then he faced forward, removed a pen from his breast pocket, and stuck it in his mouth.

"What do you want me to do?" Rance finally asked, his phone swaying in his hands with the weaving Suburban.

"I want . . . ," Dorsey started, staring ahead, biting the pen. After a few more seconds, he took the Bic out of his mouth. "Have London Station find Dale and pick him up. And for God's sake, don't say a word about this latest Maya-Dale rendezvous to anyone. Especially Meredith. Yet."

CHAPTER 33

"*QUAND?*" KASEM KAHLIDI ASKED INTO HIS BURNER PHONE, PARTING the curtains with a finger. He was watching the long concrete steps of the Alexandra Road public housing estate. Below the long sweep of terraces, he could see a few pedestrians under the streetlamps at ground level.

With the phone pressed to his ear, he listened to the infuriating answer from the Sheikh's assistant in Paris.

"*Trois jours! C'est intolérable!*" Kasem protested.

In three more days, he wanted to scream at the little French-Saudi fuck, *she may well be back in Tehran!* But he also knew it wouldn't matter what he said. The Sheikh was a billionaire, not a superhero. His vast riches could only do so much. Still. Kasem was now the Sheikh's head of security operations. These people worked for *him* now. Time to make that fact a little clearer, he thought.

The Quds man let fly at Claude, shouting, telling him to move things around, hurry the hell up. Or else.

Or else what? thought the Sheikh's personal UK bodyguard, Hassan, as he watched TV from the sofa. The big Saudi had been loaned out to Kasem, reporting in from his flat in London. Now he turned his smooth bald head at the outburst, copping a glance at the Iranian spy to whom he'd been seconded.

The bodyguard spoke only a smattering of French. But to really understand what a principal was about, he believed, you didn't need the spoken word. And watching this former Quds man, right now, Hassan had seen enough.

Ungrateful little shit.

Yes, Hassan knew, the Iranian wanted to free his woman. In a hurry. But for a supposedly calm, cool Quds arms dealer, Hassan thought the man had already taken way too many risks. That smash-up on the doctor's houseboat had been nuts. Now, here he was holed up in the middle of Camden, talking about taking down a Hezbollah cell. Nuts.

The Saudi thought this as he absently listened to *Celebrity Juice* on the British telly. The Iranian was popping off at Claude, the Sheikh's operations man in Paris. Little shit. Did the Iranian not think poor old Claude had a breaking point?

And this latest outburst after all the Sheikh had done for the Quds man. Who the fuck did he think he was, ranting and raving like that? *Get a grip, mate.*

The Saudi-English bodyguard cranked up the volume with the remote as a signal for Kahlidi to bloody well calm down.

It didn't work. The Iranian was still raving mad. Hassan gave a half turn and a hard squint, putting the Quds colonel on notice. Kahlidi noticed that. He turned away toward the wall, but kept on tearing Claude a new one.

Need he remind this Iranian that the Sheikh had ponied up for this Vrbo through one of his holding companies by offering *ten times* the going rate—simply because Kasem just had to have it, *today*?

Had he already forgotten that the Sheikh had moved heaven and earth to tap the head of his militant wing to free up friends from Nablus, then used his own jet as a ferry service to smuggle Kasem out in a huge equipment case like Carlos Ghosn? Hassan himself had even let the Iranian borrow his own pistol, under the directive of the Sheikh. Ungrateful fuck.

And here was this supposedly suave Quds bigwig, cursing a blue streak at the Sheikh's man in Paris just because the Hamas helpers wouldn't be here for three days. *Soleimani's adjutant*, Hassan thought. *Doubt the late, great general would have put up with that shit.*

"*Je suis désolé*," Hassan heard Kasem saying into the phone when *Juice* finally went to commercial. The Iranian repeated it two or three more times into the phone, taking a more apologetic line with Claude.

More like it, Hassan thought then, lowering the TV volume. Maybe his side glance *had* done some good. Or maybe Claude was finally standing up for himself over there in Paris.

Either way, things got quieter. Kahlidi had hung up, surely exhausted from all that complaining. Or was he? Hassan heard the Iranian saying something else now, a whisper, hoarse, in English. He turned. The Iranian was waving a hand at Hassan, looking through the crack in the curtains at the big, front-facing picture window.

"Hassan, *come here!*" the Quds man half shouted as he backed away from the crack. "Look," Kahlidi said when Hassan arrived at his side. "See there? All the way down at the street. See that guy carrying the white bag? I recognize him—he's Hezbollah. Looks unarmed, out for a little shopping. I told you we'd find them!"

Hassan took a careful look and nodded his big bald head.

The Quds man was putting on his jacket, checking to see that it hid the pistol, Hassan's pistol. "Let's follow," Kahlidi said. "He's going to lead us right to her."

"What, and take down a cell with one pistol between us? You mental, man?"

"Let's just see, do a little reconnaissance. Maybe it's only one or two men guarding her. Might be an easy snatch," said Kahlidi.

Easy for you to say, Hassan thought.

Dale followed at a distance, doing his best to keep a bead on the suspected Hezbollah man with the white bag as he rounded the corner into the Alexandra Road complex. He'd chosen the lane closest to the railroad tracks, where the terraced apartments rose to their full height.

"Evening," an old man said in passing, headed in the other direction. The old fella looked the part of a British pensioner—short-sleeved plaid button-down shirt, big knobby nose, news cap, booze-ravaged complexion. Classic civil-servant type.

And civil-servant types, thought Dale, tended to be nosy—to dislike men with long hair and grizzled beards in scuffed-up leather jackets. Dale hated the idea of standing out. He turned right into the car park, disappearing behind a hedgerow.

Perhaps a lucky move, the CIA man thought a few seconds later. At least from here he had a better view of the creeping, climbing outdoor staircases. He'd also be able to see where exactly White Bag was going.

There, Dale thought a few seconds later.

White Bag was climbing a staircase a hundred yards farther down, disappearing now and then as he made the turns on the landings at each floor. He was trotting in a cadence, like he had a few more flights to go.

At that section of the complex, the stairs climbed eight stories at a subdued sixty-degree angle. Dale was sure he'd at least see which apartment the thugs were using, then be able to intensify his surveillance. The moment Kahlidi showed his face, which seemed even likelier now, Dale would pounce, throw the Iranian's ass down those concrete steps, zip-tie him, gag him. Then—and only then—would he call London Station. And, of course, he would tell Meth to get her ass to London, out of Beirut.

You're welcome, thought Dale.

Dale trotted along the driveway, looking ahead and left, trying to keep an eye on the white plastic Superdrug bag. It would be too obvious, he thought, to simply follow up the same set of stairs. Better to jog left, choose a parallel rise, then make his way over in a side approach. But he needed to hurry the hell up.

How the fuck do these people sleep with that racket? The CIA man wondered thirty seconds after he'd gotten to the top, still winded from running the eight floors, subdued sixty-degree angle or not. One of the trains had just rushed by to the west. Another was bearing down from the east. He paused to catch his breath and scan the terrain below. The wind was brisk at this height. It pushed his hair around.

White Bag had disappeared down a corridor on the third floor in the neighboring apartment section to Dale's right. It made sense to Dale that if they were holed up in a kidnapping warren, they'd need a lower floor, so neighbors didn't see them dragging prisoners up the steps. To disguise his destination, Dale had kept climbing higher, like a spectator toward the nosebleeds, making sure he got the full picture.

Having reached the eighth floor, he tried to move laterally, over to the block of apartments where White Bag had disappeared. The CIA man was thinking that the best tactical surveillance approach would be from above, since the Hezbollah terrorists wouldn't be able to see him without exposing themselves on their own broad terrace—if they were in fact down there. But then the weird architecture blocked Dale from moving sideways to the next block.

To get over to the other side, Dale realized he'd have to run across the three-foot-high wall at the edge of the terrace, in full view of its oc-cupant. He didn't like that idea since he'd create a stark silhouette. But he didn't see another way. He hustled across it like a rat on a phone wire, finally stopping in the relative safety of the stair landing.

Well, Dale thought when it was done, ensuring the Beretta was still secure in his waistband. *At least I'm probably in the right apartment block.*

He decided to go higher to find a good surveillance spot. If his gut was right, he'd probably see Kahlidi here within the next day or two. *After all,* he was thinking as he trotted up, looking at his own feet, *I'm not here to assault a Hezbollah cell on my own. I'm just here to—*

All sentient thought ended there.

Dale was suddenly doubled over, gasping, struggling for air.

Retching, he looked up to see who—or what—had just hit him. But his head snapped sideways with another blow, a crushing smack into a concrete wall.

A big man was coming at him, blotting out the lights. Dale tried to kick the assailant's knees in. But the kick was a mistake. The heavy man turned, squatted, and caught Dale's leg. He shoved it up, and threw Dale to the ground. Dale rolled to the side, hoping he could just run for it, thinking he'd been made by the Hezbollah cell, had really botched it.

He got to a knee, sprang up, took two shaky steps toward an escape. He couldn't understand how the hell he could have possibly been made.

Until he ran straight into Kasem Kahlidi.

The Iranian shoved Dale back, reached to the small of his back.

Dale had already started to make the same move, going for the Beretta tucked in his belt. But while his hand went toward his belt, his arm was wrenched painfully. The big bald fucker was back there, behind him, spinning him around.

The giant had Dale's arms pinned, swinging Dale back and forth, ragdolling him. Dale grunted, tried to get away. He heard Kahlidi saying something behind him. But he couldn't quite hear the Iranian over the giant's noisy grunts. While getting tossed around, Dale hadn't yet let go of the gun, but he knew Kahlidi was back there, that he'd see it. There wasn't much time. Dale tried a reverse headbutt. It was like hitting a wall. It did nothing but hurt.

The big man was trying to turn Dale, make it so he'd be facing Kahlidi. He shouted something in Arabic that Dale didn't catch. Dale saw Kahlidi raising his pistol, aiming at Dale, but the Iranian had kept his voice low, his teeth flashing in the dim light. Dale didn't know what he was saying. Nor did he care.

Impotently, Dale pulled the trigger of the Beretta that was pinned behind him, worried he might even shoot himself. The gunshot echoed closely off the bare concrete walls. He had no idea where the bullet went.

The giant saw the threat. He grabbed Dale's hand again, wrenched at his wrist. Dale squeezed another shot before the Beretta fell, clattering on the cement. He could see Kahlidi rushing toward him, his gun still raised, his teeth still flashing. And then he was gone.

Tat-tat-tat. Tat-tat-tat. Tat-tat-tat.

Three-round tactical bursts. Loud and ringing. Masonry flying all around them.

Kahlidi had disappeared as soon as he heard the shots, ducked away around the stairwell. The giant slammed Dale one more time into the concrete. Another burst of gunfire. The giant paused, crouching to take cover himself when a huge chunk of concrete flew by them. He pushed Dale against a separate wall, in shadow, blocked from whoever was shooting at them from higher up the steps.

The knife, Dale thought then, grunting as the big man shoved him hard into the concrete. The giant was raising an arm, shoving his meaty hand against the bottom of Dale's jaw. Dale groped for the knife that was still buried in his hard leather sleeve.

The big man shoved Dale's head back. The giant's hands were around Dale's neck.

Jesus, Dale thought, his face purpling, hoping he'd hear more of those bullets ricocheting . . . anything to change the dynamic. His instinct was to raise his hands, do anything it took to get the vise to ease off. But the bastard was just *so . . . fucking . . . strong . . .*

It took every ounce of Dale's discipline to fumble with his sleeve, bend his wrist, force the butt end of the knife against the wall so the blade poked free of the lining. With another nudge, Dale felt the sharp tip of the blade cut his fingers. He was starting to see dots at the edges of his vision. He knew he only had a second or two left. He pushed his elbow against the wall, freeing the tip of the knife another inch from the long sleeve. The knife was coming forward. He felt the bulbous edge of the handle now.

Grabbing the handle through the sleeve fabric, Dale swung up, burying the exposed knife tip under the huge man's chin. It barely penetrated at first. But then the big man had made the mistake of loosening his grip, instinctively bringing his hand up to the wound.

Just enough of a break. Dale shoved the sticking knife up, hard, shredding the sleeve. The giant fell to the ground, gurgling, blood spilling down the front of his shirt through his thick hands, his bulging eyes looking up at Dale even as he slumped to the floor.

With his back to the concrete, Dale slid against the wall, gasping, still short of air. He sat on the floor just a few feet from the dying giant, flexing his jaw. The giant twitched his arms and kicked his legs three more times until he faded out altogether.

Tat-tat-tat. Tat-tat-tat. Tat-tat-tat.

Pockmarks sprouted on the wall. Concrete chunks bounced. Instinctively, Dale collapsed to his stomach, coughing out masonry dust. He crawled toward the edge of the landing where he could get a look up the steps. He inched closer to the stairs. There were three armed assaulters running up the flights in the block over from his. They were carrying stubby machine pistols, not AKs. They looked organized, well dressed, like cops.

MI-5, Dale thought with a wave of relief, there to finally take on the Hezbollah cell. *Thank. Fucking. God.*

CHAPTER 34

MAYA'S VOICE SOUNDED COOL AND RUSHED THROUGH THE UHF AS SHE transmitted halfway up the concrete steps. "Another AK shooter on the terrace," she said. "Take him."

"Mine," Caleb answered. He was carrying a machine pistol, terrible at a distance, but the man was standing in the open, firing into the staircase. The *katsa* unloaded a five-round salvo. Brass shells skittered down the concrete steps. The man on the balcony, White Bag, spilled backward, disappearing below the low wall.

"I've got a runner," Matthias said from down in the Vauxhall van at street level. "Looks wounded, hobbling down the steps, coming down toward you, Caleb."

Maya stopped and looked at the stairs. A hundred hours of surveillance tape had made her recognize that silhouette, that gait, the shape of that head. A fuzzy notion at first because the man seemed to be limping. But clearer now.

She was looking at Kasem Kahlidi.

She was sure of it. And he was hobbling right toward them. *Why?*

Werner'd been right, she thought in a flash. The old Caesarea boss had stalked Maya to her place in Tel Aviv after she'd angrily deserted Werner in Capernaum. There, standing in her doorway, Werner had told her of Mitz's lead on Dale's passport in the UK, coming in from a Lexicon hack in the US Passport Office. Werner insisted that Dale would lead them right to Kahlidi.

At the time, standing there at her threshold in Tel Aviv, Maya had wanted no part of it. Sick of Werner's tactics, she'd nearly slammed the door shut on the Caesarea boss who'd raised her. But then he'd made his ultimate pitch. "Either you track Dale, my dear, or another *kidon* will."

Maya knew what that meant. Any other *kidon* would kill on sight. The CIA man had taken down Ari just a few weeks back, nearly killed two more years ago in Sharm el-Sheikh. Only weeks earlier he'd literally chewed up Maya's own leg. Dale hadn't made any friends at Mossad, that was for sure. But she knew who he really was. They didn't.

Now, seeing Kahlidi hobble down the steps in a hurry, it didn't matter. Werner had been right. Dale had led them right to the Quds spy that held the key to understanding *Taniyn*. She would deal with the repercussions of all that later. For now, she just had to bring Kahlidi back alive.

"*Cease fire! Cease fire!*" she screamed. "I'm coming up. Caleb, *grab him*! Get the runner! That's our target. That's *Kahlidi!*"

"But Dale's still up there," Matthias added. "He's probably armed. We heard those shots. I can get an angle with the rifle from down here from the van. I can take him."

"*Matthias!*" Maya shouted sharply into the radio. "My orders were *nonlethal* on CIA. They still are. You copy?" She noted the dead air, the pause. She didn't have time for it. "*Copy!*" she nearly screamed.

"Copy," said Matthias, thinking he'd never seen Maya lose her cool like that.

Dale was crawling sideways on the concrete stair landing, through the growing puddle of the big Arab's blood. Another burst of AK fire scattered concrete dust over his head. He'd raised himself to an elbow, barely, and could now see that the shooter was on the terrace to his right.

Hezbollah fighter. Raising an AK, threatening the MI-5 people.

The fuck you will, thought Dale, taking orders solely from his own anger.

Dale found the doc's Beretta, tried to recall how many shots he might have left. The short-barreled pistol wasn't much of a weapon, but it would have to do. He rose to a knee, testing whether he had a drop on the terrorist with the AK on the terrace. But just as he looked, he heard rapid fire from behind and below. AK-man was suddenly spilling backward, disappearing below the ledge.

MI-5 had taken him.

Nice! Dale thought, coughing. Chalk one up for the good guys.

Kahlidi can't be far, Dale thought then, staggering to his feet, coughing. He breathed huskily, tried to swallow. It felt like some critical part of his windpipe had been flattened in the giant's grip. He limped slowly to the landing with the little Beretta out in front of him. He saw Kahlidi on the next flight down, bent, wounded, hobbling over the middle tier of steps.

Dale knew the MI-5 cavalry was down there somewhere. But the confused architecture of the building meant they could be coming from anywhere. Kahlidi still had a pistol in his hand. The Iranian was looking down, leaning on a wall as he entered the next landing. What if he got away? Or worse, what if MI-5 took him *out*? After all this—Meth would lose the agent she'd so desperately wanted to exploit. Being this close, Dale knew that would kill her.

This is for you, he thought.

Dale launched himself down the steps, into the dark of the landing. Kahlidi was still there. Dale leaped on the Iranian's back, wrenched his arm behind his back, tackled him. Kahlidi's pistol dropped to the cement steps. Dale scrambled for it.

Kahlidi had just enough time to raise his head, get to a knee. Dale used the pistol to whack the Iranian across the back of his head, knocking him back down. Dale wanted to hit him again. But he stopped himself. Meth needed Kahlidi alive.

Dale was hurriedly getting his backpack off now, going for the flex cuffs. Once he had the Iranian bound, he'd jump up and signal the MI-5 officers with his arms waving.

But then, just as he cinched the cuffs tight around Kahlidi's wrists, the world changed.

Dale's muscles locked in place, paralyzing him.

A jarring, vibrating shock took the CIA man's breath away. His hand had sprung open of its own accord, useless. His mouth had locked shut. Dale's only ocular sense had retreated to a single sheet of flaming orange.

Then, abruptly, the cool black night was in front of him again. His senses flooded back in. Dale smelled cordite, tasted the iron tang of blood in his mouth. He realized he'd collapsed to his stomach and clenched into a ball. His leg hurt. In his senseless contraction, Dale had stabbed himself with his sleeve knife. His only thought was to pull it free. But he didn't have time.

And then the world went orange again, blotting out everything.

Dale convulsed, writhed, scrunched into a fetal. Every muscle in his body seemed to contract at once, muscles he didn't even know he had. A thought had flickered during that one-second break. *Electric. Taser.* But that was as far as the thought went. He couldn't stop clenching his teeth now.

The orange blaze went away. Cold black night again. Dale raised a timid eye, counting to three, waiting for his night vision to return—or worse, the next shock. A few quiet seconds passed. He was able to use his neck again.

He looked around, drooling on himself. Kahlidi was gone, only a pool of blood in the spot where Dale had taken him down. He dry-heaved, spit, got to his hands and knees, wincing at this new pain in his thigh from his own knife.

Everyone was gone. It was just Dale, alone on the steps, struggling to get his body back in line. He forced himself to sit up. He looked down the stairs, tried to get his night vision to cooperate. Lights were coming on all over the apartment block. Kahlidi's pistol was gone, but Dale could still feel the bulge of his Beretta in his belt.

A shadow. Someone in black was running, a man over his shoulders in a fireman's carry. They had Kahlidi. Another person followed. Both of the MI-5 people were sprinting like alley cats. The second runner stopped and turned, looking up toward Dale through the slit of a balaclava.

A woman, Dale thought, noting the long, slim frame in his sights. He saw the curved hip, small face, bulge of escaping hair under the mask. A familiar shape. Dale realized he'd seen that runner before, something about the gait, the swing of the arm as she held the weapon. But mostly he recognized the shape of her body from behind.

Maya had found him again.

Another burst of AK fire from the terrace forced him to take cover on the floor. Another Hezbollah man was firing from the terrace. He was shooting wildly down the steps from a reckless standing position. But he wasn't aiming at Dale. He was shooting down toward the street, toward Maya.

Dale drew the Beretta from his belt. How many shots had he left? He couldn't remember. *At least one or two . . .* He wasn't sure what to do about Maya. But he knew what to do about Hezbollah.

He rose to a knee and steadied the pistol against the concrete wall, aimed the short barrel carefully as the man with the AK kept firing at Maya. Dale held his breath and steadied his wavering arm against the wall. He squeezed off four pistol shots before the Beretta's slide locked open, smoking and useless.

But AK-man was down.

Still on a knee, Dale looked back toward street level. Maya was gone now. Dale checked the terrace. AK-man was gone too. Once his ears had stopped ringing, he realized things had gotten quiet. Dogs were barking. Another train was coming, still pretty far off, he thought.

Then he heard a police siren.

Reluctantly, Dale breathed deep against the pain in his ribs and spit one more time. He pushed himself to a knee and felt the sear of the cut in his leg. He still had his knife poking out of his sleeve and shoved it back in place.

Sirens. Cops. Dale couldn't afford that. He needed to move fast, to

get after Maya and Kahlidi right away. An encounter with the local con-
stabulary would cost Dale days as they sorted through the mess of a
bunch of dead Hezbollah terrorists. He needed to hurry.

As Dale got on his feet, a woman limped down the stairs, headed
right at him.

She stopped in horror, eyes wide.

Dale was ready to lunge for her, thinking her another Hezbollah
threat.

"Please," she said in accented English over the sound of the sirens.
She had her hands up, a long, dark button-down shirt, hair covering
most of her face. Half her right leg was covered in a bandage. She raised
her hands higher.

"Please," she said again. "Just let me go."

Dale looked at her for a few seconds. She was ghostly pale. Her hair
was bent sideways. "Kasra," he said, barely recognizing the rasp of his
own voice.

Horrified, Kasra shrank from Dale, turned back in the other direction, limped as quickly as she could. Dale limped faster, grabbed her by
the shoulder.

"I'm not a threat," he said. "My name's Dale. I came here for Kasem.
Kahlidi. He's a . . . friend." She tried to jerk away from him. The sirens
were getting louder. "I'm an American," he added quickly. "Kasem was
with me. I was helping him. He . . . well, I need to help you now. I need
to get you to safety. To America, to him. It's why I'm here. To bring you
back."

She'd at least stopped resisting him for the moment. Dale wondered
what other lie he could tell her. "We came to rescue you," he said.
"Come with me. We're going to get you away from all this. But there's
not much time."

"Two are dead up there," she said, shakily. "But one got away. Where
is Kasem? Where are the other people that were with you? We should
wait for the police."

"We ran into trouble. They had to leave with Kasem. Your kidnappers put up a battle. But we have to go. Now. The police will turn you

over to the Iranian embassy. You don't want that." Dale could now see police lights flashing a block away. And that goddamned dog wouldn't stop barking.

She nodded at the blood on his thigh. "My leg's damaged. I can't go fast."

"Neither can I," said Dale. "But we have to."

CHAPTER 35

IT WAS THE LIGHT THAT WOKE MEREDITH.

At first it was little more than a sensation, a curiosity, a bubble that passed by as she lay in the cool, unhurried dark of a weightless state. But then the bubble hovered nearer, enveloped her, grew to a buoyancy that pulled her with it. She thought it a rude interloper, tried to turn from it. But it followed her.

Some reptilian instinct told her she was waking—and that something was wrong. Without even realizing it, she'd tensed her arms, flexed her knees, girded for the worst. She cracked one eyelid, then the other.

Her heart contracted into a single cold thump.

Her first rapid gasp smelled of paint. She tried to sit upright but felt the pinch on her upper arms. She attempted to raise her ankles—first in a kick and then in a pull toward her abdomen. But they were restrained too. Her heart pounded, faster, louder, it . . . beeped. She turned her head, feeling sweaty dampness under her hair. She saw a machine monitoring her heart rate, an IV tube in her wrist.

And the rude light. It was in the hand of a woman, shining directly into Meredith's eyes. Then it went away with an abrupt click. A plastic tube started worming its way through her lips. Meredith's first instinct was to bite its head off.

Water was squeezed into her mouth. She thought of spitting it out. But then, guiltily, she swallowed, easing the pain of her crackling throat. When the tube was removed, she turned to the woman who held it. "Where am I?" she croaked.

The woman didn't answer. She'd already turned away to adjust something on the beeping machine.

Memories came together. The planned dinner with the Lebanese port agent, Cassius, the near crash in the Mini, the attack from the men in the street, the abduction. The more Meredith thought, the more the fragments fell into place—and the faster her heart raced. *They have me. IRGC. Quds.* She thought of John and Grace and . . .

The machine at the side of the bed was beeping frantically.

She looked around the room. Another bed like hers, empty. Over the length of her body a yellow hospital gown, white sheets tucked over her legs. The sensation of a lurching movement. *Dizziness*, she thought at first. But then she felt it again, heard a low rushing noise, saw the woman by the machine steady herself with a hand on a wall. The movement shifted direction.

A ship.

Testing the theory, she noticed the painted cable conduits, the bolted hunks of equipment, a yellow battle lantern near the ceiling, stenciled numbers.

A warship.

"Who are you? What is this?" croaked Meredith.

Meredith's attendant threw a few switches on the machine to stop the beeping. A door opened. A big man, dark beard, plaid shirt, steadying himself against the ship's roll.

"Good afternoon," the man said with the careful pronunciation of a non-native English speaker.

Meredith glared at him.

"I'm sure you have many questions," he said. "My name is Levi. As soon as the doctor says you are ready, we will take you ashore for a meeting."

"What meeting?" she said, regaining her voice. "Who are you?"

The doctor was back in view now. She was holding a bent plastic bottle with a wide mouth before Meredith's eyes. The doctor said something to the man at the door in a foreign language. Meredith didn't understand the words—but recognized their rhythm.

"The doctor wants to know if you need to . . . use the bottle. Like restroom," Levi translated.

"*Ken*," Meredith said, using the only Hebrew word she knew. "But at least have the decency to step outside."

The gray Israeli Navy Panther helicopter flared on the rooftop of Matcal Tower, then squatted heavily on the three struts of its landing gear. With rotors still whirring, Meredith stepped out of it in the snug dress she'd worn for the Cassius dinner, feeling conspicuous. Across the gravelly roof, she saw a gaggle of military uniforms near an open door. They were waving, telling her to head toward them. Levi stayed right behind her.

The flight from the ship had been brief, about twenty minutes, she guessed, since they'd taken her phone and smartwatch. From a low altitude, Meredith had watched the long, smooth swells and cloud shadows on the whitecaps. Then the rolling sea was replaced by creamy waves, yellow beach, brown desert, mottled settlements, shining skyscrapers, and finally, this building.

Back on the ship, Levi had handed over her possessions. The plastic bag was light because they'd taken away her Glock. Now, choking in the tang of turbine exhaust, the rotors streamed her hair and ruffled her skirt as she leaned forward. She kept one hand against her thigh, holding the fabric down.

Inside, a water bottle was pressed into her hand. Uniformed IDF officers led her down a crowded hallway, Levi still following. The officers were smiling, gesturing her forward, as though she were some visiting dignitary who'd come to shake a few hands and slap a few backs. She went through corridors, elevators, people at desks. She made it to a door where Levi stepped aside with a nod. Werner Davidai was standing there, leaning against the threshold to his office, holding out his hand in greeting. He was smiling.

Meredith passed by him briskly, refusing eye contact, unwilling to shake the old man's hand.

They brought Meredith coffee, which she gulped down, and a sand-wich, which she ignored. In a life filled with deception, she wondered if this was all some elaborate Mossad mindfuck.

Werner's office was on a high floor. Beyond, she could see the mod-ern high-rises of Tel Aviv. After those, the Med, darkening with gray western clouds, obscuring a low sun. The view reminded her of Cowles's office, though without the tennis courts.

She coughed before she spoke. Her forced rest had done away with the fever. But she'd give them no credit for that. "I can't wait to hear your justification for kidnapping a United States intelligence officer," she said to the Caesarea boss.

Werner looked at her, his bald head canted to the side, one eye nar-rower than the other, making him look half-mad, she thought.

"Well. Mrs. Dale," he said. "We meet at last. For real."

Meredith kept her eyes level and said nothing.

"I saw you in the lobby outside the director's office in Langley the last time I was there," said Werner into the void. "I'm very sorry we didn't get to speak then."

"Mr. Davidai. Please get me back to my station. Obviously, you know where that is."

"I do. And I will. But we need to talk first—it's important for me to show you something."

"You'll show me nothing," said Meredith, clearing her rasping throat. "And we aren't having a meeting. For God's sake, you fucking kidnapped me. Take me back. Now."

"I had you picked up for your own protection. I'm sorry, Ms. Morris-Dale—but it had to be done covertly, quickly."

"I don't need your help."

They stared at each other. He still had one eye narrowed. "Look," he said. "Your agent in Beirut, Cassius. He works for us. And he told us that Hezbollah is looking for you, that they're actively casing your ho-tel, even as we speak. They have a nasty habit of kidnapping American CIA officers."

"As does Mossad, apparently."

"We acted. To save you. And I did you the favor of keeping your cover solid. I got you out covertly—because I wanted to talk to you."

"You should have gone through Beirut Station . . . Cowles."

"There wasn't time. Sorry we've alarmed you."

"I'm not alarmed. I'm angered. There's a difference. And there will be repercussions. For everything."

He nodded. "The repercussions might not be exactly what you think. Please. Let me—"

"You surveilled me at home in DC, on my vacation," shot Meredith. "You think I don't know about that? Yes, Mr. Davidai. There will be lots of repercussions." She coughed weakly into her fist.

"They said you had a fever of 103," said Werner. "We pumped you full of vitamins and penicillin while you slept. I'd thought about receiving you at my home, up in Galilee, as it might be more restful. But in the interests of time . . . Are you still feverish?"

"Other than being a prisoner, I feel fine. May I leave now?"

"I'll get you back to your Beirut hotel once it's safe—or I can drop you anywhere else you want to go. But you need to see something first."

"This isn't going to work. Beirut Station's already looking for me."

He'd already looked away, scrolling through his computer, reading e-mails. "Yes. But not for a while. Cassius told your case officer that you canceled, that you were sick and wanted to stay in your hotel. I know you have a flight to Paris in three days. For now, just let me—"

"Three days. Paris. That's very specific information you have." She supposed they knew she was a NOC with no regular reporting cadence in the embassy. But how did he know about her flight?

Werner peered at her over his half-lensed glasses. "We know all about Ms. Margot Henri's interview schedule," he said. "But that doesn't matter—I promise to have you back very soon. And by then, you'll be thanking me. Trust me, trust me."

"It doesn't help to say it twice," she said, wondering what else they knew.

"May I call you Meredith?"

"No."

He leaned back, his head angled to the side again. "Ms. Morris-Dale, I really do promise to get you safely back to Beirut very soon. And we won't break your journalist cover. But we needed to meet, you and I."

"We could have met a long time ago, sir. You've known my exact whereabouts for the past few months—along with my family's."

"But that was before . . . well, you'll see. Trust me, you'll thank me," he said.

"Mr. Davidai, we know everything you've done. And you're not going to get away with any of it. Or this. You've done permanent damage to the relationship between our respective organizations."

"You will soon understand why."

"Jesus Christ," she said, exhaling, coughing again.

"The King of the Jews, born not too far from here," he mumbled, fixated on his monitor.

"And Judas? He was from Galilee. Like you, right?"

The Caesarea boss chuckled. But he kept looking at his monitor.

"Look at me," she said, feeling the pulse rise in her ears.

The old man was reading intently, as though she were some lowly subordinate whose time belonged to him.

"*Look at me*," she repeated angrily. He did. She leaned forward, thrust her finger at him. "You broke the faith. You attacked the United States. You attacked my family. And *me*."

He swiveled his chair back and forth. He looked up at the ceiling, as though evaluating what she'd said. Then he spun abruptly, turning his back to her. He was looking out the windows behind his desk, over the gleaming spires of Tel Aviv. After a long pause, he swiveled back, hands clasped over his midsection. "We don't know each other well, Ms. Morris-Dale."

"How I wish that were true, Mr. Davidai."

"What I *do* know—especially after meeting you—is that if you thought your country was facing an existential threat, you'd have made the same calls I did. I can see that about you already."

"I wouldn't attack an ally, kill innocents, spy on my friends, go after an allied officer's family, for fuck's sake. I think I'd take a little more careful aim than you."

The Caesarea boss removed his glasses, twirled them in his hand. "We know Dorsey tasked you with vetting the National Intelligence Estimate. And you've seen our intelligence on *Taniyn*. We also know you had corroborating intel that you didn't bother to share with us in your zeal to get the Iranian deal done."

"You don't know as much as you think."

"I know your government is about to sign a deal with the zealots in Vienna, propped up by the NIE. The NIE you were to vet, the one you passed along, despite our intelligence on *Taniyn*. And I mean *you* personally, Ms. Morris-Dale."

"Well, Mr. Davidai, let me be the first to inform you that I was *fired* from my job to vet the NIE. They took me off it. They certified that deal over my objections. Maybe you should ream out one of your spies for missing *that*."

The chair swiveling stopped. *Score*, she thought.

"Regardless," said Werner. "You had the very source to vet what we were saying, the very thing that should have given your administration pause for continued negotiation with the Iranians. But you withheld your source. It didn't agree with your politics."

"Really." She crossed her arms and coughed.

"You're the ones who broke the faith," he said.

"I don't know what you're talking about."

"I believe you call him Atlas at CIA."

It was her turn to stay still.

The Caesarea boss turned to his monitor and replaced his reading glasses. He read aloud, " 'Lieutenant Colonel Kasem Kahlidi. Born 1982 to a wealthy family in Golestan. Finishing at the top of his secondary school class, he entered Oxford on a scholarship provided by Hadish, an IRGC front company. He studied languages at Oxford. After a master's degree from the Department of Politics and International Relations, he entered service with Quds as the adjutant to General Qasem Soleimani.' "

Werner glanced at Meredith to gauge her reaction. She gave him nothing.

"'Among other things,'" Werner continued, "'Kahlidi acted as Soleimani's chief foreign weapons importer, where he set up the front companies that would eventually import the components for Hezbollah missiles, including their newest, *Taniyn*.'"

The Caesarea boss glanced up at Meredith then. "I believe you know, Ms. Dale, we assess *Taniyn* to be a nuclear weapons initiative for use by Hezbollah. But of course you know that. We gave you our intelligence. In good faith. In trade for nothing."

She didn't respond.

He went back to reading. "'In April of this year, Lieutenant Colonel Kahlidi disappeared off all communications and international financial nets. Surveillance teams report his residences in Paris, London, and Beirut have gone untouched. Regular IRGC comm intercepts indicate Kahlidi's location is unknown to the Iranian government. A MOIS counterintelligence team has been actively searching for Kahlidi's whereabouts since his disappearance with concentrations on his residences and operational contacts in Beirut.'"

He paused in his reading, waiting for Meredith to say something. When she didn't, he said, "You'll like this next part."

She crossed her legs.

He continued. "'The date of Lieutenant Colonel Kahlidi's disappearance coincides with COMINT intercepts indicating an American raid into western Iran, near the village of Alut. The American incursion is assessed as an exfil op, where Colonel Kahlidi defected to the United States along with Cerberus, the long-running American agent enabling the joint CIA-Mossad op called Stuxnet. We further assess that Kahlidi was recruited by the same CIA case officer that was running Cerberus as the lead agent in Stuxnet.'"

Werner looked up at her. "By that, of course, the writer means John Dale, your husband. But we try not to use proper names in our reports—for the sake of allied discretion."

"He's my ex-husband," said Meredith.

"You had all that intelligence, Ms. Dale," said Werner, peering over his glasses. "You had Kahlidi as an agent, run by your own *ex*-husband. You even had him in *custody*, snatched right along with Cerberus. And when we came to you with critical intelligence on *Taniyn* that showed how the Iranians might arm up Hezbollah with a potential nuke, you did nothing—even though we know Kahlidi helped create the weapon. If anything, you tried to stop our defensive response. You came to Beirut. You directly interfered with our operations to kill the threat. You interfered with *my* operation on that convoy."

Meredith stared out to sea, past his head. The revelation that Mossad thought John had been Kahlidi's handler for years had sent her reeling. But she knew not to show it. "Believe me, Mr. Davidai," she said, "if I had access to Kasem Kahlidi right now . . . I'd be very pleased to interrogate him myself."

"Well, that's good to hear, Ms. Dale."

"Oh? And why is that, sir?"

"Because. He's downstairs waiting for you."

CHAPTER 36

MAJOR SIAMAK AZAD TIGHTENED THE KNOT ON HIS TIE AND PULLED
the seatback up to its most uncomfortable position. Having finally broken out below the overcast, the Iranian MOIS major now looked out
the window as the Dassault Falcon 20 banked left, entering the airport
traffic pattern. Through the oval glass, Siamak saw the cool gray Med.

The Falcon's engines whined as the plane decelerated in its approach
to Beirut Hariri. Siamak heard the flaps come down with a clunk. His
ears popped. He checked his phone to see if he was low enough for a
signal yet and saw that he wasn't. He tapped his fingers. He couldn't get
on the ground fast enough. London had been a disaster.

There, just nine hours earlier in this same jet at the private Luton
Field, Siamak had landed at two a.m. GMT. Per Maloof's orders, he'd
boarded the front-company's Falcon jet in Dubai, having already
slipped into his business cover. His visa, expedited through the foreign
ministry, had listed a meeting with BP to work out oil shipments now
that the deal in Vienna was about to be signed.

The real purpose of his trip had been to finally transport Kasra
Khani back to Tehran. Under Maloof's verbal orders, Siamak intended
to install Ms. Khani in Evin Prison, where she'd get a proper interrogation, sure to yield better results on the whereabouts of Kasem Kahlidi.
But when Siamak had finally hit the ground in the UK, his phone had
buzzed right off his lap, reordering everything.

The first voice mail had been from Shahid, Siamak's London Hezbollah cell leader. The militiaman had sounded terrified, shouting to be

heard over gunfire, breathing raggedly. Siamak could even hear a woman screaming in the background, presumably Kasra Khani herself. They'd been under attack, Shahid had kept screaming. A raid.

"We're blown! They're shooting! They're . . ." And then a rustle, as though the phone had been dropped. After that, disjointed gunfire. Then silence. The recording ended there.

Several texts of a similar vein were stacked in Siamak's inbox. One was a video clip from Tahir, shot vertically. It showed Shahid firing from the terrace with an AK-47, shooting down. The camera angle shifted, zoomed in on a stair landing. A man was contrasted against dark concrete, lit by a phosphorous outdoor bulb.

The video had gone in and out of focus. But for about three seconds it showed the man on the landing clearly, stepping into the light. The man had been moving to a firing position, aiming a pistol. Siamak froze the video on the face of the man in the stairwell. He zoomed in.

It was the CIA officer Maloof had identified from the SVR file, John Dale. Dale's hair was shorter than in the SVR workup, his beard a little grayer. He was wearing a leather jacket, aiming a stubby pistol toward Tahir, who'd been holding the phone, capturing the image. The video had broken when Tahir had ducked. But it had been enough.

The camera angle had shifted back to Shahid, clutching his gut, mouth gaping, gasping as he died. There the video had stopped, a drama seemingly unfinished. But another text timestamped a minute later had filled in the blanks.

Shahid is a martyr, it said. *Allahu Akbar!*

The Iranian major had then frantically checked the police blotters for Camden, specifically for any mention of violence at the Alexandra Road estate, site of the safe house. There'd been entries about police responding to calls, reported shots, but few worthwhile details. Siamak had gone onto Twitter and Telegram, searched through hashtags for Alexandra Road.

That's when the extent of the disaster had become clear. Media had made it to the scene, reporting "three as yet unidentified men being examined by Metropolitan Police detectives." No mention of a woman.

The gunfight had gone down at ten p.m. local—when Siamak had been comfortably soaring at 30,000 feet in this cushy private jet.

No mention of a woman. No body, no sign of Kasra Khani. The conclusion had been inescapable: CIA, led by Dale, had raided Siamak's Hezbollah cell specifically to take Kasra Khani. That would seem to confirm, Siamak thought, Maloof's theory that John Dale was Kahlidi's handler, that they'd come specifically to get Kasra Khani with Kahlidi's intelligence on Hezbollah.

So John Dale was in London somewhere, having now taken Kasra Kahni.

And John Dale was Kahlidi's handler, working closely with him.

And John Dale's wife was in Beirut.

Two could play the leverage game.

After deplaning, Siamak grabbed his bag and walked toward the chain-link fence, toward the parking lot, trying to spot Nabil's old Toyota. There was a row of red-bereted Lebanese army troops standing at the gate before the parking lot, snub-nosed machine guns slung lazily over shoulders, hands in pockets, knowing not to mess with anyone that came out of a private jet with an Iranian tail number.

As Siamak walked past them, he asked Nabil whether Meredith Morris-Dale had returned to the hotel where they'd been surveilling her. Nabil said that she'd been gone for two days but hadn't checked out yet, indicating she'd be back.

Once in the car, Nabil pushed the straining Toyota hatchback toward the airport exit, headed straight for the *dahiyeh*, his home, where they would plan their next moves. But along the way, Nabil sensed there was something amiss with his Iranian friend. Something had gone wrong. He decided to ask about it.

In response, the Iranian put his hand on Nabil's knee. "We have three new martyrs, now, in London. You didn't know them. But they were our brothers. We will, of course, be making all the martyr payments to honor the families."

Nabil nodded and drove. The wide street was necking down into the narrows of the slum, where many martyr posters hung from rusted lampposts. "How?" Nabil asked.

Siamak stared vacantly out the window. "As soon as Meredith Morris-Dale gets back to her hotel, we'll know."

CHAPTER 37

RAIN DRUMMED ON THE ROOF OF THE HOUSEBOAT. AN OCCASIONAL gust forced the ungainly craft to creak against the pier. Listening to dribbling water in the middle of a London canal, Dale was lying on his back on the built-in sofa, his leg raised and bandaged. He was staring up at the roof, trying—yet failing—to get some sleep. Despite being awake all night, the cocktail of jet lag, Adderall, and adrenaline had made it all but impossible.

But most of all he was awake because he wanted to tell Meth about Kahlidi. She hadn't accepted his calls—and he'd intentionally destroyed his phone an hour ago.

"*Mate*," Jason Spring, Dale's MI-5 contact, had whispered when Dale had called the Brit at seven a.m. "We had a visit from some of your FBI friends in the early hours. They're looking for you. You know that, right?"

Perhaps, Dale had admitted to himself then, Operation Crack Fall had been a little too cute. He'd quickly told Spring it was all a mistake, a mix-up of aliases that he forgot to clear, standard interagency confusion.

"Think it's more than that," the MI-5 man had said, not buying it. "They say you were in on a suspected Mossad raid last night up in Camden. Now I don't believe a bloody word of that crap, but they—"

Dale hadn't let the MI-5 officer finish the sentence before wrecking his own phone.

The motherfuckers, he'd thought, tossing its remains in the stinking waterway so it couldn't be tracked. *The motherfuckers!*

He should have seen this coming, he'd thought as the phone fragments sank into the murk. They'd always looked at him a little sideways when he'd described the escape from that goddamned horse ranch, as though he'd somehow had a hand in it. They'd squinted at him dubiously when he'd described the way Kahlidi had shaken him loose off the back of that horse.

And now, here they came again, cleaning up the gunfight mess at Alexandra Road and finding that Mossad had been chasing down Kahlidi. And, of course, they'd concluded that Dale had been on Mossad's side. An accomplice, a foreign agent—leading the Israelis to Kahlidi. *The bastards!*

And then another notion had chilled Dale. With a pang of stunning marital clairvoyance, Dale had suddenly realized that if the CI spooks now thought him a Mossad mole, then those same spooks had probably already made the Maya connection based on the thing in Hana. And if so, then the spooks would have brought the *entire thing* to Meth as a matter of national security.

Which meant that right about now, Meth would be thinking Dale was a Mossad spy.

And a cheater.

Dale wasn't sure which accusation to hate more.

Now he stared uselessly at the ceiling of the canal boat, listening to the rain, waggling his foot, wondering how long he could stay here now that they were looking for him. And where would he go? After springing for the airfare and the bike—assuming he'd get it all back—he now only had about ninety GB pounds left. He'd never expected to be running for *weeks* here. He'd thought he'd be back in the embassy within the next day or two, getting reimbursed.

Now he was really fucked. He'd need serious untraceable resources, cash, a clean passport to get to his little old hovel in central France until this whole goddamned thing blew over. He'd have a lot of explaining to do. And as a man being hunted by MI-5, he needed to get moving, soon.

A shame. The houseboat had had all the makings of a good hide after fleeing the scene with Kasra on the Triumph. Kasra had suggested it, given him directions to the canal as Dale had roared ahead of police sirens. She'd said Gulrajani had taken her to it once. She'd also said the doc rarely went to it at night, since she thought it was a place for his affairs.

Perfect, Dale had thought from behind the handlebars, speeding around a corner, trying like hell to remember to stay on the left side of the road. Once they'd arrived at the vessel, he'd smashed the window over the head and wriggled through, feet first.

"I got the phone," Kasra said now, entering the boat, her head poking through the open door. She came down the short ladder with an effort, wincing at the pain from her tender calf. She then untied the hijab disguise she'd improvised by cutting the seams of a pillowcase.

"See any cops?" asked Dale.

"No," she said, shaking off the rain. "Just the usual bobbies up at the main entrance to the hospital. I went by the pharmacy, got the stuff. Don't worry—no one recognized me."

"Good," said Dale. "Let's eat fast. We'll need to get moving soon."

"To the embassy?"

"Yeah," said Dale, looking away. He'd promised her he could keep her away from the British police and the meddling Iranians by getting her to the US embassy. But he had to clear a secure path with Langley, he'd warned, since Kahlidi was a foreign spy. And that might take a day or two. So far, she'd accepted that, knowing Kasem to be a Quds man. He wondered how much longer she'd believe him.

For now, at least, she nodded and said nothing else. She lit the galley's gas stove, emptied a can into a pot.

Sonofabitch, thought Dale, shaking his foot furiously, listening to the rain and the hum of the stove burner. He really needed to talk to Meth to straighten this mess out.

"Here," said Kasra, handing him the box with the prepaid phone. While he got busy ripping it open, she lifted the sheet from his legs.

Under the covers, he was wearing nothing but his boxer briefs. She removed the bandage on his left thigh, a few inches above the knee. With the iodine she'd purchased, she swabbed the wound yellow.

"That cut is still bleeding," she said. "You may need stitches. Even with the coagulant I picked up, the bleeding might not stop."

"Just slather the crap on there and wrap it tight," said Dale.

Kasra did as he asked, then went back to the stove.

Dale powered up the Android phone and waited for the Vodafone signal. Once he had it, he dialed Meth, hoping he might get lucky since she wouldn't recognize the number. *Nope.* Straight to a long beep. She was still freezing him out, hadn't even sent him a keep alive response. She'd gone into full-on passive-aggressive mode. Small wonder.

He dialed another number to a phone he knew would be answered. But it was a call he'd been dreading.

"Good morning, this is Midshipman Fourth Class Goodman," a young Annapolis plebe said. Dale could imagine the skinny kid manning the desk in the front entrance—quarterdeck—of Bancroft Hall at three a.m. Dale asked the midshipman of the watch to go get Midshipman Second Class Grace Dale. The CIA man faked himself as Commander So-and-So with the superintendent's office, an emergency.

Grace was rushing through her military greeting a minute later, voice hurried.

"Grace," Dale interrupted her. "Stop. It's okay. It's just me. Dad." Dale could see that Kasra was listening to him, eavesdropping. He didn't care. Even strange American officers had families.

Comprehension in Annapolis took a few seconds—but only a few. His kid was sharp. "Dad. What are you *doing?*"

Just like Meth, Dale thought in a blink. "I'll explain later. It'll all make sense—promise. Look, Grace, have you heard from your mother? I *really* need to talk to her. Really."

"Yes," she said.

Dale's heart leapt.

"I had a text from her a few days ago," Grace added. "Why? Dad—what's going on?"

"Everything's fine. I'll have to explain later. I just need to talk to her."

The line stayed quiet.

"Everything really *is* fine, Grace," Dale added. "We're both okay. We'll both be back soon."

Dale's daughter took a moment before whispering her reply. "*Are you, Dad? I mean really?* I'm probably not supposed to say this . . ." The whisper got quieter. "There was an FBI agent here yesterday. He told me I was supposed to call if you checked in."

Dale swore to himself. *Crack Fall. Too cute.*

He had to think carefully about his response. Kasra was obviously listening. So was Grace.

"Yeah," Dale said with his eyes screwed shut. "Don't worry about that, though. It's just a misunderstanding. I've been working closely with FBI. I just haven't been able to check in on time yet. Now have your mother call me on this number, okay? It's urgent. Very, *very* urgent. I mean it. Get a pen. Ready? Country code four-four . . ."

"Here you go," Kasra said, forty-five seconds after Dale had hung up. He'd spent the interlude staring at the ceiling. "Sit," the Iranian woman said with an amused half smile. "You need to eat. You look really pale."

Dale grunted into a sitting position and accepted the soup. "Thanks. But we should get going—soon."

"To the embassy?"

Before Dale could come up with a plausible answer, he felt the boat rock and spring against its moorings, nearly spilling his soup.

He raised a finger to his mouth, shushed the Iranian woman. Carefully replacing his spoon, he signaled her to get to the head and lock the door. He silently removed his blanket as she crept away, her eyes wide. Through the porthole Dale scanned the dock, seeing nothing. He felt the boat rock again. He cursed himself for calling MI-5's Spring that morning, surely giving up the trace . . . should have already been on the run by now. The boat listed back to the other side. Or maybe Hezbollah had gone back to the doctor. Maybe *they* were here.

Clad only in his underwear, Dale moved to the corner of the galley, out of sight of the boat's entrance, waiting for the door to get kicked in.

If it was cops, he thought, then that was it, the jig would be up. He'd just have to accept the consequences—a dank cell in some British jail where he'd endure a hundred hours of pointless interrogations while the lead on Kahlidi got colder and colder. Thinking about that interrogation, a dozen quick explanations Dale might give started whipping through his head. He thought them all stupid.

He thought of the big Arab he'd knifed in the stairwell, the kidnappers. Did Hezbollah know about Gulrajani's lair?

He grabbed a steak knife out of the block and waited. He heard footsteps on the deck, keys jingling, the door swinging in.

Keys jingling.

Dale put the knife back on the counter.

"Hello, Doctor," he said, moving quickly to block the door behind Gulrajani.

CHAPTER 38

"WELL, KASEM," MEREDITH SAID, SMILING. "SO NICE TO SEE YOU AGAIN. How you holdin' up?" She put her hand on the Quds man's upper arm and gave a small squeeze.

The Iranian turned his head, avoiding her. Now, from this angle, Meredith could see the contusion at his temple, the purple bruise under his jaw. An enormous swath of bandages bulged from the upper thigh of his right leg.

When Kahlidi didn't answer, Meredith looked up at Werner. "You said he was lucid, right?"

"Perfectly lucid," said Werner. "Come on, Kasem, let's hear you talking again."

The Iranian kept his eyes closed and shook his head in small, pained increments.

Werner looked at the two IDF soldiers standing to either side of the gurney. "Captain—you're sure he's all right now, yes?"

"The drugs should be out of his system," said the captain. "We even fed and washed him, like you asked."

"Excellent," said Werner. He leaned forward, close to Kasem's face. The Caesarea boss placed a grandfatherly hand on the younger Iranian's head. Kahlidi tried to shake it off, weakly. "Come, come, Colonel. I've brought an old friend for you. Show some manners to the lady."

Kahlidi kept his face toward the wall.

"Now don't be like that," said Werner. "The lady's already seen the tape of our chat from early this morning. She now knows much more about your *Taniyn* project. Do you not remember our chat? Captain, lean him up a bit more. Let's get him in a more attentive posture, jog his memory. And please—give us some privacy."

Kahlidi was sitting at a seventy-degree angle now, arms and legs shackled to the gurney's rails. The door clicked as the attending IDF medical officer left. The Quds officer blinked with an effort.

"Ah, there you are, Colonel. That's better," Werner said. The Mossad man then turned to Meredith. "I think you'd agree this morning's interview tape was fairly clear. But I'm sure you want to question Mr. Kahlidi yourself. And, of course, I'd like to avoid CIA accusing us of creating a deep-fake composite recording." The Mossad man smiled.

Meredith was shocked at Kahlidi's bruised face. Long a proponent of enhanced interrogations, she now felt a wave of revulsion.

She motioned Werner outside, into the hallway. Through the two-way mirror they watched Kahlidi, who had yet to move a muscle. The medical officers scattered when they saw the Caesarea boss and his curious American guest in the borrowed, unmarked IDF Army officer's uniform.

"Would you mind, Werner, if I had some time alone with him?" Meredith asked.

"Of course, Ms. Morris-Dale," the Caesarea man said. "Maybe you can get him to tell us what the Iranians intend to *do* with *Taniyn*, now that we know how deadly it truly is."

"I'll try. But if it's going to work, I need to be alone with him. Can I ask you to turn off all the video cameras? He needs to feel safe with me, see that I'm comfortable. I'm his original recruiter. I'd sought to build a bond of trust with him that I'd like to use."

Werner glanced at Kahlidi through the glass, then smiled at Meredith. "If I say yes to that request, what are the odds you'll believe me?"

"Low," she said. "But will you do it anyway?"

He nodded. "Give me ten minutes."

"Kasem," Meredith said after a cup of coffee in the break room where she'd gamed out her strategy. She scooted her chair close to the gurney's side. "It's just you and me now. No recordings, I promise. Now. Tell me honestly—how are you feeling? Did Mossad do this to you? Werner said your wounds happened during your snatch. Should I believe him?"

The Iranian kept his swollen eyes shut and whispered something. Meredith strained to hear it. She asked the Iranian to say it again, moving close to his mouth. "I'm . . . not talking to you," he breathed.

Meredith recoiled, sitting upright.

"Kasem," she said, leaning back in. "In case it hasn't dawned on you, I'm your *only* way out of here. Do you really want to spend the rest of your life in a Mossad prison? I should think our old deal for three million and an anonymous life in the US is looking pretty good about now. Too bad you walked."

The Iranian's head shook. Barely. He whispered again, asked her for water. She signaled through the one-way mirror for someone to get it. Once a bottle was in her hand, she leaned forward, helped him drink from a straw.

"I'm your way out of here," she repeated as she held the bottle. "Now let's get back on track with our deal. Beginning with you telling me a few things."

The Quds man shook his head, spit the straw out of his mouth. He shut his eyes again, turning away, whispering. "Meredith . . ." She leaned over him to hear. "You . . . always . . . *lie.*"

She leaned back in her chair. She crossed her legs, then uncrossed them. She took a swig from her own water bottle and looked at the Iranian's face. But his eyes were still closed. After another few seconds, the CIA woman hovered over him, positioning her face directly over her recruit. "You're the one who betrayed me. John. *Us.*"

Kahlidi didn't move in response. She sat back down and watched him, waiting for him to say something. Nearly a minute passed before she saw his mouth moving. He seemed to be grunting, preparing to speak, finding the right word. Meredith leaned in again, positioning her ear close to the Iranian's mouth. "Where . . . is Kasra?" Kahlidi whispered. "What . . . have you done with her?" His eyes stayed shut, but his mouth remained parted.

"You know what happened to Kasra. She's probably back in Iran by now. In fact, she should be one of the reasons why we need to get you back in Quds quickly, where you can execute our deal. We may not be able to get her to the US now, but you'll be able to protect her. Right?"

The Iranian was still facing the wall, unmoving.

"Kasem," Meredith said to the back of his head. "*I'm* not the reason Kasra is back in Tehran. MOIS just happened to find her before we did. That's not *my* fault. You have to believe me."

"You used her as bait," Kahlidi said hoarsely. "And now she's gone. Because of you. Because you . . ." His voice died away. He shook his head, rustling the pillow.

"What do you mean I used her as bait?" she probed, standing now, leaning over him, trying to get a read of his banged-up face.

"John could have got her, brought her back," said the Quds man. "He had her in his sights, right there. Now she's gone. I—"

"What are you talking about?" she interrupted, grabbing his chin, forcing him to face her directly. "What do you mean John was right there?"

Trapped in her grasp, the Iranian shook his head briskly, trying to free himself. But he was weak. He let out a quick breath through pursed lips.

"Kasem," she said, squeezing his face harder. "What the fuck are you talking about?"

"I just realized," he said. "You really don't know what I'm talking about."

"Why did you just mention John?"

"Because," the Iranian said. "Your husband was in London with the Mossad people. He did this to me."

"Goddamnit, Werner!" Meredith shouted at the Caesarea boss some thirty-seven minutes later. "How could you withhold that part of the tape from me?"

The sky had dimmed. In the window behind Werner, small rectangular office windows formed checkerboards on the dark Tel Aviv skyline.

"Meredith," said the Caesarea boss. "My interrogation stayed focused on *Taniyn*. You saw the whole tape. Once I got what I was looking for, I stopped and got to work with the IDF general staff on our next military moves to stamp this thing out before it's too late. Besides, he needed medical attention for the bullet in his leg. I didn't have much time."

"You didn't debrief the team you sent to get him?" she asked, dark eyebrows compressed.

"I've had no time for that. I've been in strike planning meetings. We're going to bomb every SA-5 site in Lebanon. That takes some work."

"I don't believe you."

Werner shook his head. "Look. Meredith. You know I only care about *Taniyn*. Once Kahlidi confirmed its capabilities, we've gotten very busy around here. I'm sure you can imagine."

"I can imagine many things, Werner," she said. "Did Kahlidi say anything about Kasra during your interrogation?"

"Who?" asked Werner, one eye squinted.

"Kasra Khani, his girlfriend. Kahlidi didn't mention her to you? I find that hard to believe."

"Hard to believe? Meredith, Kahlidi has only heightened our worst fears about Iran and Hezbollah—and the Vienna deal. Why, for God's sake, aren't we talking about a response to Iran right now? And why would I have ever asked a Quds colonel about his love life?"

"How many *katsas* were in the London snatch when you picked Kahlidi up, Werner?"

Werner paused. Then sighed. "Three."

"And you had no idea John was there? Remember, sir, I know you were spying on me. And my family."

"Are you back to trusting the Iranians more than you trust us, Ms. Morris-Dale?"

"Knock it off."

Werner looked down at his desk blotter. "My dear, you now have the intelligence on *Taniyn*. Kahlidi gave it to you."

"He only confirmed it's radiological-capable. We have no idea how they're going to deploy it or what its intended target is . . . or if they've even gotten a warhead into Lebanon."

"I don't care."

"What if they already have a weapon ready to go? You consider that? The moment you attack, they use it. We all go nuke. Think about it. You need better intelligence. I still think we can use Kahlidi for that."

He waved her away. "Perhaps it's time we got you back to Beirut Station so you can stop your insane nuclear deal and expose this thing to the world. We can find a way to covertly insert you back to Beirut. You could wake up in your hotel room like nothing happened."

"You *will* get me back to my hotel. But not before you come clean with me on just what the relationship is between Mossad and my ex-husband."

"We're wasting time."

"I already know you followed John to Hawaii, stayed on him, even . . . even after I'd left for the mainland. I'm now thinking you met him in London as part of some plan. *Why?*"

Werner sucked on a cheek, pausing. "Meredith," he said finally. "Do you expect me to believe that you don't know about John's relationship with . . . ?"

He stopped speaking when she shut her eyes.

"Werner. If this is one of those 'the spouse is always the last to know' kind of things, then just go ahead and tell me."

Werner said nothing, his face neutral.

"John and I are *divorced*," she added. "Just in case that tidbit somehow slipped your omniscient intelligence agency. Now . . . tell me about this relationship."

Werner blinked at her. "You really don't know about your former husband's history with Mossad? The op where I first met John?"

"Where *you* first met John."

"Yes. Me."

Meredith looked down. "Werner, are you telling me that John actually *works* for you? That he . . ." So many ideas had broken loose in her head that she couldn't finish the sentence. The "French" woman in Egypt, the Maya Shaheen overlap in Hawaii, the Mossad assault on the horse ranch with John there . . . And now, John happening to be in London during another Mossad assault.

"Wait," Werner said, watching Meredith, shaking his head emphatically. "It's not what you're thinking."

She pinched her own leg, digging in her nails, wondering if she could draw her own blood. She kept her eyes down, shaking her head.

"John *doesn't* work for us," said Werner. "Far from it. But we . . . Well. He worked *with* us once. On Stuxnet. And, I'll admit this much, I . . . wanted to recruit John. And I did send someone after him. But that was because I thought John was Kahlidi's handler and I knew Kahlidi was the key to *Taniyn*. We were desperate. You know that."

Meredith breathed deeply. "I need to know everything," she said through the exhale. "The truth." She placed an open hand on Werner's desk. "Please," she whispered, willing her voice not to break.

It took the better part of an hour for the Caesarea boss to fully recount the seven-year-old Sharm el-Sheikh op where he'd first met John Dale. A long, halting hour with frequent interruptions for Meredith's cross-examination.

And now, knowing he would want the American woman as an ally to counter *Taniyn*, the Caesarea boss promised her he'd find out the full story of what had gone down in London too. He swore he really *didn't* know the details of the snatch—but that he'd be happy to make some calls. He sent Meredith to a break room and punched his secure speakerphone button.

A few minutes after that, Meredith resumed her seat in Werner's office, where, the Caesarea boss admitted, Kahlidi's account had been correct.

According to the lead *kidon* on the case, Werner explained, John *had* been there in London. But the *kidon* swore Dale had been unharmed. Yes, they'd had a firefight with the Hezbollah cell. Yes, Dale had been there. But he'd been left alone, uninjured. Meredith now knew everything, Werner assured her.

When he'd finally finished, Meredith nodded and cleared her throat. "This *kidon* who led the snatch in London, the one you just spoke to. Is she a woman?"

"Yes," Werner said after two long beats. "I think you know, we believe women make for good cover in our foreign ops."

Meredith nodded once. "And Werner," she said. "Tell me. Was this *kidon* the same one who'd been working with John on the Egyptian Stuxnet op, staying with him at the resort in Sharm el-Sheikh? I believe the alias she used was Analise Beauchamps back then. Correct?"

"Correct," said Werner after a pause. "That's her."

"And," Meredith went on. "Is this *kidon*'s name . . . Maya Shaheen?"

Werner hesitated before answering. "Yes," he finally said. "Maya Shaheen."

Meredith's eyes fell to the carpet below Werner's desk. She studied the weave, noted an old coffee stain. She then looked up at the Caesarea boss. "And where is Ms. Shaheen now?"

"Here. In Tel Aviv."

Meredith nodded. "Good. I want to meet her."

"Is that really necessary?"

"Yes," she said. "It is."

CHAPTER 39

BUT NOT, MEREDITH THOUGHT, BEFORE FRESHENING UP.

To keep her cover solid, Werner had let the CIA woman use the living facility reserved for the Caesarea boss in the bunker beneath the building. He'd led her there personally, snagging a female Army captain along the way who was instructed to provide anything the visiting American might need. Quietly, after the Caesarea boss had left, Meredith asked the pretty young captain if she might borrow her lipstick.

And now, after a dark transit across Tel Aviv, she faced Maya Shaheen through a courtyard's iron security gate. The Caesarea boss was at Meredith's side, ahead of her, muttering the usual words of introduction with a bonhomie that felt, to both women, forced.

Maya was taller than Meredith—long-limbed, dark-haired, self-possessed of an inner calm. *Lithe* was the word that came to Meredith's mind, noting the woman's tapered legs, olive complexion, elongated nose.

But not necessarily young. Those eyes, the CIA woman thought instantly, put her at about thirty-seven, maybe even older. The eyes were canted and dark—lovely—yet betrayed by a certain weariness.

After a very firm handshake, Maya led Meredith across brick pavers, a dripping fountain, a second gate, and finally, to the Mossad woman's front door. Through a tiled foyer, past a spotless galley kitchen, Meredith's eyes circled the room. No obvious trace of a man. Scant food on the open-shelved pantry shelves. A hardbacked Hebrew book, open to the midpoint and facedown on a coffee table.

A chair was pulled out with a scrape. Meredith realized Werner was motioning her to sit at a table. Maya was already seated, legs crossed. She was looking up at Meredith.

Werner dispensed with small talk. He gave a short explanation of how Meredith had come to be in their presence. He told Maya that Meredith now knew the backstory, about the Sharm el-Sheikh op on the A. Q. Khan network.

"Now we have some tactical matters to discuss to deal with Kahlidi, what to do with him," he said. "But before we begin, you should know, Meredith, that Maya has submitted her resignation. She is here, ah, *voluntarily*, if you will." The old man attempted a smile. It went unreturned.

"Is that so?" Meredith said, eyes still on Werner, addressing him as though Maya weren't in the room. "She quit?"

"Yes," he said. "A few days ago."

"Then what was she doing in London?"

"A favor," Werner answered. "A favor. For me."

"And for John," Maya said, her first words at the table. "For his safety."

Meredith didn't much like the way she pronounced *John*. The Israeli's version had a French quality, more like *Jean*. "Oh? And how's that?"

Werner shifted in his chair. "You already know," he said to Meredith, "that we believed John had been controlling Kahlidi as a CIA asset when he was still in Tehran. So, when we got intelligence that John was in London, I wanted a team of *katsas* to surveil him, thinking he'd lead us to your Quds spy. I asked Maya to lead the op, since she'd worked with John before."

"Since she'd worked with him before," Meredith repeated automatically.

"Where are our manners?" Werner asked after a delay in which he'd recrossed his legs twice. "Maya, you have at least ten bottles of my wine. And perhaps some cheese and bread. The lady here has been through quite an ordeal. Why don't we—"

"I'm not hungry," said Meredith. "Let's just talk."

"Mrs. Dale," said Maya, "I believe I can speak plainly about why Werner sent me to London."

"That would be refreshing," said Meredith, coughing once.

"The assault on the horse farm," said Maya. "Your safe house. It was a big mistake. You must know that I was very much against it. I thought it tactically reckless and strategically disastrous."

Meredith felt her pulse rising.

"But you must also understand," the *kidon* went on, "when we learned John was there at the horse farm, it confirmed our belief that he was Kahlidi's handler, that he'd been running Kahlidi all along. We'd already been surveilling John to get to Kahlidi, but we'd only *suspected* John's involvement. Until the horse farm."

"*Surveilling* John. And for how long were you following him?"

"Since the meeting with Dorsey fell apart," Werner said after loudly clearing his throat. "Since I knew your director wouldn't give up Kahlidi as a source—even though we've been staring down the barrel of *Taniyn*. Even Dorsey just . . . ignored me. It was clear CIA had no intention of sharing the take you were getting from Kahlidi. After you and Dorsey met with our director here in Tel Aviv, it confirmed our initial instincts. You would refuse to share Kahlidi with us."

"That's right," added Maya. "Without official cooperation, I went to Hawaii last month to corner John, thinking he might . . . work with us. Together, like before."

Together. Like before. Meredith looked away.

"John overreacted," the *kidon* went on. "He assaulted us, evaded. We concluded that we'd been right, that he was Kahlidi's handler, that you'd been there in Hawaii debriefing John, just before you were recalled to Langley. It was the only thing that made sense to us."

Meredith was looking through a gap between Werner and Maya, into the modest kitchen, forcing her hands to stay still.

"And later," Maya went on, "during the raid on the horse farm, John fought fiercely, killed one of our *katsas*, wounded two others. My entire force wanted revenge on him. So, when Werner wanted a team to snatch

Kahlidi from John in London—I decided to go personally, for John's safety. I was worried about your husband."

"Ex-husband," Meredith said.

"In any case," Maya said, "that's what I meant when I said it was a favor to John. I wanted to protect him. From . . . us."

"But how did you know John was even there?" Meredith asked. *When I didn't.*

Werner held up a gnarled hand. "With all due respect, Meredith, I'm afraid I can't allow Maya to answer that question. I'm all for a long-overdue air-clearing among allies . . . but not . . ."

Maya put her hand on Werner's. "Let me. A fair question, Meredith . . ."

It was the first time Maya had used Meredith's name. The Israeli rolled the *R*.

"And if at the root of that question," the Mossad woman continued, "is whether John coordinated with me ahead of time, tipped me off like an asset . . . I can assure you he did not. We used standard intelligence methods to track John to the UK. The same methods we used to know you were in Beirut. We simply assumed he would be with Kahlidi at a UK safe house. We know you use many safe houses in London."

True enough, thought Meredith. "And how did you leave things with John? Werner said he was left unharmed. But what does that mean? What was he doing?"

Meredith noticed the barest quiver in Maya's cheek. The first hint of emotion she'd seen since arriving at the Mossad woman's apartment.

"I'm sorry," Maya said. "You don't know? Haven't you spoken to him?"

Meredith's heart thumped. "No. CIA thinks John is an agent of *yours*. I've been asked to limit contact with him, so we haven't spoken. How do you know he was okay?"

"I know because . . ." Maya paused to pull some hair behind her ear. "I know because I spoke to John yesterday. He told me he's hiding but safe. In the UK—with Kahlidi's woman."

"You called *her*, John?" shouted Meredith through the phone. "Are you fucking insane? You know damn well CIA suspects you of playing footsie with Mossad and you think the best thing to do is to call Caesarea's top *kidon*?"

Werner had finally relented, giving Meredith a burner Israeli phone to use. She was staying in the visiting officers' quarters in the bunker below Matcal Tower now, finally alone, sitting on her bed in the borrowed Israeli army uniform.

Dale was lying on a bed of his own in the back bedroom of a Marriott suite, rented via the doctor's credit card. Dishes from room service were spread across the desk. Dale's leg was raised from the mattress, properly sutured by Kasra after the doc had given her the medical supplies. Along with his wallet.

"*No*," said Dale, instantly irritated by the tone. The phone call had woken him from a fitful sleep. "*No*, I didn't call her."

"John. Stop lying to me. Just stop. They've already explained to me the Sharm el-Sheikh op. And I know all about Maya in Maui. I've spent the last three hours with the woman. I doubt I'll ever know everything, but if you think you're protecting some old op now, don't bother. I can't *believe* you called her. Do you know how this *looks*?"

"Meth," he retorted groggily. He'd finally come down from the Adderall. Now he wished he hadn't. He checked his watch—one a.m. in London, three in Beirut. "What choice did I have? I've been trying like hell to call you. You haven't picked up, not once. You didn't even return my keep alive signal. What the hell was I supposed to do?"

"But you called *her*? Do you know how that's going to *look*?"

Meredith's tone shook the rust from Dale's head.

"Well . . . no," he said. "Technically I *didn't* call her. Maya happened to give me a protocol once—a secure protocol to reach her—in an emergency. You know, tradecraft, working through a server to establish contact. And it's a goddamned good thing I had that lifeline, Meth."

"Tradecraft. A *protocol*. Jesus, John. You *are* a Mossad spy. I can't fucking believe Rance was right about you."

"Knock it off."

"What the hell did you think you were doing in London anyway?"

"Isn't it obvious? I was going for Kahlidi. I told you he'd be going back for his girl. I came to get him. I came to get him so I could fix your goddamned problem and get you out of Beirut alive."

"I don't need you to fix my goddamned problems. *Ever.* You ditched the FBI. Rance and Dorsey already think you're a Mossad asset. And that's before your latest . . . *tradecraft*. Jesus, John."

"Yeah, well . . ."

"It was just about the stupidest thing you could do," Meredith went on. "Sometimes I wonder if you *ever* look before you leap. Honest to God, John, do you *ever* think?"

That did it. A surge of adrenaline nearly bounced Dale's head from the pillow. "*Maya* answered me, Meth. *You* didn't."

Oh no, he thought one second later, holding the phone very still. He hurried to cover himself. "I tried everything, Meth. I even called Grace. I left my number with her. I wanted you to call me. I was looking all over for you."

"Jesus, John. You involved *Grace* in this mess? You told our daughter to lie to the *FBI*? Right there in the hallowed halls of Annapolis, your shared church of honor, you're using her like an *asset*? Are you fucking kidding me?"

"*I didn't want to!*" he shouted, sensing his deepening hole. He thought about hanging up to cut his losses. But after a long, shaking breath, he said, "I'll ask you again, Meth, what choice did I have? I was trying to get to you. You weren't picking up. I'm dying out here. For *you.*"

Three or four seconds passed where Dale thought he might have recovered. But then Meredith was back on the line, sounding clinical, the cool professional. *Well*, Dale thought. *At least the fight's over.*

Hopefully.

"Neither of our phones are encrypted," she said tonelessly. "But I need to know your status. Report it to me."

"Both our phones are burners. We should be okay."

"My burner phone," Meredith said, "was handed to me by the head of Caesarea. Think about what that means, John. *Think.* Just give me your status report. Carefully."

"Fine. Knife wound to upper left thigh, ambulatory, medically dressed. Police looking for suspects near the incident. I have your . . . *witness.* She's in similar condition. Leg wound. Ambulatory. Medically dressed. We're in a safe spot for now. We probably have another forty-eight before we have to move. Risk level yellow-three. There's my report."

"Yellow-three. All right. Thank you."

"And while we're at it, I need you to clear a friendly path for me," said Dale. "The embassy, preferably. You need to make them understand. Got it?"

"I'm making a path. But not for the embassy. I've got a lot to figure out here first."

"Whatever. I just need a way out of here, Meth."

"Someone's already on the way, coordinating your egress. Should be there around nine local. Just stay put."

"Good," said Dale. "Thank you. Who's coming?"

"Maya. Your handler," Meredith said just before hanging up.

CHAPTER 40

"*DODA* SAYS YOU CAN WISH ON THE SEA JUST LIKE YOU CAN WISH ON the fountain," said Dil. The girl spoke in the careful French that her *doda*, Maya, had taught her.

Meredith's bare feet were sunk into the muddy shore, her borrowed Israeli officer's trousers rolled to the knee. She held the seven-year-old's hand by her side. "*Un vœux? Comment?*"

Dil squinted up at her. "First you close your eyes," the girl said. "Then you think up your wish." She opened her fist to reveal a coin. "You're supposed to blow on it before you throw it into the sea. That's what my *doda* says."

"*Mais oui,*" Meredith returned. The baking brown hills on the far side of the Sea of Galilee reminded Meredith of Daït Aoua, a Moroccan lake in the Atlas Mountains. She'd camped there once with her out-doorsy mother while her father had been away for a diplomatic pow-wow in Cairo. "I think your *doda* is right. May I wish on it too? You can still do the throwing."

After a few seconds of consideration, the girl nodded.

Meredith knelt. She'd cast more than one wish into that Moroccan lake herself, once upon a time. The seven-year-old opened her fist to reveal the ten-agorot coin. After they both blew, Dil cocked her arm and tossed the coin into the water, leaving a barely perceptible splash in the freshwater lake known as the Sea of Galilee. Dil was a lefty, like Grace, Meredith noticed.

"I wished for a trip to Australia. To see a kangaroo," said Dil.

Still kneeling, Meredith stroked the girl's head and smoothed her windblown bronzed curls. "Didn't your *doda* tell you that you're not supposed to share your wishes?"

"I forgot," said Dil. "Can we do it again? Do you have another coin, madame?"

"*Non*," Meredith said, stroking the curls, smiling. "*Je suis désolé*. I think your wish will still come true. But just in case, I'll make sure to get you another coin. *D'accord?*"

"I believe I hear it coming, madame," said Dil, eyes searching skyward.

"*Qu'est-ce qui vient?*"

"*Un hélicoptère, madame. Un hélicoptère avec ma doda!*" The girl let go of Meredith's hand and splashed ashore.

Against the pink clouds of a dying afternoon, Meredith spotted the black Eurocopter. Dark and futuristic, it raced through terrain gaps at low altitude, zeroing in on Werner's property with daring speed, as if on a raid. Meredith hastened to a jog, following Dil, who was already sprinting up the hill to the house.

Rotors whipped the grass into silver ripples. A door slid open as the aircraft settled on its wheels. Out hopped Maya, dressed in jeans, sunglasses, and a light military-style overshirt with epaulets. The Mossad woman walked quickly toward Werner's house, carrying a soft-sided attaché case and nearly colliding with Dil. Meredith watched as Maya knelt to hold the girl in a long embrace. Then the pair headed into the house, holding hands.

Two middle-aged men in khaki followed. Though Meredith didn't recognize either, she'd been told whom to expect.

And after the Israelis came John. Hunched under the rotors with a limp, he was wearing a ratty old concert T-shirt. He'd slung his backpack over one shoulder and a scuffed leather jacket over the other. He was looking around, squinting in the sun, turning his head back and forth as his hair flew sideways. Then he saw Meredith. He kept on toward the house.

It took three more hours before the couple was finally alone, confidently free of the Mossad listening devices they'd assumed to be everywhere. Werner had introduced them to Mitz, head of the Mossad foreign agent division called Junction. They'd also met Galin, CO of the military intelligence wing known as AMAN, which ran the Unit 8200 SIGINT detachment.

Werner had forbidden shoptalk at the dinner table. Instead, his wife Rachel at his side, he'd forced them to sample his Galilean wines. Holding glass after glass to the light, the Caesarea boss had rambled on about minerality, acidity, malolactic fermentation, phenolic compounds, the terroirs of Israel and Lebanon.

Dale had stifled yawns and thrown secret glances toward Meredith.

After dinner, Werner had declared an hour's recess before the real meeting was to begin. Dale had tried to slink away, to make it down the hall to his guest room for some solid sleep. But Meredith had intercepted him. She'd dragged him down to an old rowboat on the lakeshore, where, she'd insisted, they could talk. Privately. Finally.

Now, in the gloaming of eight p.m., John had rowed his ex-wife thirty yards offshore. A low sliver of moon hung over the Jordanian hills. Dale balanced the dripping oars on the splintered gunnels and let the boat drift.

Having barely spoken since John had arrived, Meredith leaned forward and grabbed his hands. "I shouldn't have ripped into you when you were in London like that," she said, shifting her face to look directly into his eyes. "It was fucked up. I apologize."

Dale pulled his hands free and looked out over the lake, still saying nothing.

"I screwed up," said Meredith. "But in my defense, John, it's been a miserable couple of weeks. I even got sick. Really sick. I'm still not great." She forced a cough. "But I know better. I shouldn't have lit into you. I'm not making excuses. I'm apologizing."

Dale remained looking away.

"Look, John," she said. "I admit it. I fucked up. I snapped, took it out on you. But it was wrong. I really am sorry. Okay? *Okay?*"

"Fine," said Dale after a ten-count. "Apology accepted. Can I get to bed now? Would that be all right with you? And good old Mr. Werner?"

Meredith stared at him. A stray voice from the shore brought an unintelligible human utterance across the water. The security people, she supposed, walking along the bank. "This may be our only chance to talk," she said quietly. "Alone. Even Mossad can't bug a rowboat."

"Oh yeah?" said Dale, glancing down the length of the oars. "But fine. You've said your piece. I forgive you. And we're finally both out of harm's way. Now let's keep it that way. What time's our flight tomorrow?"

Meredith glanced toward the shore again. She thought she could see the faint glow of a cigarette moving near the water. "Take us farther out," she said. "You know how sound travels."

Dale sighed, then rowed vigorously, grunting.

"Far enough," said Meredith in a half whisper a minute later, kicking his foot. "Come on. We can talk here, just keep your voice down."

"You sure?"

"Yes. This should do it."

"What about snipers? I think they could still get a drop on us from the house."

"*John,*" she whispered. "*Quiet.*"

"We may have found a loophole in their security. I could keep rowing to the other side of the lake," said Dale. "That's Jordan, right? I know Jordan fairly well. They based the Sycamore op in Jordan. But I guess you know that now."

"*Quiet.* I mean it."

Dale slumped back and looked up at the sky. A few stars were visible.

The wind had strengthened on this flat part of the lake, farther from shore. Meredith put a hand over her hair, trying to keep it in place. She cleared her still tender throat. "Okay. Now. *Quietly*, tell me about your reunion with Kahlidi in Tel Aviv. When you saw him—how was he? How would you gauge his attitude?"

"How would I know about his attitude?" Dale whispered back.

"You were with him for two hours."

Dale boated the oars with a clunk that seemed unnaturally loud. "Was it that long?"

"Yes. According to Werner."

"Our jailer?"

"*Shh.* It's not like that. You know we both need to stay off the grid for a while. This place works."

"People already think I'm a Mossad asset. This ought to really clear things up."

Meredith coughed into her hand, shattering the peace. "Just tell me how Kahlidi was when you saw him in Tel Aviv. Pretend you're his case officer and I'm your boss. I *am* still your boss. Technically."

Dale leaned forward, elbows on knees, sighing. "You saw Kasem. You saw how fucked up he was."

"Yes. And he's still my agent, my responsibility. I'm trying to assess his capability. Do you think Mossad ruined him? It looked like they nearly beat him to death."

"*I'm* the one that fucked up his face," said Dale. "I pounded his head against the steps. I had him in cuffs—until your good friends here tased me." He nodded his head toward the lights of Werner's house. "Before we were forced to endure the longest wine tasting in history, did they mention *that* to you?"

"They said they used nonlethal means on you," she whispered.

"That's rich."

"I thought Mossad wounded Kahlidi. During his interrogation."

"Maybe. But Mossad's a little too slick to leave marks," said Dale quietly. "You'll notice they didn't leave any on me either. Wind's picking up. We're drifting in."

She nodded. Dale rowed the boat farther out into the lake.

"What about the London egress?" Meredith asked when he'd boated the oars again. "Tell me about it. How'd they get you up here?"

"A van showed up at the Kensington Marriott," said Dale. "Before I knew it, Maya was handing out Israeli passports, briefing us on our new legends, just in case something went wrong. I couldn't tell where the airport was. They put hoods over our heads clamped by tight earmuffs. Kasra was crying, worried about ending up in Evin Prison. She thought it all a MOIS trick."

"How much time did you have alone with Kahlidi in Tel Aviv?"

"About an hour. They spirited us over to a hospital on base to treat our wounds. I'm fine, by the way."

"What was Kahlidi's reunion with Kasra like? I asked Werner to give them plenty of alone time."

"He cried. She cried. They hugged. Et cetera. I left the room."

"Did Kahlidi say anything to you when he saw her? He must have been shocked."

"He couldn't stop thanking me for bringing her in. One of the reasons I left."

"Anything about me?"

"He doesn't like you."

"Right."

"Meth," said Dale. "I see where you're going. But if you're still thinking of running him as an agent, I'm not sure it'll work. He's an emotional train wreck."

A sudden gust flung Meredith's hair forward. "It was stupid of you to go for him in London. On your own," she said, taming her hair.

"Did it without thinking." He gave her his lopsided grin.

She looked away from it.

Leaning far over the thwart, he said, "Have you talked to Grace yet? I'm worried about my last conversation with her."

"Yes. She's fine. I took care of it."

"And the FBI? She freaked about that?"

"I told her not to worry, to just tell them she hadn't heard from us. I backed up your story. Used my special code with her, where she knows not to ask anything else."

"Special code."

"I'm sure you have something similar with her."

He shrugged.

Meredith looked back at the dim shore. She gathered the loose strands of her hair again, replacing them behind her head. "John," she whispered, "did you get a chance to meet the girl, Dil? We spent the day together. Maya's niece. I think."

Dale shrugged. "I saw her go off down the hall with Werner's wife. But it's not like I made conversation with a five-year-old."

"Seven."

"Whatever. No, I didn't talk to her. As you might imagine, Maya and I aren't the best of friends since her fellow *kidons* tasered the shit out of me."

Meredith nodded. The wind twirled the boat.

"Let's get the hell out of here," said Dale. "I'm glad we all made nice with Mossad again. It's been real. Now what time's our flight tomorrow?"

"John," she said, squeezing his knee. "I still need to run Kahlidi, get him back into Iran."

They both listened to the glop of the waves against the hull. "That's not going to happen," Dale finally said.

"He's my recruit. It's my job to get him back in the field."

Dale put the oars back in the water, rowing silently, looking over his shoulder toward the center of the lake. After a few more pulls, he stopped and sighed. "I heard the nuclear deal with Iran is about done. You shouldn't even need Kahlidi now."

"It's precisely because of the nuclear deal that I need Kahlidi now," said Meredith.

"Of course," said Dale, shaking his head.

Meredith leaned farther forward, lowering her voice. "The deal doesn't cover Hezbollah. And it allows for uranium enrichment to certain levels. Our official US policy is to—"

Dale held up a hand. "Meth. Stop. Let's just go home. Please."

"John," she whispered. "Hezbollah has built a set of very scary missiles. They're radiological-capable. They could use nuclear material that's *legal* in the new Iran deal, easier to smuggle in. That would turn these missiles into Hezbollah dirty bombs—targeted at Israel, right now."

"So? I'm sure Kahlidi will be happy to tell you about them. Give his intel over to Mossad. They can send people in to take the damn things out before anyone knows anything. It's their stock and trade."

"Kahlidi knows about the weapons—but that's it. He's been out of the game too long to know their plans. Quds has a new man in charge. It's why I need to get him back inside. To keep ahead of this."

"You're not the only section chief, Meth. Let your bosses take care of this."

"My reputation is shot in Langley. And they'll want 'observable data.' I don't have that. But I do have an idea how to get Kahlidi back over the wall. It means I need to go back to Beirut. Tomorrow."

Dale picked up the oars again. "No."

"What do you mean, *no?*"

He stroked the oars twice, then stopped. "I'm not letting you go back to Beirut. I came all this way to get you out of there. It's why I went for Kahlidi."

Meredith put her hands on his forearms. "I appreciate that. But—"

"Let's get out of here, Meth. Dorsey trusts your instincts. Always has. He put you in the job. Tell him. Let him prosecute it."

She waited a few seconds before responding, then pointed toward Werner's home. "You see all those lights up there at the house?"

He nodded.

"They're going to go to war based on what they know so far. Werner's one click away from going full scorched earth."

"Maybe he should."

"John. If Israel goes after Hezbollah, they'll hit back with this thing. Then what? Israel uses their own nukes on them in Lebanon. Iran goes berserk, hits targets all over the Gulf. That drags us in . . . along with the Syrians, Russians, Chinese. This can't happen."

Dale listened to the wind hitting the water, thinking about what she was saying, meeting her eye. It was a few seconds before he spoke. "Well . . . still. Mossad can handle it."

"Kahlidi is *my* agent. He's only going to operate because of *my* deal with him."

Dale sighed and looked up at the stars. "Fuck," he said.

"I know. But hear me out. I've talked Werner into something that can head this off, long term, a joint CIA-Mossad op. But it's highly unconventional."

"Not like the rest of this."

"You see them all up there at the house? They're here for me, for us. Werner promised me he'd go along with my idea."

"A promise from Werner. He's really done a number on you. On us."

"For what it's worth," said Meredith. "He's worried about your reaction to my proposal. He thinks you're a loose cannon."

"Good."

"And before we get back to shore, I swore to Werner I could get you on board."

"On board."

"Yes."

"With what?"

"Our new op."

CHAPTER 41

DESPITE A MILD HANGOVER, ED RANCE HAD RISEN EARLY ON WEDNES-
day morning for his daily run around Augarten, the elegant old baroque
park at Vienna's urban core.

It was, for him, a mandatory ritual, the fulfilment of a personal
pledge. On his fiftieth birthday the CIA division chief had sworn to
himself that he'd complete three miles in under thirty minutes, every
day, unconditionally, no matter where he found himself in the world
until the day he took his pension. That ten-minute-mile pace was to be
his redline, the Rubicon at which the advancing legions of age would go
no further.

That had been two years ago—and the defensive line, sadly, had
begun to show cracks.

Why, just twenty-four hours ago, sluggish from a late-night brandy
with the State boys after a long day, Rance had scared himself with a
dangerously slow time through the park. Technically, he knew, he *had*
missed the ten-minute pace—but the ambiguities of a loose shoelace
and unexpected tram-crossing had left him with a veneer of denial.

No more of that. This morning, on this run, the CIA man was determined to set things right. Now, pushing himself, feet pounding on a
bucolic Victorian avenue lined with chestnut trees, he stole a rapid
glance at his smartwatch. Much to his satisfaction he saw that he was
performing at a surprisingly strong clip—a near nine-minute pace, one
he hadn't seen in at least five years. Incredulous, he checked again. But
it was true.

And not far to go either. Up ahead, looming in the early morning mist, he could now make out the fifty-foot World War II former gun mount called—with Teutonic practicality—*der Flakturm*, the Flak Tower. The ugly concrete stack was Rance's finish line in Vienna, the end of the three miles. If he could reach it in less than thirty seconds, he realized now, then the nine-minute pace was his. It would be like turning back time.

With glory so close, he pumped his arms wildly and clenched his toes for an extra inch of stride. For this last fleeting *Flakturm* dash, Edward Ronald Rance gave it everything he had. And once finished, heaving, spitting, bent over, his smartwatch confirmed the tally: nine-minute pace. He raised one fist in celebration while the other stayed pegged to a knee.

I'm back, he thought, bent, spitting, fist swaying overhead.

Gasping, he looked up at the misty sky and watched a triangular flock of geese fly over. They were headed east. An augury? He smiled. His true destiny had always lay, he believed, in the East.

After all, it was the Near East Division as a clandestine nonofficial-cover officer where he'd begun his career. From there, he'd gone on to a chief of base assignment in Tashkent, where he'd helped lay the groundwork for the Afghanistan invasion under Jeff Dorsey. Staying east, he'd become deputy chief of station in Baghdad until Dorsey had picked him to run the Counterproliferation desk with its focus on Iran. Rance had always managed to be in the middle of the action and always emerged the stronger for it. And the action had always been in the East.

Surfing this pleasant wave of nostalgic achievement, watching the birds disappear into the low morning sun, he thought of the latest Eastern success. *His* Iran deal.

For, though it might not make the papers, it was *his* back-channel contact that had been the deal's real clincher. *He'd* been the one to midwife the relationship with Walid Zafir, the shadowy Iranian intelligence man who'd helped inform the American policymakers.

True, the Iranian wasn't an official agent or even asset of CIA just yet. But Rance had made the initial moves to recruit this murky peer into a vital contact, a liaison, someone high enough in the Iranian government who could relay signals, say the things that couldn't be said by diplomats—just like the old Russia hands had done in the Cold War. And the approach had been *his very own* idea. The credit would all go to *him*.

What an unlikely turn, he thought now, getting his breath under control, stretching a hamstring. The Zafir op had been started as a defensive move, a bulwark against the Atlas mess. Rance, Dorsey, and especially the director had all feared Meredith's botched Atlas recruitment might somehow infect the nuclear negotiation. But with Zafir, Rance had assured them, they'd have a back-channel relationship that might cushion that blow, offer amends—quietly among peer intelligence services, an insurance policy of sorts.

But so much more than that now. Even though Rance's secret Zafir meetings had dragged on with endless circumlocutions, the Iranian had eventually come to a startling point. Just five nights ago in a Krugerstrasse hookah bar, he'd dropped, "There are those of us within the Republic who are ready to turn the page." He'd then gone on to tell Rance—in so many words—that the Supreme Council was ready to sign, that any further negotiation points were just bluster for the rabid *pasdaran* back home. The Iranians wanted the deal. It was just as Rance had said weeks ago: *For every Lenin, there awaits a Gorbachev.*

Walid's pronouncement was just a signal. They'd all known that. "Hell," Vorhees had countered, "it might even be a deliberate deception." But that's when Rance had taken center stage with the State people. They were in his world now, and he wanted them to know it. *This is what I do*, he'd said. *And I'm telling you, this is real.*

Hopkins had agreed. Eventually they all had agreed. And then, just yesterday, having weighed all the factors of intelligence—Meredith's and Mossad's included—Dorsey had allowed Rance's signature to grace the final NIE endorsement. With that, the National Clandestine Service's official position could be summarized by its concluding sentence: *We assess that the inspection regime specified in the Joint United Nuclear*

Cooperation Agreement sufficiently contains the Iranian ballistic missile threat.

And now, at *der Flakturm*, still trying to get his lungs to behave, Rance stood upright. *Finally*, he was thinking as his breathing returned to normal. Finally, he'd found the way to put the mess that had been his career for the past eight months behind him. Thanks to his big win with Zafir, he could now sweep away that dreaded Russian honeypot business, the embarrassing exile to babysit the State negotiators, Meredith's unforgivable loss of Atlas . . . even his own failed marriage. All of it would be replaced by his pivotal world-beating role in Vienna. He was back. In the East. Back, baby!

Energized, he stood and slapped *der Flakturm* in a one-way high-five.

But just as his hand touched the concrete, he heard wheels grinding on gravel, the roar of an engine. Surprised to hear a car in the pedestrian park, he turned and saw a black Audi with lights flashing in its grill. It came straight toward him. Rance recognized the man behind the wheel from the embassy—DSS security. The agent's hand remained in his jacket as he got out of the vehicle. He'd drawn a machine pistol. *Why the fuck is—*

"Mr. Pine," the DSS agent called, using Rance's diplomatic cover. "I have orders to bring you in. Now, sir. CRITIC level two."

"Oh my God," Rance moaned in the embassy conference room thirty minutes later. Blowing against his still damp shirt, the air-conditioning accentuated the icy pit he felt in his stomach. He had to turn away. He could no longer look at the horrid image Dorsey was sharing on the videoconference screen. He let his face collapse into his cradled hands, then took one more glance through his fingers.

There, on the screen, was Meredith Morris-Dale—slumped, bruised, pale, staring defiantly up at the camera with one bruised eye, the other hidden behind a dirty hijab. Her kidnappers had draped a dark cloth across her body, one bare knee poking out. Her arm wore a metal shackle at the wrist, a chain that disappeared somewhere off to the side. Beside her was a folded newspaper, the French-language Beirut daily called *L'Orient-Le Jour*, dated two days earlier.

"*How?*" was all Rance managed to say.

"Exactly," responded Dorsey on the left side of the split screen now that the image had gone. It was three a.m. in DC and the head of the National Clandestine Service looked morose—tie gone, chin stubbled, shirt rumpled. On the right side of the split screen was Cowles, the Beirut chief of station. At ten a.m. local, Cowles wore a brightly colored golf shirt.

"Like I told Jeff," Cowles said. "Her last report was six days ago. She was due in today. We don't know when exactly she was snatched."

"*Snatched*," Rance repeated dumbly. His hands had yet to leave the sides of his head. How often had he feared just such a thing for himself? Though he didn't like Meredith Morris-Dale—at all—he nonetheless harbored a grudging respect. And here was this tough, feisty, fearless officer reduced to . . .

"But *how?*" asked Rance. "How did we get this photo?"

"I think you know, Ed," said Dorsey, "that her NOC was as a French freelance journo. She wanted to poke around the ports, work our agents in Beirut, look for nuclear smuggling loopholes as part of the NIE vet. Am I missing anything, Dave?"

"No," said Cowles. "You have it right. She wanted to stay in non-official cover since she didn't want the Israelis or Lebanese Intelligence to see what she was doing."

"Yeah," said Dorsey. "I personally approved the op . . . urged her to keep it quiet . . ." The spy boss looked down and shook his head, shutting himself up. Rance had never seen the chief like this. Never.

"Her kidnappers," the spy boss said after a moment, eyes pink, "call themselves *Août Noir*."

"But how'd the photo even come in? I mean, how did *we* get ahold of it?" asked Rance.

"Apparently, they called the bogus number on Meredith's press credential. It routed straight to her contact at DGSE. Duty officer called me at home ninety minutes ago. The three of us and the director are the only ones that know so far—at least in our government. Obviously, we have no control over who else the kidnappers are talking to. I'd have to assume that includes the Israelis."

"Why? What do they even want?" asked Rance.

"Reparations. They want us to put up ten billion to make up for all of the damage caused by the port explosion and the Israeli strikes in Beirut. They assume we're behind everything Israel does, of course. Bastards made their demands over the phone to the French agent that took the call. I don't know how accurate it really is. But that's all we have so far. And obviously we're not going to negotiate."

"So—she's blown, then?" Rance asked.

"Blown," said Dorsey. "Either she got burned by someone or—and I hate to even say this—they beat it out of her. One way or the other, they know she's one of us, which makes her even more valuable." Dorsey's head dropped and wagged in a long, slow shake.

"Jeff," said Rance. "Meredith's as tough as they come. We'll get her."

"We will," agreed Cowles.

"Shit," added Rance. "*Août Noir* . . . Black August. I take it that's a reference to the port explosion. You think, Dave?"

"Probably," said Cowles. "Or it could be a reference to the present month. Either way, we've never heard of them."

"Haven't heard of them? How's that even *possible*?" shot Rance.

"All it takes in this country is a few thousand bucks to start your own private militia."

"So fucked up."

"I've already got the team working to find out who *Août Noir* is," said Cowles. "Believe me, we'll find them, Jeff. We'll get the bastards."

"Fucking Hezbollah," said Dorsey, still looking down. "Iran's private army . . . Well, the Iranians can go fuck themselves when it comes to this Vienna deal." The spy boss raised a red-rimmed eye to the camera. "Ed, let Hopkins know we need more time on the vet. Invent whatever story you want . . . I don't care what you tell him. Just stall it for now."

"What about the Israelis?" Rance asked, mortified at the prospect of telling Hopkins any such thing. "They were part of the ransom demand. Anything from them?"

"Not so far," Dorsey said. "But we haven't exactly been on speaking terms with Mossad . . ." The spy boss looked away. He told them to wait a minute, went off camera. Then he came back a few seconds later and lit a cigarette—right there in the middle of the smoke-free HQS building.

It's that bad, thought Rance.

The spy boss took two puffs before going on. "Dave, do you have a way into Mossad's Beirut station? A contact? Anything? We need to move fast here. This thing gets to the media, to the politicians . . . we're fucked. We may never get her back."

"No direct contact," said Cowles. "But the Lebanese Intelligence Directorate probably does. We think the director over there is on Mossad's payroll."

"I wish we were up Mossad's ass the way they seem to be in everyone else's," said Dorsey. "After this, by God, I'm thinking we may need to start an Israeli desk."

"Agreed," said Rance.

"Do what you have to do," Dorsey added to Cowles after another puff. "Mossad probably has people in Hezbollah. I don't know if they'd be willing to help us out here. I'd sure like to get them to try."

"Mossad has people everywhere in Beirut," said Cowles. "They probably could help."

"Right," said Dorsey. "But no way am I going to ask the director to call the pricks. Not putting him in that position after . . ." The spy chief stubbed out his unfinished cigarette as though coming to his senses. "Dave, tell Ed about your last known contact with Meredith. Let's start there."

"Sure," said Cowles. "Six days ago, Meredith was supposed to have dinner with an asset at a safe house down near Sidon. You may recognize the code name—Cassius. He said she called to cancel. Too sick. Last I saw Meredith, she did look ill—feverish, coughing, you know. And then you guys took her off the NIE and gave her orders for R&R. I thought she'd gone back home, slipped out, still in her NOC."

"What about John Dale?" asked Rance. "I know we still haven't re-established contact with him. But assuming we do . . . do we tell him? He's next of kin . . . wherever the hell he is. Then there's the daughter too, at the Naval Academy. I could send someone to—"

"Too early for next-of-kin talk," shot Dorsey. "If John turns up, we'll brief him in. Shit, we might even be able to use his Mossad relationship for help. But getting Meredith back is the only thing I want us thinking about right now."

"Agreed," said Cowles.

"We have to move fast," said Dorsey. "Let's not forget what happened to Buckley." The spy chief chomped on the end of a blue Bic pen at the mention of the Beirut chief of station who'd been kidnapped and killed by Hezbollah thirty-odd years back. It'd been one of the darkest days in CIA history. Until this one.

"If we want to keep this small and fast . . . then what's our next move?" asked Rance.

"I briefed the director thirty minutes ago," said Dorsey. "You can imagine what that was like. He wants this kept under wraps, total silence. He doesn't even want the White House to know about it until we at least have a game plan. Given the Iran thing, timing is . . . Well . . ." He cleared his throat again. "Let's talk potential ops. Dave, tell me how you're set up there for counter-terror."

For thirty minutes the three senior CIA men discussed the possibilities of moving in the deadly forces that could kick in doors and crack heads—*knuckle-draggers*, in Agency parlance. They outlined the concrete actions they could take now, moving the Special Activities Center teams at their direct disposal without having to ask for permission. Cowles promised to surge his case officers into the streets, to beat bushes, to overturn stones, to shake up assets, to find the bastards called *Août Noir*. To find Meredith. Fast.

And assuming they could find her, they talked about forcible rescue, a secret assault, spoken in the clipped, acronymic dialect of American defense: DOD, CENTCOM, SOCOM, DEVGRU, FBI, HRT, SAC, Delta. Dorsey said he wanted it all, everything the United States national security establishment could muster, by God. Everything.

But *everything* would take major approvals—and with the Iran deal, those would be a bitch to get. All three men knew it—none dared voice it.

Until someone had to. When the elephant was larger than the room itself, the spy boss looked visibly sick, ashen, pen angling down from his lips like the sinking needle of a barometer.

"For now," he concluded with visible effort, "this whole op is a covert contingency—no one says anything. Because as much as I hate to say this, the director made one thing very clear: the *strategic* priority is still the Iran deal. He wants Meredith as much as we all do. But he called the nuke deal 'our core national security interest.' But by God, if the director doesn't move everything for this . . ."

And that's when Rance decided to pounce. The lightbulb had flashed early in the meeting, but he'd waited for just the right moment. Now, the word "director" triggered him.

"Jeff," Rance erupted with a raised index finger. "Wait. I think I have the play. A move to get her back—quick and quiet. No policymakers."

Dorsey said nothing, merely lifted an eyebrow.

"Let me take this to Walid," Rance continued. "If this is a Hezbollah splinter—then why don't I just lean on him? The Iranians should be able to do something. I know it's unorthodox . . . but would you approve a pitch like that? Would the director? I could get it together. Quick. Probably in the next few hours. Worth a shot."

"I like it," said Cowles, relieved that it might redirect his own heat to find the kidnappers himself. "As long as this really is a Hezbollah splinter, then yeah, the Iranians could lean on them for a release."

"I don't know . . . ," said Dorsey, levering the pen in his fingers. "I'm not sure I like the idea of admitting this to Iran. How the hell could we trust them with this?"

"We're about to trust them in the deal," said Rance. "And I've got rapport with Walid. This is the perfect use of the back channel. We can keep the deal moving forward, keep everything away from State. But I understand the sensitivity. I won't do it unless the director approves."

"I think Ed makes a lot of sense," reiterated Cowles, sensing momentum. "And I'll still see if we can get an officer in touch with Mossad as a backup. But I can't guarantee it."

"Keep me close on that, Dave," said Rance. "I don't want Mossad to taint the Iranians. If they come in too hot, they could ignite a war. So be subtle."

"I can do subtle."

The two men both looked at Dorsey. The spy boss had resumed chewing on the pen, his tired eyes staring into space off camera. "All right," he said after a while. "Dave, you work Mossad in Beirut. Ed, you work Walid in Vienna. I'll tell the director the play, make sure he's on board. He'll appreciate the creativity. But remember," the spy chief said, "speed is life. Meredith's life. She's family. You get me?"

They did. They hung up.

I am so fucking back, thought Rance.

CHAPTER 42

AND THAT'S WHAT RANCE WAS STILL THINKING BEHIND HIS DESK SOME two hours later. He'd showered and dressed back at his hotel. The DSS bodyguard had shadowed him the whole way, even waited in the suite's salon while Rance got ready. With that haunting image of Meredith still in mind, Rance rather liked the idea of his own security.

But back over at the Grand, he played it cool, acted like nothing was amiss. He spent a half hour rubbing shoulders with the State people. They were all in a good mood, expecting the deal to be done in a matter of days. And even though they were still going through the endless logistical minutiae of a proposed inspection regimen, Rance found them all a little giddy. They didn't know what he knew. They were just State people.

He looked around for Walid, hoping to bump into him. He saw a half dozen of the Iranians wandering around in their gray Nehru suits. He saw the deputy foreign minister with the white beard talking to Hopkins. Hopkins nodded at Rance when the CIA man crossed the room. *So fucking back*, Rance said to himself, checking his watch. But no Walid.

Rance hustled to his embassy office at nine to make a few calls. Though Dorsey had said not to worry about John, Rance was always a little worried about John, whom he believed to be a Mossad mole.

Walid had quietly complained about the Mossad attack on Hezbollah in London to Rance, but they'd both agreed it shouldn't have any impact on the deal. They'd agreed to keep it on the down-low, aligned that Israel shouldn't be rewarded by throwing off the negotiation.

Now Rance called his MI-5 contact in London for an update, hoping to get some info to trade with Walid. He started by asking about Dale, who'd also mysteriously disappeared in the UK, right around the same time as the Mossad attack. Fishy.

No, the MI-5 man said, they hadn't seen the French passport of Etienne Crochet, Dale's alias, pop up again—which must mean Dale was still in the UK somewhere. Yes, they'd sent a man by the hostel where Dale had checked in. But there'd been no sign of him.

As far as the evidence went, said the MI-5 officer, they had a couple of dead Hezbollah terrorists and the body of a knifed Saudi known to be on the payroll of Sheikh Abdullah, the shady Saudi financier who was trying to overthrow Mohammed bin Salman. The gun battle at Alexandra, MI-5 had concluded, looked to be some sort of turf war, maybe a weapons deal gone wrong.

"Well—good riddance," said Rance, mildly disappointed.

"Too right," said the MI-5 man.

After hanging up, Rance prepared his Walid approach, scratching out a few ideas on a legal pad, gaming out moves. He wanted to make sure he knew what Meredith had been up to before getting snatched. He called Rick Desmond, Meredith's number two in Langley, for background.

The young analyst seemed a little flustered in talking to his boss's boss. But after some prompting Desmond ran through the same intelligence Rance had already seen about the Israeli missile suspicions. The whole *Taniyn* paranoia—nothing worthwhile. Desmond hadn't heard from Meredith in a week.

He'd mostly been curious about the status of Meredith's Atlas op. The kid had the nerve to ask Rance about it, mentioning something about a Kurdish cover story he'd concocted. The nerve, bringing that up to Rance's level. Rance had told the kid to get back in his lane, in so many words.

After jotting a few more notes to himself, Rance checked his e-mail. A message from Dorsey, written vaguely. The DCIA had approved Rance's idea, it said. *Cleared to make the approach.*

All right, thought Rance, rubbing his hands together with relish. Time for the big call to Walid. Rance's back-channel contact had given him a number to call. "In case you ever have the need to speak urgently," the Iranian had said.

Rance punched the number pad.

"This is a pleasant place to stroll," said Walid as their loafers crunched along the gravel of the Augarten an hour later. Rance had thought it significant that the Iranian agreed to meet him so quickly.

"Yes," said Rance. "I like to run here every morning, for exercise. I know the park well."

"You run every morning, do you?"

"Indeed," said Rance.

Walid turned his head halfway toward Rance. "You are very fit. And young, for someone in so senior a position."

Rance nodded and walked. He thought briefly of that morning's nine-minute pace.

Walid two-handed his own belly for a second. "I should run every day too—but then it would interfere with my smoking." The Iranian smiled and chuckled.

Rance chuckled. Walid retrieved a pack of smokes from his own jacket and offered one to Rance, who demurred. The Iranian lit up. They spoke in pointless circles about weather, hotels, airline food, the best places to go for summer vacations.

"Have you ever been," asked Rance, searching for a transition to the matter at hand, "to the mountains east of Beirut? I'm told that's a good place to escape the heat."

Rance noticed that Walid took a few seconds before composing an answer. A good sign.

"I have," said Walid. "Things can get very hot on either side of those mountains. Damascus in August? Hot. Beirut in August? Hot. In fact . . . I find that August is always hot. Even in Beirut, August is hot."

August. Beirut. Hot. Why say those words so specifically—and repeat the month four times? It was time to raise the Meredith issue, get down to business. This was the play.

They were walking along the circular drive that led to the old stately ceramics factory that looked like a set from *The Sound of Music. Der Flakturm*, site of Rance's glorious nine-minute pace, was just on the other side of the chestnut trees.

"Mr. Zafir," Rance began after two more steps. "I'm afraid that like the British a few days ago—we may now have a bit of a Hezbollah problem ourselves. We seem to have . . . lost one of our own people to them . . . and they appear to be . . . holding our officer for certain, well, *demands*."

Walid kept walking and smoking, smiling genially. For a half dozen steps Rance wondered whether the shorter Iranian had heard him. The American thought about leaning down a little, speaking louder, but this wasn't the kind of conversation where you did that.

Walid removed the dilemma. "That is quite a problem, Mr. Pine," he said.

"Yes," said Rance. "Quite. And I just think it would be great if we could work together to solve it. I think we've gotten better at working out problems—our two countries. What else are we doing here in Vienna now if not working out problems?"

"I see," said Walid after a few more steps, still smiling. "So you think *I* can help solve this problem of your missing officer for *you*, Mr. Pine?"

"As a matter of fact, I do," said Rance, pushing his hands into his trouser pockets. "There seems to be a group in Lebanon that has taken matters into their own hands. They call themselves *Août Noir* . . . a splinter of Hezbollah, we believe. You've heard of them, I trust?"

Walid smiled and walked, said nothing. Somehow, the heat hadn't made the Iranian sweat, Rance noticed.

After Walid didn't respond, Rance added, "*Août Noir* seems to have taken this officer of ours. They're making ransom demands. You can see how that might be . . . problematic."

"I do see that," said Walid, walking, listening to the ceaseless grind of cicada bugs. Rance was determined not to say anything now. The Iranian needed to offer something. He'd gotten the message—hadn't he? The gravel crunched. The cicadas buzzed.

Smiling, Walid finally said, "I have been meaning to ask you about something as well. Something you could perhaps help *me* with, Mr. Pine—since we're now talking about solving problems."

"Oh? And what's that?" Rance took a quick dab at his forehead before shoving his hands back into his pockets.

"I think you would agree," said Walid, "that one of the lowest points of the relationship between our two countries was when the great general Qasem Soleimani was . . . shall we say . . . *killed.*"

"Yes," said Rance, worried that this was headed off in a weird direction, since the US had whacked Soleimani in a drone strike in early 2020. "I would agree that that was a tough moment in our history. I know you had a great deal of respect for the general. His death was a shame. An unfortunate outcome."

"Indeed," said Walid, walking, smoking. "A very unfortunate outcome." His bearded smile had faded when mentioning the general. But it was back now. "And did you also know that we've had people go missing? We've lost many scientists. Fates unknown."

"Mossad . . . ," said Rance, exhaling audibly. "What they did to Dr. Farzad was—"

"Yes, killed with his wife on vacation. The barbarity. And did you know, Mr. Pine, that sometimes our scientists will just go missing completely? There was one a few months ago like that. His name is Rahimi. Are you familiar with this scientist?"

Rahimi. Cerberus. Fuck!

"Mossad," moaned Rance, shaking his head, eyes locked on the gravel. "So much trouble."

"A constant obstacle to peace," agreed the Iranian. "And, right around the time Dr. Rahimi disappeared, so did one of our most talented officers, an adjutant to General Soleimani. Like the general, this officer was very dear to us. Even dear to me. Perhaps you know of him?"

Kahlidi! Fuck!

"No," said Rance, fists now balled in his pockets. "Why should I know something about this officer?"

"Well, I don't know, Mr. Pine," said Walid. "But he's the biggest problem *I* have. And a friend of mine suggested that you, personally, might help me overcome it. The missing officer's name is Kasem Kahlidi. A lieutenant colonel in the Quds Force. Are you sure you don't know of him? Or Dr. Rahimi?" The Iranian was looking up intently at Rance now. The smile was long gone.

The CIA man remained impassive, walking, sweating. "No, I'm afraid I've never heard of either of these men. Why would you think I had, Walid?"

"A mutual friend—a *Russian* friend—suggested something to me. But who knows if he was just bluffing. You can't trust anyone in this business."

"No," agreed Rance.

The Iranian had stopped walking. He smiled again and offered his hand. "Well, Mr. Pine. You have lost an officer. And so have we. What if we were to help each other get each of these officers back home to their families?"

"This is a fucking disaster," Dorsey said when Rance got him on the videoconference just sixty-two minutes later. The spy chief had abandoned a meeting with Pakistani intelligence at a discreet DC State office when Rance called. "You're telling me that Walid actually raised Atlas? Now of all times?"

"I'm afraid so," said Rance. He'd ordered the DSS man to drive like a maniac to get back to the embassy as soon as he'd let go of Walid's soft hand. As a matter of self-preservation, Rance hadn't told Dorsey that Walid had used the *R*-word, Russians, prevaricators of Rance's greatest shame—the honeypot business.

"So what does it mean?" asked Dorsey.

"I suppose it means that they want us to offer up Kahlidi," said Rance. "His implication was that they could help us with Meredith in return."

"You mean the bastards had Hezbollah take Meredith to orchestrate a swap—because they *think* we have Kahlidi. And why do they draw that conclusion all of a sudden?"

"I don't know," said Rance.

"Could the Russians be fucking with us? Tipping the Iranians off? All the trouble we had a few months back with the Cerberus extract? Your honeypot?"

"Does that really matter right now?" Rance quickly shot. "You said speed is life, Jeff. I'm working at top speed on Meredith here. She's all that matters now."

"Right," said Dorsey after a two-second silence. "So what did Walid have to say specifically about *Août Noir*? Does he know these bastards?"

"Walid wouldn't comment in any useful way. But he also didn't deny having heard of them either. His overall signal seemed to be that we can all keep this below the line without interrupting the deal if we can work the trade."

"But we don't have anything to trade. What did you tell him about Atlas?"

"I didn't tell him anything."

"But you think they could probably swing getting Meredith back—if we still had Kahlidi?"

"I do. It's an obvious quid pro quo. But we don't have the quid."

"And they have the quo. Fuck," said Dorsey.

"Fuck," repeated Rance.

"Well, how did you leave it with Walid? When's the next time you're going to see him? We need to move fast."

"I haven't set up another meet with Walid yet. But there are a lot of ceremonial functions around the deal going on here this week, as you can imagine. The IAEA board of governors is hosting a reception tonight. Walid made a point of saying he'd be there with the foreign minister. I think he's expecting a counteroffer."

"You mean you haven't said anything to Hopkins about slowing the nuke deal down yet?"

"No," said Rance. "I'm only thinking of Meredith now."

"Right. I suppose we can still shut the deal down if we have to. I'll say something to the director. What about Cowles? Has he made any progress with Mossad in Beirut?"

"I haven't heard from him yet. You have to figure it'll take time to get the word out."

"I never know what to figure with Mossad. They're probably already surveilling Cowles. And I'd wager they're surveilling you and Walid in Vienna."

"Could be."

"But," said Dorsey, "Israel's part of this too—whether we like it or not. The quote unquote reparations demand for the port disaster is aimed at them as much as us. What if I called Werner myself? I hate to do it after the way he hit us. But if anybody could pull off a raid on these fuckers and get Meredith back quick . . . it's Werner."

"Jeff," said Rance, "Werner's head is surely on the block since he fucked up the hit on the Hezbollah aid convoy. He may not have the juice to go kinetic these days."

"The guillotine hasn't fallen yet," said Dorsey, pushing his sleeves past his elbows.

"But if you call Werner," said Rance, "you won't know how far it will go before things unravel. He may force you into backing off the NIE, raise a stink about all their missile intelligence again. Werner always negotiates, just like he tried to do in Langley when this mess started. It could wreck the whole deal."

Dorsey stared straight at the camera. His face seemed suddenly large. "You think I give *two shits* about this deal now, Ed?"

Rance looked away.

"It's late enough over there that I might be able to catch Werner before he goes to bed," said Dorsey. "Let's just see what he knows about this *Août Noir*."

Well, thought Rance. If Dorsey goes off the reservation with Werner, then it won't just be Werner's head that will roll. And considering all the collateral that Rance himself had earned of late with the director, it seemed to him in that very moment that perhaps it was a good idea if Dorsey *did* go off the reservation.

"Okay," said Rance. "I suppose it's worth a shot. Should we reconvene in an hour?"

Outside the embassy gates on Liechtensteinstrasse, Rance found a place that sold *döenerkabobs*. He stuffed one down right in the street for lunch, maneuvering his fingers carefully to keep the mustard on the tissue paper while the DSS man stood a few feet away. Then, still upset at having heard the *R*-word, he went for a walk around stately Liechtensteinpark with the DSS man following him before getting back up to the videoconference SCIF.

"Hi, Dave," Rance said when he saw Cowles on video next to Dorsey's empty chair on the left side of the split. Rance hadn't expected Cowles to join. He wasn't sure he much liked the idea of Beirut Station horning in on this thing.

"Okay," said Dorsey, somewhat breathless, sitting down in a heap. His shirt was still a mess, but the boss appeared to have shaved. His cheeks were rosier, his eyes brighter. "I had the call with Werner. And it may just be the break we need—if we act fast."

"Great," said Rance and Cowles simultaneously, echoing the chief's newfound vigor.

"Dave, before we begin, I have to tell you about something. It's kind of ugly and I don't have the time to go through the rigmarole to get all the classification papers in order, so I'm going to just trust you. It stays between us. We good with that?"

"Sure," said Cowles, leaning forward in the Beirut embassy SCIF.

"All right," said Dorsey. "About a month ago, Mossad did something really stupid . . . beyond the pale . . ." The spy boss continued to tell Cowles all about Cerberus and Atlas and the suspected Mossad raid on the Virginia horse farm–safehouse when they lost Kahlidi. Throughout, Cowles displayed the appropriate outrage.

"But," Dorsey added after finishing up the story. "Werner finally copped to it this morning."

"Shut up," said Rance. "He admitted to the hit on us? Really?"

"Not in so many words," said Dorsey. "But you know, in our way, he more or less admitted to it. As much as he ever will."

"Wow," said Rance. "This is big. So, since he was being so honest— did you ask him if they have a good Junction agent in Hezbollah?"

"Yeah, I did. But he wouldn't go that far," said Dorsey. "Not yet. But more to the point, Werner knows about this *Août Noir* cell. He says it's legit, a Hezbollah splinter, true believer Shias loyal to the original ayatollah, the real deal. And he's made a wild suggestion. That's why I need you two now. It relates to what we were discussing earlier, Ed. And I think we can probably wire it up fast. *Really* fast."

Rance was on the edge of his chair. He was worried Dorsey was about to tell him that Werner would go into attack mode, launch his shock troops on this offshoot terrorist cell in Beirut. In which case, Rance's credibility with Walid would be shot—and the deal with Iran would most certainly fall apart. *His* deal.

But, on the other hand, if that happened, Dorsey would be toast— way, way off the reservation. *Be careful*, thought Rance.

"Well, what does he suggest?" Rance inquired.

"Get this," said Dorsey, leaning forward. "Werner told me they have Atlas—fucking Kahlidi himself—in custody, there, in Tel Aviv."

"*What?*" Rance shrieked. His voice had come out higher than he'd wished. He got it under control, quick. "So they did get Atlas in the Virginia raid?"

"I don't know," said Dorsey. "They got him somehow."

"Must have been Virginia," said Rance, wringing his hands. "Dale *did* help them, then, didn't he? The bastard."

"For now, I really don't give a shit about Dale. We don't have time for any of that. I only care about Meredith—and Werner's suggestion."

"Which is what, exactly?" asked Rance.

"A swap."

"A swap?" Immediately suspicious of any idea originating with Werner, Rance added, "How?"

"Werner's willing to give Kahlidi over to this Hezbollah splinter to put things right with us. Swap Kahlidi for Meredith. If you can lean on the Iranians to pay this *Août Noir* splinter off, then the Iranians get Kahlidi back while keeping their money in the Hezbollah family. We get Meredith back. Mossad rebuilds their relationship with us. Everybody wins."

The light blinked behind Rance's forehead for the second time that day. He still didn't trust Werner. But that didn't matter because this was very, very good news. It had the potential to clean up the Kahlidi mess, even the *R*-word. It would make it look to the Iranians like Mossad had been to blame for the Atlas botch. And it would keep Rance's relationship with Walid solid. Best of all, it would make Rance's back channel the linchpin to pulling it all together. He, Edward Ronald Rance, would be at the center of—

"Jeff," Rance blurted. "I think Werner's suggestion is brilliant. We can do it all through my back channel. We can do the whole swap in private, just the intelligence people. None of the politicos even need to know about it, right?"

"That's exactly what I'm thinking," said Dorsey. "Keeping it small is critical. And fast. I'll have to tell the director, of course. And he may share it with the White House, but it will stay very quiet—no politicos. We keep it dark. You think you could get your man Walid to go for it? I'd sure like to give the director some hopeful news about this mess."

The White House!

"Hell yes," said Rance quickly. "I'll even orchestrate that swap. Myself."

CHAPTER 43

"WHO IS *AOÛT NOIR*?" MALOOF ASKED FROM HIS OFFICE IN TEHRAN. "What have you learned?"

Siamak was at the Iranian embassy to Lebanon in Jnah, the secure satellite radio phone to one ear. The Russians had gifted the Iranians with a new communications suite with fresh encryption, now deployed at the Lebanese embassy. They all knew Israel's Unit 8200 would eventually crack it too. But for a few weeks, at least, they believed themselves safe, and Maloof had insisted they speak on a secure line.

"I have men watching everywhere," the major answered, his voice muffled by the small, airless communications warren in the basement. "*Août Noir* is a new splinter, a small one. Devout warriors, according to the whispers we're hearing. But we don't know them. We have feelers out, looking."

"How could you *not know* them?" shot Maloof. "How is that even *possible*? How could the man I have running counterintelligence in Beirut not know about a splinter cell among our own people? What's that agent of yours . . . *Nabil* . . . what's he even *doing*? Why haven't you abducted the Morris-Dale woman yet?"

Siamak wiped a drip of sweat from his nose and shook his head. As he'd already reported to Maloof, Siamak had had his men on Morris-Dale's hotel day and night. Nabil's cousin was a farmer in the Beqaa Valley. He had a flatbed Ford they were using parked at a construction site that neighbored her hotel. But the woman hadn't been back for three days.

"Sir, this *Noir* cell grabbed the woman first, on their own, thinking she was just a journalist covering the port explosion, according to their demands. We didn't see that coming."

"And now the brigadier wants to swap this woman for Kahlidi!" Maloof thundered. "Walid Zafir's brilliant idea—pitched it to the Americans without running it by me first, the rat. Kahlidi's old personal friend. Major, can you *understand* what will happen if Kahlidi comes back like that?"

With the phone now two inches from his ear, Siamak said, "Yes, sir. We'll have Kahlidi, the traitor, in custody. That will be good."

"*No!*" Maloof cried. "It will *not be good!*"

"I don't understand," said Siamak, clearing his forehead of moisture.

"Kahlidi will be released by *Mossad*," seethed Maloof. "Not CIA. Forty-eight hours ago, a Quds unit in Iraq found a dead Kurd with a photo of Kahlidi in his pocket."

"Maybe the Kurd was a fake to—"

"That doesn't matter! The brigadier is convinced the Kurds sold Kahlidi to the Jews instead! That discovery's a disaster, it's—"

"But, sir, how could the brigadier—"

"The Zionists have even sent over their own picture of Kahlidi!" shrieked Maloof. "Looks to have been tortured to within an inch of his life. No one's ever come back from a Zionist prison before. Now the brigadier thinks Kahlidi's a hero! A *pasdar*! A shining *fedayee*! The brigadier is thrilled at the thought of getting this hero back!"

"But . . . if he was tortured, Kahlidi must have broken and told the Jews everything about *Taniyn* by now. That's the same as saying it straight to CIA. Surely the brigadier sees that."

"He does! But all he cares about right now is the loyal *fedayee* who survived the worst Mossad could throw at him! Think about what this means for *you*, Major Azad."

"Sir?"

"Don't be a fool! *You* kidnapped Kahlidi's woman. Your cell shot her, left her for dead. Who knows where the hell she is now? Do you think Kahlidi's just going to *forgive* you for that? With his connections he'll have you in Evin Prison before his plane lands in Tehran!"

"But we saw Dale in London, trying to get the woman," shot Siamak, his breath a little faster. "We agreed he was doing it *for* Kahlidi because Kahlidi is a CIA spy. Like you said when—"

"I only said he was a spy as a *theory!*"

"But, sir, Kahlidi's information must be how CIA and Mossad have been targeting the scientists. I even have the cell phone video with the American, Dale, that shows—"

"Destroy that video!" shrieked Maloof. "Cut ties with your London people, now! Stop making martyr payments to them. Hear me? I tell you all of this for your own good, Major."

"Stop the martyr payments? But, sir—"

"You *never knew them.* Hear? Blame the fight on the dead Saudi. Their crazy English shootout could very well screw up the Vienna deal on its own. Why did you seize Kahlidi's woman in the first place? If I were you, I'd destroy all evidence that links you to that Hezbollah cell."

Siamak squeezed the phone handset so hard that his arm shook.

"Now," said Maloof, calmer, wheezing over the secure connection. "There is one way I can think of to stop this madness. It's the only way I see to help you out, to stop Kahlidi, who you think might be a spy, even if the brigadier doesn't."

Siamak grunted.

"This *Août Noir* cell," continued Maloof. "At least they're in Beirut. You can still stop this swap from happening if you find them before the prisoner swap."

"Not if the brigadier wants the trade to happen," said Siamak, closing his eyes, thinking of his wife and son up in the northwestern Sunni district.

"Exactly why you have to kill the CIA woman! Have your man Nabil wire up that delivery truck you've been using for surveillance. Blow the whole cell—and the woman along with it."

CHAPTER 44

MEREDITH AWOKE TO THE SOUND OF THE MUEZZIN CALL. THE VOICE singing through the tinny speakers was clear enough that she guessed it was about a quarter mile from the spartan room where she now lay.

The song reminded her of her adolescent years in Rabat, living in the condo complex set up for American diplomats. Even now, out of habit, she couldn't stop herself from humming along. She couldn't help herself from translating the rising, falling, vibrating voice of the celebrant who'd always sounded so mournful to her young ears:

Allah is great.
I testify that there is no God but Allah.
I testify that Muhammad is the prophet of Allah.
Come to prayer. Come salvation. Come to the best work.
Allah is most great.
There is no God but Allah.

She noted the slight difference between this call and the ones in Sunni Morocco. This *adhan* added the "work" phrase, a line unique to Shias. And while Meredith didn't know exactly where in Beirut she was, she guessed that this *adhan* version put her somewhere in Beirut's southern Shia quarter.

Stiff from her night on the hard floor, she angled herself on her elbows, listening to the chant, taking note of the empty room.

Greeting her again, she saw the lighted rectangle. The rising sun had formed it each of her three mornings on that floor. And over the course of the day, she knew, the rectangle would march toward the cracked wall, then bend at the corner. That's when the late afternoon rectangle would kick in from the opposing western window.

She stretched her arms over her head, looking up at the high slitted openings, well out of arm's reach. She took a deep breath. The air was relatively fresh today, having blown westerly from the sea. That was good. Sometimes it delivered disagreeable odors from the eastern city center, another geographic indicator.

The mournful *adhan* finished, echoing off into eternity. Meredith pushed herself into a seated position. She could hear the honk of cars somewhere on the street, the occasional vibrations of a truck. Starving, her stomach growled. She guzzled a bottle of water to shut it up.

With no watch or phone, the competing east-west rectangles and morning *adhan* wails were her only indicators of time. But then, she supposed, they were enough. She knew her visitor would arrive shortly.

And she was right. Just three minutes later, Meredith heard dead bolts moving, keys jangling, the doorknob spinning. A woman dressed head to toe in a flowing black chador carrying a woven bag entered. Only her eyes were visible above the adorning hijab's extra face scarf. But the eyes were enough.

"*Bonjour*, Maya," Meredith said.

"*Sabah alkhayr*," Maya returned in Arabic.

The Mossad woman unfastened the draping black chador and dropped it to the floor. She knelt to attend to her bag.

Beneath the chador she wore tapered pants with cargo pockets and a long-sleeved button-down shirt. Her torso was thickened by a Kevlar vest. A holster was strapped to her thigh. Within it, a .22-caliber Beretta with a suppressor was Velcroed in place next to the barrel.

The Mossad woman withdrew an orange, a granola bar, and a newspaper from the bag. She put the items in front of Meredith. Despite her ravenous hunger, Meredith reached only for the French Beiruti daily, *L'Orient-Le Jour*.

"You should eat," Maya said, watching the CIA woman. "You're looking quite gaunt."

"That's the idea," Meredith replied, turning a page with a noisy rustle.

Maya let her read in peace.

"It says here there may be a possible delay in the nuclear deal," said Meredith after a long squint. "Have you heard anything else about that?"

"Not really," said Maya. "Al Jazeera's reporting the IAEA board of governors has accepted the production limits on the new solid fuel *Kheibar Sheban* missile. But they now say that several signing parties are late in their reviews. I suspect the delay is really just . . . you."

Meredith put the paper down and stretched the stiffness from her arms. Her own dirty chador lay beside her in a heap since she'd used it as a pillow. She was otherwise clothed in the dress she'd been wearing on her way to see Cassius eight days ago. It was dirty, torn at the hem. Her feet were bare.

She noted the digital camera around Maya's neck. "Ah," said the CIA woman. "That's why you brought the newspaper."

"Afraid so," said Maya. "The Iranians are leaning on us, having stepped in for the Americans in the negotiation with *Août Noir*. They want another photo."

"And how is it negotiating with the Iranians?"

"So far, so good. We—I mean *Août Noir*—are asking Iran for funding, telling them we intend to do more for the local economy than current Hezbollah—that kind of nonsense."

"Sounds like progress. No Hezbollah intermediary, then?"

"No. We've made that a condition. IRGC has passed us off to a local negotiator now. Our SIGINT pinpoints him at the Iranian embassy in Jnah but it's new encryption and we haven't decoded it yet. We think he's MOIS counterintelligence since he keeps asking for clarifying information about *Noir*. He's tried to bait us into meeting with him, but we're finding ways to head that off. If we can't, Mitz's Junction people will be ready."

"Right. All the same, I'd rather not have to meet a MOIS man."

"Of course not. But our cover is solid. We'll all play the part. Mitz's agents out there will protect you."

"What about the other *Noir* demands? Does it sound like the Iranians will fold?"

"The Iranians agreed in concept to pay off *Noir*. If that happens, then *Noir* will release you to the Americans and we'll release Kahlidi to the Iranians. Mitz's people say the Iranians have been motivated, negotiating in a hurry, going back and forth with your man in Vienna, Rance. They've even proposed the exchange logistics. We have people sourcing plans for that."

"Perfect."

"Yes. Mitz's Junction group is very good. They're trying to get rid of the demand to meet in person *before* the exchange. Afterward, okay, but not before. We're offering up proof of life instead. Rance has also asked for that."

"And, speaking of Rance . . . Anything new coming from CIA?"

"Werner says the US is sending a helicopter carrier and its flotilla to the eastern Med." The Mossad woman smiled. "Just think, Meredith. Your face has launched a thousand ships."

"Well . . . ," Meredith said, massaging a bruised cheek. "A few anyway. How does my face look? The swelling feels down."

"Put your hood on and I'll take you to the lav. You can see for yourself."

Horrid, Meredith thought once she'd removed the blindfold. The Israelis had pumped her full of blood thinners. And then, once the drugs had taken hold, she'd submitted to a few blows from a very contrite Mossad *kidon* who'd been billed as an expert on such things. But the blood thinners had worked—much of her face was swollen and bruised.

Maya moved Meredith down the hall, back to her locked room. The CIA woman was to be kept locked and blindfolded for authenticity. Junction leadership wouldn't allow her to see the Israeli double agents that guarded the safe house, which was fine with Meredith. She guessed there were just two of them who seemed to watch soccer on the TV in the front room all day while Maya did the attendant work.

Once resettled, blindfold off, Maya helped Meredith put the metal shackle on her wrist.

"We can get you a mattress," the Mossad woman said apologetically as she aimed the camera. "It wouldn't be great, but it would be better than the floor. There's a thin one in the other room."

"No," said Meredith, holding the front page of *L'Orient* by her face. "I need to be stiff and tired when I show up at the exchange. I have to sell this to CIA too, for this to really work. By the way, it looked like the swelling in my lip is down. Maybe we should get one of those gentlemen up front to hit me again before we do the photo? I can keep the blindfold on."

And a few hours later, bringing another lunch that Meredith again refused, Maya said, "We got the photo off to the respective parties, including the Iranians. Some techs enhanced the bruises. But we're worried about photoshopping you too much. You can understand."

"Yes," said Meredith, licking the growing swell of her lip. "Don't photoshop anything. Please. It has to be real for this to work. Any other news since you sent off the photos?"

"No," said Maya. "But we're getting close to closing a deal. All parties seem to be cooperating now."

"Good," said Meredith. "And how about John? Is he cooperative?"

Maya paused. "Less so," she said.

"This should all be going down at night," John Dale said to Werner Davidai.

They were still in Capernaum at Werner's home by the Sea of Galilee. But now, the fallow fields north of the house had been transformed into a dusty military bivouac. The slope teemed with olive tents and military vehicles. Three Panther helicopters rested on a flat spot, their rotors drooping, almost touching the long switchgrass. At the extreme northern end of the field, five towering radio antennae had been erected, casting long shadows.

"I wish you could tell that to your Mr. Rance," said Werner. "He's been the go-between on this. The Iranians talk to Rance, he talks to me, and then it spins the other way back round."

"With Rance running things, what could go wrong?" muttered Dale. The CIA man wore an unmarked IDF infantry uniform and olive ball cap, unlike the IDF snipers, who wore berets.

"Well," said Werner. "Your Mr. Rance deserves props for making the Iranians cooperative. And everyone's agreed now on a full daylight exchange. It will ensure all parties are clearly visible, no tricks, keeping it clean." With a three-foot wooden pointer, Werner tapped a spot on the laminated map that covered his dining room table. "We were thinking here, this area."

"That's stupid," said Dale, after a ten-second study of the spot. "IDF and US Marines have the tactical advantage at night. Why would we cede that advantage?"

"You must remember, Mr. Dale, *Août Noir* are the terrorists driving the conditions. And *we* are *Août Noir*. We must be convincing. It must be real. Would it make sense for a low-budget terrorist group to cede an advantage like that to the Zionists?"

"Okay . . . what about ISR then?"

"Reconnaissance? Limited. Again, we felt it prudent to negotiate that point to lower the temperature in general, speaking as *Août Noir*. We've all agreed to suspended air operations—no drones, no air defense radars, nothing during the hours surrounding the swap. Hezbollah included. That's a win for us. Hezbollah has SAMs deployed everywhere around there."

"What about regular airport traffic?"

"Your State Department has negotiated an airport shutdown with the Lebanese for at least two hours."

"I still don't like the idea of this happening in daylight," muttered Dale.

"You've made yourself abundantly clear, Mr. Dale." Werner moved the pointer to the south. "But remember, you're still inserting at night, this beach. And you'll be all set up long before the sun rises."

"I still don't like it."

Werner sighed. "It's just the prisoner exchange itself that will be in daylight. And it should be quick. We do these often, Mr. Dale. You'll have to trust me."

Dale looked down at the map on Werner's dining room table, marked up with red and blue dry-erase stripes. As a security precaution, he hadn't been allowed to attend the full briefing with the other IDF officers earlier that morning. Werner had agreed to this briefing as a favor to Meredith to keep the jittery American CIA man from going sideways.

"What's this heavily populated area here, to the east?" asked Dale.

"That's what we call the *dahiyeh*," said Werner. "It's all Hezbollah territory, completely run by them. Our Junction people are there with Meredith, posing as the *Août Noir* terrorists. In this neighborhood, here, to be precise." The pointer tapped on a crowded section of town.

"Looks like a shithole," said Dale. "Nothing but shacks and narrow alleys."

"Yes. This section to the east of them is Shatila, a Palestinian refugee camp. To get to the exchange, they'll be driving through it for authenticity, so real Hezbollah fighters can bear witness. Authenticity is crucial, of course, if we're to pull this off."

Dale looked warily at the Israeli.

The Caesarea boss added, "We're keeping a close eye on her. We know what we're doing."

"Wouldn't it be safer to do the prisoner swap up to the north, closer to the US embassy? You're the *Août Noir* cell setting the demands. Why not demand that?"

"Mr. Dale, why would a Hezbollah splinter choose to be outside a Hezbollah area? We have to *think* like Hezbollah. Mitz and I agree that the airport is a fair middle ground. Rance has agreed. We can all get in and out quickly. And it's still Hezbollah territory. It will be safe."

Dale shoved his hands in his pockets. "I guess you have to pick someplace for it," he mumbled.

"Indeed, Mr. Dale. Now. Shall I go on?"

"Please."

Werner pointed to a corner to the northeast of the Beirut airport. "We are thinking that the American chopper with Rance will touch down here, to the west. I'm told your helicopter carrier *Kearsarge* has been ordered to the Lebanese coast from the Ionian Sea."

"Only *one* helo?" asked Dale.

"Yes. Another condition. One aircraft from each country and only enough troops for personal security. Again, we are trying to keep this from escalating."

Dale nodded.

"The Israeli helicopter with me and Kahlidi will be here, to the south," continued Werner. "The Iranians have chosen trucks that will take Kahlidi across this field, to the executive jet terminal."

"And the exchange itself?"

"We were thinking here." Werner pointed to the north end of the Beirut-Rafic Hariri International Airport, which sat south of the city, by the sea. "We want to do it in the center of the tarmac for this executive terminal here, away from civilians, possible disruptors. We think that's the safest option for all of us." He raised a hooded eye toward Dale. "Especially Meredith."

"Maybe," said Dale. "As long as I'm on overwatch."

Werner ignored the comment. "Then the two prisoners, Meredith and Kahlidi, will walk, alone, from their respective vehicles past each other to the waiting delegations, who will be next to their aircraft here . . . and here." He slapped the map with his wooden pointer to indicate the American spot. "We think that keeps this whole op safe."

Safe. Dale studied the map in silence for fifteen seconds. "This building has the best sight line. About three hundred meters . . . well within range of an M-24 sniper rifle. I want to set up on the roof . . . here. Not a super easy shot, but in this heat, no wind . . . it would work."

"There's no concealment on that roof."

"But you said there was no airborne ISR," said Dale. "No one would see me from below."

"There may not be drones in the air, but we're all flying into the field. If anyone spots anything on those buildings, the whole exchange will be off. I can't have it."

Right again, thought Dale, annoyed and fidgeting. He leaned farther over the table. "Okay. Here, then." Dale ran his finger over a clump of trees to the north. "Elevation's not great, but there are plenty of places to hide. And the range is still in the envelope. I'd call it three-fiftyish. We can cut the fence there . . . walk down this perimeter road. Climb the back of this hill. It's a good ingress."

"All right," said Werner. "I'll get sat imagery updates to make sure there are no Hezbollah people active in that area, and assuming that's the case, we'll plan on that spot." He made a mark on the laminated map with a dry-erase marker. "But you'll want to check with Reu to make sure he agrees."

"*Reu*? Who's *Reu*?"

"Didn't you meet him at the range this morning? Commander Reu Klein, our Flotilla 13 team leader supporting this op. I told him to introduce himself. You're supposed to be in the ops tent in an hour for prebrief. He didn't tell you?"

"We weren't doing much talking over in that field this morning. Just zeroing in our scopes. But I did, at least, meet my English-speaking spotter."

Werner grunted. "Reu's not too happy about bringing a guest along for this op."

"Tough shit," said Dale. "A deal's a deal."

CHAPTER 45

SIAMAK RODE IN THE FRONT SEAT, IDLY WATCHING THE OLD APART-
ment buildings that were so crowded together they looked like one
seamless concrete wall. The only individual property markers were
strings of laundry that billowed from the windows like ragged nautical
flags among the checkered posters of martyrs.

But the buildings were not all the same to Nabil. He'd lived here for
all of his thirty-one years, having survived countless Israeli bombing
attacks. And to him, each one of these narrow streets had a unique story
to tell.

Behind the wheel, the Hezbollah counterintelligence leader hung
up his phone and tossed it on the dash. He concentrated on the crowded
street, maneuvering his dented Toyota through the Haret Hreik neighborhood with the expertise of a safari guide. Avoiding obstacle after
obstacle, he threaded through leaping children, steaming food carts,
heedless old women, and beeping scooters.

"This will have to be our last stop," he finally said.

"Why?" asked Siamak.

"Because we've already hit everyone from here to Laylaki today. But
this last stop may be the one. Kareem knows a lot of people. Everybody
shops with Kareem."

"Where's his building?"

"There. That's his place." Nabil pointed toward an electronics shop
at the bottom of a faceless concrete building. Hanging above it was a
poster with the face of Imad Mugniyeh, the Lebanese brother who'd

bombed the US Marine barracks near the Beirut airport in '83. He'd finally been martyred in '08 when a joint CIA-Mossad team killed him in a Damascus car bomb.

There was nowhere to park—but that was no bother. Clad in his long-sleeved black T-shirt—an indicator of his Hezbollah rank—Nabil drove the hatchback onto the sidewalk. Seconds later, a flock of slow-moving pedestrians streamed around the Toyota, as though it had been sitting there for years. He and Siamak got out of the car and joined the flow.

"That's Kareem there," said Nabil, pointing to a man in a black T-shirt and embroidered jeans. The merchant was leaning against his shop with a look that suggested the world had long ago bored him. Over his head were more martyr posters, three young men whose faces had become the size of bedsheets hanging like flags from makeshift wires. Siamak didn't recognize any of them, but guessed they'd once lived in the building.

"*Kareem!*" Nabil called, garrulously extending his arms.

Still looking bored, Kareem pushed himself from his lazy lean and embraced Nabil. He then dutifully snatched the latch with the long pole he used to pull down the garage-style metal security door.

"*Salaam,*" he said to Siamak in the comparative dark, after the door had roared shut. Kareem found two plastic chairs and threw on the lights. They spent fifteen minutes on small talk, assessing the prospects of the Lebanese football club, Ahed.

"No," the bored merchant was saying when the football talk had run its course. "*Inshallah,* I wish I could help you. I haven't seen anyone come in and buy a digital camera in months. People only use phones now. Who are these brothers?"

Siamak repeated the words "Black August" in French, Arabic, and Farsi. "You're sure, Kareem? You're sure you've never heard anyone talking about a new movement—nothing even close to that name?"

Leaning on a glass counter filled with dusty Chinese gadgets, Kareem's eyes shifted. Nabil was an important member in the security brigade. And he was with an IRGC man.

The merchant touched his hand to his heart and looked at Siamak. "I'm sorry, *Effendi*," he said. "I wish I could help. But I don't know anything about this."

"What about her?" Siamak asked, showing that morning's proof-of-life photo on his phone. He zoomed in on Meredith's bruised face with his thumbs. "You've never seen this woman around here? Never? She's a French journalist investigating last year's port disaster. She may have been down here, interviewing people."

"No, *Effendi*. I don't know her. There are no French ladies shopping down here in this neighborhood, as far as I know."

"Kareem," Nabil intervened in a low voice. "We *have to* find this lady. She's not really French. She's a Zionist spy. You don't know *anyone* that could have taken her? Maybe someone around here buying a lot of new equipment besides cameras? Maybe walkie-talkies or burner phones? Security systems? Nothing bad will happen if you give us a tip. *Effendi* speaks truth. He'll take care of you."

Kareem looked harder at the photograph. "*Ana asf*," he said with a final touch of his heart. "I wish I could help, but I . . ." And then he glanced again at the phone in Siamak's hand. "Huh," he said, tilting his head.

"What?" asked Siamak.

"*Effendi*, may I see your phone myself?" Kareem asked Siamak.

After the MOIS major handed it over, the merchant zoomed in tightly on the photograph.

But he wasn't focused on Meredith's face. He was focused on the lower left corner of *L'Orient-Le Jour*. Kareem maneuvered the zoomed photo to show a partial patch of the newspaper's barcode, just below Meredith's right hand.

"Brothers," said Kareem, "have you considered tracing this code?"

CHAPTER 46

RANCE TRIED TO LOOK OUT ONE OF THE TWO SMALL WINDOWS INSIDE
the MV-22 Osprey, but the centrifugal force of the aircraft's gut-
wrenching bank pasted him right back to his seat. When the hybrid
airplane-helicopter finally leveled, the CIA man looked resolutely up at
the Marine Corps staff sergeant sitting across from him. Though em-
barrassed, Rance wasn't about to let these jarheads think he was just
another suit from DC.

He certainly wasn't *wearing* a suit anyway. Before landing at Turkey's
Incirlik Air Force Base in Dorsey's jet a few hours earlier, he'd changed
into his reinforced khaki trousers and short-sleeved black nylon shirt.
And when the Osprey had been waiting there at the end of the runway
with its twin rotors turning, Rance had run up its back ramp like he'd
done it two hundred times before.

"*Kearsarge* off the port side, sir," said one of the pilots through the
intercom into Rance's helmet. "Stay strapped, sir. It's about to get dicey."
The aircraft banked again, then dropped altitude and slowed sickeningly.

Rance burped into his fist. He could see nothing, but he felt the
pressure difference in his ears. The aircraft bucked through turbulence.
And then, a half minute later, it unexpectedly hit the ship's deck with a
thud so fierce the CIA man thought they'd crashed.

The cargo door lowered. A humid stew of gassy exhaust and ocean
wind blew in. The Osprey had been chained to the flight deck. It now
rocked back and forth with the ship's motion.

Rance unstrapped and ran down the ramp like he was splashing onto a Normandy beach. Finally on the flight deck, still nauseous, he was relieved to see that people in uniforms were running toward him. One of them had silver stars on his collar points.

"Mr. Pine," the Marine brigadier screamed over the rotor wash, seizing Rance's hand in an iron grip. "Good to meet you, sir. Follow me. We're this way."

This way meant the interior of the ship's superstructure. Rance was hurried by the general's aide behind him through a dizzying array of thick metal bulkheads, narrow hatches, polished tiled floors. "Langley's on the horn," the general said over his shoulder. Jerking his large square chin, the general motioned Rance to follow him up a ladder. "My intel center's up here," said the brigadier. "And when you're done with your call, let's sit down and go over the final plan."

"Roger that," said Rance, hustling to keep up.

Once to the top of two more ladders, the ship rolled left—slowly—then righted itself. Rance wanted to show the general he had his sea legs and tried to keep his hands by his sides as he walked. But the ship's sudden list in the other direction threw him into a wall, smacking his shoulder against the jagged mount of a coiled firehose. The general was too busy punching a code into a cipher lock to notice.

Five Marines jumped to terrified attention in the intel center. The general waved them all off with an *at ease*. "Videoconferencing system's set up over there," he said to Rance. "Now, just hit enter and your call will start. Sound good?"

Rance found the chair and waited for the Marines to clear out before hitting enter. When he finally did, he found himself looking at Dorsey and Cowles in split screen, just as if he were back in the embassy in Vienna.

"All right," Dorsey said after a few polite questions about Rance's complicated DOD travel arrangements. "Ed—are the Iranians still in alignment with this thing? Anything new from Walid?"

"Just a note that *Août Noir*'s agreed to the exchange," said Rance. "Sounds like we're all set with it. Executive terminal at Beirut Hariri. We should be good to go."

"Great," said Dorsey, slapping his left hand over his right fist with a flinty smile. "Then it's on. I just spoke with Werner. Kahlidi's with him, all set for the helo transit. Provided we get that last proof of life, I trust you have no problem getting there at about fifteen-hundred local?"

"Shouldn't be a problem," said Rance. "I've got a briefing with the Marine general right after this. Sounds like it will only be like an hour transit from *Kearsarge*'s position off the coast. He said we're steaming east at flank speed."

Dorsey ground the fist into his other hand. "Perfect. Now, Dave, I want you to keep your SAC team on alert in case this thing goes sideways. But no *visible* force. Just get them armed and ready. And remember, keep all of this away from the ambassador. No State people."

"Got it," said Cowles. "Beirut Station will be ready, boss."

Dorsey nodded. "And Ed, you need to keep Walid and the Iranians from going all wobbly on us. I still don't trust these fuckers. But if it gets Meredith back, then I'm happy to sing *Kumbaya* for two fucking hours. Okay?"

"Roger that," said Rance. "I got this."

"It's on," Captain Reu Klein said to Dale after hanging up in the aft torpedo room of the Israeli Navy submarine *Tekumah*.

The sub was cruising at five knots, one hundred feet below the Mediterranean surface, two hundred nautical miles southeast of Rance on the USS *Kearsarge*. "Captain says the weather's a little windy but there's no shipping traffic. We're cleared to surface."

"Surface," Dale repeated, in a profound exhale of relief. Though an experienced diver, the prospect of having to egress the submarine through the torpedo tubes had left him quietly terrified for the past hour.

The rest of the Flotilla 13 men had sensed it. They'd regaled Dale with one story after another about comrades who'd occasionally been stuck inside the mortifying tubes. And even though he suspected they'd just been screwing with him, the mere chance that they weren't had left Dale shaken.

The bucking IAF Panther helo ride from the Sea of Galilee to the jittery night hover over this submarine forty miles out at sea had been bad. The spine-tingling twenty-five-foot drop into the cold, tossing waves in the dark had sucked ass. The confused scramble up the sub's side netting from the heaving rubber boat had truly been a shitstorm. But the thought of being trapped in a dark, claustrophobic torpedo tube a hundred feet underwater as they equalized pressure was . . .

"So," Dale said, cracking his knuckles. "Just to confirm—you're saying we're *definitely* getting ashore by rubber boat?"

"Yes," the crusty Flotilla 13 commander answered. "We're only three clicks offshore now. Our contacts should have the van ready on the beach already. We'll be all set up in the hide north of the airport in . . ." The commander checked his massive dive watch. "I'd say about three hours. Around oh-two-hundred local time."

Dale nodded. These were, perhaps, the first complete sentences he'd heard the leathery old frogman speak. Up until now, Dale hadn't been convinced the Israeli knew English.

Reu's hands closed on Dale's shoulders like a vise. He roughly spun Dale around. The commander pulled a zipper on Dale's back and cinched down the strap that held the rubber-cased sniper rifle and M-4 rifle bundled together. Two of the other Flotilla commandos stood by, already suited up, grinning when Dale nearly stumbled under Reu's harsh equipment checks.

"Listen, Mr. John," said Reu as he tucked a strap on Dale's combat vest. "Just stay with me and we shouldn't have any trouble. Okay?"

"Okay," said Dale. "I want no trouble."

CHAPTER 47

"IF THIS IS THE LAST PHOTO, THEN HOW WILL I PROVE I'M ALIVE FROM now on?" Meredith joked.

Maya simply grunted. The Mossad woman didn't seem happy at all, even though she'd arrived just fifteen minutes earlier with good news.

Clearly in mission mode, Maya had announced the updates as though reading from a teleprompter: Kahlidi was in Capernaum with Werner; John and the Flotilla 13 snipers were in position; the USS *Kearsarge* was now off the Lebanese coast. And finally, the Iranian executive jet was over Iraqi airspace, on its way to the Beirut executive terminal. It was all going to plan. Good news.

"Meredith," Maya said now from behind the digital SLR camera. "You look a little too . . . happy. You shouldn't even have the trace of a smile if you're held captive by terrorists."

"Right," said Meredith. She pinched her sore lip, causing her eyes to water.

"Better," Maya said, snapping the picture with that morning's fresh edition of *L'Orient-Le Jour* in front of Meredith's face. "Will you eat something today?"

"Yes," said Meredith, leaning against the wall to undo her wrist shackle. "I suppose it would be good to get my strength up."

"I agree," said Maya. "When I come back from lunch I'll bring something worthwhile. Also a pair of shoes for you. Now I need to go get this photo over to them. Excuse me."

The Mossad woman returned a few hours later dressed in her chador. After removing it, as usual, she knelt and emptied the contents of her bag. But this time, there was a larger round item wrapped in foil and a pair of used women's Nikes. Ravenous, Meredith's mouth watered at the aroma of baked bread. She distracted herself by lacing the old sneakers.

"What's that?" said Meredith, motioning toward the foil, unable to help herself. "It smells so good."

"*Manousheh,*" said Maya, unwrapping it on the floor. The Mossad woman had removed the Kevlar vest she typically wore in order to lean over more comfortably.

"It's Lebanese flatbread," said the Israeli woman. "I hope you don't mind but I'm vegetarian—so this is just cheese and nigella seeds. I brought it for you. Can we split it?" She sat cross-legged on the floor across from Meredith and spread out the food in a picnic.

"You've never eaten with me before."

"We're finally celebrating," said Maya. She parted her lips with a warm smile. Meredith hadn't seen that before either. "This is our last supper together."

The CIA woman returned the smile and pulled apart the leavened bread. They ate and drank in silence for a few minutes. Meredith could hear the two Junction agents outside, posing as kidnappers from *Août Noir*. Their primary activity in posing as Hezbollah militants seemed to be watching TV. Soccer. Always soccer. Meredith was entirely sick of listening to it.

Over the roar of an announcer celebrating a goal on television, she swallowed a hunk of flatbread and said, "Maya—I've been thinking about Dil. I got to spend some time with her when I was at Werner's place. She's darling. So sweet."

"Yes," said Maya. "Dil told me as much. She said the two of you made a wish together at the lake. She also told me she wished for you to come back one day. She says you promised her another coin. She's expecting it."

"Oh, is she?" Meredith smiled through the pain of her swollen lip.

Maya continued eating, nodding. After a few more bites, she added, "To have bonded with Dil in so short a visit makes me suspect you're a very good mother, Meredith. In fact, Dil is still asking about you. I spoke to her this morning."

Meredith nodded and held a piece of flatbread a few inches in front of her mouth. "That's nice to hear," she said. "Tell Dil I already miss her." She washed down more flatbread with a swig of water.

"I will," said Maya, looking down at the foil.

"And," added Meredith, "I hope you don't think this too forward, Maya. But I suppose I've also been wondering—who will ultimately raise Dil? Werner and his wife seem in good health, but she's so young . . ."

"Only seven."

"Yes. And then that got me to wondering . . . Where are Dil's parents?"

Maya finished off another piece of flatbread and then stopped eating. She placed her hands in her lap, not far from the Beretta strap on her thigh. After a moment, the Mossad woman looked up at Meredith's swollen eyes. "Meredith—why would you ask me about Dil's parents?"

"Just wondering about a sweet child, that's all."

"Wondering about the sweet child's parentage, to be precise."

"Yes. Wondering . . . I suppose I was wondering if *you* are Dil's mother . . ."

"But you already know I'm her *doda*."

"A *doda* is an aunt," said Meredith. "And I've done the math. Werner said he'd lost a son, in a raid ten years ago. Dil's too young to be Werner's granddaughter. And . . . well . . . Dil *looks* like you. She's beautiful . . . very fortunate that way . . ."

The two women looked into each other's eyes for a long moment.

"You can tell me the truth," Meredith said, breaking the stare. She brushed a lock of dirty hair from her forehead. "If I can take a beating from Mossad and a fake kidnapping . . . I can take just about anything." Meredith attempted a grin, but her lip hurt. She let the smile drop.

Maya hadn't moved, Meredith noticed.

"To understand Dil," the Mossad woman finally said, "I think you first have to understand me."

"Ah," said Meredith, looking away. "So that's a yes, then. You are her mother. And . . ." Meredith stopped talking, stared at the filthy old running shoes on her feet.

"It's not what you think," said Maya.

"Oh? And what do I think?"

"Meredith, you're never going to see me again after today."

"I don't know about that," said Meredith, still looking at the shoes. "I was hoping that we'd reestablished the relationship between Mossad and CIA. After this, maybe we'll—"

"No," said Maya. "We won't. Trust me. I'm no longer part of Caesarea. I resigned, remember? I don't want this life anymore. After this, you will never see me again. Or Dil."

Meredith nodded slowly. "So formal. But all right. What will you do now? What's your new life going to be like?"

"I want to be a good mother," said Maya. "Dil needs one. I want to be a good mother to her like you've been to your daughter."

"Thank you," said Meredith. "You should do that. A girl needs a mother . . ."

"Of course. But, Meredith—I am *not* Dil's biological mother. She calls me *doda* because I'm closest to her. That's all."

"You just said you—"

"I said I would *be* her mother. But I'm not her biological mother."

"I'm a little confused," said Meredith.

"That's because you don't understand me."

"Care to help me out with that?"

"All right. You see, *my* mother was Lebanese. She was a Maronite Christian who lived near Fatima Gate, just north of the Israeli border. She met my father when they were both traveling to Athens, both in school. After they fell in love my mother emigrated to Israel to be with him. They were married in Jerusalem and had me a year later. My father was a pilot—in Werner's squadron. He was shot down, taken prisoner—by Hezbollah. They . . . tortured him. To death."

Meredith stayed very still. She could hear the vehicle traffic increasing outside, the inane soccer broadcaster in the next room roaring away. "I didn't know that," she said. "I'm very sorry."

"Yes. We were all very sorry. My mother was *so* very sorry, *so* sick with guilt, thinking her own country had caused her husband's death, that a month later she took her own life. Growing up, everyone told me it was ill health—but I know what really happened."

"I'm sorry, Maya. I had no idea."

The Caesarea woman nodded, took a sip of water. "And then, orphaned, Werner took me in, adopted me. But as he raised me, he pulled me into—well, what I eventually became. A *kidon*. An expert. Werner honed every skill I had—my looks, my athleticism, my schooling—into that one purpose. To be a *kidon*. To avenge my parents. And I wanted that too."

"Werner may have done that," said Meredith, "but I sense he loves you like his own daughter."

"He does love me as a daughter. In *his* way. But he really loves me for what I became, for what I represent. Not for who I am."

"And Dil?" Meredith asked. "Where did she come from?"

"Poor little Dil is a refugee. One of our patrols found her wandering around the streets in the *dahiyeh* after a car bombing. Her parents had been killed when one of these rickety buildings collapsed. She was only four at the time. She had no idea what had happened, of course, only that her mother was suddenly gone, that her home had suddenly been wiped off the earth. The men brought her back to Israel, and Werner . . . adopted her."

"So, Dil is technically your stepsister."

"Yes. That's what an American would call her in legal terms. My stepsister."

"And you're going to raise her now. You've resigned from the service. I see."

"Yes," said Maya, taking another sip of water. "I won't let Werner mold Dil into a Mossad operative. This has to stop somewhere. *He* has to stop somewhere. Fortunately, I have a place to the south, a hideaway in the Negev. Dil and I are going to get away from all of this. I'm going to bring her up in a pure, pristine place. In the Negev. And that's why you will never see me again."

Meredith nodded and looked again at her shoes. "I see," she said. "Did you know that Dil wants to go to Australia? See a kangaroo?"

"Yes, of course I know. And I will take her."

"I hope that . . . I hope that it all works out for you, Maya. And Dil."

"But before I go," said Maya, her long, straight nose canted shyly down. "I sense that you wish to ask me about someone else. Not just Dil."

Meredith continued looking at her shoes, shaking her head slightly. "I have no right."

"I can tell you about John," said Maya. "About our relationship. It is not hard to be honest with you. You are a good listener."

Meredith looked away, letting her eyes wander to the slit of light at the top of the opposite wall. She brushed her hand under her sore nose. "It's none of my business anymore. John is his own man. You don't have to tell me anything."

Maya leaned forward and placed her hands on Meredith's dirty shoes. "Meredith, please. Look at me."

After Meredith's eyes had settled onto Maya's, the Mossad woman continued. "John is an honorable man, Meredith. It's important that you know that. It's important to know that I tried to seduce him back in Egypt, years ago. He wouldn't have me, despite all my training. I tried to flip him. He wouldn't stand for it. He must surely have told you all about it. It was . . . tradecraft."

Meredith continued shaking her head, sadly. *Tradecraft.* "He wouldn't tell me." She grabbed Maya's two hands. "Well. It has all led to this. This operation will be . . . important. Strategic. As intelligence people, this may be our greatest collaboration ever."

"Yes," said Maya. "Because of you. It is all you, Meredith. But we still have to get you back home in one piece for it to work." The Mossad woman smiled, warmly.

Meredith returned it, despite the crippling pain of her lips.

Maya shuffled to her feet and zipped her Kevlar vest back into place. Checking on her equipment pockets. Over this, she draped the chador and checked the holster strapped to her leg.

"Hezbollah men are obsessed with their mothers," she said. "I'll be the one driving you to the exchange this afternoon. The thought is that the chador will make me look like a martyr's mother in the car. We'll have a martyr poster in the window. You'll be hidden in the back."

"All right," said Meredith.

"When we get to the tarmac," continued Maya, "you'll get out, walk to your waiting helicopter while Kahlidi walks the other way—and that will be it. Your agent will finally be in place back in Quds. So. I'm glad we got the chance to have this . . . goodbye chat. It would have been much harder in the car."

"Much harder, yes. And where are you going now?"

"To get the vehicle. It will be parked out front. It's old and beat up. But it's armored—on loan from our Beirut station just in case. I'll see you at three-thirty."

"How far off is three-thirty? I can only tell time by the muezzin call."

"Here," Maya said, removing her gold wristwatch. "No more proof-of-life photos for us. Take this."

Meredith looked at the small gold watch after Maya left. She had only two more hours to go. They would feel like a lifetime, she thought.

CHAPTER 48

"TELL *EFFENDI* WHAT YOU TOLD ME," NABIL SAID TO THE BOY.

The boy looked up at Siamak. The MOIS officer was a forbidding sight in his dark green uniform and long-billed cap.

Though Beirut-based IRGC officers were careful to keep a low profile among the Hezbollah militiamen they controlled, Siamak had put the uniform on before leaving his home in West Beirut that afternoon. If the lead was as strong as Nabil had suggested on the phone, then there was a good chance he would get to confront the *Août Noir* brothers—and, surely, an upstart Hezbollah splinter cell would respond respectfully to the uniform.

"*Effendi* really needs to hear it himself. Tell him just like you told me," Nabil coaxed the shy boy, stroking his head. "Now—you're a good boy. Go on. Show him the picture and tell him. Just like you told me."

It now occurred to Siamak that the uniform may have been a mistake. He judged the boy to be about twelve—and terrified of these men who wanted so desperately to speak with him.

The MOIS major removed his Browning pistol belt and set it on a table. Then he removed his hat. He turned to face the boy with his hand on his heart. "It's all right," Siamak said, forcing himself to smile. "I have a son like you. His name is Ali. And I promise I won't bite. Do you like *Star Wars*?"

The son of a devout Shia family, the boy wore the full-length, open-necked long shirt called a *thobe*. It was dirty, likely the only garment he owned, Siamak thought. "Yes," he said.

"Which character?"

"The Mandalorian."

"Brother," Siamak said, hand still on his heart. "Ali loves the Mandalorian too. Now, this is important. You can tell me."

With one more glance toward Nabil, the boy withdrew a cheap Android phone from his pocket. "I was watching the newsstand all morning," he said quietly to Siamak. "I was on the far corner, sitting on the curb, playing a game on my phone. That's what Fouad told me I could do as long as I kept an eye out." The boy looked up at Nabil for support.

"Fouad is his watch commander," Nabil said to Siamak. "Works for Said. Fouad is the one I have manning the truck outside the hotel now. But go on, boy. Show *Effendi*. Tell him."

"Okay. I took a picture of everyone that came from sunrise until nine o'clock who bought a newspaper, just like Fouad said I should." The boy looked up again. "This is her, *Effendi*," the boy said, holding up the phone. "She's the only one that bought the *L'Orient* paper there before nine o'clock. She bought it and two bottles of water, put them in the bag. See?" The boy handed the phone to Siamak for closer inspection.

The Iranian greedily zoomed in with his thumbs, trying to get a look at the woman's face. She was clad in a full chador with a hijab scarf pulled carefully over her nose, only the eyes visible. By virtue of the other citizens standing nearby, Siamak could see she was much taller than the average *dahiyeh* woman. Her body seemed thick, almost like a man's. It was hard to judge her age.

The MOIS officer looked at Nabil and smiled genuinely. "Well, at least we have our first look at *Août Noir*." The smile faded. "But I suppose it's too late. The prisoner exchange is only about an hour from now. And this woman could have gone anywhere. Still, I'd like to make sure we reward Kareem something for coming up with the idea about the newspaper barcode."

The day before, when Siamak and Nabil had visited the electronics shop, Kareem had printed off the blown-up barcode image. He'd told

Siamak to take it to the newspaper for analysis. And after Nabil had e-mailed the image to a Hezbollah brother that worked at *L'Orient*, they'd learned that the barcode was an indicator of daily printing lots for the newspaper—and the destination of the lots.

This one had made its way to only five newsstands in southern Beirut, two of which were in the *dahiyeh*. Nabil's watchers had been on a rotating shift outside them ever since.

"It may *not* be too late, *Effendi*," said Nabil. "Tell him what happened next, boy. Go on. Don't be afraid. Tell him."

The boy nodded. He spoke so quietly that Siamak had to lean toward him. "I followed her. Stayed back, like Fouad taught me. But I saw her enter a house. A small one, not one of the tall buildings. It was on Burj al-Barajneh, over near the Palestinian camp. Less than a half kilometer from the newsstand."

Siamak knelt and looked intently into the boy's eyes. The MOIS officer put his hands on the boy's shoulders. "You are a *pasdar*," he said. "The very best. But Burj al-Barajneh runs in many directions. Do you have anything else to go on? I need to go find it, quickly."

"Yes," the boy said. He opened his phone to Google Maps. "I dropped a pin. The house is here, *Effendi*."

Siamak studied the location and looked up at Nabil's glittering eyes.

"Why did it take so long to get to us?" Siamak asked.

"Forgive the boy," said Nabil. "He has the GPS phone, but he ran out of data earlier today. The kids buy data whenever they get a few pounds, which isn't often these days. He walked all the way here with his information. It took him hours."

Siamak looked at the twelve-year-old. "I will pay for your phone service from now on, my little *pasdar*," the MOIS officer said, smiling widely. "Forever."

"Should we go now?" asked Nabil.

"I will," said Siamak. "I want to talk to these *Août Noir* brothers. But not you. Get Said to drive me in that fast Mustang of his."

"He'll be happy to do that, *Effendi*. He's obsessed with that noisy, gas-guzzling thing."

"Good. Tell him to come get me. And to bring his AK."

"But what about me?" asked Nabil.

"I want you," said Siamak, "to get up to West Beirut, relieve Fouad, and bring your cousin's truck down to this *Août Noir* safe house—just in case they won't listen to me."

CHAPTER 49

DALE LOOKED THROUGH THE SCOPE, PUTTING THE RETICLE ON THE taxiing Iranian business jet, a Falcon 20, marked only by its "EN" tail number. Through the scope he could see a few dark forms in the round aircraft windows. He couldn't make out faces, just the dark shapes of heads.

With the heat waves shimmering up through the scope, Dale absently wondered if he could take one of the Iranians out. Just for practice, he moved his right hand slowly forward and clicked the scope's elevation wheel twice.

"What are you doing?" whispered the Flotilla 13 spotter next to him, hearing the faint clicks. They were both covered in camouflage netting, nestled into the dirt under a wild ficus grove.

"Nothing," said Dale. "Just curious if I could make the shot."

"It's weird that the Iranians are the first ones to arrive," said the spotter. "And it's creepy the way the airport is shut down. Never good when things get quiet in Beirut. I don't like it."

"Me neither," whispered Dale. "I could shoot these guys now before our team shows up. We'd be the only ones who'd know it. How it should be done."

But then the CIA man heard the distant whop of rotors. "Shit," said Dale. "Too late. Can you rate that helo with your spotter scope? I can't make it out with my bare eyes."

"Not really a helo," said the spotter, rustling under the net as he shifted his long telescopic lens. "It's . . . weird-looking. It has rotors like a helicopter . . . but also regular wings. I think you call it an Osprey? Looks like it's headed in for approach now."

Dale looked up and made out the distant aircraft's two enormous propellers now. "You're right," Dale said. "An Osprey. American Marines."

"Semper fi," said the spotter, grinning, proud of himself for knowing the famous Latin motto.

"Ooh-rah," returned Dale.

After slowing enough to rotate its engine nacelles to convert to vertical flight, the enormous American aircraft set down on the eastern side of the runway. The two opposing aircraft now faced each other across the tarmac, a hundred meters apart.

"Did Reu report the arrival of the Americans?" Dale asked the spotter. The Flotilla 13 commander hadn't trusted the American enough to have his own radio.

"Yes," said the spotter. "He said the IAF helicopter is almost here too."

The Osprey's rotors finally slowed. Its rear cargo ramp came down and touched the tarmac. Two US Marines decked out in everything they'd need for combat except their M-4s stood outside the ramp, blinking under their helmets in the bright afternoon sun. Then one of them waved to the interior of the Osprey, signaling that it was safe for its VIP passenger to egress.

Dale watched as Ed Rance walked down the ramp wearing a short-sleeved black button-down.

"Tell me," Dale said to the spotter, watching Rance through the scope. "You think I could hit that guy in the black shirt in the foot from here? I'll bet you a pile of shekels I could take off that right foot. Just the foot."

The spotter shifted his lens to look at Rance's legs.

"Nah," said the Israeli. "I wouldn't take that bet. I think you could easily hit that foot. How about something smaller?"

"Like his balls?"

Meredith looked at Maya's watch. It was a little after three o'clock—not so long to go now. To minimize the chance of Hezbollah interference, the plan was to stay in the safe house for as long as they could. They estimated the drive to the airfield at thirty minutes—and they didn't want to be too early. The less the Iranians saw of the fake Hezbollah splinter *Août Noir*, the better.

Meredith looked at the familiar rectangle of light coming in from the room's western side. The breeze had been coming from the east today, bringing in the varied smells of squalor. The last hour in this miserable hellhole, she thought, would be a long one.

She checked the timepiece Maya had given her again, watching the sweep of the second hand out of utter boredom. She slumped against the wall, counting the seconds, listening to the scooter beeps, the car horns, the truck rumbles. It was another warm August day. Without the sea breeze, the room was getting hot. Meredith crossed her legs and listened to the traffic, trying to distinguish the sound of one vehicle from another.

And then, surprisingly, one car stood out. It seemed to get louder, a heaving exhaust, coming closer. Meredith wondered if she was simply deceiving herself because she wanted so badly for Maya to finally get there. The car's racket got louder still. Then she heard it idle for a moment and thought it sounded like one of the old American cars she'd grown up with, a big V-8. Then the engine went quiet. She thought she heard a car door. Another one. Then nothing.

Maya had said the vehicle would be armored, heavy. Probably need a big V-8, thought Meredith. *Finally getting out of here.*

Her hope rose further when she heard the soccer men in the front room moving around. They turned down the TV for the first time since she'd been locked up in this miserable place. Then she heard what sounded like a door slamming. In a near Pavlovian response, Meredith sat against the wall, facing the door, tightening the shoelaces, waiting for Maya to come in, trying not to smile so it wouldn't hurt her swollen lips.

Meredith heard the keys rattling the lock, as usual. But then the door didn't open the way it usually did. Instead, it opened a mere crack. She could see the whites of a man's eyes looking through it.

The door opened further. A man in a headscarf, black shirt, blue jeans, and white sneakers came through it slowly, shutting it behind him very quietly, carefully. It was the first look Meredith had ever had of one of her fake captors, one of the Mossad Junction agents in disguise.

The man hurried across the floor toward her. Meredith wasn't sure what to do. "*Tranquille,*" he whispered, reaching down toward her, grabbing her arms.

Once she was on her feet, he continued in rapid French. "There's someone here. Come. We need to put you somewhere." He opened the door carefully again and led her through it.

She was in a carpeted dark hallway now, the first time she'd ever seen anything in this safe house other than her own room. She could see shadows on the wall, sunlight coming from the front room. She heard voices. The man in the sneakers pulled Meredith by the arm, rushing her down the hall, a finger held to his mouth that told her to stay quiet. With infinite care, he opened another door and nudged Meredith through. It was a room just like hers. But unlike the room in which Meredith had been sequestered, this one had a twin bed.

"*Passez dessous,*" the man whispered, pointing under the metal bed frame.

The voices down the hall seemed to get a little louder. It sounded like Arabic to Meredith. "Where's Maya?" she whispered before sliding under. "*Qu'est-ce que c'est?*"

The man kneeled and angled his face so he could hear her under the bed. The black scarf around his head dangled down. "People have come," he whispered. "We have to treat them as guests. But don't worry. We'll get rid of them. Just hide here in case. *Tranquille, tranquille.*"

Dale watched the Israeli Panther helicopter winding down now after its quick landing. With the airport closed to any other traffic, the helicopter hadn't even bothered to enter a normal traffic pattern. It had flown right to the designated spot on the executive field about fifty meters from the Osprey.

Its rotors ground to a halt, the whine of the turbines dying away. Through his scope, Dale saw Werner step out with another IDF officer. Werner was wearing a civilian straw hat with a black band, like a fifties gangster on a Havana holiday. *Old school*, thought Dale, grinning.

From his hide three hundred yards up the scrubby slope, Dale watched Werner and Rance shake hands while the Marines and IDF soldiers stood around the aircraft. Rance was using his hands while he talked, pointing at things. He and Werner seemed to keep their distance from one another.

Dale checked his watch. Three-thirty. Only a half hour to go. He raised his scope to the open gates for the terminal and the access road beyond it. The Israelis had said Meredith would be arriving in an old, beat-up Mercedes 300. They'd promised it would be armored too. It had better be. Dale raised his scope toward the far gates of the field but didn't see it.

CHAPTER 50

MEREDITH COULD FEEL HER HEARTBEAT THUMPING AGAINST THE GRAY tiled floor under the bed.

She could still hear the voices of the men in the front room. She couldn't make out the words, but she recognized the cadence of Arabic. And the cadence was getting faster. It was beginning to sound like an argument. She'd caught the Arabic word *shaqiq*, "brother." She heard it over and over. But the pace still suggested argument.

Between brothers, men. There was no sign of Maya, no feminine voice out there.

The male voices got louder, faster. And then Meredith heard an angry yell, a big thump, as though the TV had been toppled. She felt the thump vibrate through the floor, startling her. She heard another loud yell, then something worse.

A gunshot. Two shots. Three shots, returning fire with a separate sound. Then nothing.

They're Mossad Junction agents, Meredith thought, her mind racing, her heart thumping against the floor. *They've been prepared for trouble from the beginning. They couldn't have been surprised.*

She scanned the room, pressed one swollen eye against the tile, looked down the length of the floor. Like the room where she'd been held for the past four days, this one had high slitted windows. She recognized the lighted rectangle on the floor.

She could reach the windows if she stood on the bed. But just as quickly she rejected the idea. She'd never be able to get through either of the narrow slots.

This room had a closet. But it had waist-high saloon doors and nothing else inside. She'd be less exposed where she was, under the bed, lame as that was.

The bed, then.

She searched the underside of the mattress over her head. It was an old-style frame with long, wavy metal springs running horizontally. There was a metal support bar in the middle of it held in place with two simple screws—not even screws. They were more like pegs. Meredith was able to make the crossbar slide to an angle, then pull it free.

She heard the other bedroom door open with a crash, the room where she'd been staying before they'd moved her to this one.

Oh Jesus Christ, she thought.

"This is it!" she heard a man yell in Arabic. She heard the clank of her old shackle chains. "Keep looking!" the man shouted again.

Meredith hugged the metal bar to her chest, panting, thinking. Quietly, she rolled to her side and inched all the way under the bed, as close to the wall as possible. She clutched the metal bar, tested the end of it with her thumb to see if it was sharp. It wasn't. She heard footsteps coming down the hall. She held her breath.

The door opened. Two sets of shoes. One man wore white high-top sneakers, the other shined black military combat boots. Neither spoke when they came in. Boots went right to the closet and nearly ripped the swinging doors off their hinges.

Sneakers came right toward her.

Meredith took one last breath and squeezed the metal bar. And then everything became bright. The man had ripped the thin mattress from the frame.

Meredith rolled to her stomach, hiding the bar under her chest.

"Here! Here!" the man was shouting in Arabic. Meredith felt rough hands on her arm, tugging at her. Now a second set of hands on her ankles. They were yanking her out from under the bed, sliding her along the floor like a rolled rug. She stayed facedown, hiding the bar.

One of the men forced her onto her back with a strong jerk of her shoulders. Meredith used the momentum of the roll to swing the bar as hard as she could. She hit a young, bearded man in the face. He had sunglasses hanging from the nape of his T-shirt. When the man took the blow, the sunglasses went flying. Stunned, he slapped Meredith across the face with an open hand, saying something she didn't understand. She managed another backhand with the bar to the side of his head, but it wasn't much.

He caught her arm, bent her wrist painfully. The metal bar clanged to the floor. Meredith tried a long-forgotten move to entangle her legs with his. She thought she might roll, to get him to the floor. Then she might be able to scramble to her feet and run for it. Her chances out on the street were surely better than this.

She was almost into the maneuver when another set of hands had her by the collar of her dress. It was the man in combat boots. His pants were green, his shirt green with markings—a uniform, she realized—an Iranian uniform. He was shaking her hard, slapping her.

I'm part of a prisoner swap, she was saying to herself. *Maybe this will be okay. Maybe they just wanted to free me from this splinter cell to hand me over.* She willed herself to say nothing.

"Stop it, stop it!" the man started saying in English. "I know who you are." Meredith stopped struggling against him. *He knows who I am. He's an Iranian. This is a prisoner swap.* She looked down, determined to avoid his eyes.

Her head snapped sideways, painfully. The Iranian had hit her hard, closed fist, just to the right of her nose. She screamed in pain. The other man had her arms pinned back as they muscled her to her feet and against the wall. They shoved her into it, face first. The younger man was tugging at her arms, holding them in place behind her. *This is all part of the exchange*, she said to herself. *They're just going to rough me up. You don't have to . . .*

They pushed her toward the door.

This is the exchange. We're just going to the exchange, the mantra went on.

Sneakers kicked the backs of her knees and knocked her to the floor. He gripped her wrists tightly and stretched her arms over her head. He kneed her between the shoulder blades, shoving her against the wall.

No! she screamed inwardly. She jerked a hand free and tried to raise it. The man grabbed her by the fabric at her back and hit her. Her head bounced off the wall.

Uniform was suddenly close to her. He had her face in his hand. He was pinching her cheeks together harshly, forcing her to look at him. She shut her eyes, determined not to give him anything.

While the other man held her arms together, Uniform pried her swollen black eye open with the finger and thumb of his right hand. "I know you," he said. "Meredith Morris-Dale. CIA. Hello."

She jerked her head, shutting her eyes again. She felt something cold and foreign against her forehead. Her eyes opened. She was looking down the barrel of a pistol.

Her chest was heaving. She held her breath, shut her eyes.

Blown.

She swallowed hard. Her dry throat clicked.

But at least I can go with dignity.

She felt the metal tap against her forehead and ground her teeth. "If you tell me just one thing, Mrs. Meredith Morris-Dale. I might let you live," the man said. The Iranian spoke with a slight British lilt, almost like Kasem.

Kasem, she thought, cursing herself. Fucking Atlas. It had been such a brilliant plan. Her plan.

She thought of Grace and John. John, who'd warned her about this; he'd said it was the stupidest goddamned plan he'd ever heard, begged her not to go through with it. Begged her there at Werner's house like she'd never seen him do before.

Now she ground her teeth, waiting to die, every muscle in her face clenching.

She felt the pistol grip smack against her forehead. She swallowed again. *Not going to say a goddamned thing*, she thought. *Not a scream, not a tear, nothing.*

"Listen to me," the man said. "I want to know about Colonel Kasem Kahlidi. I want to know how he ended up with the Jews."

Nothing.

Siamak tapped the gun barrel against her skull. He thought of the planned prisoner exchange less than an hour from now, of Maloof. But Maloof's orders weren't the reason he was going to kill her now. "You think you can do anything, don't you?" Siamak seethed through clenched teeth. He put his hand around her neck and shook her.

Meredith kept her eyes shut. She turned her forehead. The gun barrel shifted to her temple. The Iranian's hand was still on her neck.

"You trick all of us, don't you? You use us, don't you?" He bounced the barrel off her skull, hesitating. If Kahlidi really was a spy, Siamak was thinking, then he would be the very worst kind. If he was welcomed back as a hero, who knew how much damage he could do? But then he thought of Maloof again, and of his son, Ali.

Siamak shook Meredith's neck harshly. "Did he tell you how to kill my brothers in London? Were you his controller? Is that how you learned all about our little project here in Beirut, in Laylaki? If you tell me, I might let you live. You don't have to die today."

Either way, Siamak thought, Maloof would survive, the old fox. At least he wouldn't need Nabil's truck to kill the woman—that would save killing some innocents in the *dahiyeh.*

Meredith finally raised her chin to him. She looked him in the eye for the first time. *Maybe I will say one thing to him,* she thought as she struggled for air.

Through her swollen bloody eye she looked at him. He was young, almost handsome, dark brown eyes and thick black eyebrows. Like Kasem. She decided she would give him just two words before dying: "Fuck. You."

She clamped her eyes shut and gulped one last breath through her constricted throat.

"*Au revoir.*" The Iranian pulled the hammer of his pistol back.

Meredith heard an ear-shattering bang.

CHAPTER 51

"WHERE THE HELL ARE THEY?" DALE WHISPERED TO THE SPOTTER THAT lay in a prone position next to him.

"Nothing on the nets," the spotter whispered back after adjusting the squelch.

Dale watched the tarmac intently through his scope. The white Iranian Falcon jet sat perpendicular to the Israeli and American aircraft, two hundred meters across the striped concrete. Though the Iranian jet's engines had been shut down, a squat auxiliary power unit vehicle had been plugged to it, keeping the aircraft systems running. Beyond, in the shimmering distance, Dale could see the paved access roads that led to the field. The one to the west was gated with razor-topped wire, facing the parking lot. The other had a lowered arm manned by Lebanese Army regulars in red berets.

Iranian fuckers have air-conditioning, thought Dale, swinging his scope back to the white business jet. He chanced a slow swipe of his forehead, removing an annoying sweat trickle.

Now four-fifteen, the heat was up to full blast. They'd been lying in this tall grass beneath the trees since sunrise, moving only to adjust scopes, suck water from a blister pack, or piss into the shallow dirt holes under them.

"Check with Reu," Dale whispered. "They're more than fifteen minutes late. This is totally unsat."

Dale's spotter, a Flotilla 13 chief warrant officer, keyed his microphone and whispered in Hebrew. "No update," the commando said after a half minute of radio jargon. "Command says the package hasn't checked in yet."

Dale moved his scope from the Iranian jet to the open cargo ramp of the Osprey. Rance was still out there, talking to Werner, standing in the shade of the aircraft's huge twin vertical stabilizers. Two Marines stood to either side of the senior spies.

Dale shifted the scope another centimeter toward the Israeli helo. It too had its cargo door open. Dale saw now that an IDF officer in a beret was trotting over from the helo, heading to Werner, moving his mouth, probably saying something. Dale watched as Werner and Rance looked at their watches and took in whatever beret-man was saying. Dale focused on Rance's face. It had turned sour.

"I'm going down there," said Dale.

"*Mamash lo!*" the chief whispered harshly. "You can't blow our cover. Sit tight, Dale."

"Negative. Sorry, Chief. I'm going down there."

The spotter let out a long string of Hebrew curse words that washed pointlessly over Dale.

"Look," said Dale. "I'll inch back toward the trail. Then I'll circle down to the perimeter road and slip through our fence breach. Once I'm down that low, the Osprey will block the view from the Iranians. Now let your team down there know a friendly's coming in."

"*No!*" the spotter whispered harshly, grabbing at Dale's ankle.

But Dale had already started backing out of the camo net.

As promised, Dale descended the back side of the small hill, out of view of the airfield. He ran in a crouch, keeping low in the tall, dry grass.

Beirut Hariri had been built on a raised platform of level fill dirt. After combat crawling down a shallow, descending gulley, Dale caught the perimeter road just below the runway and broke into a sprint. He found the section of fence the Flotilla team had cut the night before and rolled under it.

Popping to a knee, he looked up to see a US Marine at the ramp of the Osprey pointing an M-4 at him. Dale brought his arms out in front of him. "*American!*" he shouted.

Rance turned, made a face, then said something to the Marine, who lowered his weapon. Dale sprinted toward them, meeting them in the shade of the Osprey's vast tail assembly.

"What's going on? Where are they?" Dale half shouted at Rance and Werner.

By now Rance had a phone pressed to his ear. He glanced once at Dale, turned, shook his head, and continued his phone conversation. He walked to the far side of the aircraft for privacy.

With Rance out of earshot, Dale turned to Werner. "Where are they? What's going on?"

"We don't know," said the Caesarea boss, fanning himself with his straw hat. "But that doesn't mean anything's wrong—yet. Rance is talking to Walid Zafir, his Iranian MOIS contact, right now. There doesn't appear to be a cause for concern." He replaced the hat on his head.

Drenched in sweat, Dale unbuttoned the Israeli military overshirt and dropped it to the tarmac. Beneath it he wore his Radiohead at Wembley T-shirt. The Marine that had pointed the rifle at Dale stepped forward and handed him a water bottle.

"What did Rance say when he finally saw me?" Dale asked Werner when alone again.

"You don't want to know."

"Seriously," said Dale after emptying the water bottle. "Did he tell you I'm a fugitive or something? Are these Marines about to arrest me?"

The old Caesarea boss grinned and lowered his voice. "I'm afraid your career as a Mossad spy has been cut short. But it went to plan. He thinks you engineered this whole thing. He bought it."

"What *exactly* did you tell him?"

"Just what we rehearsed. I told him you used Maya to find Kahlidi, then threatened to expose us to Dorsey if we didn't offer up Kahlidi for Meredith. I told him you pulled a weapon on me when you found me at Capernaum. That seemed to be the clincher for Rance. He said that was typical of you."

Dale looked around to make sure Rance was still out of earshot. "Whatever works."

"Bought it lock, stock, and barrel. But he seemed irritated. I don't think he likes you."

"That's a fair way to put it. But thank you."

"As you say, Mr. Dale. A deal's a deal."

"They haven't heard anything," said Rance as he came around the corner of the Osprey, pocketing the phone in his black nylon shirt. A gust of hot wind blew his red-blond hair to the vertical then flopped it back down. He looked at Dale briefly, then his watch, then Werner. "Still nothing from *Août Noir*?"

"Nothing," said Werner. "We're trying to make contact but no one's picking up."

"Shit," said Rance. "At what point do we start to worry about this swap?"

"Yesterday," said Werner.

Rance looked at Dale, about to say something.

But Werner spoke first. "The good news is that the Iranians don't seem to have heard anything either. They seem to know as little about *Août Noir* as we do. Let's just give it time."

Rance's phone buzzed. He looked at it before answering. "Okay," he said. "Cowles is calling. His teams have been looking all over for *Août Noir*. Maybe he's got something."

"Maya's not answering?" whispered Dale after Rance had gone to the side of the huge gray aircraft again. "How the fuck is that even possible?"

"She'll come through," said Werner. "She always does." He jerked his head when Rance came back around the corner, signaling Dale to stay quiet.

"I don't know how much longer we can keep the airport closed," said Rance, his face flushed in the heat. "The Lebanese minister of transportation is crawling up the ambassador's ass. Cowles is running out of excuses for her. Not sure how much more time we really have here."

"Tell the Iranians to call the transportation minister," said Werner.

"We all know Hezbollah controls this airport. The Iranians can swing an extension."

Rance thought for a moment before pulling his phone back out of his pocket. "Not a bad idea," he said, dialing and turning away.

Dale looked over at the main Hariri airport. Fifteen airliners were at the gates, but the taxiways were quiet. The red berets at the swinging gate were smoking their cigarettes. Dale was starting to see some maintenance and service vehicles moving about, a few baggage handlers standing around. He looked to the right of the terminal and noticed a parking lot with a half dozen service vehicles.

Come on, Meth, he thought. *Don't do this to me.*

CHAPTER 52

MEREDITH FELL BACKWARD.

The sensation that most invaded her mind was one of acrid smoke. She realized she was coughing. Her ears were ringing. Another loud bang. Disoriented, she had no idea what was happening. Her ears rang, she coughed, tried to make out anything at all. Through the smoky fog she realized she was looking at the form of the Iranian who'd been about to shoot her a few seconds ago. He was down too, on his side, also coughing, blinking. Then he raised his head and saw her.

Meredith dove on him, going for the gun that was still in his hand. She was on top of him, helped by gravity. The Iranian was trying to raise the gun at his side. She gripped his wrist, pinning it to the floor.

But he was stronger than her. His arm raised higher, nearly lifting her. She shifted one of her hands to gouge savagely at his eyes, clawing at them like an animal while she twisted to the side. The gun went off right next to her head. It had missed. She rolled away. He was getting to his feet. Meredith went to the foot of the twin metal bed frame and hurled it on its side, shoving it toward the Iranian.

There was another shattering bang. A bright flash. Four cracks of rapid gunshots, then a fifth, a sixth.

Meredith had been behind the bare bed. Now she looked through the weave of the metal frame, through the smoke. The Iranian in uniform was on his back. He wasn't moving. The one in sneakers was crumpled near the closet, a puddle of blood under him.

Maya was lying against the far wall dressed in her chador, her pistol by her side, still in her hand.

Meredith coughed and threw the bed aside. She put a foot on the uniformed Iranian's head. She picked up his Browning pistol and shot him three times in the chest. She moved to the other man and kicked his head. He was already dead. But she shot him through the chest anyway, the aim a little off because her arms were starting to shake.

She dropped on her knees next to Maya, who lay on the floor puddled in her draping black chador. Meredith scooted forward and held the Israeli woman's face in her trembling hands. She could see that Maya was alive, blinking, her head framed by the hijab. Her long, solemn face incongruently composed.

"Are you hit?" Meredith asked.

Maya let go of her pistol, leaving it on the ground. She moved her hands slowly over her chest. She coughed. "I think I took a round to the vest," she said. "It just hurts. I don't think it was a straight-on shot."

Meredith peeled the chador from Maya's body and looked at the vest, noting a shredded equipment pocket. "What happened?" she asked.

Maya coughed and winced before she spoke. "Our men up front are down."

"What's this smoke?"

"Flash-bangs. I wasn't sure what I'd find when I kicked in the door." The Israeli woman coughed again.

Meredith nodded. "The guy in the uniform is IRGC. We're blown," said Meredith.

"No," said Maya. She inhaled a shaking breath. "We're not. I heard some of the argument before I came in. They think we're *Août Noir* still. We can still make the exchange. But we need to hurry."

Meredith helped Maya to her feet. The Mossad woman took a moment to lean against the wall, breathing deeply, coughing. She seemed to summon an inner strength and rose to her full height. She ejected the mag from her pistol, slammed home a fresh one, and raised it as she headed out of the room. "Stay low," she said, wrapping herself in the chador, one hand bracing her ribs.

Carrying the Iranian's Browning, Meredith followed Maya to the front of the safe house, staying low, sweeping for targets. Bright light slanted through a high window. The two dead Junction operatives were lying on the floor, limbs twisted at awkward angles. One had been taken with an ugly headshot. Maya checked both of them for vitals. She shook her head.

She moved low and carefully to a spot below the window, then raised herself to steal a glimpse outside. She collapsed back down into her crouch and swore in Hebrew.

"What?" asked Meredith.

"We'll have to go out the back," said Maya. She stood and bolted the front door. "Can't get to our car. Bunch of men in black shirts coming down the alley. Must have heard the shots. Get my bag out of the other room. We have to go. *Now.*"

Clad head to foot in their black chadors, the two women found themselves in a narrow alley of the Haret Hreik neighborhood, dodging hanging laundry, men lazing on door stoops, and children playing everywhere.

"How's your Arabic?" Maya whispered as men in black T-shirts ran past them in the other direction, headed toward the safe house.

"*Hasananaan,*" said Meredith. "Not much."

Maya switched to Arabic, speaking simply and slowly. "We can't walk too fast," she whispered. "They might all be watching us. They see the Hezbollah people. They know something's wrong." The two of them bumped into a throng of shoppers near an open-air market.

Meredith nodded, tightened the hijab scarf over her bruised face, and tucked it under the all-encompassing chador. She kept walking as calmly as she could.

"Here," Maya said after another thirty meters. She'd stopped at a crowded produce vendor. "You shop," the Mossad woman whispered in slow Arabic. "I'll get an update on our status to the team at the airport. Stop here. Stay at this fruit stand."

Meredith nodded. She now stood shoulder to shoulder with twenty other draped Muslim women, fondling apples and pears. The air smelled smoky, roasting vapors from a nearby food cart. After three minutes, Maya was back, tugging at Meredith's chador. Her eyes looked strange.

"What?" whispered Meredith, staying focused on the fruit.

"My phone's out," Maya said in low English, holding an apple. "It was in my vest. Bullet nicked it. And my spare was in the car. We'll need another way to communicate."

Meredith looked at the watch on her wrist, the one Maya had given her. "It's four-fifteen. We need to get to the exchange right now."

Maya nodded. She barked a price at the fruit vendor. He countered and shrugged. Maya and the vendor haggled while two bearded men in black shirts were walking past them. They were shouldering their way through the crowded market with halting glances.

After they'd passed, Maya told the fruit vendor she didn't like his price and turned away. Meredith waited ten seconds, then followed.

They were next to each other again, walking shoulder to shoulder down the street, Maya's eyes darting. They passed a crowded alley. Maya stopped walking.

The Mossad woman pulled Meredith into the alley. There were still pedestrians here, but mostly parked cars. Maya walked down the narrow sidewalk, her eyes sweeping back and forth.

"That one," the Mossad woman said, nodding to a silver Honda Accord from the early eighties. "Stand behind me. Raise your arms. Use the chador. Block the view." A noisy scooter came puttering by. Maya waited for it to pass.

Meredith stretched out her arms, shielding Maya with the black fabric like a raven drying its wings. Meredith heard glass shatter. The door opened. Maya was already behind the wheel.

"Keep your chador up," the Mossad woman said through the broken window. With a quick glance, Meredith could see that Maya had already pried a plastic trim piece off the steering wheel and was yanking at wires. Fifteen seconds later, the car was running.

"Keep your face covered," Maya said as Meredith got in. "There were black shirts everywhere on that street. They're looking all over for us."

Nabil hung up the phone and shifted the big flatbed into third. He'd been on his way to meet *Effendi* and Said at the *Août Noir* house that the boy had marked, following his orders. But then, when Nabil had still been a few blocks away from it, his phone had rung. Other brothers had been inside the house already. They'd found Said. And *Effendi*.

The words had had a startling effect on Nabil. He'd held the phone to his ear for ten or fifteen seconds, even missing a turn while he drove the big flatbed that had been so carefully fixed up by the Jordanian bomb maker. Nabil held the phone to his ear and said nothing, even after the brother who'd called had hung up.

Effendi. A martyr.

And Nabil knew what he had to do now. His cousin's truck was wired. And he knew exactly where the infidels were going.

To the airport.

CHAPTER 53

"WE'RE LOOKING ALL OVER FOR THEM," WERNER SAID TO RANCE AND Dale. "We've surged what agents we have into the street."

It was four-thirty. They'd managed to keep the airport closed with Iranian help, but Walid had called Rance to tell him the delegation was anxious. They wanted to see Kahlidi. Now. After hanging up, Rance looked morose.

"Why not show them Kahlidi?" Dale asked. "It will at least buy us some time."

Rance looked at Werner. "What do you think? He's your prisoner."

"We've given them our proof-of-life shots of Kahlidi. They know we have him," said Werner, fanning his face with his old-school hat.

"Yeah," said Dale. "But they don't know we have him *here*. If it buys us more time, I say we get his ass out here on the tarmac. What's the harm?"

Werner fanned himself for another five seconds, then replaced the hat on his bald head. "All right. It's up to you, Mr. Rance," said the Caesarea boss. "You have the relationship with the Iranians. And this is your deal."

Rance nodded his agreement, privately wondering if his long-sought propriety for this prisoner exchange would still turn out to be a good thing. He walked to the side of the Osprey and made a call to Walid, his Iranian contact sitting in the air-conditioned jet across the tarmac. As Werner and Dale waited, Dale used the small binoculars around his neck that the Marine lieutenant had lent him. He looked intently at the Iranian jet, wondering about the people inside it.

Rance returned, the phone still in his hand, cupping the mic. "They want us to walk Kahlidi out where they can see him plainly. I said we'd do it as an act of good faith. Okay?"

Werner nodded. Rance said something into the phone and hung up. Werner called to an IDF captain loitering in the shade twenty feet away, telling him to get Kahlidi ready.

"Let me do it," said Dale as the captain approached. "Let me take Kahlidi out there."

Rance and Werner both looked at him. "Why?" asked Rance.

"So he doesn't do anything funny," said Dale. "I know him. He won't fuck with me."

Rance shrugged. "Sure, whatever. I don't care. Werner?"

"It might be a good way to keep Kahlidi in line," said the Caesarea boss. "Even though he's wounded, he's crafty."

"Right," said Dale, already heading to the Israeli helo. "But tell your man Reu up there what we're doing. I don't want him sniping me."

Werner relayed the instructions in Hebrew. Rance watched as Dale trotted to the Israeli helo and emerged with Kasem Kahlidi, Atlas, former adjutant to the late, great General Qasem Soleimani. Meredith's once and future spy.

Squinting through his Ray-Bans, Rance was shocked at Kahlidi's bruised face, visible even from this distance. The Quds man was walking with crutches, Dale helping him along at his side. As Rance watched, his phone buzzed again. He looked at the screen. Dorsey. Rance excused himself from Werner's side and went to the side of the Osprey for privacy.

"Dale's here," said Rance to his boss. "Yeah, he's fine. But there's still no sign of Meredith or the *Août Noir* fuckers. Yeah. Dale's out there on the tarmac showing Atlas to the Iranian delegation. What's that, Jeff? Sorry, bad connection again. I said Dale's out in the center of the tarmac, close enough to the Iranian jet they can see him but not so close that . . . Oh hey, Jeff, hold on. Something's happening. Something's up. Let me call you back."

Standing next to Kahlidi, looking at the Iranian jet as the hot wind blew his hair around, Dale heard a crash. He snapped his head to the right, into the wind.

Though distant, the sound was messy with metallic clanks and scrapes, like a train of shopping carts had been toppled in a parking lot. With Kahlidi leaning against him for support, Dale held the Marine's field binoculars up to his eyes. Five hundred yards away, a Honda Accord had smashed through a gate that led from the parking lot at the main terminal. Its headlights were flashing. It was speeding crazily toward them.

Squinting through the binoculars, Dale could see a woman in a black chador behind the wheel. Beside her in the front passenger seat was another woman pulling off a face hijab and waving it around like a black flag out the window. The woman's dark brown hair was fluttering around her head.

Meth.

Dale dropped the binoculars to the ground. He spun around and faced the Israelis and Americans some hundred yards behind him. He waved his arms crazily at them, shouting, "Friendly! Friendly! It's them!"

He pulled Kasem close, whispering into his ear. "You betray Meredith this time, Kasem, and I will personally be on the next mission to Tehran. And you'll never see Kasra again. Got it?"

Leaning on his crutches, the Quds officer nodded twice.

"Good," said Dale. "Now signal your boys on that plane and be prepared to be welcomed as a hero."

Kasem nodded again. He waved one arm at the Iranian jet, which now had a set of movable stairs at an open door. Walid emerged at the top of the stairs and acknowledged the wave with a lazy hand. "They're all right," Kahlidi said, putting his arm on Dale's shoulder to stay up. "They're not going to want any trouble. I recognize the man on the stairs. He knows me well, trusts me."

Dale lowered his arms and watched the Honda approaching up the tarmac.

"But Meredith needs to honor my deal too," said Kahlidi. "You tell her that, Dale. I'm going to be looking for proof of that money—even if I can't touch it for two years. And Kasra had better be happy when I come out. You tell Meredith that. She listens to you more than you think."

Dale was still looking at the approaching car.

"And, for what it's worth," added the Iranian. "I'm glad Meredith made it out."

But Dale had stopped listening to Kahlidi. His eyes remained fixed on something else, a movement from the side, about a half mile away. It was a white flatbed truck, entering the taxiway after passing by the corrupt Lebanese Army soldiers who'd just waved it through as though it belonged on the runway. It had come in from the entrance on the opposite side of the field. Dale left Kahlidi standing there on his crutches.

He sprinted at full speed toward the approaching Honda.

CHAPTER 54

"ALLAHU AKBAR," NABIL WAS REPEATING TO HIMSELF QUIETLY, OVER and over while he drove. One glaring gesture at the Lebanese soldiers and they'd known Nabil was with the Iranians. They knew not to fuck with him. They'd waved him through.

Now Nabil was almost to the tarmac. The Honda Accord was to his left, maybe a kilometer away, headed toward the military helicopters and the private jet at the other end of the taxiway. Nabil had caught a glimpse of the woman in the passenger seat. She was the Zionist spy, the one whose picture they'd been flashing around the *dahiyeh*, the one who had killed *Effendi*. He'd seen her waving a cloth out the window, signaling the aircraft at the end of the runway. He had an occasional glancing view at the other woman, the one behind the Honda's wheel. She appeared to be in a full chador, her face covered by a hijab. He guessed she was the one who'd been at the newsstand, then.

Nabil adjusted his course, approaching the Honda at a shallow angle.

He had one more chance. And he would give it everything. Everything. *He*, Nabil, would join his brothers in glorious martyrdom.

The car was getting closer.

Thinking of his mother, the Hezbollah man held one hand on the wheel and fixed one hand near the button mounted just below the dash. He kept his fingers planted firmly on the big blank metal spot just below the AM radio, careful not to touch the red plunger until it was time. He removed his hand only once, to shift the truck into fourth gear.

Meredith had thought the truck an innocent airport vehicle at first. It was a big dually, white, with a load on its bed like any service vehicle might have. It seemed only natural that after she and Maya had broken through a razor-topped chain-link gate that *some* airport maintenance vehicle would sally forth to chase the two women down.

But now, looking straight ahead, Meredith saw a man running, on foot, coming straight toward her. He was sprinting, waving his arms just as wildly as she'd been waving hers out the window. She released the hijab she'd been waving and let it fly behind the car. It fluttered away like a detached flag. She recognized the man coming toward her, recognized the way his arms and feet moved. It was John.

"John's running toward us!" she shouted to Maya.

Her nose and mouth shrouded by the black hijab, Maya merely nodded. "What's he doing? He needs to get out of the way," she said.

But then the veering flatbed caught Maya's eye. "*Chara*. That truck's trying to block us," she said.

The Mossad woman sped up, staying far to the left of the taxiway, hoping to squeeze past the big vehicle without tumbling off the earthen berm. But it was rapidly becoming clear that there wouldn't be enough room. The truck's intercept course was solid.

Looking away from John, Meredith twisted her neck to study the approaching vehicle. She could make out a figure behind the wheel. His black hair streamed in the wind. He was bearded, wore a long-sleeved black shirt, the trademark uniform of the Shia warrior.

"He's Hezbollah!" Meredith shouted.

The CIA woman pulled the Browning pistol she'd taken from the dead Iranian from beneath the chador. She was about to aim when Maya leaned over with her arm on Meredith's hand, holding down the gun.

"*Don't!*" the Mossad woman shouted. She suddenly slammed the brakes. The car shuddered to a screeching stop. Meredith was flung into her seat belt.

"Put the gun down," shouted Maya. "You're supposed to be the prisoner. You don't want any of those soldiers up there to see you with a gun. Now get out! *Go!*"

"What do you mean *get out?*"

"*Get out! Now!* Run that way! Run toward John. I need to take care of that truck." The Mossad woman pushed Meredith with both hands. "Don't you see? That's Kahlidi out there in the center of the tarmac, waiting. That's John, coming for you. You're the exchange. It's going down right now. I'm supposed to be the *Août Noir* terrorist. You're the key to this whole thing. For God's sake, it's everything we've worked for! Get out, Meredith, go! *Go!*"

Meredith leapt out of the car and ran for it.

The truck was fifty meters away now, speeding in from the side. It had changed course slightly, veering directly toward Meredith as she ran. The CIA woman pumped her arms, used everything she had, the black chador billowing around her until it came loose and fluttered away.

But the truck kept coming. It was aiming directly at her, intending, it seemed, to run her over. Meredith had nowhere to go.

But then she saw Maya's Honda. Its tires were screeching, leaving two black trails on the beige tarmac as it raced toward the truck. Now the Honda was on the intercept course, headed toward it like a wheeled missile.

The venerable old Accord had made it all the way up to forty miles per hour when it smashed into the door of the big Ford flatbed with a noisy thud. The thud was loud enough that Meredith stopped in her tracks.

With her dirty skirt blowing around her legs, Meredith turned. The big flatbed had tried to maneuver, but between the impact and its abrupt turn, it had flipped onto its side. The Honda's entire front end was smashed. The car lay at a diagonal on its right side. Meredith watched as Maya scurried out of the broken driver's window of the Honda, her pistol in her hand. She climbed on top of the sideways truck, firing down into the cab, the chador billowing about her.

And then the truck blew up.

The Mossad woman was blotted out, engulfed in a crackling orange fireball. The blast's heat wave knocked the air from Meredith's lungs. The pressure wave sent her flying five meters backward.

She was on her back, senseless. She exhaled smoke, having breathed fire like the very dragon she'd been chasing, *Taniyn*. Her eyelashes singed and stinging, she couldn't shut them for the swelling. They just stayed open, unseeing, dumb to the world. Sightlessly, she stared up at the cloudless blue sky, unable to process anything at all.

For the first time in her entire life she was uncomprehending, numb, disembodied. She would realize one day that the sensation had lasted only a few seconds in real time. But in that moment, it felt much longer, as though she'd entered the mysterious ether that divides life from death.

And then the sense was broken. John's face, smeared with dirt, was suddenly blocking out the sun, the flames, the drifting black smoke. Backlit, Meredith couldn't quite see his expression. And had she been able, her mind wouldn't have been able to interpret it.

She only noticed that John's hair was hanging down, touching her forehead, almost tickling it. He was shouting something very close to her face—but the ringing in Meredith's ears squelched out all meaning. Her eyes twitched because his hair was hanging down into them.

She felt a squeeze at her upper arms. Her head fell even further, sagging away. The airport was suddenly upside down. She could see a white jet. It was moving, rolling, taxiing. Beyond it were helicopters. But they weren't moving. And they were upside down.

The inverted view changed abruptly. Now she saw black smoke, more of the orange fireball floating up into the sky like a blazing balloon. She felt the heat and smelled the oil burning. And through it all she was, somehow, off the ground, floating. It took her five more halting, smoking breaths to realize why.

John was carrying her.

EPILOGUE

One month later

"BY THE LEE!" SHOUTED GRACE DALE FROM THE COCKPIT AS SHE WORKED the winch to tighten the jib sheet.

Up on *Mollymawk*'s stunted bow, Dale watched the mainsail's boom swing. Overhead, he could hear the sail's crackle as it filled with wind. Close-hauled, *Molly* leaned into the new starboard tack, slicing through the green Chesapeake. Dale inched on his butt to the elevated side, alive with the feeling of salt spray on his beard, grinning.

Must be eight knots, he thought, looking at the foamy waves that raced by. He looked back at his daughter, who stood at the helm. Grace leaned forward to tighten the jib sheet with a few more hand-cranks of the winch, trimming the sail until it was flat as a wall. Dale looked up at the puffy white clouds and breathed the fresh sea air deeply, contentedly.

But as much as he enjoyed the smell of the sea and the lash of the wind, it was the sight of his daughter in command of his boat that had given him joy. He'd made it back from his week in the Outer Banks right on time that Saturday morning, surprising his daughter as much as himself. There, at an Annapolis marina, Grace had joined her father for a Labor Day weekend of sail, with an intent to stay across the bay at Tilghman Island, a respite from the Academy's rigors.

"What's that land?" Dale called, standing, holding a backstay to steady himself as *Molly* shrugged off yet another swell. He was looking at a distant head, wondering if it blocked the cove he'd been looking for.

He saw Grace look down at the GPS chartplotter. But she didn't answer Dale. Instead, she was speaking into the VHF radio, the microphone to her lips. Her eyebrows were slanted into a consternated V.

She turned, looking astern, toward the horizon, the binoculars now to her eyes. And then Dale saw for himself what his daughter had been looking for. The speck of a boat on the horizon. A flashing blue light.

"Well, what did they say?" he asked her thirty seconds later. She'd just replaced the radio microphone in its cradle. Now she was coming about, into the wind, letting the jib and mainsail luff like laundry on a line. Dale had the binoculars to his eyes. He could see the orange-and-gray boat speeding toward them, a white wake flying behind it. Coast Guard.

"They said to heave to," said Grace. "It was a specific call to *Molly-mawk*. On channel twenty-two alpha."

"And you *answered* it?" shot Dale with growing alarm. He could think of at least five nautical violations on *Mollymawk* for which he might be fined. He'd been dodging Coastie patrol boats since his boat had touched at Nags Head.

"Of course!" shouted Grace from the base of the mast, where she'd now busied herself with gathering up the dropped mainsail. "Dad—I'm almost a naval officer. Do you honestly think I'm not going to listen to the United States Coast Guard?"

The small patrol boat was alongside a few minutes later. Grace and Dale boarded it as one of the guardsmen took the helm of *Molly*, awaiting a tow.

There followed a rapid, bucking, howling ride to a Coast Guard wharf on the east side of the bay. The other patrol boat sailors said little to Grace and Dale, other than that they were under strict orders to get them to Andrews, ASAP. The orders had been stamped by the commandant himself, they said reverently.

"Dad," Grace whispered when she saw the MH-60 Jayhawk helicopter waiting for them by the wharf with its rotors already whizzing, "is this because of the FBI?"

No, Dale thought. *It's because of your mother.*

Grace looked out the helicopter's window and did a double take. The Coast Guard helicopter was coming into its low hover, preparing to land. But Grace thought she could see her mother down there on the tarmac at Andrews, just across the Potomac from DC, waiting for them.

Grace had been told that her mother had built up so much vacation time that she was in a "use-it-or-lose-it" situation. Supposedly, Grace recalled, her mother was to spend two weeks in Baden-Baden, there to soak up the mineral waters of the German spa town, do yoga, get massages, and generally decompress. But Grace suspected it was a lie. The young midshipman couldn't quite picture her mother doing that for two weeks straight.

And now, as if in confirmation of those doubts, there was Meredith. She was leaning on a Humvee at the foot of the base operations building, wearing a dark trouser suit and large black sunglasses. Grace could see her mother's hair blowing in the rotor wash as the helicopter settled on the tarmac.

The Dale family reunited in a VIP suite off the base operations center. Grace knew better than to ask what this was all about. She contented herself with a long hug with her mother and noted her father's nervous twitches as he stood by the window, looking out at the runway.

Meredith revealed that she'd made dinner reservations. The trio were to meet in four hours at Across the Pond, a Dupont Circle Irish pub just walking distance from Meredith's brownstone. Dale, both women knew, had a fondness for Guinness Stout. Meredith's choice of restaurant had been subtly crafted as an inclusive nod to him. All three of them knew it.

Thus arranged, Meredith pulled the key for her Volvo from her purse and asked Grace to drive it home for her. She would meet Grace there. But, Meredith announced, it would be a few hours before Grace's parents got home. She and John had some business to attend to first.

"How will you two get back to DC, then?" asked Grace.

"Don't worry," said Meredith. "We have a car waiting for us."

A black Suburban with an Agency driver, to be exact. Knowing he'd be dressed in his ragged sailing attire, Meredith had bought John a completely new outfit. In the back of the Suburban a pair of black gabardine trousers, a blue oxford shirt, and a size forty black blazer had been hung on a hanger. On the seats next to it had been the rest—a box of new shoes, wool socks, and an expensive leather belt. Meredith had splurged on the shoes. She couldn't respect men that wore bad shoes. She'd also brought along scissors, a razor, and shaving cream.

The SUV stopped in front of a modest two-story home on a secluded court off the Georgetown Pike. The house was just over the fence from the football field at Langley High School. On Friday nights, Kasra Khani had learned, she could hear the crowds now that the American football season was in full swing.

After passing by the security man at the entrance to the home, Dale was shown to the bathroom. And, following ten seconds of reflection—an interval where he literally stared at his shaggy reflection—he decided that Meth had made a few good points on the drive over from Andrews. And she'd gone to all of this trouble of buying him the clothes. Perhaps, Dale told himself as he looked at his own face, it would even be fun to surprise his daughter at the pub later by arriving with a sartorial splash.

With all these thoughts singing through his head—along with many others—Dale took the scissors to his beard. He then turned to his hair.

"Why, John Dale," said Kasra Khani when Dale stepped into the big open kitchen. His cheeks were pink and smooth. "I wouldn't have recognized you."

Meredith hurried to brush at her ex-husband's coat and flatten the lapels. Then she put a hand to his smooth jawline. "I can't believe it," she said. "I didn't think you'd actually do it. And you even trimmed your hair. A little lopsided, but—why, John—it's almost hip."

"Don't get too excited," said Dale, running a hand across his mouth, his cheeks reddening. "It will all be back by winter."

The security man dropped the Saturday edition of the *Washington Post* on the kitchen island. "Ready?" he asked. "Should we do the picture inside or out?"

"Out," said Meredith.

Dale, Meredith, and Kasra stood on the back patio. Per Kahlidi's request, Dale had placed Kasra in the middle. He held up the paper. The security man took the shot.

Back inside, Kasra served them lemonade on ice after Meredith had ducked out to make a call. Dale knew it had been a call to Dorsey. While staying polite, Dale sensed that Meth was now in a hurry.

"Your mother didn't want to come down?" asked Meredith.

"No," said Kasra. "She's still jet-lagged. Sleeping upstairs."

Meredith nodded. Kasra's mother had had complicated travel arrangements. She'd flown from Tehran to Turkey, then India, then Canada, and finally the US. "Does she understand what she's doing here?" asked Meredith.

"She was born in 1961, the height of the Shah's power," said Kasra. "My mother has lived in Tehran her entire life—so, yes, she understands. And of course, she knows not to ask."

Meredith nodded and took another sip of her drink. "And work? How do you like Walter Reed?"

"I have a lot to learn," said Kasra. "They do things differently here. I would have preferred to work in pediatrics."

"But you understand why we had to start with Walter Reed."

Kasra nodded. "Of course I do. American military."

After a few more polite questions, Meredith abruptly asked the security man to leave. It was time to get down to business. Once he'd departed, leaning on the kitchen island, Meredith said to Kasra, "Kasem has dropped another message. I'll need your help with it again."

"What does he want to use for a code this time?" Ms. Khani asked.

"The month and year that you two first met," said Meredith.

"Oh," said Kasra. "I'm not sure I can come up with that. We were just kids. It would have been the first day of school . . . fifth grade?" She came up with a proposed date.

Meredith ran off to make another call to Dorsey, then promptly returned. She was looking at Dale. "He's waiting for us," Meredith said. "Let's hustle."

Dorsey received them in a fourth-floor SCIF at five o'clock. He was sitting at a table by himself, sleeves rolled, tie at half-mast, a discarded jacket strewn over a chair. He stood when Meredith pushed open the vault's foot-thick door. She immediately noticed that he had a thick folder open in front of him. His reading glasses were sitting on the papers.

"Jesus," said Dorsey, shaking Dale's hand. "Is that you, John Dale?"

"I know, right?" said Meredith from the other end of the table. Her bruises had dimmed enough under the makeup, and the swelling was gone. The military hospital at Ramstein Air Base where she'd conducted her debriefs had taken care of that. But the second-degree burn she'd suffered from the explosion had left a permanent reddish patch on her neck, just under her chin. Dale had called it a permanent hickey, a beauty mark.

"Don't get used to my clean shave," said Dale. "Or this thing." Dale flipped the laminated ID card around his neck, letting it collapse back down to his dress shirt. "I'm here for one reason only."

Dorsey shot a glance at Meredith, then nodded. "Yeah," he said. "I know. Have a seat. We'll cover your retirement options in a minute. Okay?"

"Sure," said Dale, scooting into a chair.

"So, how was the take?" Meredith asked Dorsey, once both men were seated. "Worth it?"

"Very worth it," said Dorsey, leaning back on two legs of his chair. "Sorry, John, for plucking you off the Chesapeake in such a hurry. But you know sometimes Atlas only gives us our hit if he sees you with his girl, holding that paper. His rule, not ours."

"I know," said Dale. "But I didn't see it coming *today*. I'd hoped to take my daughter out sailing for the weekend."

"Well, it's because he has something hot. He knew it—and he wanted to flex his leverage before giving it up. Like I said. His rules, not ours."

"And," said Meredith to Dorsey. "Do you agree with Atlas? Was it worth plucking John from the sea?"

The spy boss had folded his hands across his narrow waist. "So fucking worth it . . ."

And then Meredith witnessed a very rare thing. Dorsey smiled at her. It made him look ten years younger, she thought.

"I take it you spoke to Werner too?" she asked, returning Dorsey's smile.

"Yeah," said the spy boss. "Twenty minutes ago. He's moving chess pieces around. But I expect they'll intercept the ship in the southeastern Med, right after it comes out of the Suez Canal, well before it gets to that Syrian port, Latakia."

"Not us? Why not our Navy?"

"Well, that was Atlas's idea, believe it or not. He offered an interesting analysis in this last message. And I think it's probably right."

"And what analysis is that?"

"Hang on," said Dale. "You guys are having an operational meeting. I shouldn't be here. I don't want to—"

Dorsey held up a swift hand. Even Dale obeyed that hand.

"Atlas says it has to be Israel," said the spy boss. "Well before Flotilla 13 can board a ship with spent nuclear fuel pellets bound for Damascus, the Iranian crew will scuttle. They'll claim the Israelis sunk it, international crime, outrage, yadda, yadda. No one has to fire a shot."

"Right," said Meredith. "Just the Israelis being the Israelis—the maritime intercept wouldn't come from any special intelligence we Americans might have."

"Exactly," said Dorsey. "Now, on the one hand, Atlas is just being careful, protecting himself. But on the other, I think his characterization of how the mullahs will see this is spot-on. They're constantly at war with Israel. But a US-Iran naval battle would be a big escalation. Even the appearance of one."

"Makes sense."

"And," added Dorsey, "it gets better."

"Oh?"

"Yeah. Atlas said that when Israel moves to take out specific *Taniyn* sites, the mullahs will get the signal that the jig is up. They won't want to get caught with their pants down in front of the international community, not after all the hoopla they've made of their peaceful intentions. Atlas says they'll kill the whole program and simply convert those modified SA-5s into anti-ship missiles. Provided they have any left after the Mossad raids."

"So Werner is definitely going in to take out whatever *Taniyns* they've already built."

"Oh, you better believe it," said Dorsey. "But I'm not sure how much he'll share with us first."

"Fair enough. What did he say about Atlas's information on *Taniyn*'s ultimate target?"

Dorsey sighed. "Werner said he admired their thinking."

"That's very Werner."

"Yeah. Isn't it?" Dorsey looked at Dale, as though suddenly aware of his presence. "Look, John. I know you're not cleared for any of this—for now—but I want you to hear it. Atlas is your agent. And this is a very big deal."

"Atlas is temporarily my agent," said Dale. "I thought we were here to talk through who would be running him next. After I'm out."

"He'll always be your recruit," said Dorsey, as though Dale hadn't objected. "And just so you have a sense of perspective of what *you've* accomplished, I think you need to hear what Atlas has given us. Okay? Then we can decide about who should run him going forward."

Dale looked toward the table. He could see Meredith in the corner of his eye, looking at him. He kept his eyes down and, after a few silent seconds, nodded.

"Meredith," said Dorsey. "Why don't you bring John fully up to speed on the whole op? Atlas may be John's recruit—but he's only in position now back in Quds because you authorized his snatch in April. And we three are the only ones who know about his new position. The three of us shouldn't have any secrets when it comes to Atlas, right? So go on, tell John—assuming you haven't already." Dorsey burrowed his eyes into her.

Meredith met Dorsey's eyes. She nodded, then looked across the table at her ex-husband. Having shaved the beard, his face had an uneven color, sunburned at his nose, lighter at his chin.

"John," she began. "Long before we snatched Kasem in the desert in April, he'd been working on a plan for deadly Hezbollah missiles in Beirut. Specifically, he was helping them modify old SAMs, converting them into hypersonic cruise missiles."

Dale still had his eyes down, pretending that he was hearing all of this for the first time. It was the deal he'd made with Meredith back on the Sea of Galilee. He nodded once.

"Maya," continued Meredith, "managed to steal engineering plans for these Hezbollah missiles from a scientist in Paris who the Israelis ended up assassinating. I'm not sure she ever told you about that."

Dale breathed deeply, his eyes still down, trying hard not to look at Dorsey's reaction.

"Well, the plans Maya stole indicated a missile that could be converted into a nuke. But the details for the warhead itself were technically indeterminate. We knew that Kasem could tell us everything we needed. But of course, Kahlidi ended up in the wind, ruining everything."

"Yeah," said Dale. "I'm familiar."

Dorsey grunted.

"Well," continued Meredith. "Your idea to track Maya down as a way to recapture Kahlidi was brilliant, John."

"Truly brilliant," said Dorsey.

"And," continued Meredith, "once you learned that Mossad had taken both Kahlidi and his woman in London, it changed everything. For the good."

"Maya was a brilliant recruit job, John. I had no idea you'd set up a protocol with her way back in Egypt to bring her in as a potential agent for us one day. Well done. Hats off."

Dale nodded. His face turned a darker shade of pink.

"Yes," said Meredith. "The fact that Maya trusted you enough to get you in front of Werner did much more than just save my life."

Dale swallowed and stared at a blank spot on the wall.

"But not only that," continued Meredith, "you somehow managed to convince Werner to send Kahlidi to the Iranians in exchange for freedom from *Août Noir*. *That* was a game changer for all of us."

"Seriously," said Dorsey. "It was a brilliant bit of deception, John. You need to hear about the results we're getting from your plan. They're huge."

"Yes," continued Meredith. "Huge results. Now, since we've held up our end of the bargain by meeting Kahlidi's demands—the deposited money, Kasra's agent relo package—we're really starting to see just how valuable this take is. Jeff and I just wanted to make sure you understood that."

"Yeah," said Dorsey, removing a Bic pen from his breast pocket. "Tell him about the take."

"Right," said Meredith. "First of all, we confirmed that the warhead in the plans Maya stole *was* designed for radiological use. But in a highly unconventional way. Suffice to say that Quds intended for Hezbollah to pack it with spent nuclear fuel pellets from an Iranian LEU waste site."

"A fucking *dirty* missile," said Dorsey. "Go on, Meredith, tell John about the targets."

"Right. Well, in our take from Kahlidi we've learned of various targeting contingencies driven by Quds, for use by Hezbollah. Some of them are very creative—they even surprised Werner."

"Damned creative," said Dorsey, a spark in his eye. "Tell him about this latest one." The spy boss was leaning forward, chewing furiously on the end of the blue Bic.

"Well, according to Kahlidi, the Supreme Council's latest idea," said Meredith, "is to launch multiple conventional rockets into Israel after a terrorist incident designed for escalation. That would in turn trigger an Israeli air strike on Hezbollah, they believe. And then, along with the next retaliatory rocket attack, Hezbollah would also slip in a *Taniyn* missile with a warhead of spent nuclear pellets. The missile would be aimed at the Negev Nuclear Research Center—Israel's nuclear reactor."

"Yeah," said Dorsey. "See? Hezbollah would finally get to nuke the Israelis without anyone even knowing they'd done it, making it look like Israel's own disaster. And, of course, they'd love the irony of Israel having a meltdown while Iran has to run everything through IAEA, per the deal. Fucking genius."

"What about that deal anyway?" asked Dale, looking for something innocent to say. "Is it done yet? I tried not to watch TV on my boat."

"Still not signed, still dragging on," said Dorsey. "IAEA found another enrichment site. We're asking State to rework the inspection requirements. The damn thing may never get done. But Ed Rance has a solid back channel in the Iranian delegation—saved our bacon to have someone we could communicate with for Meredith's swap."

"That Rance is something," said Dale.

"Yeah. He's done an amazing job over there. Now Ed says the Iranians will sign as soon as we're ready. But because we know about the spent fuel threat, we're going to add a bunch of inspection requirements in there for their waste treatment facility."

"And that," said Meredith, "is also how the Iranians will get the message that we know about their *Taniyn* dirty missile strategy. They will know that we know—once we start putting onerous requirements on spent fuel inspections. But they'll assume we got our intel from Mossad, from this ship that's on its way to Syria, as we speak."

"The one you guys said the Israelis are going to intercept?" asked John, doing his best to look amazed.

"Yeah. That one," said Meredith. "But we'll all look the other way, of course."

"As it should be," said Dorsey, chewing the pen. "And *that* is the kind of op my Counterproliferation team does. Our finest work in a long while. And for that, I can thank the two of you. Both of you."

"Nah," said Dale. "This is all Meredith."

"Don't bullshit me," shot Dorsey. "I know you went after Mossad to get Meredith back at first. But in the process, you managed to recruit this Mossad woman *and* Atlas. Hell, Dale, you even got Werner working for us, in a way. And then when some crackpot Iranian officer and his Hezbollah thugs tried to break up the *Août Noir* cell on his own, Maya, your recruit, stepped in. But Maya, well . . . we're all a little sick about her. She was a good one."

"She was," said Meredith.

"But look where we are now," said Dorsey. He looked at John. "Somehow, you managed to get the best of Mossad working for us. It was a brilliant bit of tradecraft, John. Fucking brilliant. I had no idea."

Dorsey thrust his hand at Dale, smiling, his face twisted into something nearly unrecognizable.

Dale looked down at the outstretched right hand. After a moment's hesitation, he gripped it and shook.

"All right," Dorsey said, the smile already fading as his hand withdrew. "Now I know, Meredith, that you have to get going. You finally get to go on your leave for real, just like I promised."

"Thanks," said Meredith.

Dorsey looked at Dale. "But we have just a little more business to discuss, John." The spy chief moved his thick folder aside to reveal two brown envelopes. One of them was large, a half inch thick, legal-sized. The other was a normal A4 with a clear address window. Dale thought it looked like a bill.

"This," Dorsey said, tapping the big envelope, "has all the paperwork you've asked for from personnel. You'll have to sign a phone book's worth of legal crap, naturally—nondisclosures and so forth—but the upshot is that you'll officially be retired. Pension restored. Clean break with my gratitude for a fine career of service. Especially this last op."

"Great," said Dale, reaching for it.

"But this one," said Dorsey, tapping the small envelope, blocking Dale's reach, "is just one page. If you sign it right now, I won't even have to deal with legal, which, believe me, is a reward all its own."

Dale leaned back. He crossed his leg, looking at the expensive shoe on his foot. He kept his head down and swallowed.

"Listen, Mr. Dale," said Dorsey, the volume of his voice rising, "I will only ask you this one time. And my ask is this: please don't leave us. Within this envelope I have prepared your reinstatement letter as a case officer, already signed by me. And as God is my witness, I hope you'll sign it."

The spy boss stood up and dropped a fresh pen on the table in front of Dale. "Now I'll leave you two to discuss this. Meredith, I'll see you in a couple weeks when you get back. And I promise not to interrupt your vacation . . . this time."

The heavy SCIF door closed with a solid thud. Dale looked up at Meredith. "Jesus, Meth."

"What?"

"You and Werner sure got your deepfake on that poor bastard, didn't you?"

"*We* did, John. You were part of it too . . . just maybe not as big a part as Dorsey *thinks*. Now which letter are you going to sign?"

"Which one do you think?" asked Dale, meeting her eye.

Meredith grinned. "I'm not about to tell you what to do."

Dale nodded once and paused. Then his hand drifted toward the smaller envelope. "Well, I suppose I should at least *read* it."

Meredith reached forward and touched his arm, smiling wider.

"Hey," Dale said, tearing open the small envelope. "What's all that stuff about you going on vacation for a couple of weeks? I know I'm not supposed to ask . . . and I'm sorry if I'm prying. I was just . . . surprised to hear you were going on leave."

"Oh that," said Meredith. "I'm going to Sydney."

"*Australia?*" shot Dale. "You serious? Don't tell me you're moving over to work on some kind of China problem already."

"No. Not yet anyway."

"Then what? Why Sydney?"

"Because," said Meredith, "I promised a seven-year-old girl she'd finally get to see a kangaroo."

ACKNOWLEDGMENTS

I would like to thank my agent, Scott Miller, for his advice and encouragement in developing this novel. His industry acumen and literary instincts are indispensable. The same can be said of my editor, Tom Colgan, whose peerless judgment is at the very peak of his profession, likely never to be equaled. My heartfelt appreciation also goes to Jessica Mangicaro, Lauren Burnstein, and Tina Joell of Penguin Random House for their tireless efforts in promoting this work. In my estimation, their job is harder than mine.

Writing can feel like a very personal and solitary endeavor. I would like to thank friends and fellow writers Bryan Tomasovich, Don Bentley, Mark Greaney, and Stephen Coonts for their encouragement, perspective, and counsel.

For research support, I wish to thank Dr. Charles Feicht on matters medical, John Kuhn for his background in US special operations, Nahshon Davidai for Israeli culture, and Houssam Nassif for a deep dive into Beirut. Finally, while I promised not to reveal their real identities, I cannot close without thanking Eli, Rachel, and Ari for their collective insights on Mossad and IDF. You inspire us all.

GLOSSARY

Alut, Iran—Small Kurdish village near the border with Iraq.

AMAN—The Israeli military intelligence arm that supports the Israeli Defense Force.

AOR—Area of Responsibility—designated geography for a military operation.

Août Noir—French for "Black August," this is a fictitious Hezbollah splinter cell operating in Beirut.

Baradar—Farsi for "brother," a term of comradery.

Caesarea—Operational section of Mossad. It was developed as the single group within Mossad that deals with sabotage, targeted killings, and espionage.

COMINT—Communications intelligence.

CPC—CIA Counterproliferation Center charged with stopping the spread of nuclear weapons.

Dahiyeh—Arabic for "suburb," it is the Shia district in Beirut's southwestern quarter.

DGSE—French General Directorate for External Security, subordinate to the Ministry of the Defense. Responsible for military, strategic, and signals intelligence. Also responsible for counterespionage outside of national borders.

Effendi—A term of respect that signifies nobility, especially in former Ottoman Empire countries.

Flotilla 13—An Israeli unit of naval commandos charged with clandestine operations (equivalent to US Navy SEALs).

HEU—Highly Enriched Uranium. As defined by the US Nuclear Regulatory Commission, HEU is uranium enriched to at least 20 percent uranium 235, which is a higher concentration than exists in natural uranium ore.

HQS—Agency shorthand for CIA headquarters in Langley, Virginia.

HUMINT—Human intelligence reporting through agents.

IAEA—International Atomic Energy Agency. A UN-chartered organization that monitors the development of nuclear materials and compliance to the nuclear nonproliferation treaty (NPT).

IDF—Israeli Defense Forces.

IR—Infrared.

IRGC—Islamic Revolutionary Guard Corps. IRGC was formed by the Ayatollah Khomeini as a parallel military force, since the Shah's military could not be trusted. IRGC has since evolved into all service branches—Air Defense, Navy, Air Force, Army. The IRGC has been officially designated as a terrorist organization since October 2018 by Bahrain and Saudi Arabia and since April 15, 2019, by the United States.

ISIS—Islamic State of Iraq and Syria also known as ISIL. Sunni Muslim revolutionary army operating in northern Iraq and Syria.

ISR—Intelligence, Surveillance, Reconnaissance.

Jnah—Neighborhood in Beirut that houses the embassy of the Islamic Republic of Iran.

Jon—A Farsi term of endearment appended to a given name, equivalent to "dear" in English.

Junction—Mossad group that runs foreign (non-Israeli) intelligence agents.

JWR—Joint War Room, the command center where the multiple intelligence and operating functions of Mossad and the IDF come together to facilitate tactical coordination.

Katsa—Mossad case officers who recruit and operate foreign sources. Also referred to as "collection officers."

Kidon—Hebrew for "bayonet," *kidons* are specially trained Mossad operatives, from the unit called Bayonet, who operate in foreign countries with special military training.

Laylaki—Neighborhood in Beirut suspected of housing covert, illegal Hezbollah missile assembly sites.

LEU—Low Enriched Uranium. As defined by the International Atomic Energy Agency, LEU is the basic material to fabricate nuclear fuel. It consists of uranium hexafluoride that is a white-gray, waxy solid at standard temperature and pressure. LEU is made by enriching naturally occurring uranium to improve its ability to produce energy for peaceful purposes.

Lexicon—Mossad spyware program operating in foreign governments.

M-4—Standard assault rifle for the US military, 7.62mm.

Matcal Tower—Israeli defense headquarters in Tel Aviv.

MI-5—intelligence agency charged with internal security and domestic counterintelligence operations for the United Kingdom.

MOIS—Ministry of Intelligence and Security, the Iranian intelligence service.

Mossad—Hebrew for "the Institute," Mossad is Israel's sprawling intelligence agency, equivalent to the US CIA.

NCIC—National Crime Information Center, an FBI database of criminal justice information available to law enforcement.

NIE—National Intelligence Estimate. An NIE is the intelligence community's best assessment on an issue related to national security. NIE sources are vetted by the CIA's National Clandestine Service.

NPT—Nuclear Non-Proliferation Treaty, administered by the UN.

ONI—the Office of Naval Intelligence. ONI collects, analyzes, and produces maritime intelligence for decision makers and warfighters in the US national security establishment.

Pasdar—Farsi for a revolutionary of the Islamic Republic, guardian of the revolution, used as a term of respect.

Pasdaran—Farsi for Islamic Republic revolutionaries.

Quds Force—The Iranian intelligence service charged with foreign intervention through paramilitary forces. Quds (or Qods) Force means "Jerusalem Force," after the Israeli holy city that they someday hope to conquer. It is tasked with intelligence activities, unconventional warfare, and foreign operations.

RQ-170 Sentinel Drone—CIA variant of a long-range drone operated by the US Air Force to provide ISR in hostile locales.

S&T—shorthand reference to "science and technology," the groups within intelligence agencies that analyze the capabilities of foreign military and intelligence systems.

SAC—Special Activities Center, the CIA paramilitary arm.

Salaam—Arabic greeting, short for *Salaam Aleikum*, "Peace and God be with you."

SAM—Surface-to-air missile.

SIGINT—Signals Intelligence.

Stuxnet—Joint Mossad-CIA operation to cripple Iranian uranium enrichment programs.

SVR—Russian foreign intelligence service, equivalent to the CIA, headquartered in Moscows's Yasenevo District. S Directorate SVR agents operate in secret under nonofficial cover. PR Directorate SVR agents operate in embassies under diplomatic cover.

UHF—Ultrahigh Frequency, the radio frequency between 3,000 and 300 megahertz. UHF bands are used extensively in public safety and military radio communications.

Unit 8200—The signals intelligence unit of the Israeli Defense Force. Its operations would be equivalent to the US National Security Agency (NSA) or the United Kingdom's Government Communications Headquarters (GCHQ).